Books in the EMPIRE Series

by Richard F. Weyand:
EMPIRE: Reformer
EMPIRE: Usurper
EMPIRE: Tyrant
EMPIRE: Commander
EMPIRE: Warlord
EMPIRE: Conqueror

by Stephanie Osborn:
EMPIRE: Imperial Police
EMPIRE: Imperial Detective
EMPIRE: Imperial Inspector

by Richard F. Weyand:
EMPIRE: Intervention
EMPIRE: Investigation
EMPIRE: Succession

Books in the Childers Universe

by Richard F. Weyand:
Childers
Childers: Absurd Proposals
Galactic Mail: Revolution
A Charter For The Commonwealth
Campbell: The Problem With Bliss

by Stephanie Osborn:
Campbell: The Sigurdsen Incident

EMPIRE
Imperial Police

by

STEPHANIE OSBORN

STEPHANIE OSBORN

ISBN 978-1-7340758-2-3
Printed in the United States of America

Cover Credits
Cover Art: James Lewis-Vines
Back Cover Photo: Fritz Ling

Published by Weyand Associates, Inc.
Bloomington, Indiana, USA
July 2020

CONTENTS

Foreword

Dialogue in scenes that are common between this trilogy and previous trilogies written by Mr. Weyand in this series is used verbatim, in order to maintain the content of this book as a stand-alone story.

In The Beginning

Nick Ashton was from the city of Norwich, on the planet Flanders, in the Allemagne Sector. It was a relatively nice city, on an average planet, in a sector that was neither Earthside, nor farside, and not that far from Sintar. It was neither rich nor poor, relatively stable politically and economically, and as such, his family had found it a good location to raise children for several generations. Nick Ashton was the latest product of that family, and an only child. His doting mother ensured his intellectual progress, and his loving father taught him calm discipline and determination.

At the age of ten, Nick discovered that the Ashtons' neighbors in a quiet subdivision of Norwich had their house burgled, and considerable quantities of household goods robbed as a consequence. Since their son Andrew was Nick's best friend and playmate, he saw quite a bit of the investigation, which ultimately led to the capture of the burglars, if not to the recovery of all the stolen goods.

Seeing young Nick's interest in and curiosity about the investigation, a quick discussion between father and mother resulted in the father introducing Nick to the investigating detective, who took a liking to the boy. Meanwhile, the mother introduced Nick to classic mystery novels, ranging from ancient texts by Arthur Conan Doyle and Agatha Christie to those by more modern authors. Quickly, Nick was hooked.

More, Detective Waterford stayed in touch with the bright youth, answering questions and mentoring him.

So Leya and Hans Ashton were not surprised when, a year

later, Nick declared he wanted to be a detective when he grew up.

Ten years later, Dominick "Nick" Xavier Ashton, formerly of Norwich on Flanders, was a rookie officer in the Imperial Police, in the sixteenth year of the reign of Empress Ilithyia I. Not just a rookie, but a soggy-green-behind-the-ears rookie, fresh out of the Empire's police academy. But he was not without gray matter; he'd been the top cadet of his year with a certain amount of ambition – specifically, to become a detective – and as a consequence, had drawn the attention of the Imperial Police on the capital planet of Sintar. So instead of returning to Flanders – he had no close family left there; his parents had died when the house in which he'd grown up got struck by lightning and burned down overnight, shortly before he had graduated from the police academy – he'd been assigned to the Imperial City office on Sintar, though not to the Imperial City Police Department, which was... somewhat separate, though he hadn't understood why, at the time.

His superior was Captain Lee Harding Carter, the veteran officer over all of the beat cops, an older, grizzled man who tended to mentor the rookies whenever possible. This resulted in considerable respect from most of the younger officers, though the captain was somewhat overlooked, if not outrightly scorned, by the older ones. Ashton sometimes wondered why Carter wasn't farther up in the hierarchy; he was old enough, and had the experience. So he had asked Carter that once, and Carter had replied it was because he preferred looking after the young ones like Ashton, just coming into the system, to try to ensure they stayed...safe. Given the fact that the rookies were generally either assigned experienced partners, or placed under experienced investigators – sometimes both – the statement had made little sense to Ashton at the time. Ashton had also noted the wry, almost sardonic smile Carter wore as he made the statement, and puzzled over it, but Carter hadn't offered additional explanation, and Ashton had nothing else from which to reason, so he let it drop, deciding he was only more confused by the "explanation" than he had been by the question.

It wasn't long – only about three months into the job – before Ashton began to see what Carter had meant.

"...But wait a minute," Ashton had said, as he watched the inspector survey the crime scene of his "first investigation." Not, he thought, that he was actually the one doing the investigating; he had simply been the first officer on the scene after the emergency call. One of these days, though, he promised himself, he would be.

"What's the matter, kid?" Imperial Police Inspector Ron Thomas said. "Ain't used to seein' dead bodies?"

"No, not used to seeing dead bodies labeled 'random violent crime' when they've taken a clean double-tap to the head by a professional's .25 caliber airgun," Ashton declared, annoyed. "This is just like that murder a year and a half ago, over on the east end. I know, because I did a case study on that at the academy, my last year. VR imagery and all."

"Did you, now?" Thomas said, walking over to stand in front of Ashton. "So you're an expert, eh?"

"No, sir, but I know what random crime looks like, and that ain't it," Ashton averred, standing up to the other man. "That was a professional hit. Probably done by a guy named Bron–"

"That, kiddo, was a random violent crime, and you'd do well to remember it," Thomas said, dropping his voice in both tone and volume; the result sounded menacing in the extreme.

"Cops what don't remember it tend to find themselves the victims of random violent crime their own selves. Do I make myself clear?"

"But sir–" Ashton tried again.

"Hey, Stash," Thomas called to one of his team, "come escort young Ashton out to the street, please. I want him to stand guard and keep any civvies from marching all over our random violent crime scene."

"You bet, Ron," Stanley "Stash" Gorecki declared, coming to Ashton and taking him by the shoulder. "C'mon, kid, you heard the inspector."

Ashton was hustled out of the suite, down the hall to the elevator, and thence down to the street by the big, burly Gorecki. There, the older man took hold of both of Ashton's shoulders.

"Now you listen here, squirt," Gorecki said in a low voice, nearly a growl, and just as intimidating. "You're new, or you wouldn't be standing here beside me right now. You're no detective. You're barely even a cop. Hell, you're nothing but a punk kid. They say you're smart, but I ain't seeing signs of it, 'cause you still got a few things to learn. One of those is, when an inspector tells you something, you say, 'Yes, sir,' and don't question it. Another is, the situation is what we tell you it is, no more and no less. So don't go putting something into it that the inspector says ain't there. Got it?"

Ashton glared at him. Gorecki squared his shoulders…and scowled.

"I said, you got that?"

"Yeah, I got it," Ashton grumbled.

"Got it, what?"

"Got it, *sir*."

"Good. Now you stay here like a good little rookie and make sure nobody comes inside unless me or Inspector Thomas says so."

"Yes, sir."

Ashton was stuck on guard duty, without a break for food, water, or hygiene, for the next six hours straight.

"Gorecki?! Oh hell no! Stay away from him!" his friend and roommate, fellow rookie Peter Stone, declared. "Do not do anything to draw his attention!"

"Why?" Ashton wondered.

"When he shows on your doorstep, it's bad news, Nick," Stone said. "Haven't you been paying attention to the grapevine among the rookies?"

"No. You know me and all that rumor crap."

"Yeah, but sometimes it has things you need to know, Nick. You already realized something was wrong about the detective..."

"No shit."

"Well, from what I can tell, that sort of thing runs through the whole damn department, at least what's on Sintar. And Gorecki?"

"Yeah?"

"He's their enforcer."

"*What*?!"

"Yeah. You heard me. I heard some of the older guys talking in the men's room; they didn't know I was there, 'cause I was in a stall, takin' a dump. So I know this is no rumor: If one of the police officers, or for that matter, almost anybody, civilian or otherwise, goes against Kershaw or Stanier, or any of their cronies on the Council, Gorecki gets sent in. If he and his goons don't do it personally, he knows who to bring in to, uh, 'clean

5

things up,' is the way I heard it." Stone shrugged. "It's entirely possible this guy you think really did the murder was one of those clean-up guys."

"And you're sure, Pete?" Ashton pressed, shocked. "You're saying the force is corrupt from the top down! I mean, I went into the force to catch criminals, not help enforce their rule!"

"No joke. It's why I'm transferring back home at the end of the year, or as soon as I can get it arranged," Stone noted. "I kinda think it's gonna take longer than that, but I've got the paperwork in; I just have to wait for a slot to come open. At least there, I know they're honest. I thought working in the capital planet's headquarters would be a big perk, help me along in my career and be a nice bullet on the curriculum vitae, but this sure ain't what I thought it was."

"But are you *sure*?!"

"I can't say a hundred percent, Nick," Stone said, "but think about the story you just told me. The detective basically threatens you with 'random violent crime,' then calls Gorecki over to escort you out? That's showing Gorecki who you are, in case he needs to know, in future."

"Damn. You're right."

"Yeah, pal. Now Gorecki knows exactly who you are. Trust me. You do not want to get his attention again. Believe me, Nick, it's nothing but bad news if you do."

Around his work shifts for the next few weeks, Ashton went back and reviewed his case study on the earlier cold case murder in private for his own satisfaction, and realized that there was definitely a similar *modus operandi*: in both cases, the murder victim saw nothing coming, had no evidence of elevated vital signs per VR data, and had received two shots to the back of the skull from a weapon that did not leave residue, resulting in essentially instantaneous death. There were rumors in both instances of stray handymen, delivery persons, or utilities workers wandering in the area, which made him suspicious.

Digging even deeper convinced him, as he had become convinced at the academy, that a certain con artist named Josip Bronsky, a.k.a. Joey Bronze, was responsible.

Born in Odessa Sector, Bronsky's mother had deserted him soon after. His father, Mikhail, was a con man and brought Josip up in his footsteps. They left the sector when it got too hot, and Mikhail was killed by an angry mark when Josip was in his teens. Josip landed on Wollaston.

As a young man in the Estvian-controlled city of Savanna on Wollaston, Bronsky had started off as a small time crook, but had shown a certain skill for the con; while they knew he was running the cons, no Imperial investigator could ever find enough evidence to nail him. And given the political environment on Wollaston, it proved easy for the sharp-witted youth to play both ends against the middle, sometimes scamming Sintaran supporters, sometimes Estvian, carefully walking a tightrope between the two and never taking sides himself.

So he had quickly moved from small-time, penny-ante stuff into the big leagues, conning richer and richer victims, sometimes alone, and sometimes with the help of one or more skilled – or unskilled – cronies, usually attractive females that went with Bronsky to various nightclubs and parties. Speculation among those trying to apprehend him varied on whether they were also his lovers, and if they knew they were taking part in a con.

And business – and life – had been good for Bronsky.

Until one of those cons had gone wrong.

Johnston Eustace Petticord, who had emigrated from elsewhere in the Empire of Sintar, and who was a strong supporter thereof, had not fallen for Bronsky's scam. Somehow, he had figured out that his friend Mia was *not* a young billionaire heiress from Travers World, ripe for marriage; it never even occurred to Bronsky that someone might check to find out that there were no heiresses of significance on Travers World – it was far too rural in general, and had too few inhabitants, for anyone as wealthy as that. For that matter, Bronsky himself hadn't bothered to check…which taught him a significant lesson: Don't just wing your con, make sure your background story is good enough to withstand scrutiny.

More and worse, however, was the fact that Petticord had friends in powerful places; if he turned Bronsky and his lady compatriot over to the police, it would have meant a sure conviction and many, many years of imprisonment.

But at least on Wollaston, Petticord also had powerful enemies due to his political stance. And he traveled in, and on, a world where men and women were not afraid to take what they wanted…or hire it taken. Given the political intrigue rampant on Wollaston, and the fact that he was a major political player for one side, Petticord had had a price on his head for over a year from the other side; he had simply been fortunate so far, in that he could hire better bodyguards.

So when Petticord had immediately realized there was a scam going down as soon as Bronsky told him about "Bambi's" purported background, he looked into the con artist's past and learned the truth. Then Petticord had summoned Bronsky and confronted him. He had subsequently been stupid enough to draw on Bronsky, evidently planning to hold him for the authorities to take into custody.

Bronsky had responded in kind. And proved faster.

Slipping the desired proof of Petticord's death – an hereditary signet ring; the Petticords were an old, well-pedigreed, and very wealthy family from Adonar, on the Earthside of the empire – from Petticord's finger and tucking it into the secret pocket of his jacket, Bronsky executed the escape plan he always developed when working a new con, thankful that Mia wasn't with him to slow him down. He made it out of the house and off the grounds before the alarm was raised.

From there, he headed straight for the house of Albert Armstrong, an émigré from the Kingdom of Estvia who had come to Wollaston expressly to restore the Wollaston system to that star nation, and the mortal enemy of Petticord. There, Bronsky showed the ring to the guard at the gate, then to successively higher members of Armstrong's staff, until he finally reached the man himself.

The reward had been substantial, more than enough to offset the loss of the con.

Not that Mia ever knew.

But it had done something to Bronsky that he didn't expect. Only in the aftermath, when he walked out of Armstrong's house alive and considerably richer, did Bronsky experience the adrenaline rush, the surge of endorphins.

Bronsky discovered he enjoyed killing.

The police suspected Bronsky at first; he had been a known associate in the weeks leading up to Petticord's death, and a known con artist. But he was not known for murder. And when the signet ring turned up missing, suspicion fell on Armstrong's people. However, while the rumor was well known, Armstrong was not stupid, and had been careful to leave nothing that could be traced to him or his staff of enforcers. Further, his Estvian sympathies were largely shared by the police force in Savanna, and there was no serious desire to point a finger at such a staunch supporter of the "Wollaston for Estvia" movement.

The fact that Mia had gone missing did not help the development of any case against Bronsky. He simply claimed that she had gotten homesick and left Wollaston, and he didn't know where she'd gone.

Bronsky was lying, of course. He was good at that. Mia had never left Wollaston. But no one was ever going to find the body, either. Armstrong and his people had helped him see to it. And he had learned a lot in the process.

In the end, the Petticord murder had become a cold case, and Bronsky was smart enough to leave Wollaston and head for what he expected to be far better pickings, especially for someone who wanted to change "careers."

Imperial City on Sintar.

No one knew the details except Bronsky himself, of course, but Ashton had some serious intelligence, imagination, and a distinct aptitude for investigation instilled by his late mentor Detective Waterford – who had lived just long enough to see Ashton graduate the Imperial Police Academy – and it didn't take a great stretch of that imagination for him to suspect what had happened. For it was a demonstrable fact that Josip Bronsky had not resorted to con schemes upon making landfall on Sintar. He also had had no problems setting himself up in a new life on his new homeworld...which, to Ashton, spoke to being paid off handsomely by someone on Wollaston, though he couldn't determine who, let alone prove it.

Bronsky, or Bronze, as he now preferred to be known,

dropped out of sight for a significant amount of time after arriving on Sintar. There was no evidence of employment, legal or criminal – or much of anything else – for nearly a year... though Bronze continued to maintain an apartment in the neighborhoods west of the Imperial complex.

Then Wang Li had been killed.

And suddenly Joey Bronze had surfaced again.

It all appeared innocent, his resurfacing; when approached by any authorities, Bronze claimed to have cleaned up his act, got some specialized training, and become a consultant of some sort. Ashton dug and dug, but had a hard time determining who Bronze was consulting *for*, let alone how. But in fairly short order, Bronze had ditched the leased apartment and bought an upscale condo in Imperial Park East. His lifestyle began to change concurrently.

I dunno, Ashton considered, studying his display in VR, *all the info on that seems to go around in circles. Maybe I need to get back to my current case and my cold case and quit worrying so much about Bronze himself. If he did it, the clues will be there. I just have to find them.*

So he pulled up all of the known information about both cases and settled down to look at the details and try to correlate the information.

And it was at that point, when he dug into the two victims themselves and compared the cases, that Ashton was shocked at the correlations. Both victims had been involved in efforts to bring to light corruption in government. Her Majesty Adannaya III had evidently had an investigation ongoing into medical matters, the young sleuth decided, though it had been somewhat before his time, and apparently hadn't come to a head until the reign of her successor Ilithyia I had forced the issue. That had been when the principal information source, Wang Li, formerly of one of the major pharmaceutical firms, had met with unexpected "random violent crime."

This most recent murder had been another whistleblower, this time in the university education field, likewise for Ilithyia I.

Both had been shot twice in the back of the head. Both had died essentially instantaneously.

Son of a bitch, Ashton thought, grim. *I bet I know just exactly what sort of "consulting" Bronsky is doing. And somebody in the government has a vested interest in maintaining the status quo, and they're willing to take out anybody trying to make a change. At least, anybody they can get to,* he decided, thinking of the Empress herself.

The next day, the news was full of the death of Empress Ilithyia I.

Whenever a leader died unexpectedly, regardless of the time period, planet, or regime, there was always a concern that there could be unrest. So the Imperial Police turned out in force, creating a show of presence to keep the streets quiet. So Ashton and his roommate stayed busy for the entire week – by which time the new empress, Ilithyia II, had been duly installed and announced, if not yet formally crowned, and her predecessor laid in the Imperial Mausoleum with all due respect, pomp, and ceremony.

When that was over, things settled down.

And Ashton had a chance to think.

Two whistleblowers, both working with the Empress, he considered. *Or at least, with her investigatory teams. And I was only just starting to dig out any other murders – assassinations, really – that fit the same modus operandi. But even so, I found a couple. Double-taps to the back of the head, .25 caliber, no evidence of residue from the weapon so probably an airgun…* He broke off. *So there's evidence of a conspiracy to fight back against the Empress' reforms,* he thought. *And that's just from one assassin. How many others might there have been?*

And then another, even more dreadful, thought hit him.

They said that Empress Ilithyia I died of congestive heart failure. But these days, what with the state of the medical arts, I'd have thought that was just not a problem, that they could have cured her without difficulty. Especially with the resources available to the Throne. What if… he stopped, gathering his thoughts, not sure he even wanted to think it, *what if it wasn't really heart failure? At least, not natural heart failure? What if the heart failure was induced over time, by something someone was slipping to her? What if Ilithyia I was assassinated, too, to get her out of the way? Maybe somebody thought they could slip somebody into position if the Empress died suddenly and didn't name an heir?*

In the end, however, he couldn't figure out how to access any information to tell him, one way or the other. He was only a lowly beat cop and simply did not have the ability to find out who had had access to Ilithyia I, or what medications she had been given, or even what had been in her food and drink.

Those should have been closely guarded, he realized, *but if somebody really high up is doing this, they might be able to sneak it in. But I'm not gonna find it. Only an inspector could…and at this point,* he frowned to himself, *there's not a one of the damn bastards that I would ever trust to even hint to, about this. Maybe Captain Carter. I dunno.*

So he filed it away in the back of his mind, in case he ever did get the chance, and turned back to his quiet little investigations of the two assassinations about which he did know a few things.

Ashton only became more and more convinced that Josip Bronsky, upon his arrival on Sintar, had ditched con artistry and found someone to teach him a thing or two about assassination, though he had no idea who, or where, or even how. But while all of the trends pointed that way, by the time the various "investigators" – excuse for investigators, in his considered opinion – were done with the crime scenes, there was no evidence left with which he could work.

He sighed and put both cases away.

One of these days, he thought. *Maybe one of these days, I can properly close a case. Maybe I can close* this *case.*

Round Two

It had been just over a year since the incident with Stash and Inspector Thomas, and coming up on a year since the death of Empress Ilithyia I, and other than the odd pickpocket or domestic dispute, Ashton's shifts had been relatively quiet. His roommate Stone had – finally – recently managed to transfer to his homeworld, and Ashton had spent most of his off hours for the last week getting ready to move to a new apartment, though he hadn't filed the information with the department yet.

By this point, he was basically a beat cop, having left his rookie status behind at his annum anniversary with the department, some months prior – though he hadn't been moved into the investigatory division like he'd hoped. Other than the official change of status in his records, there had been no other recognition of the day…somewhat to his disappointment. He was supposed to be an assistant to Inspector Thomas according to all the paperwork, but Ashton had gotten no requests to attend Thomas for a case since that one incident, nearly a year prior. Which, he decided, wasn't surprising at all. *I don't want to work with a dirty detective any more than that detective wants to work with a straight cop. But I do still want to be a detective, dammit! Now, if I could just figure out how to go about requesting assignment to a different investigator without getting Gorecki on my case, I might get someplace. Maybe I'll go by and feel the Captain out about it, at the end of my shift.*

Meanwhile, he tried to concentrate on doing a good job as a

beat cop, and developing a social life. He dated a good bit, mostly outside the force, but never managed to find a woman that seemed to "click" for him.

Until one morning when another cop, passing by in the break room as he stood up from fetching the coffee from the under-counter cabinet, pinched his ass, then turned and grinned.

Officer Tabitha "Tabby" Koch was a tanned honey-blonde, around half a foot shorter than Ashton's six feet, with big blue-green eyes and pearly white teeth that showed when she grinned. And that grin was making it plain that she thought Ashton was cute, if not downright sexy. And in turn, it made her downright sexy.

Ashton was instantly smitten.

"Hey, big guy," she said, continuing to grin. "Sorry about that. I never could resist a tight, round ass."

"Hey yourself," he responded, matching her grin. "I'm just glad you think it's tight and round."

"Oh, definitely. I thought I was gonna dislocate a knuckle when I tried to pinch it."

"I *was* doing a reverse squat, after all."

"True, true! I'm Tabby Koch. Pleased to meet you."

"I'm Nick Ashton. Likewise."

"There's an empty table in the corner, and it's fifteen until the morning brief. Wanna join?"

"Sure."

He promptly ascertained that her beat was in the arcade next to his, then invited her to join him for coffee at a convenient café during their next break.

She accepted.

They laughed and talked and were almost late going back on duty... but not before they'd arranged to go out to dinner that night, once they got off work.

Thus began an intense relationship that lasted several months…

…Until Nick discovered that Tabby was General William Kershaw's niece.

"Holy shit, Nick, I can't believe you didn't know that!" Peter Stone, who would be leaving for a slot on his homeworld in just a few days, told Ashton one night after a particularly hot date. "And he dotes on her! She's the daughter of his favorite sister, and word has it, he was the father figure after her dad got killed on Wollaston! I was wondering why the hell you were dating Kershaw's niece, given everything you've said about your personal ethics!"

"Aw, damn," Ashton said, perturbed. "Well, at least she doesn't take after him."

"Buddy, I hate to tell you," Stone said, solemn, "she most certainly does."

"No," Ashton averred, deeply disturbed by the accusation. "I don't believe you."

Stone shrugged.

"You're the one wants to be a detective. Find out for yourself. Just do it before you get in over your head."

So on his next day off, he arranged that it should not coincide with Tabby's, and then spent the day doing "case studies," as he told her. "After all, I need to keep my hand in, even if I'm not seeing much but street shit."

He also didn't tell her that the case studies were hers.

It wasn't so much that he believed Stone – although, admittedly, Stone had never lied to him, and had helped him in a few close shaves, into the bargain – as much as it was that he wanted to prove to himself that Stone's accusations weren't true. It troubled him to think that an innocent Tabby might get undeservedly tarred with her uncle's filthy brush. So he sat down at the desk in his bedroom and checked into VR, digging out as many of her records as he could legitimately access, all the way back to her police academy days.

Tabby Koch had done well at the police academy, there was no doubt about it. She was smart, and quick, and knew what she was doing – which wasn't surprising, given who her uncle was. But in the end, you could do well in school and not so well on the street, and the real test for academy graduates was how they did on the street.

There had apparently been no question that Tabby would return to Sintar; several other sectors had made offers, but she had turned them all down. She had been in the class six months behind Nick's, so she'd been on the beat around three-quarters of a year at this point.

Her first case had been under Inspector Ron Thomas. It had been labeled a suicide. Knowing Thomas' predilections, Ashton dug a little deeper, pulling the forensics and coroner's reports and studying them. The first thing he checked was the top-level coroner report, then he sat back in dismay.

IMMEDIATE CAUSE OF DEATH: A knife wound which penetrated the left ventricle of the heart.

DETAILS: Width of incision was between 1-2" and some 5-6" deep; rear wall of ventricle was fully penetrated and interior front wall was cut but not penetrated.

OTHER CONTRIBUTING FACTORS: None.

OTHER ADDITIONAL INJURIES: Some bruising in the throat and clavicle region.

TIME OF ONSET: Approximately 10:20am.

TIME OF DEATH: Approximately 15 sec after onset.

LOCATION OF INJURY: Between the third and fourth ribs on the left posterior portion of the thoracic wall, immediately adjacent to the left scapula.

DESCRIBE HOW INJURY OCCURRED: Subject self-inflicted the injury.

MANNER OF DEATH: Suicide.

"Damn," he muttered to himself, "that was blatant. What the hell did the guy do to deserve that?"

Another quick side search verified that the victim had been an employee of the principal weapons maker for the Imperial Marines. More importantly, he had been contacted by a member of the Empress' Staff for information regarding the testing processes for some of those weapons.

"Oh. Well, that explains it," Ashton all but snarled, face twisting in disgust and anger; he and Stone had had several very private discussions of how matters laid in Imperial City, the military situation being only one, especially after a minor disaster in one of the systems toward the Rim. "He probably blew a whistle, and they got him for it."

Then he saw the evaluation that Inspector Thomas had written on Tabby, and the room spun as the blood seemed to leave his head.

The rookie Tabitha Koch was extremely helpful and caught on to the nature of my work very quickly. Unlike some recent recruits, who sometimes seemed to believe themselves detectives in their own rights, Officer Koch was smooth and polished, and did not try to explain away the crime scene, but did exactly as she was told with no demur and no complaints.

"Shit," he whispered in dismay.

Several additional case studies produced similar results.

Evidently Tabby was completely inured in her uncle's ways, and content to go along with the flow and the corruption. Ashton felt sick to his stomach. He had been serious about Tabby, and had been thinking about whether or not to take their relationship more intimate, maybe even asking her to marry him. He would have invited her to meet his parents, but they had died when the house in which he'd grown up got struck by lightning and burned down overnight, shortly before he had graduated from the police academy; it had been the reason he had not gone back to Flanders to begin work.

Then a thought hit him.

She's regularly working with Thomas, and I'm not, even though I'm supposed to be assigned to him. And she's gotta know half the upper echelons, given who her uncle is. And her first come-on was really blatant. Fun, and sexy, but blatant. What if she was told to get my attention? What if she's either spying on me, or trying to sway me to their way of doing things? SHIT!

"Hey, Pete?" he called then, standing and heading toward the living room. "You here?"

"Yeah, Nick. What's up?" Stone asked, coming out of the kitchen with a beer.

"I need to ask you something…"

"…Yeah, Nick, that's why I thought you needed to know," Stone said, after Ashton had told him what he'd found, then explained his concern. "That's exactly what I was afraid she was doing. Either way, spying or influencing, it ain't good for you, man. Watch out for that chick."

"Hell," Ashton said with feeling. He had felt like they had something, something good, and now he found she had likely been fooling him the whole time. It hurt badly; he had trusted her, and it sure looked like she'd betrayed that trust from the beginning. *Before, really,* he thought, deeply pained. *Her whole intent looks to have been to turn me, one way or another. Well, at least it explains why she never wanted to talk about her family. In a lot of respects. Let alone bring me home to meet 'em.*

"Hey, I'm sorry, buddy," Stone said softly, putting a hand on Ashton's shoulder. "But look at it like this – better to find out now, while you have a chance to break it off, than later, when you'd tied yourself to her."

Ashton had to acknowledge the wisdom of that.

The next morning, he managed to avoid running into her by dint of being late to work. He slipped into the back of the morning briefing under Carter's shift opposite, and stood in the rear of the room, where he could slip out just as quickly.

As soon as Carter ended the shift briefing, Ashton ducked out the door and headed for his assigned beat, hoping to stay on the far side of the arcade from Tabby's beat.

Then the emergency call came in.

It was very early in the morning, before any of the shops or businesses had opened. Since Ashton was already out on his general patrol in the arcade level, with an experienced beat cop only a few blocks away on the street level above, dispatch contacted him – he was less than a block from the site of the emergency, just around the corner – and he hit the pedal on his arcade cart, zipped around to the location, and entered the building.

"I'm Officer Ashton, from the Imperial Police," he barked as soon as he passed the – surprisingly – unlocked door. In the corner, several people were crouched next to a security guard, who sat on the floor, seeming a bit confused. Then he noticed the trickle of blood running down the side of the guard's face.

Uh-oh, he thought. "Who's in charge, and what's going down?" he continued aloud.

"I am," an older woman said, rising from the guard's side and stepping forward. "I'm Anne Roberts. I run the museum; I'm the direct descendant of George Roberts, Personal Secretary to Empress Kolbesdeka, over four centuries ago." She pointed. "Our security guard, Michael Anders, was patrolling around the Sigil, and just as he turned, someone knocked him on the head. We're not sure how long he's been out."

"Not long," Anders said. "I never blacked out. It just stunned me."

"What's the Sigil?" Ashton wondered.

Roberts and Anders stared at him.

The building, as it turned out, was a tiny museum dedicated to the Throne – The Museum of the Throne, it was called, lack of imagination notwithstanding – and run by the family of a former Personal Secretary to the Empress in one of the earlier reigns of Empresses, when matters were a bit more feudal. Kolbesdeka had been one of the more famous of her era, responsible for consolidating the holdings of the Empire, and more importantly, more formally codifying the rule of law under the Throne. Most of the exhibits were memorabilia, heirlooms the family had kept over the years, passing them down from generation to generation as treasures.

Of those treasures, none was more precious or more revered than the Empress' Sigil, a signet ring from Empress Kolbesdeka, dating from the days before everything was done – before it *could* be done – in virtual reality, and given to the Personal Secretary. It was a sign of his authority on her behalf, established by no less than an Imperial Decree. It was not only a sign of her favor, but could be used as an ink seal denoting her authority on documentation, or in wax seals on formal documents or envelopes. The mark of that Sigil on anything was the same as the Empress' signature, at least in that era.

The system had been superseded eventually by ever more sophisticated electronic means, but the Empress' Sigil was still looked upon as a legitimate means of conveying authority, and no Empress had ever contravened that original Imperial Decree, but it was no longer used. Which, Ashton decided, was likely why he had never heard of it before.

"What about security alarms?" Ashton wondered.

"We're not sure," Roberts said, puzzled. "It didn't go off. I have a call in to the security company to see if there was a glitch or something. It was pure luck that several of us came in early to work on the design for a new exhibit."

"Mm. So if you were hit on the head," he said to the guard, "I guess you never saw the guy who hit you?"

"Well, just as I hit the floor, I did," Anders admitted. "I guess he expected to knock me out, because he wasn't careful to stay out of my line of sight. It wasn't really clear, but I got a decent look at his profile as he turned."

"So it was a he."

"Yeah. Tall, moderately muscular, lean. He just walked over to the display case, paused and looked like he was in VR for a moment, the lock clicked, and he reached in and grabbed the Sigil and sauntered out. Wasn't more than five, ten minutes before the others came in."

"He sauntered out?! He didn't run?"

"No, sir."

"Can you pass me an image of his face in VR? Meet me in channel 621."

Anders entered the VR channel and produced a "photo" of his assailant. He held it up for the young policeman to see.

Moments later, Ashton found himself looking at a familiar face.

"Shit!" he exclaimed, exiting VR, then he turned and ran out of the museum.

That face had been familiar from Ashton's youth. It was the head of the gang that had burglarized the house of his playmate Andrew, one Bill Jakes, according to his old detective mentor. What Jakes was doing on Sintar, Ashton wasn't sure, let alone why he was after something so valuable and historic; that hadn't been the Jakes Gang's *modus operandi*. But it was a fact that Detective Waterford had not been able to capture him, out of the entire gang.

More, Ashton was sure he had seen a certain familiar face – familiar from mug sheets Waterford had shown him – if considerably older, on the side street of the arcade only moments before. A face that matched the one he'd just been shown in VR.

He jumped into the arcade cart, released the brake, and slammed his foot onto the accelerator, headed back the way he had come, as fast as he could go.

"...And he already captured and arrested the perp?" Inspector Thomas asked Anne Roberts an hour later.

"Yes, and returned the Sigil into our custody," Roberts said, delighted. "It was on the burglar when he was captured – he hadn't had time to get rid of it yet. And the problem with the alarm was at the security company; they accepted this month's payment, then shut off our service anyway! We've already changed companies, and that won't be happening again!"

"What about your guard? He loyal?"

"Oh, he and his family have been with us for years," Roberts said. "Ever since my ancestor worked for the Empress. The

Anders always make sure they have at least two children, and one goes into the Marines, then into the Imperial Guard, and the other works security for the museum."

"That's...good, then," Thomas said, throwing a grim glance at Gorecki. "I'll just go see about things back at Headquarters, I suppose."

"Thank you so much for your time, though. You need to promote that young officer! He knew exactly what he was doing!"

Outside the museum, the pair piled into a police cart and headed for the main street level.

"That don't sound good, Ron," Gorecki said then.

"It's not, Stash," Thomas said, intensely annoyed. "One of our top superiors just got set back to pretty much the beginning. That Imperial Sigil is still functional; it would be accepted anywhere in the Empire. It was supposed to be collected in order to be used strategically by certain persons not in the Palace, if you know what I mean."

"I do. You want me to, ah, go see about this Ashton kid?"

"That might be a good idea."

Later that morning, right after he'd come on shift and before he'd even finished his first cup of coffee – he'd had a dental appointment, so someone else did the morning brief – Captain Carter took a look at the incoming reports in VR and sighed; it was going to be another long shift, he decided. Then a particular report caught his eye and he sat up straight in his desk chair.

Oh shit, he thought, shocked and worried. *Tell me he didn't do that.*

He read a little farther, then smeared a tired hand over his face and up into his grizzled, salt-with-a-little-pepper hair. *Of course he did. That's who he is. And that's not going to make the powers that be happy at all. I can see that handwriting on the wall – I know why that got stolen! All I have to know to figure it is how the politics work around here. Hellfire damnation. I better meet with Maia pronto, or he won't survive the week. In any sense of the word. Shit, he might not even survive the day.*

He laid down as many secure protocols as he could on the communication, then initiated the private, and decidedly unofficial, connection.

"Hey, Maia," Carter said, as she appeared in the classic nondescript meeting room of virtual reality, where he awaited her. "How ya doin', honey?"

"Pretty good, Lee; how 'bout you?" the attractive woman with bronze-toned skin and vivid green eyes replied. "Oh, and congratulations; I saw where one of your up-and-comers solved the Museum of the Throne burglary case." She smiled at Carter, then studied his face for a moment, her smile disappearing. "Uh-oh. I see that expression. He wasn't supposed to solve the case, was he?"

"No," Carter said with a sigh. "And now I've got a problem. A *big* problem, if my instincts are right."

"All right. Lemme hear the details, if you can."

"Yeah, I think I can help out, here," Colonel Maia Peterson, the Deputy Chief of Investigations in the Imperial City Police, decided, some half an hour later, after a full explanation and a brainstorming session. They were old friends and colleagues, though very few knew the fact, because this was not the first time Carter had called her on a similar errand. "I'll get things set up on this end, as fast as I can. You know what to do on that end."

"I do," Carter replied. "And yeah, I'll move fast too. Thanks, Maia. You won't regret this. He's a good kid, and shows a damn lot of promise. This one's one of the best I've sent you, I think. Maybe the best."

"Wow. Investigations, then?"

"I haven't had a chance to talk to him about it yet, at least not in depth, but if I had to guess based on what I already know of him, and the paperwork he filled out when he came on, I'd say in a big way. But because of the way things work around here, and the way his innate moral stance is in counterpoint, it just ain't gonna happen here."

"Right. I understand. I'll wait to hear from you on it, and discuss it with him when I see him."

"Roger that. And again, thank you!"

"Eh," Peterson said with a wave of her hand. "Bring me another big tin of your special-blend chili powder and we'll call it paid. I'll even make some of those chili chocolates you like so much."

"You know, if I was only a decade younger, Maia…"

"And I've told you, Lee, I'm not bothered by your age. I'm not that young these days, either."

"Lemme get to a place where I'm out of this damn mine field, then we'll talk."

"I can't wait."

"Me neither."

And she blinked out of the virtual room.

Carter sighed in mingled regret and concern, and dropped the link.

He spent the next few hours getting his ducks in a row. It was only a matter of time before a certain enforcer arrived, looking for young Ashton, and ready to take on Carter if he got in the way.

So he hacked into the security system on his office – after all these years, it was a skill that had been honed by long practice – and set it up to pick up, not what was really happening in his office, but a nondescript paperwork sequence. Even his VR telemetry was faked, so that he could tend his unblemished rookies as needed, and keep them out of harm's way.

Once that was arranged, he began setting up the paperwork to get Ashton safely out of IPD headquarters and into Maia's care...while looking like he went elsewhere. When that was finished, he sent a message to Ashton through VR, directing him to go off on a wild snipe hunt, to keep him out of harm's way until it could all go through. It wasn't a useless mission; he directed him to carry a piece of evidence to a city office on the other end of the continent. It was needed for a case being prosecuted there, by a perp from Imp City, and it would serve the purpose of diverting Ashton out of reach of those who would want his hide.

Then he began tweaking the report on the burglary...just a little bit.

Scrambling for Position

"Where's Dominick Ashton?" Gorecki demanded, as soon as he entered Carter's office.

Right. No greeting, no, "How ya doin', Lee," no nothin', Carter thought, hiding his disgust carefully.

"Uh, lemme think," Carter said, pretending to rack his brain. "Oh! That's right. That murder case on the far side of the continent – what city was that? Was it Hobarth? Anyway, they wanted some pieces of hard evidence, since the perp is from Imp City, and Ashton was free, so I sent him on a shuttle with it in a case. He won't be back until…" Carter checked the time in VR, "wow, until close on my getting off shift."

Gorecki glared at him.

"What did you want to see him for?" Carter asked casually. "I can see about handling any matters, seeing as how I'm his shift supervisor…"

"He undercut Inspector Thomas this morning," Gorecki noted, "and Ron ain't real happy about it."

"Ohh, that thing. Yes, I saw that in the reports when I came on duty this morning," Carter said, tsking appropriately. "Don't worry. I'll have a little talk with him. He's not picking up on some things like he should; I'm thinking about sending him for some remedial training. There's this retired detective on Pritani that should do well for our purpose; he used to work at Headquarters and knows the ropes around here. But you know what? I started looking, and there were no messages sent down to the beat cops' line management about that situation. Kid had no idea that anything else needed to be done but what he did, because nobody in our department had a clue."

"What?! You're shittin' me!"

Carter shrugged. He'd double-checked on that aspect about as soon as he'd ended the meeting with Maia. There had, in fact, been nothing obvious, though there had been a slight hint in a message…which he'd promptly hacked so he could delete the hint. Fortunately, no one else seemed to have seen it either. Which, he considered, really only supported what he was telling Stash.

"Nope. Not a word. I dunno if somebody forgot, or if they just thought we didn't need to know, or what, Stash," Carter said, helpful, friendly and familiar, when he really wanted to vomit. Preferably in Gorecki's shoes. "Granted, Ashton didn't handle it the way you might expect, but I really don't think the fault was his. Somebody didn't pass the word. It wouldn't have mattered if it was Ashton or any other of the rookies – remember, he hasn't even been here a full year yet!" *That was a flat-out lie,* he thought. "– Or hell, it coulda been some of our experienced beat cops. They'd probably have done the very same thing."

"That so?"

"Without any heads-up? Sure," Carter said, shrugging again. "If I was in your shoes, I'd be looking to see who flubbed the dub on the communications end of things. Not passing on essential information to the appropriate shifts is a great way to get somebody blown to dust bunnies on the street. Somebody you don't want blown to dust bunnies." Carter glanced around, then leaned forward and murmured conspiratorially, "And I don't mean somebody on the obvious side of the force."

"Hm. You got a point," Gorecki decided. "Maybe I need to dig into this a little further, make sure where things went wrong, so it don't happen again."

"Sounds like a plan to me," Carter agreed. "Meanwhile, I can promise you, you won't be having any more trouble out of Ashton. I'll see to that personally. He'll be gone for a while, here, and if and when he comes back, oughta be a little more…in line."

"Right," Gorecki all but snarled. "See to it. Or I will."

Carter drew a deep breath and let it out in surreptitious relief as Gorecki stalked out of his office.

"…I'm sorry, Nick," Lee Carter, the Imperial City office captain over the local Imperial Police beat cops, told the young police officer when he finally returned, toward the end of his shift. "You're a good kid, and a good cop. Idealistic. What some call a 'boy scout,' though I'm not sure where that old term comes from. Unfortunately, this is the wrong organization for that."

"So…what? I was supposed to let a thief – of a valuable, historic heirloom – go free?" Ashton said in shock.

"Keep your voice down, son," Carter murmured, glancing at his closed office door and hoping it was sufficiently soundproofed…especially when added to the surreptitious hack he'd performed on the surveillance equipment in his office. "I'm trying my damnedest to keep you alive, right now. No, but yes, is your answer. You've already seen it; you're too observant not to have done. You *know* the answer to that question. Or at least, the expected answer around here."

"Yeah," Ashton grumbled, face closing in a scowl. "I just thought you were different."

"I am. *Look* at me, son," Carter demanded, pointing at his hair, as Ashton continued to mutter under his breath. "See all this white on top? See the crow's feet, the frown lines? Where do you think I *got* all that white hair, dammit? I'm not *that* old!

Why do you think, at my age, I haven't gone farther up the ranks? Why do you think I choose this job over some fancier one, with a more important-sounding title? It's so I can keep the newbies, the ones like you, *safe*! I'm not so far from retirement, Nick; maybe a decade, decade an' a half, out. I could go ahead and take early retirement and be done. And as sick as I am of this shit, if I can get you safely where you need to be, I probably will. Listen: do you know who Stash Gorecki is, Nick?"

"Oh damn. Yeah," Ashton said, growing quiet.

"Do you know he came to see me this afternoon, to find out why you solved the case? Asking for you *by name*?"

"Uh. No, I hadn't heard. That's…not good news."

"No, it isn't. I managed to divert him and send him off on a different track, but it was hard. As soon as I saw the report, I started setting my ducks in order for this, or I wouldn't have managed to divert him at all. And you might well be dead already."

"Um…thanks, Captain?"

"You're damn straight," Carter said, stern. "And that is why you're going on detached duty to the Imperial City Police Department. You're lucky, as it is, that I got you away from the office before Stash got here! If I hadn't sent you off on that courier duty, I'd have had to stand here and watch, pretending to approve, while he beat you senseless…if not outright killed you. Listen close, and remember what I'm about to tell you, or you're a dead man walking: You stumbled across the solution to the theft because the perp pulled a cocky, stupid stunt – which, to be honest, he did, so that works in our favor – and you're still too green to realize what you were supposed to do. And," Carter added, thinking about phrasing, "no word came down to the beat cops about it, so you didn't have any instructions beforehand. So you're going offworld to Pritani for 'training.' There's an old pal of mine, a retired detective outta HQ there who does training – not really, but it works for our purposes now – really strict, and I want you to work under him, so that when you come back, you'll have sense enough to see what you're supposed to see…and then I'll shape you up to doing what you're supposed to do. That's the official story. Got it?"

"Yeah."

"What?"

"Um. Sorry. Yes, sir. I'm…" Ashton paused. "It's a lot to take in, sir. But I'm trying hard."

"Good. 'Cause what's really gonna happen is, I'm sending you over to Imp City's force. ICPD has some excellent detectives, and you'll get trained right, over there, without all of this 'do only what we tell you' shit."

"Yes, sir, I understand, and I'll remember it. But if I'm over at ICPD, how…?" Ashton began, confused. "I mean, well…how's that any different?"

"Because it's a separate organization, reporting to a different part of the hierarchy, and they work much closer to the Imperial Guard and the Empress's staff," Carter explained. "They're straight and they're clean. You'll fit in there, and be happy. If you're smart, you'll make it a permanent transfer. In the larger scheme of things, you'll still be in the overall organization, but it'll suit your personal morals much better. So let me suggest it, in the strongest possible terms: *transfer*." He paused, then added, "Oh, and while I'm thinking about it, I know Stone transferred out this morning…"

"Yes, sir."

"Were you planning to move your living space?"

"I was, sir. In fact, I'm almost done. I just have to move a couple last things, fill out the change of address paperwork and leave it with you, and it's finished."

"Do it. Tonight. As fast as you can get it done. Do not – repeat, do not – leave a forwarding address with anybody, because according to the story I've set up, you're going offworld anyway. And once you've got your stuff in the new place? Do. Not. Go. Back. For anything. So make sure you get it all on the first go."

"Yes, sir." Ashton paused, trying to gather his wits. *And thank God I hadn't shown it to Tabby yet,* he thought. *As busy as we've been, I don't think I'd even mentioned it. She probably expected me to ask her to move in once Pete was gone.* Then he brought himself back to the present and tried, "Um, sir, when…? The transfer…?"

"Effective immediately," Carter ordered. "I want you out of here as fast as we can get you out. I got the paperwork ready – and hidden – around prepping for Gorecki's visit. Go clear your locker right now, and report straight to ICPD headquarters. You'll be interviewing with one Colonel Maia Peterson, Deputy Chief of Investigations."

"But…"

"Don't worry about looking like you went offworld. Peterson is an old friend, and she's taking care of that for us over at the spaceport, with some of her people. Just go, and try to stay out of sight. Throw your off-duty clothes on until you get there."

"…Yes, sir."

Ashton rose, a hangdog expression on his face, and Carter came around his desk to meet the younger man, taking his hand.

"Godspeed, son," he murmured, barely loud enough for Ashton to hear. "Good luck, and watch your back. You may be in a different org chart, but these goons are still in the same city with you."

"Thank you, sir," Ashton said, and headed for the door.

As soon as Carter saw Ashton safely out the front door of Imperial Police headquarters, he sat back down at his desk and logged into VR.

There, he began filling out a very special form. One that pertained only to him, for a change.

Once he had submitted it, he leaned back in his desk chair with a very tired sigh.

Here's hoping, he thought.

"So you're interested in investigation, Officer Ashton?" Colonel Maia Peterson asked.

"Yes, ma'am," Ashton admitted. "My mom was a huge mystery fan, and she sicced me onto 'em, too. I've read so many old classic detective novels – everything from Sherlock Holmes, Hercule Poirot and Agatha Christie, to Philip Marlowe, let alone the more recent stuff, like that Peter Popinjay character; who writes that? Oh! Seneca Flandry. I thought it was cool, and then I discovered there was a real-life method there…and I was hooked."

"You know those are only fiction…"

"Yes ma'am! But the real thing is even better, from the couple of cases I've helped out with. I think so, anyway."

"And you'd like to go into that side of things?"

"Absolutely. Only…I want it to be…real." He paused, then added, "And straight."

"Captain Carter said he suspicioned you would," Peterson admitted, noting the addendum but deciding not to comment on it. "All right. Let me see, here, then…" She took on the blank look of someone working in VR for a few moments, then resumed focusing on Ashton. "Okay, there; I've put you in the fast track for investigative work, and I've called several of our detectives – the ones that aren't on a case...or other diversionary tactic," she shot a glance at Ashton, who nodded understanding, "at this moment – and they'll be coming by here so I can introduce you. I'll assign you to their department, and you can be a kind of assistant and adjunct to their work. An investigator, but not a detective – not yet. You have a few ranks to move up through, first."

"That sounds great, ma'am. At least here I've got a chance. Thank you so much."

At the Imperial City Spaceport, a young man in an Imperial Police uniform and a brunet crew cut was seen off by an older man and woman, who hugged him, kissed him, and told him to be careful. The young man picked up an oversized duffel and slung it over his shoulder, then went through the gate and boarded a shuttle. The older couple waved through the gate windows as the shuttle revved up, then lifted off. The woman dashed tears from her eyes, and the man put his arm around her.

Then they turned and left, headed for the concourse exit.

The young officer rode the shuttle up to the Sintar Spacelines craft, the SSS *Imperium*. There he boarded the star liner and ducked into the nearest head, locking the door behind him. He opened the duffel, revealing two small cases, one soft-sided, one hard. Plopping the soft-sided case on the sink, he opened it and pulled out a set of well-worn, casual civilian clothing, stripping off the police uniform, folding and placing it in the case, before donning the fresh clothing. That case was fastened, placed on the floor next to the duffel, and replaced with the hard-sided case.

This case held makeup, wigs, and more. He pulled off the brunet wig he wore, revealing a completely shaved head. The wig went into its place in the case, and an auburn wig pulled out, in a longer style.

This went on his head, secured in place with some double-sided tape, and the man fished brown-colored lenses from his eyes, revealing bright blue eyes. The discarded lenses went into a special small case, which was in turn tucked into a recess inside the suitcase.

Then he set to work on his face, removing makeup, thoroughly cleansing his face, then starting again and adding wrinkles and bags under his eyes, as well as copious freckles.

When he was finished, he picked up the empty duffel and turned it inside-out, revealing what looked like a completely different duffel. The makeup case and the clothing bag went inside, and it was fastened.

Ten minutes after "Nick Ashton" had entered, an older, ginger-complected deckhand exited the head and made his way to the shuttle about to debark, headed back for Sintar on leave.

Peterson introduced Ashton to several of the detectives in the Imperial City Police force, and he was duly impressed by all of them, but the ones with whom he instantly bonded were Eugene Demetrius and Stefan Gorski.

In addition, there were two other detectives who were commuting between Imperial City and Charia, the main city on the other big Sintaran continent of Hartug; there was a major murder case going on there that apparently started in Imperial City, at least in terms of planning. Detective Jill Amundsen and

Inspector Taylor Haptman were ostensibly part of the Investigations department as well, but currently spent little time there, and most of their time in the courts of Charia.

"So I'm afraid it may be some time before I can introduce you to them, Nick," she told him.

"That's all right, ma'am; it's something to look forward to," he replied with an understanding grin, and she chuckled.

"Somebody's enjoying this, huh?"

"A chance to meet and work with straight investigators? Oh HELL yes, ma'am!"

Peterson also introduced him to several of the other investigators in the department that had not yet made detective: Peter Rassmussen, Roger Armbrand, Timothy Jones, Darrell Osborn, and Rich Weyand. Of those five, the most experienced were Rassmussen and Armbrand, both of whom held the rank of Sergeant Investigator, and were thus higher rank than the other three.

"But given your time in your previous position, Nick," Peterson told him, "you're closer to their level. So once you get your feet on the ground and show us what you can do, I don't have a problem bumping you to Sergeant Investigator, too."

"I have an idea," Demetrius suggested. "It's nearly shift end; why don't we all go out and grab drinks, and maybe dinner, at the local hangout and get to know each other? Then we can go help Nick, here, finish moving. Maia, you got a problem with that?"

"Not at all, Gene, provided you watch out for problems with the Imperial Police," Peterson noted. "Remember where Ashton, here, is 'on loan' from...and why. Assuming he doesn't apply for a permanent slot in ICPD, which I hope he will. Even then, we might still need to help him watch his back. After all, he's not even supposed to be on the planet now."

"Right," Gorski agreed. "Yeah, no worries. We'll look out for 'im and keep it – and him – on the down low. This ain't our first rodeo like this. Gonna come with?"

"I'm not sure yet," Peterson noted. "I still have to tag up on some stuff to do with Ashton, and it might run me too late. Elvis gets...temperamental...if I'm late with his din-din."

"Elvis? Wasn't that an old-Earth music star?" a confused Ashton wondered, and the others laughed.

"Yeah, but that's not who she's talking about!" Rassmussen all but guffawed.

"Her cat," Gorski chuckled. "Blue point Oriental. He's temperamental on a good day. If she's late with his dinner, he barfs in her shoes."

"Or bed," Peterson added, rolling her eyes.

Another laugh went up, and this time, Ashton joined in. Peterson grinned ruefully.

"I liked the name. What can I say?" she said with a shrug. "He's my kitty tranquilizer when I come home from work on a bad day. It's better than drinking myself under the table every night."

"True words," Gorski agreed.

"Well, you know the hangout," Demetrius said. "If you get a chance, swing on by and join us. Even if only for a few minutes."

"Will do, but don't expect me, just in case I don't make it," Peterson said with a smile. "You lot go on and assign Ashton a desk and get him settled in, then head out."

"All over it," Gorski affirmed.

"...No, we never did get anything on him," General William Kershaw, the head of the IPD on Sintar, told his superior, Imperial Police Chief George Stanier, at about the same time as

Ashton was meeting the detectives. "Even though he's been here for years and years. Not for lack of trying, lemme tell ya. Smart bastard. Carter never quite went the way we wanted him to go, but he never quite crossed any lines, either. Still, I can't help but think how many kids he sent over to Imp City PD."

"Yeah, but those were the rejects," Stanier pointed out. "The ones we didn't want. And let's face it, Imp City isn't big enough to bother us too much. We're the main precinct for the Imperial Police, after all."

"True."

"So let's get rid of another one, and go ahead and accept Carter's retirement," Stanier decided. "We can put somebody in that position that we know is gonna do exactly and only what we want him to do, and be done with it." He paused, then added, "And when Officer Ashton gets back from his training, if he still doesn't get it, we'll take care of it then."

"Right. Done," Kershaw said, approving the form; in VR, it came across as checking the approval box on the form with a pen, when it was the electronic file that was in fact flagged as approved. "Be thinking about who you want to see in that position. I'll come up with a list of candidates by tomorrow morning."

"I think replacing him won't take long," Stanier agreed. "But I just had a thought…"

"What?"

"Carter *has* sent a bunch of rookies over to Imp City. What if Ashton really isn't going offworld at all, he's just going over there? He ducked out on your niece this morning, and that's suspicious, according to what you told me earlier. She had him strung along pretty good, there, we thought."

"Oh, that's right. And he's a problem child," Kershaw said, considering. "Hm. Good point."

"If he really hasn't gone anywhere except 'next door,' then we need to go ahead and take him out. Otherwise, he's liable to get us in trouble by blabbing to the wrong people. Especially about that attempted theft of the Sigil. We don't need the Empress' staff finding out about that."

"True…" Kershaw shrugged. "His home address is on file with the department. We can always have a cooking-fuel explosion outta the apartment kitchen, overnight…" He shrugged again. "Then it doesn't matter. One way or the other, he's out of our hair."

Stanier nodded.

"Make it happen," he declared.

Repercussions

"…Yeah, Lee, we got Ashton eased in and going," Peterson told Carter a few hours later, in the same nondescript VR meeting room. "And Gorski said he'd help him finish moving later tonight, so he wouldn't be alone at his old place, just in case. Given the lot that went with 'em to dinner, I expect there'll be easily half a dozen on moving duty, so it'll go fast. And they're good, so they'll stay out of sight, and keep *him* out of sight. Did you get the rationale sent, that will hopefully get the goons off his ass?"

"I did," Carter said, "and got the feedback that they bought it…I think. I hope so, for his sake, anyway."

"That's good, then."

"Yeah."

"What's your next step?"

"Oh, I've already taken it. I expect it to be approved any moment."

"What's that?"

"I've applied for early retirement. Given they've never been quite sure of me, I expect they won't hesitate to accept it. The faster they can get rid of me, the better." Carter paused, then sighed.

"Hey, what's wrong?" Peterson asked.

"I just feel bad for all the great kids like Ashton that'll come later," Carter admitted. "Because you know they're gonna put a hardcore stooge in this job, once I'm gone."

"Well, we'll see," Peterson said with a shrug. "Meanwhile, I–"

"Hold on a sec," Carter said, glancing to one side. "I just got a notification."

"Standing by."

Peterson waited while Carter's avatar assumed a blank look, as he checked the reason for the notification in a different channel. When he came back, he smiled.

"That's that," he told her. "My application for early retirement has been accepted, with my accrued leave to commence at the end of my shift today and run through until the official termination date. I'm done with this damn place. When we're finished here, I'll pack my personal things in a box and leave this office behind for good."

"Congratulations!" Peterson said with a wide smile. "Do you have any celebratory plans?"

"No, not really…"

"Good. Come over to my place about two hours after you get off shift. That'll give me time to finish my own shift, then get home, feed Elvis, and prep a nice dinner. We'll celebrate together." She shrugged, then added, "I was gonna see about swinging by the pub; all the guys are getting to know Ashton before they headed out to finish his move, and I was invited. But I think I like this idea better."

Carter grinned.

"It's a date."

"It better be."

"I've been thinking," Gorski said, as the group headed out.

"I knew I smelled something burning," Demetrius said with a smirk. "Let's hear it."

"Well, my gut is saying we need to go get Nick, here, moved out of his place before we go off to the pub, just in case. If they suspect anything, it'll be the first place they look for him, so we need to get it clear, *now*."

"Mm," Demetrius hummed, considering. "Now that you mention it, my gut agrees. Yeah, Stefan, I think you have a really good idea there. Guys?" he addressed the rest of their party, "are you up for this? Anybody who doesn't want to help can just head for the pub and get us the back room..."

"Which we need somebody to do, anyway," Gorski decided.

"I'll go take care of the back room," Rassmussen offered. "You want the one near the back entrance, right? The 'backmost back room'?"

"That's the one," Demetrius confirmed. "How about the rest of you? Going with us, or to the pub?"

It turned out they were game to go to Ashton's apartment and help move him.

So the rest, led by Gorski, followed Ashton to his old apartment, where they helped him load and grab the last few boxes, and transfer them to his new place; with all of them working, it took only about forty-five minutes.

As Carter had instructed him, he didn't leave a forwarding address with the old apartment superintendent.

And he applied for, and was approved, to change his VR contact channels.

Once they left the boxes in Ashton's new den, they headed for the pub...covertly. Demetrius led the way through a series of back alleys, private arcades, maintenance tunnels, and mews, to the back door of the Laughing Cat Pub. Slipping inside, they found that Rassmussen awaited the group, and he promptly led them into the pub's "backmost back room," as he termed it; Ashton found from the conversation that this sort of thing was not necessarily unusual, when the detectives wanted to gather during an active undercover investigation or the like.

In short order, a waiter – their usual, it appeared, named George – came in and took orders for food and drink.

The gathering at the local pub was fun, full of jokes and laughter, and Ashton was glad to get to know the people with whom he'd be working in the immediate future. When it was over, Gorski and Demetrius personally escorted Ashton back to his new apartment.

"Stay put tonight," Gorski told him at the door of his flat. "Crash early, if you can. We want to make sure everyone thinks you're not on Sintar any longer."

"Right," Ashton agreed.

More than an hour after the two experienced detectives left Ashton at his new apartment, a figure dressed in head-to-toe black, gloves on hands, face hidden under a balaclava, small kit tucked under one arm, slipped from the shadows on the street and into a particular apartment building. It headed up the fire escape to the correct floor for his apartment, then headed for the apartment door, rapidly hacking the lock and entering the darkened apartment.

There, it headed straight for the kitchen. The kit came out, and a device was pulled from it, the timer on it set, then it was fastened into the interior of the oven.

The mysterious stranger left the way it had come.

Late that night, a maintenance man let himself into the now-empty apartment that Ashton and Stone had once occupied, to check out the flat for any needed updates or repairs, as well as strip certain amenities that needed replacing before a new tenant could be installed.

He planned to be there all night, working on the apartment.

In the end, he never went home.

In the wee small hours the next morning, in Imperial Park West a few blocks south of the Imperial University, an explosion rocked the building that had been Ashton's old home, an explosion within the very apartment in which he had lived.

Maia Peterson's apartment was only a couple of blocks away, and the concussion was loud enough to rattle windows and loose items in her bedroom.

"SHIT!" Lee Carter exclaimed, lunging into a sitting position and dislodging a startled little Siamese who had been snuggling against him, even as Maia also sat up, pulling the covers to her bare chest. "What the *hell* was that?!"

"Dunno," Maia said, puzzled. "Whatever happened, it was a mighty big boom."

"It sounded fairly close," Lee noted. "Let's see what we can find in the news feed."

The police assistant chief and the retired police assistant chief sat still, expressions blank, as they entered immersive VR together.

"This oughta do it," Maia said, as she and Lee sat down in virtual armchairs in front of a wall screen of sorts. "I need to get a screen for the bedroom, especially if you're going to be over often. At least this way, we can watch together."

"Yeah. But I'm betting nobody knows yet. It only just happened," Lee pointed out.

"Probably, but we can have a look."

It did take a while, but eventually reports began to come in about the incident. As soon as the news media reached the area and set up video crews, Lee gasped.

"Oh dear Lord," he all but groaned. "They got him, despite my best efforts."

"Huh?" Maia asked in alarm, turning. "Got who?"

"Nick. Nick Ashton. The kid I sent you toda– er, yesterday, now."

"Shit," Maia said, wincing. "He struck me as a good kid. Is that his new place?"

"No...oh, that's right, he was moving, wasn't he? I told him to finish up, get clear, and not to tell anybody over at IPD about it. I sure as hell hope he followed my instructions."

"Gorski an' the rest of his team were gonna go take care of that after the socializing at the pub," Maia explained. "If they actually did, then he was probably in the new apartment, not the old one. So he should be safe, Lee."

"Um," Lee said, raking a hand over his face, "Maia, at the risk of sounding like an old softie, you wouldn't mind checking, would you? As soon as I left Headquarters at the end of my shift, they took down all my links, 'cause I'm retired now..."

"You can't call the kid?"

"Nope. I don't have access. And I never got his personal info, 'cause I didn't want to risk being accused of something..."

"Okay, lemme see. Huh. He's changed his VR contact info; that's promising. But this might take me a bit..."

Ashton woke to an urgent notification in his VR, and saw that it was from Colonel Peterson. He sat up, groggy, and glanced at the clock: *3:12am. Shit,* he thought. *What's* this *all about? I'm supposed to be off duty. And how the hell did she get my new VR contact info... well, she* is *the assistant chief, after all.*

He was also nude, mildly disoriented, sitting in the dark and unable to remember where the light switches were in his new apartment – in or out of VR – and too out of it to select an appropriate avatar, so he simply used an audio link.

"Officer Ashton."

"Oh, thank God, Nick!" Maia Peterson's voice came through to him. "I'm so sorry to wake you, but Lee and I – er, Captain Carter and I – have been dreadfully worried about you."

"Um, okay, yeah, I'm fine...what's happened?"

"I take it, you're in your new place?"

"Uh, yeah..."

"Good. Because your old place was blown to dust bunnies about half an hour, maybe forty-five minutes ago."

Ashton sat up straight, suddenly wide awake.

"SHIT!" he declared.

"Yes, and according to the news feeds, one Inspector Thomas has decreed it was 'an accident by the inhabitant, who was apparently killed in the blast. Most likely a failure to switch off certain cooking appliances or the like,' given the video clip that's running in the newsfeed."

"You're kidding," Ashton said, voice flat with surprise and dismay. "That was the detective I was supposed to be assigned to, over at IPD, the one that didn't want me to do anything but what he said."

"Aha. The one Lee – um, Captain Carter – says you hacked off?"

"That's the one, yeah. And then he never used me again."

"All right. I want you to lay low for a few days, then. Stefan Gorski and I will help keep you out of sight, while still getting you up to speed with our department. We don't need these rotten cops finding out they killed the wrong guy and coming back after you until we get you a little better settled. And not even then, if we can help it."

"I won't argue that," Ashton said, perturbed, raking his fingers through his hair and disarranging it further.

"Good. I'm sorry I woke you, but I'm sure you can see why I

did."

"Yes ma'am, and thanks for being worried about me. Can you call Captain Carter back and tell him I'm okay?"

"I'll do that, Nick," Peterson said in an amused tone. "See you in the morning. Keep your head down. Wear street clothes to come in, though; whatever you do, don't come in uniform. Bring your uniform in to the locker room in a garment bag and change there, and wear a hooded jacket or ball cap or something, to minimize recognition. All right?"

"Yes ma'am."

"See you then."

"Good night, ma'am."

And the VR link broke.

Ashton pulled up the news feed to see what had happened to his old apartment, thankful he was no longer in it, and wondering who had been.

"It's all right, Lee; he's fine," Maia told her lover. "He was in the new place. Whoever they nailed, it was the wrong guy. Might have been the super, or a maintenance worker, or maybe a cleaning person."

"Good," Lee said, deeply relieved. "And yeah, you're probably right...though I feel bad for whoever it was, and their family. You told the boy to lay low?"

"Yeah. We're gonna try to keep him out of sight for as long as we can. You think they'll check to see that they got the right person?"

"No idea. I guess it depends on how cocky they are, and how good they think their hit man is. But if Ashton goes out with your people, they'll find out, sooner or later."

"I know. But better later, when we can get a bit more experience under his belt, and some buddies watching his back, than sooner, without all that."

"No argument there." Lee drew a deep breath, and let it out in a shaky sigh.

"Aw. You're really fond of the kid."

"Well...yeah. He's...he's smart, and he's good, and he has a good heart, Maia." He shrugged. "He...sorta reminds me of me, when I started. I..."

"You've been keeping an eye on him since he arrived."

"Yeah."

"And you thought you'd failed."

Lee dropped his gaze to the bedclothes in his lap. Elvis was already settling back down, across his ankles. "...Yeah."

"C'mere, baby," she said, pulling him close. "He's safe. Everything's okay now. Just relax."

And she kissed him thoroughly.

Hitting the Ground One Way or Another

The next morning, Ashton arrived at ICPD headquarters in a hooded jacket and casual wear, his uniform in a garment bag which he carefully rolled and placed in a small duffel to disguise it as much as possible. He changed in the locker room, then headed for his superior's office, where he gave his new address to Colonel Peterson.

"And if you wouldn't mind, could you pass it on to Captain Carter when it's appropriate, since I'm…well, I guess I'm officially offworld, but unofficially on loan to you guys?"

"I can, when I see him tonight," Maia agreed, "but he's not 'Captain' anybody now, you know. He retired as soon as you got your ass outta that place, Nick."

"He did?!"

"He did. Like, within an hour. And glad of it, to judge by what he told me last night." She studied the young officer for a long moment. "You know what? I'm gonna just hang on to this. Oh, I'll enter it into the formal records for Imp City, but I'll ensure it's buried deep, and has a restriction on it so nobody can see it that I don't want seeing. Lee won't have a replacement yet, and when they do replace him, it'll be somebody who kowtows to Stanier or Kershaw, you can be sure of that. And by the time they do, or by the time you've 'come back from training,' whichever comes first…well, I'll have conveniently 'lost' it."

"Oh," Ashton said, trying not to grin.

"Oh, go ahead and laugh," Peterson said, grinning herself. "You're going to find out, Nick, that this department runs a lot differently – and a lot less formally – than the one you were just in. And I'll bet you wind up liking it, when all's said and done."

"I'm sure liking it so far, ma'am. I'd never have thought of somebody over at IPD headquarters calling me in the middle of the night 'cause they were worried about me. Well, maybe Captain Carter…"

"Definitely Captain Carter. He was waiting on tenterhooks for me to let him know if you were okay."

"Why didn't he call me himself?"

"He couldn't. As soon as he was out of the building – probably before – they cut his comms to all you guys, and he'd deliberately not gotten your personal contact info to prevent either of you being accused of collusion or something."

"Oh. Aw. Well, yeah, then. I definitely am liking this department better."

"Good."

Starting that very morning, Peterson kept Ashton at his desk for more than three weeks, waiting for the hullaballoo over the bombing to die down – it had to have been a bomb, given nobody was living in the apartment, and per ICPD's official unofficial assessment by their explosives experts, it was too big to have been a gas explosion, anyway. This was all done with the help of Stefan Gorski and his team, during which time they accepted Ashton as one of their own. They were, one and all, concerned for his safety, especially after the blast; as a general rule, someone walked home with him at the end of shift, and pretty soon, at least one and often more were meeting him near his new flat to come in with him in the mornings, as well.

"What's the word, George?" Chief Stanier asked General

Kershaw. "Did we get 'im?"

"Not according to the forensics guys, George," Kershaw responded. "Apparently it was just a maintenance guy."

"But that was Ashton's apartment, right, Bill?"

"It was. It was a furnished apartment, so all the furniture and décor was there, but there were no personal items there. After the fact, we went in and found out that he'd given up the lease on it, packed up, and headed out. Evidently Ashton really did leave Sintar. And some of my people actually saw him departing from an interstellar gate, on a flight to Pritani, like Carter said."

"Really? That's good, then. Maybe he'll come back with some street smarts to add to the book smarts."

"Hopefully. We might even want to consider moving him from the beat cop line org into the investigation line, if his training pans out."

"It's an idea. We'll wait and see what happens when he gets back." Stanier paused, then delicately changed the subject. "How's your niece doing with her assignments?"

"She's doing great, George," Kershaw replied with a chuckle. "Coming right along. Already got her first promotion."

"Great! Oh, and have you heard about that new boyfriend? Some actor from a VR drama. She caught a looker, from the scuttlebutt I heard."

"Yeah," Kershaw laughed. "That one's going hot and heavy. He's even slept over a few times already."

"Do tell…"

When the news became public that the deceased had been a maintenance man prepping the apartment for a new renter, Carter, Peterson, and Gorski realized that their "laying low" subterfuge might have run its course.

"Because they know now, it wasn't Ashton," Gorski told Peterson in her office.

"Yeah," she sighed. "I'd hoped for a little longer, but there it is." She paused. "Maybe it'll work in our favor, though."

"How's that?"

"He's not supposed to be on Sintar, remember? He's on Pritani, getting trained."

"Ooo, good point. You might be right, then."

"So maybe it's time to take advantage of that notion."

"Yeah. Let's start getting him some street experience," Gorski suggested. "Might as well get as much training under his belt as we can, as fast as we can, while they think he's not here. It stands him a better chance to survive. Especially if one of us is with him."

"Go for it," Peterson agreed. "But…"

"But?"

"You think we can get him into an Imp City uniform?"

"I think we're gonna try," Gorski agreed. "Or…"

"Or?"

"Or that might be too close to how they're used to seeing him. It might not be a big enough difference. A police uniform is a police uniform, after all. And they're all part of the same pattern."

"Mmph. Good point. What do you suggest, then?"

"Simple. We can put him in plainclothes, since he's on the investigatory team. Then, if and only if we have a need for him to be formally in uniform, we'll slap his ass in an Imp City one. Maybe even a high-ranking one. Because 'undercover.' And," he added, considering, "we might ought to gin up a fake police I.D. for him, just in case. Something that we can put into the system and therefore looks real, but is an alias for him, in case he has to face off against an IPD officer while on a case. That way he doesn't give away who he really is."

"Even better. Do it."

"Yes, sir?" Ashton said, reporting to Detective Gorski in his office. "What do you need, sir?"

"It's what you need, Nick," Gorski said, gesturing to the visitor's chair. "The IPD – meaning Stanier, Kershaw and Company – now knows you weren't in your old apartment, and have probably realized you moved out, so we're going to play off the notion that you're offworld for as long as possible."

"Okay…"

"How many suits do you have?"

"Suits? Um, one, maybe two…"

"What about a sport coat?"

"I have a tweed jacket…" Ashton noted, thinking hard.

"Dress trousers?"

"Just my uniforms and what goes with my suits, sir."

"Casual dress slacks?"

"Uh, yeah, I got around four or five of those."

"Shirts?"

"Um, 'bout twice as many of those, more or less."

"Can you put together a work wardrobe that resembles what I'm wearing right now?" Gorski asked, standing, so Ashton could see the corduroy jacket, open-collared shirt, and casual slacks he wore. "Without using the uniform trousers?"

"Yes, sir, I can. Might have to buy another jacket and maybe another pair or two of trousers to get me through, but I think I can. Won't look quite as nice as what you're wearing, but you're a detective, and I'm just an investigator…"

"Good, and that'll work. Give Jones your measurements and wardrobe colors, and I'll have him see about getting the additions for you, since we don't want you out and about, shopping; he can even use the expense account, since you're an undercover project of ours. We need to get you some body armor to go under it all, too."

"Thank you, sir! I'll pay back the cost, or you can pull it from my pay."

"We'll worry about that later. For now, go to your locker and put your street clothes back on. If anybody says anything, you're undercover...which you are. Besides, you're on the investigations squad now, anyway."

"Yes, sir."

"Oh, and start growing out your hair, some. That near-crew cut thing you got, with a little length on the top, is kind of distinctive on you. Meantime, ping Adrian Mott for a wig or some extensions. Maybe even consider a beard or something."

"On it, sir."

That began Ashton's tenure as a formal investigator.

The next day, while Colonel Peterson was still trying to get a feel for him to determine an exact assignment and teaming, she sent Ashton out – complete with blond wig, in plainclothes – with Sergeant Investigator Peter Rassmussen, so that Rassmussen could familiarize him with the jurisdiction, and explain the differences in operation between the Imperial Police and the Imperial City Police.

They were walking through the arcade, which was moderately crowded at that time of day, as Rassmussen noted the differences in operation between IPD and ICPD, when Ashton stopped dead, staring. Rassmussen stopped as well.

"Hey, Nick, are you oka—" he began

"Hey! Oy! You, there! STOP!" Ashton yelled abruptly, then set off running...

...Just as a thief grabbed a woman's shopping bags from her arm and ran.

"HEY!" Rassmussen shouted, and headed after Ashton. "Stop! Police!"

The thief dared an alarmed glance over his shoulder, then turned around and ran harder.

"This...is gonna...take...a while," Ashton said, pacing his speech to his breath, as Rassmussen accelerated until he was alongside him. They managed to keep the thief in sight with difficulty; he was darting in and out of the foot traffic on the arcade.

"Yup," was all Rassmussen said in response. They cornered hard, as the thief tried to lose them in a side street of the arcade.

"Got tranqs?"

"Nope. Needs a...rifle. We're...plainclothes. An' too... many...p'destr'ns...around...to risk...a shot," Rassmussen panted. "Of any...thing."

"Wait. You gotta...baton...stashed...someplace?"

"Uh, yeah..."

"Gimme."

Rassmussen pulled his baton from its hidden pocket within the left side of his blazer, and passed it to Ashton. Ashton took it, put on a brief burst of speed, then yelled at the top of his lungs, "MOVE!" He hit the extension switch even as he twisted to the side and threw the baton on a low, straight, twirling trajectory.

Pedestrians instinctively dodged at his cry, and the baton whipped forward, spinning, right into the pumping legs of the fleeing thief, who promptly went down hard onto the pavement, smacking his head and stunning him nearly unconscious. Before he could regain his wits, the two police officers were on him, restraining him and taking him into custody.

"So he spotted the purse snatcher before you did? And then took him down?" Peterson asked later that day.

"Yeah, and yeah, he did," Rassmussen told Peterson and Gorski. "It was a standoff, and looked like it was gonna be a case of who ran outta oomph first. But Nick took the guy out with my baton, without our having to even get close. Damn, though, but the perp is lucky not to have busted a leg or something. Those batons can hurt. And for a split-second, there, he was so tangled up with the baton, he looked like he had *three* legs!"

"Sounds like Ashton is sharp-eyed and quick-thinking," Gorski said, shooting a meaningful glance at Peterson.

"He is," Rassmussen averred. "And I thought he was really easy to get along with, too. He seems like a genuinely nice guy, with a good sense of right and wrong. Not to mention sharp eyes and a lotta brains."

"I'd have to agree," Peterson said. "You want him, Stefan?"

"What, Eugene hasn't called dibs on him yet? He's got seniority; he's an inspector. I'm just a lowly detective."

"Not yet. I think he hasn't really thought about it this early in the game. He's still winding up that case over on the north side, after all."

"Aha! Then yeah, I think I do, Maia," Gorski agreed with a grin. "Assign him to me. I'll see he gets those talents honed properly."

"Great!" Rassmussen enthused. "He's gonna be part of *our* team!"

"It's a plan," Peterson said. She "checked out" for a moment, entering VR, then came back. "Paperwork implemented. Take him under your wing and train that boy to be a detective,

Stefan. Hell, train that boy to become an inspector. He's got it in him."

"Consider it done," Gorski said, pleased.

First Case

Ashton started work under Gorski immediately. The experienced detective took him in hand and ascertained what he already knew about investigation, and how experienced he already was. He took the younger man around with him to his various cases as they occurred, essentially smaller things for the time being – burglaries and petty theft, for the most part, in various areas of Imperial Park.

The crimes were largely near ICPD headquarters, which was in the West quadrant, a few blocks north of the line of the underground commuter train, though many of the investigators lived south of it. Gorski promptly began training Ashton to know what to look for, how to find and interpret clues, how to properly take evidence without contaminating or corrupting it, and how to glean as much information as possible from a victim interview.

Meanwhile, Ashton was growing his hair out, changing its style, and trying to get a bit of a tan by sunning on the roof of his apartment building – whatever he could think of to change his appearance. This included having his barber add heavy blond highlights as his hair grew. And that image of him, enhanced to make his hair even blonder, became the "official" mug shot of one "Nicholas 'Nick' Benton," investigator for the Imperial City Police Department.

It all seemed to be working; no one from the Imperial Police bothered him. And he had inadvertently walked right by a couple of Imperial Police officers just the day before.

The fact that he now had a couple of suits of body armor,

one of which he wore each day under his clothing and alternating days, helped him feel a little more confident about the encounter, especially after they failed to recognize him.

Then the call came in.

"Come on, Nick," Gorski said, coming by the young investigator's desk. "Let's go. We've got a call. Bad situation."

"What happened?" Ashton said, grabbing his tweed jacket from the back of his chair as he stood.

"Not quite sure yet," Gorski responded, already headed for the door. "Definite assault. Judging by what I was shown of the condition of the victim's clothes, probable sexual assault. Whether it was attempted or successful rape, I'm still waiting on the docs to decide."

"What does the victim say happened?"

"The victim is unconscious, likely in a coma. Apparently she fought back, and took a nasty knock on the head for her troubles. Her boyfriend found her on the floor of their apartment when he came home from work, and called for emergency help to get her to the hospital. He was afraid to move her."

"Ooo."

"Yeah." By now, they were on the sidewalk outside ICPD headquarters. Gorski stopped dead, holding up a hand. "Wait a minute."

The pair stood there for several minutes as Gorski "checked out." When several groups paused beside them, unable to get by without stepping into the street, Ashton grabbed Gorski's elbow, gently and unobtrusively pulling him out of the flow of pedestrian traffic – there wasn't a slidewalk here, directly in front of the headquarters building – into an alcove near the door; he figured his new mentor was in VR, likely getting information, and didn't want to disturb him. But they were blocking the sidewalk; transport traffic was heavy that time of day, so no one dared step into the street proper. Therefore staying well out of the way of the pedestrian traffic was wise. Finally Gorski came up for air and looked around.

"Wha? Oh. Yeah, okay. Thanks for getting me out of the way, Nick. Shoulda thought."

"No problem. What have you got?"

"That was the emergency physician at the hospital. It was definitely an attempted rape. Her clothing was shredded up, and she has bruises and scratch marks on breasts and external genitals, but no evidence of penetration, or semen."

"Evidence of pen…?"

"Bruising. Internal or…" Gorski waved a hand, "internal-external, if you get me. Nothing around the vaginal opening."

"Oh. But that should mean," Ashton considered, thinking hard. "She must have hurt her assailant pretty good, or he'd have finished the rape after he knocked her out."

"Good reasoning job, son. That's what I think, too. The hospital has a forensic physician on her case, so if she has any hair or tissue samples on her – under her fingernails, for instance, and by the way, they think they did find some – we'll get the rundown on that once it's been processed. Meantime, you and I are going over to the apartment to look for additional clues and evidence."

"Let's go, then."

The boyfriend, Owen Jackson, was being held in the hallway while three Imp City police beat cops stood guard over the door, when the two investigators arrived. They identified themselves in VR to the waiting police officers and Jackson, and the guards let them inside.

"Stay behind me, Nick, and keep your eyes peeled," Gorski told him. "We want to avoid disturbing things, and try to get a picture of what might have happened based on the clues, then we'll start looking for more details based on that. If we don't find those details, we back off again and adjust our big picture."

"Right," Ashton confirmed. "I get it."

"Good."

Gorski entered the apartment slowly, followed by Ashton. They stood by the door and surveyed the apartment, including the door, front and back.

Before them lay the den, with a couch, coffee table, two end tables with lamps, two armchairs, one on each side of the couch and at right angles to it, and a wet bar in the corner. A couple of bookcases stood on the wall opposite the wet bar, as well as a small rack containing folding tray tables; the complete set of tables remained in the rack.

The narrow coffee table had been turned over, and one leg was broken; both lamps were on the floor, one broken, both with crushed shades; the couch had been shoved back at one end, twisting the adjacent end table, and the corresponding armchair was forced well to the side, pivoted to face roughly the same direction as the couch. The throw pillows on the disarranged end of the couch had been flung to the floor in various parts of the room, but the ones on the other end still lay tucked into the corner of the couch. The upholstery of the couch had blood smears, and there were two small puddles of blood on the floor near the broken leg of the coffee table, one on each side of the table. Two coffee cups on the twisted end table had been overturned, their contents running over the tabletop and onto the floor in various places.

"All right, Nick, what happened, and where should we look

for what?" Gorski asked, somewhat to Ashton's surprise.

"Um, okay, lessee," he said, quickly collecting his thoughts. "She let a friend in for coffee. She sat on the end of the couch, he sat in the armchair, and they talked for a bit. He made a move, she said no, and he didn't take no for an answer. He tried to push her down on the couch and rape her, and she fought back, shoving him away. He fell over the coffee table, turning it over and crunching one of its legs, and she tried to get out the end, but he grabbed her – probably by the ankle, with him still down on the floor – and she stumbled and grabbed for the end table. It slid, and she lunged forward for the armchair, managing to kick him, maybe in the face. If she broke his nose, that might explain one puddle of blood on the floor…but so would a head wound, from his fall over the table. But he jumped up and got in front of her – the way the armchair is turned, she couldn't have gotten it in that position herself, but it could have slid some with her body weight – then shoved her back. She grabbed his arm to keep from falling, but then she probably either kicked or kneed him hard in the groin, and he shoved her down. She hit her head on the broken table leg, and that created the second puddle of blood…and the cranial damage that put her into a coma. But if she hit him hard enough in the groin, he wasn't going to be doing much with the personal tackle for a while."

Gorski raised an impressed eyebrow.

"Could you elaborate on the rationale for your deductions?" he asked.

"Sure, sir. There's no evidence the door was forced; she let him in. Ergo, she knew him. There may or may not be latents on the door; we probably need to check. There are two cups of coffee, one black, one with cream, so she offered him coffee; she wasn't drinking alone. Which also means there's probably the remains where she made the coffee in the kitchen someplace. There's not enough coffee spilled for the mugs to have been full when he attacked, so they sat and talked for a while. They were friends. Or at least, she thought so.

"The end of the couch next to the coffee mugs is shoved back hard enough to scratch the finish on the floor; that argues for some weight on it. He was trying to push her down and force her. That, in turn, caused the far end of the couch to smack that end table, toppling its lamp – notice how it fell away from the couch, and parallel with it? But she fought back, and probably managed to get a foot into his belly or the like and shove hard. That sent him back and over the coffee table, which turned over – I'd say he got a leg or a foot hung under it – and his weight snapped one of the legs. He hit hard, and the puddle over there," he pointed, "is either where his nose bled, or more probably his scalp, likely split under the force of the impact. That would have dazed him, and she would seize the opportunity to jump up and run. He grabbed for her ankle and tripped her up, so she lunged for the nearest piece of furniture, the end table. That's probably when the coffee mugs turned over and spilled, and that lamp fell – it fell back roughly perpendicular to the direction of the couch, in turn indicating the approximate direction of force, which was greater than the other end, because this lamp broke." He glanced at Gorski, uncertain.

"Good so far," Gorski murmured. "Keep going."

"She instinctively kicked back, probably caught him in the face, and that's how the pillow there got a blood spatter on it." Ashton pointed. "Note the angle of the spray, pointing to the location of the source. Chances are, she smashed his nose with her heel. If it wasn't broken already, it would be by then."

"Good..."

"He shook his head to clear it, sending more blood spatters from his nose and possibly the back of his head and hair, then jumped up, leaping over the coffee table and getting in front of her, fending her off with the chair from the back; he could keep her from running for help, or into the bedroom and locking the door, that way." Ashton paused, thinking. "She may have turned to run around the other end of the couch at that point. Then he shoved the chair aside and came after her before she could. Oh! I meant to ask; did she have any blood on her knuckles?"

"She did," Gorski confirmed. "The forensic doctor noted that, and her knuckles were bruised, but the skin wasn't broken. And yes, he took samples of the blood for analysis."

"So she punched him in the busted nose," Ashton said with a wolfish grin. "Good for her! But that's what made him good and mad, so he shoved her down, probably with the intent to pin her and rape her at that point...when she kicked upward. If it was deliberate intent combined with her body being off-balance as she started to fall, then her foot...maybe her knee, but if she was falling, probably foot or shin...clobbered him in the family jewels pretty hard. In turn, she hit her head on the broken table leg and it rendered her unconscious." Ashton shook his head, wincing despite himself. "That wouldn't do any favors for her skull or brain, I'd think. Anyway, the scalp laceration from the broken table leg created *that* puddle." He pointed to the second congealing blood pool. "But we already know that she wasn't actually penetrated. He was in too much pain from the head blow, the broken nose, and the kick in the crotch to finish his intended job, so he left...probably walking funny."

"And based on this scenario, what should we do, and what should we look for?"

"We get *in situ* imagery, then grab samples of all the blood stains for the lab, both coffee mugs for DNA, and look for any latents on the mugs and the front door, as well as on the tabletops. Also any hair – pubic or head – on the armchair and possibly the couch." Ashton, who had been studying the crime scene intently, now looked up at Gorski. "And we need to contact the hospitals, looking for a man of around average height – judging by the location of the coffee table to the pool of blood his head left – with a probable concussion and skull laceration, probable broken nose but certainly a couple of black eyes and facial bruising, with nosebleed, scratches somewhere on his body, and severe bruising to the family jewels."

"Why didn't she call for help in VR?"

"She was probably surprised by his attack, and once it started happening, she was just reacting, trying to get away." He shrugged. "That's how most people tend to react in a threat emergency sitch. They only make the emergency call after they have a chance to think."

"Damn, son, you're gonna be a hell of a detective," Gorski said with a grin. "Now, do you know how to take those samples?"

"Not yet, sir. I mean, we did them in the forensics labs at the academy, and I've watched you do a few things, but in the field, my own self? No. This is my first opportunity to actually do it."

"Then let me talk you through it..."

In short order, the *in situ* imagery was taken, several latent prints found and lifted, the coffee mugs were bagged, samples of the coffee taken, blood samples were taken of both pools and each spatter grouping, and several dark hairs – that did not match the victim's medium auburn hair – were bagged as well.

One of the beat cops who had been guarding the door was promptly dispatched with the evidence to the ICPD forensics lab for analysis, along with a control sample from the victim's hairbrush in the bathroom, in order to separate out the victim's DNA from her assailant's.

"And now we need to put out the hospital inquiry," Gorski noted. "Nick, come with me into VR – we'll use channel 842 – and I'll show you how that's done..."

They contacted all of the hospitals within easy walking distance of the crime scene; since there had been no reports of a bloody, battered man wandering around the Imperial Park area, let alone walking oddly, the two investigators surmised that he likely went straight to medical help, and didn't go far to get it.

On the third contact, they hit paydirt.

Dirk Leeds had been admitted to the Empress Adannaya III Hospital two hours before their inquiry. He was diagnosed with a badly broken nose, a three-inch gash in his scalp, severe claw marks to chest and one side of the face, and at least one ruptured testicle, as well as possible urethral damage. He was in emergency surgery at that time, as doctors attempted to repair the genital damage.

"Well, that explains a lot," Gorski said, crossing his eyes. "And we don't need to rush, because I don't think he'll be going anywhere any time soon."

"You mean aside from the surgery?"

"Yeah. He gave the ER docs some sort of drivel about a dog attack while he was biking, but they didn't believe him. And I confirmed it for 'em. So they're gonna hold him until we come and tell 'em what to do with him. He's goin' nowhere."

"No. But his victim won't, either. Assuming she lives, or

comes out of the coma. And even if she wakes up, she might not…" Ashton paused, sighed, then asked, "How bad was she, anyway?"

"I'm not sure, Nick. We can go talk to Dr. Aadi Botha – he's the forensic physician over at the Empress Adannaya III Hospital – and ensure our prisoner is cuffed to his bed until he's released into our custody, then go see about her, if you want to. Her boyfriend, I have it to understand, headed out shortly after we started processing their apartment, going back to the hospital. He just wanted to meet us and ensure we had what we needed, first."

"That…sounds like a good idea, sir. It's a good plan."

"If you like, Nick, when no other team members are around, you can call me Stefan. You show some real promise, and I want to mentor you…which means I want you to be comfortable around me, and not feel constrained. I'm here for any questions you have, or if you're unsure about something… and that means in your personal life, too, by the way."

"Oh! Thank you si– uh, Stefan. I appreciate that," Nick said with a smile.

"Are you sure you won't be upset if the victim doesn't make it?"

"No, sir, um, Stefan, I'm not. I think it'll probably take my mood down a few tens of notches, at least." He shook his head, his face falling despite himself. "I haven't even met her yet, but I really hope she comes out okay. But I know she could have brain damage, even if she survives…" He sighed. "Damn."

"Ah. Then you're human, and not a psychopath, like some of those jerks over at IPD Headquarters. Good. You just passed my last test. We'll do fine together, you and me."

It didn't take long to arrange for Dirk Leeds to be restrained, and a police presence placed over him, at the Empress Adannaya III Hospital. He wouldn't be going anywhere except to jail and then to trial. And the hospital forensic physician had already sent over DNA samples to the ICPD Forensics Lab for comparison to the samples taken at the crime scene and from the victim. Before Gorski and Ashton could reach the Empress Kolbesdeka Hospital, where the victim was being treated, Forensics was calling them with a confirmed match on all three sample sources.

When they arrived, the victim, Sheila Mackay, was still unconscious, though Owen Jackson, her significant other, said the doctors had more hope of a good outcome than they had had when she was admitted; she was beginning to respond to stimulus, and it was hoped she might wake soon. The two investigators stood in the ICU room with Jackson, as the battered woman lay in the bed nearby.

"That's good," Ashton said in response to the improved prognosis.

"Yes, it is," Gorski agreed. "And we have some good news for you, Mr. Jackson."

"Oh? Don't tell me you know who did it."

"We do, and he is under custody at a different hospital. He had to have emergency surgery to try to repair what your lady, there, did to him."

"What?! What did she do to him?"

"She kicked him right in the pocket rocket, hard enough to bust his balls!" Ashton said with a wide grin.

"And the rocket," Gorski added with a smirk.

"Good enough for him! Who the hell was it?"

"Guy named Dirk Leeds," Gorski said. "You know him?"

"You're kidding." Jackson gaped. "That's her coworker. They were, like, best friends. When I first got to know Sheila –

we've only been together a few months, but I think it's gonna be permanent, 'cause I'm crazy about her – well, I thought those two were an item until she explained."

"Evidently he thought so, too, I guess," Ashton noted. "Anyway, when the doctors finally release him after surgery–"

"Surgery?! You guys weren't kidding that she busted his balls!"

"Nope," Ashton averred.

"I had it to understand from the attending physician that he wouldn't be trying anything like this again," Gorski added. "I don't know that the repair is going to be completely successful, based on what the surgeon of record told me...*off* the record. He took a really hard hit to the groin. They're having to do some reconstruction, the damage was so bad. Penis and at least one testicle. And that wasn't the only damage he took. Severely broken nose, scalp laceration, claw marks to face and chest..."

"Damn." Jackson winced. "Sounds like Sheila gave as good as she got."

"Yup, just about. Once he's released from the hospital," Ashton tag-teamed his new mentor, "which may take a while given all that, we can assure you both that he'll be going straight into custody, and based on the evidence we secured, is likely to be going away for a while."

"...Good," Jackson said with a sigh. "That's...a relief."

"Iiiithnnsooootooo," the woman in the bed breathed.

All three men glanced around, startled.

"Did she just try to talk?" Ashton wondered.

"Sure sounded like it to me," Gorski said, eyebrows shooting up. "Nick, go grab the doctor! Mr. Jackson, try to talk to her!"

Ashton sprinted to the door, yelling, "We need a doctor! She's trying to wake up!" as Jackson bent over the bed.

"Honey? It's Owen. I'm right here. Sheila, baby, can you

hear me?" Jackson asked.

"Mm-hmm."

"What did you just say?" he asked, as several doctors ran in. They immediately began checking her vitals.

"Said...I th'nk so, too." Her eyelids fluttered, then parted slightly. "Dey go' 'im, righ'?" she slurred. "Go' Dirk?"

"And there's our witness confirmation. Yes, ma'am, we have him," Gorski confirmed. "You're safe now."

"Thank...you." She offered them a weak smile, as her eyes slid closed again.

Gorski gestured at Ashton, who had returned to his side, instructing him to respond to the woman.

"You're very welcome, ma'am," Ashton said, adding a gentle, understanding smile at a deeply relieved Jackson. "We were glad to do it."

Then he looked back at Gorski and smiled again.

Gorski grinned and patted him on the back.

"Way to go, kiddo," he murmured. "You just finished your very first real case as a proper investigator, all successful-like."

Ashton beamed.

This kind of case load went on for more than a year, and with that level of practice, Ashton was getting good at it. More, he was moving up in rank and status; his unofficial rank had transitioned fairly quickly, and as promised, from Investigator to Sergeant Investigator, and he was nearing a promotion to Lieutenant Investigator.

Finally the Deputy Chief of Investigations, Colonel Peterson, called him into her office.

"Have a seat, Nick," she told him, gesturing at the visitor chair across from her desk. "it's time we made some decisions, you and I."

Ashton drew a deep breath.

"Transfer, or go back," he said then.

"Yes, which also means going back as someone who has ostensibly 'learned' under a past master of the gamesmanship in the Imperial Police, at least at Headquarters," she confirmed. "And it means stepping back into that rat hole and being one of the rats." She eyed him closely. "And you don't strike me as a rat."

"No ma'am. I'm not," Ashton averred. "I'm not goin' back to that snake pit, rest assured on that."

"But there's one other option you have."

"Oh? What's that?"

"You could really transfer off-planet. Go to another sector in Sintaran space. For the most part, it's only the headquarters here on Sintar that's corrupt, because of how close it is, physically and organizationally, to the Council. Hell's bells, the upper echelons tend to be friends with the Council members. But the other sectors' departments tend to be pretty straight. And Lee and I could help you decide where you'd fit best. Hell, you could always go back to your home planet, for that matter." She shrugged. "You wouldn't have Stefan for a mentor, except long-distance, but from what I've been hearing, you might not need him now, except for that. And even that, only on some particularly hairy case."

Ashton paused, gnawing his lower lip, in deep thought; he hadn't considered that – any of that. And to be honest, going back home to work held a certain appeal; his parents were gone, but there was other family still there. The problem was, Flanders generally had a very quiet sort of population; even in Norwich, there hadn't been very much crime. Which was good, but he didn't want to sit around and twiddle his thumbs, either. Which, in turn, gave him another question.

"What's the most active police sector in the Empire?"

"Oh," Peterson said, somewhat startled by the question. "That would have to be Sintar, specifically Imperial City, hands down. Partly because of the corruption, and partly just because it's the power center. I think power is kind of like gravity; it tends to attract all the people who want it, or the money that usually comes with it, and don't care how they get it."

"Hmph. Makes sense."

"Yeah. Why did you want to know?"

"Because I don't want to sit around and do nothing but grow dust bunnies in a quiet sector, on a quiet planet," he explained. "And that includes my home planet. I don't want to stagnate, I want to be someplace where I can actually do some good. So..."

"So...?"

"So let's do it, I guess," he decided. "After all, Imp City is still part of the Empire-wide police organization, and I want to be of some use, here. Which means," he looked to her for confirmation, "I need to formalize this whole situation, so you can actually give me those ranks?"

"Exactly," Peterson said with a wide smile. "I was very much hoping you'd say that. Yes, we'll get this formalized and you placed directly into our system, rather than on the periphery."

"I've been meaning to ask – how did you do all that without getting somebody into trouble, in the first place?"

Peterson drew a deep breath.

"You aren't the first good-guy cop the ICPD has had to 'help' out of that rats' nest, Nick," she said with a sigh. "It doesn't happen real often, because they're generally pretty good at picking guys outta the Academy who have their particular corrupt leanings, but once in a great while they go for brains instead of bribery and the like. Lee and I think that's what they did with you. Sometimes they're able to get the brains to go along, and sometimes they don't. That's when Lee or one of a handful of others over at the Headquarters building pings us. Or, well, Lee used to ping us."

"So you have a system within the system?"

"Sort of, yes. Everybody in a position of authority at Imp City Police knows about it. And they know when someone is inducted into it. You're the latest, and doing well; we haven't had another inductee since Lee left, though…which says he was right about them putting a toadie in his old position. And that bodes badly for the rookies. But we can't keep you in the special system indefinitely; it wasn't designed for that. So we need to either make you fully one of us, or move you out, one way or another."

"Aha. Well, let's move in, then."

"Consider it done," Peterson said, and grinned.

Several months later, Ashton was promoted to Lieutenant Investigator; Peterson had placed him on a fast track from the very beginning of his tenure with the Imperial City Police. By this time, Peter Rassmussen and Roger Armbrand were getting close to being promoted to Captain Investigator, and several of the others had moved into Sergeant Investigator, as well. Four new investigators had also joined the team – John Smith, Hugo Weaver, Callista Ames, and Alan Compton.

"But we're still one big team," Peter had told Nick, and Roger agreed.

"Yeah, what Pete said. Even when we're all detectives, I can't see us doing anything but working together, like we do now."

"Besides," Pete added, "we might be able to help some of the others bump up their ranks, while we're at it. Kind of like what Gorski's doing with you."

Nick Ashton now settled more permanently into his work at the Imperial City Police, learning more and more and becoming ever more skilled in detection, especially with Stefan Gorski as his mentor. In a large city like that, murders were not uncommon, and burglaries and thefts reasonably frequent, so he had plenty of opportunities to hone those skills.

And as he gained seniority in "the Team," as he'd taken to thinking of it, his pay went up, his wardrobe improved in quality, and he let his hair grow more than a bit on the sides while trimming the top much closer. The blond highlights had proliferated to augment the difference, and now gave him a golden blond look, especially with the tan he tried to maintain year-round. He even grew out his beard into the stubble-length currently fashionable, and which he'd gotten Colonel Peterson's permission to do, in order to look as different as possible from the rookie officer who had started at Imperial Police Headquarters. He kept in shape in the department's gym, and as his body continued to mature, it filled out in musculature.

Some three years into his work at ICPD, few people would have recognized the lanky young, uniformed cop who worked the streets of Imperial City for IPD as this serious, well-built, talented investigator.

Unfortunately, "few" was not "none."

Teamwork and Leadership

Ray "Droppoint" Murphy was a petty thief and pickpocket who operated in Imperial City in the arcades nearest the Palace. Not that he was apt to get wallets or cash; those hadn't existed – at least on Sintar – in hundreds of years, having been replaced by virtual reality transactions long ago. Oh, some of the more rural planets in the Empire still had people who only carried actual coin, but they rarely showed up on Sintar, let alone in Imperial City. A few credits in coin was as much as most people on Sintar carried.

But that didn't mean there weren't other trinkets in pockets and on wrists and around throats – jewelry, inlaid pocket knives, and other such valuable items were easy to acquire for a skilled pickpocket like Droppoint. And he had been on a spree in recent weeks in the arcades; when one of the wealthier matrons lost a valuable bauble, matters had come to a head.

It was time, the ICPD decided, to put an end to it. But Gorski and Demetrius were already out on minor cases, having taken Rassmussen and Armbrand along to help them get a leg up on their upcoming promotions to Detective; Taylor and Amundsen were still on the other side of Sintar, stuck in a kind of courtroom hell.

So Ashton was given the job of scouting out the specific locations Droppoint was hitting, then setting up an operation to catch him.

The first thing he did was to go into VR and use the city planning records to set up a three-dimensional map of the arcade that Droppoint frequented the most, then he had the computer take all of the complaints and reports of pickpocketing and try to locate them within the map. Most of the time, the best that could be done was to highlight an area, or a store; Droppoint was very skilled, and most of his victims didn't know they'd been robbed for some little time after he stole from them.

Still, it began to give Ashton a good feel for the areas of the arcade that Droppoint preferred to hit. When he then added in the times of the robberies, and animated them, he started to see the ebb and flow of the pickpocket's movements.

And I can probably use this to command a surveillance team, he thought, zooming in and out of the model by grabbing this or that storefront. *I just need to set it up so their VR triggers their location in here, and I can follow their movements, and even tap their markers to communicate with 'em. Huh. This is pretty cool.*

Ashton decided to take the newbies, by way of providing some on-the-job training, along with Timothy Jones to help him "wrangle," as Jones put it...grinning as he did so. This meant his team consisted of relative rookie investigators John Smith, Hugo Weaver, Callista Ames, and Alan Compton.

"Now, the first thing we need to do is to go undercover and see exactly where he's hanging out," Ashton noted. "Ray Murphy, a.k.a. 'Droppoint,' is a known pickpocket, but he's good and he's fast, so he's hard to catch out. Which means that the reports we have in don't have any hard locations – the victims only know where they discover they have a missing item, and sometimes that's not until they get home. But he's been at it this time for a couple of months, and not only are the locals starting to complain, he's scored a couple of really expensive items, one of which was an heirloom bracelet from the wife of the university chancellor, so the beat cops – who are frustrated as hell – handed it off to us. The pressure's on from higher-ups, guys, so we need this collar."

"What do you need us to do, Lieutenant Investigator?" Ames asked.

"No, no, no," Ashton said with a smile, holding up a hand. "We're a team, here. There's no formality required unless we're in one of the chiefs' offices, or a department briefing or something like that. I'm Nick, and this is Tim." He indicated Jones.

"Or you can call me 'Wrangler,'" Jones noted with a smirk. They all laughed.

"Um, okay," a flushing Ames said with a slightly shy grin. "What do you need us to do, Nick?"

"We're going to all get into disguises and go scope out his activities in the arcade," Ashton explained, even as Jones gave him a surreptitious elbow nudge, which he ignored. "Once we have a good feel for where he's most likely to be, when, one or two of you are gonna become bait and see if we can't get him to fall for it. It's called a sting operation. Everybody good, so far?"

A chorus of "uh-huh" came back to him.

"Great. I brought in an expert in disguise to help us go undercover." Ashton waved an invited bystander from the doorway; he was average in height, with a clean-shaven face and shaved head. "This is Detective Adrian Mott; he's going to help us with this."

"Hi, guys," Mott said, moving to stand beside Ashton. "Call me Adrian. The key to working undercover is to look nondescript, to look ordinary, not stand out. If you're going to be undercover for a long time, you have to *be* your character, but for our purposes today, and for the next few days, we just want to make sure you don't stand out..."

While Mott worked with the rookie investigators, Jones was giving Ashton a good ribbing in the corner.

"Man, she likes you," he murmured. "She's hardly taken her eyes off you the whole damn time. She *likes* you."

"I'm running this show," Ashton pointed out. "Of course she's watched me. She's paying attention to the plan. There's every indication she's gonna be a good cop, if her academy record is any judge."

"C'mon, man. With all those blond streaks and that tan, never mind those golden-brown eyes of yours, you got the whole 'golden god' thing goin' on. She all but drooled."

"Lay off. I do not, and she did not."

"Did too. Didn't you see her blush and drop her eyes when you told her to call you Nick? Dude, she's got a thing for you."

"It doesn't matter. We have jobs to do."

Exasperated, Jones eyed Ashton.

"I've never seen you with anybody, man or woman, the whole time you've been with us, Nick. And that's been – what? A couple of years now, man. Yet I've seen you eyeing that VR actress you think is hot, so you're not, like, asexual or something. What gives?"

"What gives," Ashton told him, mildly irked, "is that my last girlfriend turned out to be the kowtowing, crooked-cop niece of the guy that runs IPD Headquarters, over in the south quadrant. And, near as I was able to tell, she was sicced onto me, rather than really being interested. She sure as hell didn't waste any time hooking up with somebody else after I got moved over here – she's on her third live-in since – nor yet try to contact me after my old apartment blew, to find out if I was okay. I'm just glad I found out before it got as far as one of us spendin' the damn night. My old mentor told me, once I got old enough, 'never stick it in crazy, son,' and as far as I'm concerned, dirty cop is even worse than crazy. But I came close, before I found out who and what she really was. I was serious. She wasn't."

"Oh. Shit. I...I'm sorry, Nick. I had no idea."

"Yeah, well. Now you do. So..."

"Yeah, yeah. I'll lay off. Sorry."

Soon the members of Ashton's team were all dressed and made up as fairly ordinary pedestrian shoppers, neither poor nor rich, and their hair was covered by either caps or wigs, depending on the officer's preference.

"Okay, good," Ashton declared, looking them over. "Good job. At a glance, I don't think I'd recognize any of you without staring at you for a few seconds. And I know you! So we should be able to fool Droppoint, who's never met any of you. Tim? Do you have the grid worked out based on what I gave you?"

"Sure do, Nick," Jones averred. "Can everybody join me in channel 227? I want to go over the areas of the arcade each person is responsible for, as well as the store fronts..."

They arrived at the arcade by ones and twos, to avoid drawing attention to a group. Each investigator moved casually to his or her assigned area using the slidewalks, and began to "shop."

No sign was seen of Droppoint Murphy until mid-morning. Then he appeared in one corner of the arcade, not too far from the west archway to the people-movers. Compton spotted him first, and used VR to send a vocal alert.

"He's here, guys," Compton notified the others. "Over by the dry cleaners."

"Right," a disguised Ashton responded in kind, sitting by

the central fountain and pretending to read in VR; in reality, he was keeping track of each member of his team in a special virtual control room he'd worked out – the entire room comprised that same three-dimensional space that modeled the arcade in miniature. He had spent some time in his off-duty evenings updating and enhancing it, and now it had the capability of tagging any given pedestrian in the arcade's security system, which currently fed even more data into the control room. He identified which pedestrian was Droppoint, and reached out with his avatar to tag it. "There we go. I'm seeing him pop up on my display, here. Keep an eye on him, but don't let him see you doing so. John, looks like you're up next in his path; keep your eyes peeled for him."

"I see him, Nick." Smith sounded calm.

"Good. He's probably moving to a particular location with lots of people; the busier the area, the more he can do without being noticed."

"That means there's an ebb and flow to the crowds of shoppers in the arcade," Ames mused.

"Right, Cally. And remember that, guys – there's a pattern, a flow, to every shopping arcade like this, and it pays to know what it is. He's studied it already and worked it out, so we're going to cheat: we'll watch his actions to tell us what that is."

"Ooo, Nick, nice call," Jones said. "I hadn't thought of doing that before."

"I had a detective mentor as a kid," Ashton explained. "My homeworld didn't have a lot of violent crime, but there were a reasonable number of pickpockets in the cities. That – and a chance to run the show and see how I do – is why I got the lead on this assignment."

"Gotcha," Jones said. "That's great. No wonder you got fast-tracked."

"But why did he come in the west entrance?" Ames wondered. "I thought his dossier said he lived in Imperial Park South."

"He does," Ashton explained. "But the majority of people coming to this arcade will be coming in from the residence structures in Imperial Park West. So he goes around and joins them by coming in the west entrance so he doesn't stand out."

"Ohh, that makes sense. Ah! Here he comes my way," Ames said, as she walked between adjacent storefronts. "Oh, but he's going right past. Hugo, heads up!"

"I got it," Weaver noted. "I think I'm gonna go over to the food cart and get a snack and a drink. I can wander around and window-shop, and still look busy, while I keep an eye on him."

"Good plan, Hugo," Ashton agreed. "Everybody, just relax. We're gonna be here for a while. If you actually see him do something, well and good, but from what I read in this guy's dossier, you probably won't, 'cause he's damn good at what he does. Right now, we're just here to get a feel for his movements, so we'll know where to set up our sting. Tomorrow, we'll rotate through the arcade areas, so he never sees the same face in the same area. Not to mention, you'll have different clothes and hair each day..."

After several days of this, they had a good feel for Droppoint Murphy's pattern. He arrived around ten in the morning each day on the west people-mover cars – which, as Ashton had pointed out the first day, comprised the main entrance from the residential district in the area – after which Murphy made his way to the far side of the arcade, stayed there until around noon, then meandered over to the higher-end restaurants off the food court, usually picking up a small, inexpensive wrap to eat himself, from the same food cart that Weaver had patronized. When the lunch rush passed, he moved back toward the west arcade entrance, where he'd be sure to catch all of the departing shoppers. His preference seemed to be the south side, Ashton noted, since most of the jewelry stores were there, also.

"...So based on all that, here's what we're gonna do," Ashton said the next morning, as he briefed his little team. "Cally, are you up for playing target?"

"Sure am, Nick!" she decreed with a cheerful grin.

She was a petite little honey blonde, adorably cute at times, very pretty without being a drop-dead beauty, spunky and strong despite her small stature, and definitely not someone to underestimate in any sense – not only did she take down most of her classmates in the sparring-combat class at Academy, she'd accepted the instructor's challenge and fought him to a stalemate. She also had more than her fair share of gray matter, so she was taking to investigative work like jam to bread. Ashton had to admit, if he hadn't been soured on relationships by Tabby, he might consider asking her out. *Fortunately the whole 'fraternization' thing went out in police work a long time ago,* he thought. *As long as we're aboveboard about it, and neither of us plays faves, nobody would blink twice. But that's a moot point.* He got his train of thought back on track.

"Good. I brought Adrian back in to turn you into a hoity-toity rich chick," Ashton said with a grin of his own. "Complete with some nice shiny baubles and everything."

"Ooo, sounds like fun," she decreed, grin growing wider. "Tell me more."

"The rest of the team is going to go in during lunch, while he's busy, and set up in the hiding places we discussed yesterday after we finished the surveillance," Ashton explained. "Cally is gonna come in *after* lunch, in her disguise as Ms. Pampered Rich-Priss, and Cally, you're gonna hit up all the high-end stores, starting with Bianchi's first."

"You mean the big, top-end jewelry store?"

"Exactly. Colonel Peterson has already worked something out with them for us, at my suggestion, and they have a set of excellent simulated diamonds for you to 'buy' and wear – ring, earrings, necklace, maybe bracelet, I dunno – but all matching, and all looking really ritzy...but not. And you're gonna put 'em on and waltz around with 'em, in and out of the clothing stores, where – since he doesn't actually enter the stores – we also have some undercover cops waiting, disguised as shop clerks. They'll have shopping bags for you, with junk in 'em that will look like designer clothing and stuff, in case anybody gets a look. None of it is real; it's some of the better knock-offs that our counterfeits division encountered and confiscated over the last, oh, year, maybe. So you'll sashay in, spend twenty or thirty minutes there, waltz out with a bag. Go over to another, spend an hour, come out with two more bags. Back and forth. Try to make sure you get Murphy's attention without seeming like you're trying to."

"Got it," Ames said, still cheerful and pleased about the assignment. Ashton promptly decided he'd found a kindred spirit.

"Along about four in the afternoon," he continued, "you're gonna meander back toward the west entrance, but you're gonna have slowed down a lot, even on the slidewalks. You're tired; you've been shopping all afternoon, you're dead on your feet. You're gonna walk right past Droppoint nice and slow, without looking at him or seeming to even notice him, and if he doesn't bite, I'll be surprised."

"But Nick," Compton asked, "if he's that good, she might never feel him swipe the jewelry."

"Which is why it's rigged," Ashton said with a huge grin. "Bianchi's installed what they call a 'thumper' on each piece. Murphy won't know, but Cally will feel it. And as soon as he makes a grab, we bust him."

Everything went according to plan. Ashton, Jones, Smith, Weaver, and Compton all got into position – as themselves, this time – within no more than fifty feet of Murphy's afternoon position during lunch, and were well hidden by the time he arrived over an hour later.

Half an hour after that, Cally Ames arrived, haute couture and all, looking like she could be the young trophy wife of a Council member, and headed straight for Bianchi's Jewelers as if she had an appointment – which, in fact, she did. Ashton zoomed in and watched from his VR surveillance room as Murphy's eyes followed her into the jewelry store. She was inside some twenty minutes, then emerged into the arcade's main thoroughfare, delightedly holding out her hand to watch the sparkle of the gemstone on it in the bright, full-spectrum lighting. Her ears, wrist, and throat also sparkled.

Next came a designer dress shop, then a fur-and-leather store, then the highest-end department store in the arcade. Each time Ames emerged, she had more packages and bags in hand.

This went on for fully three hours. As the afternoon wore on, Ames got slower and slower, appearing to tire. She went from a brisk walk on the slidewalks, to a slower walk, to finally standing and waiting for it to deposit her near where she wanted to go. Murphy began to watch her more closely, though the observation was surreptitious; if the investigative team hadn't been keeping all eyes on him, they might not have noticed.

As the clock on the jewelry store façade neared four, Ames

and her packages started to amble toward the west entrance of the arcade. She appeared to be dragging pretty badly by this time; she stared at the slidewalk in front of her, walking very slowly and seeming almost in a daze. She then managed to stumble on her high heels – they were emphatically *not* "sensible shoes" – and thereby step off the slidewalk, appearing to almost fall, just as she got even with Murphy.

Perfect, thought Ashton, pleased. *Cally completely gets this.*

Murphy put out a hand and caught her before she fell, steadying her on her feet.

"There you go, madam," he said smoothly, his manner suave and persuasive. "Perhaps you should sit down soon, and rest."

"Perhaps I–" Ames began with a smile, then jerked back, dropping the shopping bags and drawing her concealed carry weapon in one move, revealing the fake-diamond bracelet sparkling in Murphy's hand. "POLICE! You're under arrest!"

And Ashton and the rest of his team descended upon their quarry.

It was while Ashton was handcuffing Droppoint Murphy and loading him into an arcade cart to take him up to street level and a waiting police transport that a certain off-duty IPD officer, on a shopping run for her current live-in boyfriend, saw the bust going down. Tabby Koch stopped, hiding her startlement, and watched the bust along with several other pedestrians, trying to fade into the crowd.

Then, as Ashton drove off with his perp, she pinged her uncle in VR.

"Wait. Ashton was seen? Here? In Imperial City?" a disbelieving Chief George Stanier, head of the entire Imperial

Police, asked General William Kershaw, head of the Imperial Police on Sintar.

"Yes, George, he was. By my niece, who spent some time dating him and hoping to coax him into compliance, a couple of years back, if you will recall."

"Mm. So that's definitive; she'd recognize him if they used to see each other. And that's the kid that caused all the problems for Ron Thomas a few years back, too, right?"

"The very same, George. We sent Stash's people out after him, but missed, because apparently the kid really did leave Sintar. We even got security video at the spaceport of him saying goodbye to his parents and boarding a shuttle. I guess at some point, he came back to Sintar."

"Wait. Saying goodbye to his parents?" Stanier said, startled. "I thought the kid was from some podunk backwater planet... Flanders, wasn't it?"

"Oh," Kershaw said, paling as he realized the error his subordinates had made...and that he had not caught. "Perhaps they moved with him, at least initially? And he's only recently returned, but decided to work for ICPD instead?"

"Or maybe we've been had, and that bastard Carter laughed at us all the way," Stanier snarled.

Kershaw dropped all pretense at familiarity.

"What do you want to do, sir?"

"See if you can get somebody on Ashton's tail, find out what he's doing now," Stanier ordered. "He can still get us in dutch if he's told anybody about the Sigil...which, thanks to that little muffed operation, we never did get our hands on. And send somebody to find Carter and take him out."

"Yes, sir. Shall I use Stash? He doesn't have a badge now..."

"Contact him, at least. The badge makes no difference. He ought to know someone suited to handle Carter; he's been retired how many years now? It shouldn't be difficult."

"That was excellent work, Lieutenant Investigator Ashton; excellent work! You not only scoped out the perp, you set up an effective sting and took the perp into custody," Deputy Chief of Investigations Colonel Maia Peterson told Ashton in her office. The Imperial City Police Chief, Brigadier General Harold Quan, stood beside her, looking on in approbation. "And you trained our new investigators while you were at it! Very well done, sir. Very well done."

"Thank you, ma'am," Ashton said with a cheerful smile. "I appreciate your and General Quan's approval. But you know I'm doing it because people deserve to be safe."

"Of course we do, Lieutenant Investigator Ashton," Peterson said. "And that's all the more reason to approve."

"Oh, it's more than approval, Ashton," Quan added. "You're coming up on the end of your time in grade, and that just demonstrated to us that you're ready. You're now officially Captain Investigator Dominick Ashton. Congratulations."

"Oh! Thank you, sir, ma'am!" Ashton said in pleased surprise. He took General Quan's proffered hand and shook it, followed by Colonel Peterson's.

"You're more than welcome, Nick," Peterson said with a smile, reverting to informality now that the official moment had passed. "You've been a great investigator for us so far, and if you keep this up, I think you're going to wind up topping out things, one of these days, not too terribly far in the future."

"Now, get with your team and the lot of you go out and celebrate," Quan urged with a smile of his own.

But it turned out that none of "the guys" were available. Except one.

"Terrific! Congratulations!" Cally Ames declared. "Sure, I'd love to go out and celebrate with everybody! Sounds like fun!"

"Nah, I gotta go home and see about laundry, or I won't have any clean clothes to wear tomorrow. And you do not want me to show up buck naked!" Jones said with a smirk, shooting knowing glances at Smith, Weaver, and Compton. "Nor yet in already-worn clothes!"

"Um, I promised my mom last weekend that I'd come over for dinner tonight," Compton tried. "I haven't seen her in almost a month, and she only lives a couple blocks from me. Maybe tomorrow?"

"I'm meeting friends after work today," Weaver declared. "We've got tickets to see a play. Yeah, tomorrow might work."

Everyone looked at Smith, who winced.

"I had a glitch in my kitchen system this morning," he explained, "and had to swing by and grab breakfast in the arcade, 'cause nothing was working. I pinged the super in my apartment building, and he was sending a maintenance person by after work for repairs. I'm hoping none of the fresh stuff has spoiled, 'cause I'd just done my bi-weekly grocery shopping..."

"Oh geez, man," Jones said, as the others all groaned. "That sucks."

"Yeah. I'm not sure what happened; I wonder if the thunderstorm last night threw a breaker or something."

"Could be," Ashton agreed. "I hope it's an easy fix, Johnny."

"Me too, Nick."

"Anyway, why don't you an' Cally go on out and grab a brew or two, an' the rest of us will try to do something later in the week?" Jones suggested, clapping Ashton on the back. "An' congrats, pal."

"Yeah, way to go! Congratulations!" the others chorused.

Then they cleared out, and Ashton was left standing with a

happy-looking Ames, silently cursing to himself.

Nick decided to get through it by treating Cally like 'one of the guys.' Which, he considered, she was, after all. They headed out to the Laughing Cat Pub, going in the back door as usual. The ICPD's favorite waiter George, spotting the two and recognizing Nick, promptly led them to the backmost back room, seated them in a corner booth, then pulled a movable wall across the opening, effectively creating a small private room just for them.

That works, I guess, Nick decided. *This way, at least we stay well out of sight.*

"So, what's good here?" Cally wondered, picking up a menu and glancing over it.

"Most of it, I've found," Nick said. "I usually get a stout and the bacon double cheeseburger, extra fries, extra bacon."

"Heart attack on a plate? Sounds delish!" she laughed. "We'll make it two."

The food was as good as Nick's word, George was discreet and unobtrusive, and soon they were relaxed and chatting amiably. The burgers were large and juicy and filling, the stout hearty, cool and foamy, and when they were finished, both wanted dessert, but didn't have room.

"I got an idea," Cally said. "Wanna split a piece of key lime pie? I love that stuff."

"So do I," Nick agreed. "Let's do it."

When they were finished, Cally insisted on paying.

"No, no, it won't do, Nick," she said with a grin. "This is a celebration of your promotion! I'm not letting you pay for it! That's my treat!"

"All right, on one condition," Nick decided.

"What?"

"You let me pay tomorrow night."

"Why, Nick Ashton, that almost sounds like you asked me on a date."

"...Almost."

"Then I accept."

He walked her home, before heading home himself.

Reprisals

Lee Carter and Maia Peterson were an established couple by this time, though they had not made things permanent as yet. In point of fact, Lee's old-fashioned pride prevented him from formalizing their relationship – the fact that he had stagnated at the rank of captain while Maia made colonel meant that her income would always be significantly larger than his, when he wanted nothing more than to pamper and care for this woman he loved. When Maia even brought up the idea of adding him to her apartment's security system, Lee balked rather decidedly. She therefore hesitated to bring up anything more official. And yet, she recognized, it didn't seem to indicate the end of their relationship; he still wanted to be with her.

Most nights found them together, in fact, either at his apartment or hers, though occasionally, when first-thing-in-the-morning schedules conflicted, they spent the night alone in their respective apartments. She supposed she needed to sit down and try to discuss the issue with him, to at least find out why he knee-jerked every time she brought it up. But she had yet to find the right opportunity to do so.

Meanwhile, they had kept their relationship, if not completely secret, then intensely private and tightly under wraps. "Because I have a feeling we don't need to draw attention to it," Lee had told Maia, who had agreed; her own gut spoke to the same response – in Imperial City, retired IPD cops did well to keep their heads down, especially with shiny records like Carter's.

This night had been one of the "separate" nights, due to the fact that Maia had an early shift start for a meeting, and Lee had a dental appointment, followed by a sparring session at the dojo where he trained. They'd had dinner together at her place, caught up on each other's days, then Lee had gone home.

Now, after a very basic breakfast of the ubiquitous and ancient recipe for cold cereal and milk – though he had his specialties, in general Lee wasn't as good a cook as Maia, so he kept it simple – he departed for that appointment.

He never made it.

After going along the hall and down the elevator to the lobby, Carter headed out the door of his apartment building and turned left, headed for the ramp down to the medical arcade level. He stepped aside, into the mouth of an alley, to allow his tired neighbor, loaded with shopping bags after getting off shift an hour earlier, to pass…

…And felt an arm go around his throat from behind, from the alley to his rear.

"Gotcha, Carter," the assailant murmured in his ear in a deep, smirking, male voice, as he pulled him deeper into the alley, out of sight from the street. "You're done."

Lee Carter went into action.

He slipped his left hand inside the arm around his throat, turned his head and bit the inner, upper arm as hard as he could until he tasted blood, and simultaneously drove his right heel down on his assailant's instep. This was immediately followed by driving his right elbow back with all his strength, into his assailant's floating ribs; he felt several snap.

The man cried out, nearly screaming, as teeth penetrated skin, and tried to jerk back. Keeping his jaws tensed as tightly closed as he could, Carter forced the arm away from him, grabbing the wrist as he spun about, and spat torn cloth, raw flesh, and blood from his mouth. This time the other man did scream, but they were by this time deep in the alley and thanks to echoes off the masonry, any would-be witnesses would be uncertain of the sound's direction.

Besides, Carter thought, *I don't really* want *anybody seeing me do this. Not if I want to survive.*

A couple of solid punches with his right fist to his attacker's face made a series of satisfying crunches, followed by a truly nasty-sounding pop, as the abused nose of Carter's assailant broke in a gush of blood. Only then did the man drop the knife he had in his free hand in order to clutch his face, instinctively attempting to protect his nose. Carter kicked the knife aside, twisted, and threw the attempted murderer over his shoulder and into a nearby trash dumpster – there was a restaurant on the ground floor of his apartment building, and ordinances required exterior waste disposal and daily pick-up. He had no doubt but that it had been his intended resting place, but he slammed the open lid down and latched it without qualms. *If his superiors or a passer-by happens to find him, fine,* Carter thought. *If not, I'm sure the trash compactor will take care of matters during pickup.*

He fumbled in his jacket pocket, pulling out an old pair of exam gloves and an evidence bag he used to keep there for crime scenes and had never remembered to remove, then walked over to the knife as he donned one of the gloves. He picked it up in the gloved hand, stowed it gingerly in the bag and the bag equally gingerly in his jacket pocket, removed the glove, then headed for the maintenance passage into the arcade below, effectively disappearing to all and sundry.

Five minutes later, one of the restaurant workers came out to dispose of some waste, and was shocked to find someone inside the closed and latched dumpster, yelling and banging on it from within. He quickly opened the lid, and a man crawled out, cursing, his nose smashed to one side, blood streaming down his face and off the fingertips of one hand.

"What in the name of all that is holy happened to you?" the restaurant worker asked, horrified at the look of him.

"Damn mugger," he grumbled, eyes darting to and fro. "Name's Anton Davis. I just came from shopping and he took everything."

"Shall I call the police?"

"…Yeah, you better."

Half an hour later, and finally out of her bureaucratic meeting, Maia Peterson got an emergency call on the private VR channel she'd reserved exclusively for Lee Carter. She closed the door to her office and locked it, then sat back down and "checked out," as she entered the channel. His avatar waited for her in the classic nondescript room adorned with two leather wing chairs, and which they'd discussed upgrading and had yet to get around to it…

…But Lee was pacing.

And trembling. *Avatars aren't supposed to shake, are they?* she thought briefly.

"Lee! What's wrong?"

His avatar came to hers and grabbed it by the shoulders.

"Forget all that guff I was giving you about adding me to your apartment security system the other night, Maia. *Thank you,* sweetheart. Twenty million times over."

"Huh?"

"I'm in your apartment right now, and awfully damn glad to be here. Oh, and I used your mouthwash. Three times. Ieucch."

"What the hell are you talking about, Lee, and why did you send me an emergency call?"

His avatar let go of her shoulders and began to pace again. She watched him, worried.

"Well, either the IPD made Nick Ashton at some point in the last day or so, or they dug up something on me they don't like, I'm not sure yet which," he told her. "Somebody just accosted me right outside my apartment building, and given he had one arm around my throat, and the other hand held a big-ass knife, I don't think he expected me to survive the encounter."

"WHAT?!" she almost screamed. "Are you okay?"

"More or less, yeah," Lee told her. "A little shaken – okay, a lot shaken – and maybe a few bruises on my knuckles. But he's probably gonna need stitches where I took a bite outta his arm, not to mention having his busted nose set."

"So you got free and belted him a good one?"

"Oh HELL yes! Then threw him into the restaurant dumpster for good measure."

"And now you're at my place?" she confirmed. "Oh, now I get the mouthwash remark…"

"Yeah, I am, and I might need to stay here, out of sight. Or, well, someplace *other* than my apartment. For a little while, at least."

"You took one of the clandestine routes, right?" she verified.

"Hell yes."

"Okay, good. Lemme get hold of Adrian, who's our disguise expert, and some of my trusted people, and we'll just see about getting you moved in with me. I was gonna invite you anyway, at least until you got so bent out of shape about the security thing." She shrugged. "I was still gonna bring up the subject and see how you reacted. And we need to talk about that, I guess. Are…are you okay with that? Moving in with me, I

STEPHANIE OSBORN

mean?"

"Yeah, honey, I am. And yeah, we need to talk…because my reticence is, well, foolish, I guess. And I guess I need to make sure you understand it. But right now, I think you're not just my lover, you're my lifeline."

"And that's fine. All of that. But you need to lay low while we work this, otherwise they'll be after both of us. And I'll give Nick a heads-up to watch his back, too."

"Sounds like a plan, Maia," Lee agreed, finally slumping into the armchair in the VR room. Maia's avatar wandered over and put a comforting hand on his shoulder. "Damn."

"Yeah. Stay put, right here, honey," she told him, "and be compiling a list of what needs to be swiped out of your place and moved to mine. Meanwhile, I'm gonna contact my buddies."

"Okay."

In short order, Adrian Mott – who had impersonated Nick Ashton some years earlier, when he purportedly left Sintar for "training" – met with Peterson and Inspector Eugene Demetrius in her office; she'd also called Detective Stefan Gorski, but he'd been out at a robbery scene. She'd filled them in on what had happened in VR when she notified them to come to her office; while she was waiting for them to arrive, she'd likewise notified Nick Ashton of the attempt on Carter… without telling him where Carter was hiding. *Because he's a target, too, and he doesn't need to know, or he could accidentally give away both of us if they get to him,* she considered. *But Gene's an old pal who can get into the apartment, and he knows Lee, so that should work.*

Twenty minutes later, Mott and Demetrius were thoroughly disguised and on their way to Peterson's apartment to make sure Carter was indeed all right, then assist in covertly transporting his essential belongings to Peterson's place.

"...No, I'm afraid not, Cally," Ashton told Ames in the break room in private, fifteen minutes later. "Something bad almost went down early this morning, and my old bosses might be after me. I need to lay low for a while, and I need to stay away from my friends, at least in public. One almost got hurt, maybe killed, as it was. I don't want to get anybody else in a bad place, let alone hurt."

"I could come over to your place, and bring dinner..."

"No, I was supposed to pay, remember?" *Never mind the fact that I'm not ready to have a girl over to my home,* he thought. *Not after Tabby. Not yet. I gotta get past some trust issues, first.*

"Well, then you could come over...no, you're supposed to be staying out of sight..."

"Right. So let's just put it on hold, and see what's going down. If it doesn't actually have to do with me, we can try again later. It may only be a few days; try to be patient."

"All right," Cally said with a sigh.

"Yeah, I saw him," Carter told the disguised Demetrius as he and Mott verified Carter's condition at Maia's apartment shortly thereafter. "Full-on face, after which I busted his nose pretty thoroughly. And yeah, I know him. It was Switch Sykes."

"Mm," Demetrius murmured. "Definite Imperial Police ties, there. He's been suspected of being used for several assassinations, but because of his connections, we haven't been able to nail him."

"Yup, don't I know it," Carter sighed. "Which means I need to stay out of sight for a while."

"You broke his nose?" Mott verified.

"Oh hell yes. And took a significant plug outta his arm, into the bargain. If you go back to that alley, you can probably find the piece I bit out of him, complete with teeth marks, by way of some DNA evidence. I also managed to bust some of the floating ribs – I heard and felt 'em crunch – and might have done a number on his foot, too."

"What the hell did you do?!" Demetrius wanted to know, and Carter laughed grimly.

"I refused to turn into a couch potato just because I retired," he replied. "I've got belts going all the way up to black in a couple of different martial arts, and a dojo where I keep in shape and form. Picked up at least two belts since I retired."

"I'll bet Maia helped with a little of that," Demetrius murmured, a sly grin on his face. Carter snorted.

"Hey, she didn't hurt. But yeah, sometimes she spars with me. She's not somebody to mess with, either."

"Good man," Mott said, impressed. "I want you to show me those moves, sometime. I may be younger, but you've had more time to learn and get good."

"Be happy to."

"So he grabbed you around the neck..." Demetrius said. "How do you know he was gonna stab you?"

"This was in his other hand." And Carter pulled the bagged knife out of his jacket pocket.

"Shit," Mott said, as Demetrius took the weapon as evidence. "So...what? He grabbed you, knife at your back, and you stomped, elbowed, and bit?"

"Yeah. Pretty much all at the same time. I was going for, 'inflict enough pain that he's not thinking,' you know. I guess it worked, 'cause that kinda made him arch away, so I was safer from the knife. Then I twisted around until I faced him, holding the wrist that had been around my neck, popped him a couple times in the face but good, hitting hard at an angle – I was trying to break his nose – and sure enough, he dropped the knife to grab his nose when it busted. I kicked the knife outta his reach, then spun him around and threw him over my shoulder into the dumpster." Carter grinned at their disbelieving looks. "I fastened him in, grabbed the knife as evidence, then cleared out."

"You bashed hell out of him, in other words," Mott decided.

"Best I could, yeah," Carter confirmed.

"Sounds like a pretty damn good 'best,' if you ask me," Mott concluded.

"I'm thinking he's going to be needing medical attention for that arm, at the least," Demetrius said. "Probably the nose, too."

"And he'll need to get the ribs strapped up," Mott added.

"Does he know you saw him?" Demetrius wondered. Carter shrugged.

"He knows I saw him well enough to nearly punch his lights out," he said. "I expect so."

"All right, that's all I got for now," Demetrius said. "Maia said you'd have a list of items to get out of your apartment?"

"Yeah. It came completely furnished, so the list is all just some personal shit," Carter said. "There's nothing real big to worry about; couple framed photos and certificates are the biggest things, I think. Hang on and I'll transfer it to you." He blanked out for a few moments, then came back. "There. You should both have it now. It's not a whole lot, but there's some stuff there I'd hate like hell to lose."

"Mm, doesn't look like anything we can't readily bring back, just the two of us," Mott decided, splitting his attention between the two men and the VR list.

"I agree," Demetrius said. "Let's go and get the stuff and get back before they pull a stunt like they did on Ashton's old apartment."

"Right," Mott said. "Back soon, Lee. Stay put."

"Trust me. I'm not goin' anywhere," Carter averred.

They headed out.

"...Great," Kershaw grumbled, when told what had happened. "Just bloody damn great. Bumbling fool! And you know Carter saw him?"

"Considering the busted nose, I'd say so," Stash Gorecki said with a shrug. "You pretty much gotta look at a guy to smash his nose all over his face."

"All right. What's Switch's attitude right now?"

"I dunno that he's got much," Gorecki said. "He's been too busy gettin' patched up to care about anything else. Carter took a plug out of his arm, in addition to the nose."

"What? How?"

"Teeth, I understood," Gorecki told him, and Kershaw winced.

"Shit. Well, if Carter sent Ashton over to ICPD, we can't risk it. Has anybody seen Carter since?"

"Nope. Not a hair of 'im."

"Damn. All right, we'll do this the hard way, then. Contact Bronze. Tell him to clean up the failure."

"You sure you wanna do that, boss? Switch has done good work for us."

"It can't be helped, Stash. He screwed up this time. Bad. He didn't perform surveillance first, and as a result, he grossly underestimated his target. He's a liability now. Better him than us. And *find Carter and Ashton!*"

"Okay, boss."

Dwight Sykes, also known as "Switch," had reported to the nearest IPD beat cop, then gotten said cop to use an electric cart to carry him to the closest hospital emergency room. He was in considerable pain, and had barely been able to breathe, let alone walk.

"No wonder," the ER physician said, when he was done with being poked, prodded, and x-rayed. "Your nose is broken, you have three broken asternal ribs in your side, as well as two broken cuneiform bones and a broken metatarsal *and* a torn extensor digitorum longus tendon in your foot. Let alone the chunk torn out of your arm; it's going to need disinfecting and stitches, and I'll need to put you on antibiotics. That... mugger...must have done a number on you."

The doctor gave him a mildly skeptical glance, and Sykes realized she suspected that matters had been the other way around, but apparently chose not to challenge him...for the moment, at least.

"Can you patch me up, doc?" he wondered. "And...well, frankly, I'm hurtin' pretty bad, here..."

"Yes, I can do that, but the patching is going to be rather unpleasant."

"Can't ya give me something for pain, and then fix things?"

"Only to a point. You have several broken bones here, and while the tendon isn't completely detached, and should heal on its own if we stabilize that foot and you *keep it* that way, the pain medication is only going to suppress the ongoing, more chronic pain. Setting bones tends to result in brief acute pain while the bone ends are being positioned, and the only thing that will stop that is general anesthesia...which we don't want to do here, because it tends to slow healing."

"Shit."

"Something like, yes. I'd strongly recommend avoiding that

neighborhood from now on. Never mind whatever you were doing that took you there."

"Yeah, yeah, I figured," he grumbled. "Hit me with some pain shit, and let's get this over with. I wanna go home and go to bed."

"I can imagine," the physician said, rolling her eyes.

It took over an hour, and even with the maximum dosage of pain medication, Sykes was forced to agree – it hurt like hell. The nose was the worst, he decided; when it had abruptly snapped back into place, he had all but screamed like a little girl, and the nosebleed – that had finally stopped after Carter broke it to begin with – resumed in full force. Then the doctor packed it, and it hurt even worse. By the time the physician was done, his entire head throbbed like it would explode.

Strapping his ribs was the easiest; it wasn't comfortable, but it supported the ribs so that they would stay in place, and hurt less when he tried to breathe. Not that he was breathing through that nose, but mouth breathing worked, provided he didn't feel like he was being stabbed by one of his own knives every time he inhaled. Which, he realized, the strapping helped prevent. It didn't stop it entirely, but he could breathe.

Stitching up the arm wasn't too bad, either; the doctor used a local anesthetic in addition to the pain medication, and made quick work of it once she'd cleaned and disinfected it. Then she gave him a shot of antibiotic, and a prescription for oral antibiotics into the bargain. She did a neat job, but it was still going to be a hell of a scar, he decided as she bandaged it.

The foot, however, proved almost as bad as the nose. He was glad when things were finally in place and she put a boot cast on it.

Finally it was all over. The hospital sent him the bill in VR, and he paid it – which proved to be a pain of its own, at least to his bank account. It took every bit of the advance payment Stash Gorecki had given him for the botched hit, and then some, and he grumbled mentally as he paid it.

I owe that damn retired cop big time for this, he thought vengefully. *And this time, I'm gonna make it nice and slow. Stick the knife in deep and twist. Then rip. That oughta slice the bastard to hell and back. I wanna hear* him *scream like a girl, next time. Then watch him die. Slow.*

He hobbled out of the hospital's arcade level on one good foot, a crutch, and a boot cast, and made it one scant block down before he was panting, his broken ribs throbbing despite pain medications and strapping. The foot, not being elevated, was trying to swell inside the boot, and didn't feel much better than the ribs. In addition, the stitches in his arm pulled painfully every time he swung his arm.

"Dammit. This ain't gonna work," he fussed, stopping to catch his breath. "I'll never get home like this."

He turned and headed for the people-movers.

This particular people-mover only had small cars, holding a couple of people at most; it was never intended for high volume, but it would take Sykes where he wanted to go without much fuss or onlooker stares. Which, he decided, would be good about now.

Sykes waited in line for one of the people-mover cars, but several people, including at least one delivery man, saw his condition and let him move to the front of the line.

"Hey, lemme help, here," the delivery man offered. "I'm used to carrying loads of shit; I can handle this one package and still help steady you."

"That'd be appreciated," Sykes said, grateful. "I got mugged this morning and the guy made a mess of me."

"Somebody sure made a mess, all right," the delivery man agreed, and helped steady Sykes with a gloved hand as they stepped into the car together. The door closed, and the car moved off, headed for a narrow tunnel to the next arcade section. Rather than try to sit and have his ribs complain at the move, then have to stand up again while they complained worse, Sykes simply leaned his good shoulder against the wall of the car and stared ahead, down the tunnel, unseeing. He sighed, deeply tired, and he blinked slowly as the pain medication finally had a chance to do its job.

Behind him, the delivery man pulled an airgun out of his package and put two shots into the back of Sykes' head. Switch Sykes collapsed to the floor of the car like a rag doll.

The gloved delivery man caught the crutch by the pad and eased it to the floor, hit the emergency stop button, opened the door and stepped onto the maintenance walkway, before slipping away in the darkness.

After several moments, the doors of the people-mover car closed, and it continued on, diverting to the emergency path upon exiting the tunnel.

Callista Ames sat at home alone, staring at her solitary plate of food. Rather than trying to cook anything fresh, she had simply heated a prepared meal tray of mass-market frozen food she'd bought from the grocer's, for times when she was too busy to cook. It wasn't half as good as what she'd have cooked for Nick if he'd come over, and it wasn't as good as the take-out she would have gotten, had she gone to his place. But it was food, with nutrients, and it would do for now.

It just wasn't what she had hoped for the evening.

Nick Ashton sat at his dining table at home, having slapped together a cold cut sandwich with plenty of condiments. But the lettuce in his fridge was wilted and the tomatoes old and half-dried-out, and both had gone into the kitchen waste chute, which was collected, composted, and used for fertilizer on the various green spaces within the city. So there were no veggies on the sandwich, and it left the texture and flavor somewhat bland. He sighed, thinking of the nice hibachi restaurant he had planned for the evening.

He picked up his bottle of beer and slugged it, wondering what sort of entertainment might be available that night in VR, and if he could possibly manage to find something he hadn't already seen.

This is gonna get old fast, he decided.

It took about two hours for Mott and Demetrius to slip over to Carter's apartment, find all the items on Carter's list, and stuff them into the special, oversized, ship's duffels Mott had brought, carefully folded into the hidden pockets of his jacket.

Then they slung them over their shoulders and snuck back out, taking maintenance corridors and tunnels.

Twenty minutes later, they were back in Peterson's apartment, and Carter was unpacking the items and stowing them, Maia having pinged him in VR to tell him where he could put various things.

"And while you're doing that," Demetrius said, "I'm going to put out an all-points for one Dwight 'Switch' Sykes."

"Works for me," Carter said, glancing up from folding undershorts and stuffing them into the dresser drawer.

"Oh, and by the way, congratulations," Demetrius added. "Maia is a great catch, and you're a good man."

"What he said," Mott agreed.

Carter flushed, then grinned.

"We've known each other for years – met on a case, way, way back when, and clicked – but because of who and what she is, I kind of kept that friendship secret from my, er, colleagues," he admitted. "It's been smoldering the whole time. When I finally got sick of the shit and took early retirement, it kind of…ignited."

"Good," Demetrius said. "About damn time. She's been waiting for you long enough. Now lemme go see about Switch."

With Mott's help, Carter had finished putting the appropriate hygiene items in the bath, and was nearly finished stashing clothing in the closet and dresser, when Demetrius came up for air, out of VR.

"Got 'im yet, Gene?" Mott wondered.

"Somebody did, Adrian," a solemn Demetrius said in a grave, mildly perturbed tone, and the other two men stopped what they were doing to pay attention.

"Whatcha mean, Gene?" Carter asked.

"He was in the hospital getting some remedial work done on everything you did to him, Lee – stitches in the arm, the nose set and splinted, the ribs strapped, a boot cast – but somebody was apparently waiting for him when he came out. He was found, alone, on the floor of a car in the nearest low-capacity people-mover to the hospital. Two taps to the back of the head; .25 caliber, probably from an airgun. Dead."

"Shit," Carter said, shocked.

"It was Bronze, I swear it was Joey Bronze," Ashton told the rest of the team, as soon as word reached them of what had happened.

"What makes you think that, Nick?" Stefan Gorski asked.

"The double-tap to the head by a .25 caliber airgun. I did a case study on Bronze, my last year at the Academy," Ashton explained. "And I've been following him ever since, adding to that case study. I've got a whole profile on him, now. There's at least four, maybe five other hits he's done in Imp City alone. There was this guy, a lawyer, over in Imperial Park East, who was working with the Empress – boom. Double-tap to the head, airgun, .25 caliber. And a prostitute who was blackmailing one of the assistants of a Council member. Double-tap to the head, airgun, .25 caliber. And two whistleblowers for the previous Empress, one in education, one in the pharmaceutical industry. Both double-taps from a .25 caliber airgun. There's a couple others in nearby cities I've suspected, too."

"But can you prove it?" Demetrius asked. "Just on the basis of the double-tap to the back of the head? Because right now, that's all the clues we have. Yeah, it's a known M.O. for a regular executioner, but we've never been able to tie it to Bronze. Or anybody else, for that matter."

"What about the monitor in the people-mover car? In the station? There would be video…"

"Disabled. Both." Demetrius shrugged.

"And Switch never saw Bronze disable it?!"

"No. It was disabled from outside," Demetrius explained. "Apparently from the control center."

"Shit. That means it was a sanctioned hit."

"Almost certainly, yes. The nature of Sykes' injuries would have meant Carter saw him, and that, in turn, made him a liability."

"What about latents?"

"None found. The crutch Sykes was using was carefully laid beside the body, apparently to prevent breaking any of the windows or causing a lot of noise. We checked it, the car doors, the seats, the railings…nothing. No hairs, no body oils that were recoverable, no fingerprints."

"Shit."

Well, Nick?" Demetrius pressed. "Do you have anything else to give us?"

Ashton's shoulders slumped.

"No, sir. It's a distinctive style, but I know we need more, to take it to court."

"Hell, we need more to get a warrant to pick him up," Demetrius pointed out.

"Exactly. I'm afraid," Gorski sighed, "that unless we turn up some more clues to point us in the right direction, this one is going to go down as another cold case."

"Naw, man," Kendall Raines said, as he met with Stash Gorecki. "So far, ain't nobody seen either one of 'em. Are you sure Ashton is back in town? I mean, absolutely positive? 'Cause it might have been somebody that just looked like him. It's been – what? Three, four years now? People can change a lot in that amount o' time."

"Yeah, we're pretty sure. In fact, we aren't sure now that he ever left," Gorecki declared. "The boss thinks Carter pulled a fast one and transferred Ashton over to Imp City, then got out while the gettin' was good."

"Eh," Raines said, considering. "Could be, I suppose. The Imp City guys are about the most strait-laced dicks I ever saw, so it figures he'd be in with 'em, from what I hear. But no, none of my boys an' girls have seen 'em, either one of 'em. Sorry, Stash. We'll keep looking."

Matters went on like this for several days, and while Ashton had to duck into a store front once, when he spotted one of Gorecki's hand-picked gang coming around a corner on his way to work, nothing else happened that anyone could tell.

Eventually the word from Imp City's street informers indicated that the search for the two men had been back-burnered, to the considerable relief of Ashton, Carter, Peterson, and Ames.

But that didn't mean things were over.

"You'd think," Peterson grumbled, "that Gorecki and his goons getting their badges taken for that shit they did to Solisbury would have slowed things down."

"No," Carter said. "It's only going to have made them worse."

"Why?"

"Because they resent it. They're still on the payroll, but they're not official any longer."

"Oh shit."

"Exactly."

Things finally settled down after a few more days, and there were no more immediate indications of anyone from IPD coming after Ashton, so Ashton and Ames met back at the Laughing Cat, taking what Ames called "the undercover route" to get there. George met them and put them in the corner booth of the backmost back room again, closing off the folding partitions to allow them privacy.

This time, when Nick walked Cally home – continuing to take the "undercover routes" to get there – he kissed her.

The next night, at her invitation, Nick skulked his way over to Cally's apartment and she cooked for him. The first course was a simple spinach salad with a homemade champagne vinaigrette followed by a hearty, warming soupe à l'oignon. Then she served broiled tilapia drizzled with a delicate lemon-dill sauce and a delicious ratatouille on the side. Dessert was a chocolate crème brûlée. All were, according to Cally, from old family recipes.

More, she put out her good china – the set, she told him, that her mother had given her – and put flowers and lit candles on the table. The wine Nick brought per her instructions was poured into two crystal goblets, to be enjoyed with the meal.

It was by far the most sophisticated and delicious meal Nick had had since he had left home on Flanders.

It was definitely better than either the frozen dinner or the cold-cut sandwich.

After dinner, they sat on her sofa and talked.

Mostly.

The rest of the time, they did what young people attracted to one another often did, since the origins of the human race long ago, on Earth.

And that was a *lot* better than sitting home alone.

The Sandman

A couple of days – almost a full week – after the attack on Carter, Peterson called a meeting of the investigative department.

"He's back, guys," she told them. "'Jack' is back in the game."

The older detectives cursed quietly.

"What happened, and who did he get?" Gorski asked.

"Lana Rounder, head of marketing for the Flying Porker restaurant chain," Peterson said. "She reports directly to the vice president of marketing, Jack Witte. Apparently she collapsed this morning in her office and didn't respond, so they called for emergency transport to the hospital. She's already gone into a coma, her liver is failing as we speak, and they found the G.A.S. treatment in her bloodstream. The failure cascade is already starting."

"Damn," Demetrius muttered, patently distressed.

"Um, ma'am, who's Jack?" Ames asked. "And...what did the rest of that mean?"

"Okay, that's right, you newbies don't know. Lemme see. About five or six years back–"

"It started about ten years ago, Maia," Demetrius reminded.

"True, but it went on until around five years ago," Peterson averred, "we had a serial killer, Cally. Some of us started off calling him 'Jack' after the very first recorded serial killer in human history. Others, like the news media, called him 'the Sandman' after his method of killing, and that's mostly the name that stuck. We never caught him, and eventually he stopped killing, and the murders became cold cases. Until now."

"How did he kill, then?" Ashton asked.

"No one knew, at first," Demetrius said. "The victims would fall unconscious, drop into a coma, and then internal organs would start to fail, one by one, in an increasing and accelerating cascade. Eventually not enough was functional to keep them alive, and they died."

"What was the profile on his victims?" Compton asked.

"We were never able to figure that out," Gorski said. "That's why we were never able to solve any of the murders. If you have a serial killer with a known *modus operandi*, a specific method of killing, but you can't figure out why he chooses his targets, or how he actually kills beyond 'somehow he administers this toxic substance,' you're going to have a hard time solving the cases."

"Shit," Weaver muttered.

"Exactly," Peterson said. "Now, Taylor Haptman and Jill Amundsen are still on that same case that they're fighting with over in Charia, which I'm beginning to think is never gonna end. At any rate, they're out of pocket just like they've been for well over a year, now. Which hurts, because they were the leads on the Sandman killings, last time. I've pinged 'em, and they're making themselves available as best they can for us to consult, but that's about as much as they can manage. And Peter and Roger are already assigned to other cases, and they're using Tim and Darrell, which leaves the rest of you. I want *all* of you working this for me. And that's not a team of slouches. So what I've done is pull up all of the old case files and uploaded them to a 'study room' in channel 352, with tables and chairs so everybody can get comfortable and look things over. Gene, you and Stefan take Nick and go over to the latest...damn, I hate to call it a crime scene, because the place where the victim passed out may or may not be the place where the toxin was administered, but it's the best we can do right now."

"What was the toxin, anyway?" Ashton queried. "Did they ever find out what was causing the deaths?"

"Yes, the forensic pathologists did. It's actually a medicine, one of the virulosins," Demetrius said. "Used for very rare diseases, and occasionally for rare types of injuries. In this particular instance, it was developed for Griggs-Andersen Syndrome, or G.A.S., 'gas,' where the bodily organs don't know how to use glycogen correctly. So they have to be modified at the genetic level to utilize it properly, and they use a particular virulosin to do it. The doctors therefore refer to the medication as G.A.S. virulosin. The thing is, like most powerful medicines, you have to be careful and really nail the diagnosis, because in a healthy person, the virulosin can actually end up killing the organs by destroying their ability to use glycogen for fuel."

"So...it kind of...*creates* the syndrome...in somebody that doesn't already have it..." Ames pondered.

"Something like, yes," Demetrius confirmed. "Only it's accelerated, because of the viral nature of the virulosin. Whereas someone with G.A.S. might take five years to die in the absence of the cure, someone without it, given the virulosin, might last only a week. If that." He paused, then added, "I'm told it's hell to watch."

"Damn," Compton muttered.

"Exactly," Gorski agreed.

"Isn't the usual method of administering a virulosin via eyedrops?" Ashton asked, as they headed for the office building where the latest victim had fallen unconscious, hopping the commuter train to go under the Imperial Park in the process. They boarded from the IUS Imperial Center station, and would debark in the Imperial Park East station.

"It depends," Demetrius said, offhanded, with a shrug. "I'm no expert by any means, but on the last go-round of the Sandman, I had occasion to learn a lot, because I was working under Jill Amundsen. It seems to depend on what, exactly, is being affected by the disease it's intended to treat. Now, Melsbach Syndrome, yeah, it goes in the eyes, because it follows the optic nerves to the brain, and that's where the problem is. Other virulosins might treat the stomach, or the digestive tract, or the lungs. For those, you might drink it, or breathe it in in a mist, or something like that. The doctors told me you could inject it, put it in an intravenous drip, all kinds of things like that."

"So it could have been put in a drink, or in food, or even in a humidifier," Ashton speculated, thoughtful, as they exited the train at the Imperial Park East stop.

"Yes, but the humidifier would have affected a lot more people, unless it was a personal, room thing," Gorski pointed out.

"Hm."

"Exactly." Demetrius paused at an elevator, activating it in VR. "An added complication, though, is that most virulosins need to be kept cold – even frozen – right up until they're administered, in order to remain viable. Although it's possible to heat them right before administration, if the situation requires; at that point, they're pretty sturdy little buggums." He shrugged. "It's really just about preservation until it's time to administer."

"Damn, it just gets harder and harder," Ashton grumbled, as

they entered the elevator and took it up to street level.

"Now you see why we never caught him the first time around," Gorski noted.

A few minutes later, they arrived at the office building where Lana Rounder had passed out. Now hospitalized as her liver failed and other organs threatened collapse, she had worked in a restaurant chain's headquarters, as head of marketing for the chain.

"Oh, you're the detectives to investigate what happened to Ms. Rounder," the receptionist in the lobby said when they showed her their credentials; her desk sign read Amani Hayden. "I'll call Mr. Witte at once. I can't imagine what happened! Lana – she told me to call her Lana; she always stopped and chatted with me – was so friendly and generally well-liked; I just can't understand why anyone would want to kill her."

"So you already know it was a murder attempt?" Gorski asked, shooting a surreptitious, concerned glance at Demetrius and Ashton.

"Oh, Yes, sir! Mr. Witte has already called the hospital to find out her condition. They..." the little receptionist broke off, looking like she might cry. "They said she's...dying, and the doctors can't stop it. Mr. Witte was shocked, and he put out word for people to be sending up prayers and good thoughts for her, just in case they can find a way to stop it."

"Those are all good things to do, ma'am," Demetrius said in a gentle, quiet voice. "Miracles do happen. And perhaps we can find out who did it, and put an end to it."

"O-okay," Hayden sniffled, fighting tears. "I'll call Mr. Witte. His executive assistant said he was fairly pacing the floor, waiting for you."

Jack Witte was a charismatic, personable sort, obviously a promoter, but courteous for all that. It could have been all too easy for him to come across as a used-vehicle salesman, Ashton thought, but he didn't; more, he seemed genuinely concerned over the situation. And not a little stunned.

"I just can't believe it," he kept saying. "I only saw her this morning, and she seemed fine."

"Could we see her office? That was where she passed out, correct?" Demetrius asked.

"Oh, certainly, certainly. And yes, that's where she collapsed. Right this way," Witte said, heading for the elevator. "I'll show you to it personally. I just can't believe it. We had coffee together and discussed the latest ad campaign plan, just this morning, not an hour before she collapsed."

"Where did the coffee come from?" Ashton asked, jumping on the statement.

"Oh, from the company break room. Lana's assistant brought it to us."

"And you both had some?" Gorski pressed.

"Yes, of course. I drink mine with cream and two sugars, she drinks – drank – hers black."

"Dead end," Demetrius murmured to his companions.

"Yeah, dammit," Ashton grumbled under his breath.

"Did she have anyone under her?" Gorski asked. "Designers, marketers, artists, or the like?"

"She had two marketers," Witte said. "We hired out our artwork to a well-known firm."

"Who were her marketers?" Gorski followed up his question. "And were there any problems within the group recently?"

"Livy Glenn and Tristan Wall," Witte said. "And no, they all got along quite well. Ms. Glenn and Mr. Wall are fairly young, only a year or so out of university, so Lana was mentoring them. Those three made a great team."

"Here it is, gentlemen," Witte said, stopping in front of an executive office. "My own office is right down the hall, and I fear I'm expecting an important communiqué, so I need to get back to it. I'll leave you here; do whatever you need to do, and if you need me, just step down to my office. I'll stop whatever I'm doing to help."

"Thank you, sir," Demetrius said, shaking the vice-president's hand. "We'll do that."

And Witte headed down the corridor.

There was nothing especially unusual about the office where Lana Rounder had collapsed; it was fairly modern, with an executive desk and matching ergonomic chair, a number of colorful, rough print images lying on the desktop. Two recently-stained but empty ceramic coffee mugs sat on a credenza along one wall, along with several more print images; a luxurious visitor chair sat beside it. Old-style books in bookcases sat on shelves along the walls, in addition to quite a few old notebooks, each marked with a year. Ashton nosed about the notebooks; they proved to be scrapbooks of previous years' marketing campaigns.

"She likes old-fashioned print," Gorski noticed.

"Some marketing types do," Demetrius agreed. "They say it helps 'em envision it on a wall or shop window, or whatever."

"One thing there isn't, is Nick's humidifier," Gorski observed.

"Yeah, I saw," Ashton said with a stifled sigh.

"Hey, it was a definite idea, kiddo, and one we need to check up on for the cold cases," Demetrius encouraged.

"Besides, this might not even have been where the virulosin was introduced."

"But how the hell do we figure out where it was introduced?" Ashton asked, frustrated.

"Well, the stuff is going to take effect really fast, likely within hours, and the bigger the dose, the faster it kicks in," Gorski pointed out. "So if we have to, we simply try to reconstruct where she was for the last, oh, up to maybe twelve hours, and one of those places has to be where it was done."

"She was here all day," came a voice behind them.

They turned. An older woman of around fifty stood there, a salt-and-pepper brunette with more salt than pepper, and hazel eyes wearing a worried expression.

"I assume you're the police investigators?" she asked.

"Yes, ma'am," Demetrius said. "I'm Inspector Eugene Demetrius. These are my colleagues, Detective Stefan Gorski, and Lieu-uh, Captain Investigator, Officer Dominick Ashton."

"Pleased," she said, shaking hands. "I'm Lana's assistant, Joyce Abelard."

"Can you tell us if there is anything unusual here, something she doesn't usually have in her office? Anything new, any unexpected visitor, anyone you've never seen before?" Gorski queried.

"No," Abelard said. "She's had no visitors, no new projects, not even any shipments or new print proofs. Not today."

"Where did she go for lunch?"

"Her desk," Abelard said with a rueful chuckle. "She actually brought in leftovers from home, most of the time."

"Do we still have the containers the food was in?" Ashton piped up. "It might be good to test them, to make certain they were clean of the virulosin..."

"Good thought, Nick," Gorski agreed. "Do we?"

"Yes, but it was disposable," Abelard told them. She pointed. "It's all right there in her wastebasket."

"Got it." Ashton immediately knelt by the receptacle, pulling forensic gloves and some poly bags for the items. He donned the gloves and promptly began a gingerly rooting in the waste can, extracting the food-stained items and bagging them.

"What about this morning?" Gorski continued the questioning while his capable protégé triaged the trash can. "Had she been anywhere before she came to work?"

"No, she came straight from home. I met her at the front door of her building, like I always do, and we walked to work together."

"I guess we check her home next," Gorski decided. "Finished there, Nick?"

"Yes, sir; bagged and tagged," Ashton said, standing and tucking several bags into the special tote Demetrius produced and held out to him.

"Then let's go," Demetrius declared.

After the investigators left, a troubled Abelard glanced around the office.

The wastebasket was almost completely empty, where the young investigator had dug around for Rounder's food containers and utensils, but they had left the various print proofs alone, on both the desk and the credenza. Nothing unduly untidy caught her eye, though she absently noted that Rounder and Witte must have moved to the credenza to look over some of the advertising, since a dried coffee ring now stained the top of that cabinet. She sighed.

"I guess I'd best clean that up," she murmured to herself. "Somehow I doubt Lana is going to be back to do it herself, by the sound of things."

As the trio of investigators moved through the arcade on the slidewalk toward the building that Lana Rounder had called home, a woman sitting at an outdoor café sipping a cappuccino with a male "companion" watched them move past, then started in surprise.

"Wait a second, sweetie," she told the john. "I need to check on something real quick."

"What? I haven't done anything wrong," the john said, then smirked. "Yet."

"No, no, it's not about you. Just wait a minute."

"Okay, if you insist."

"I do."

The woman dropped into the blank-eyed expression of VR immersion.

"Stash! Stash, where are you! Come quick! I think I see him!" she called. Finally Gorecki appeared in the nondescript gray VR room in response to her emergency summons.

"All right, all right, don't get y'r panties in a wad. Assuming you're wearing any. I'm here," he grumbled. "What the hell do you want, Jeannie? I thought I told you not to bother me at work. I don't like it when my ex bugs me in the middle of something."

"That cop you're trying to find! I think I see him! He went right by me at the café!"

"Which one? Carter or Ashton?"

"I don't know which one's which! The young, good-looking guy!"

"Ashton. You sure?"

"No! That's why I'm in full VR! You got his picture, right?"

"Aha. Yeah, lemme dig that out."

The VR depicted Gorecki patting down his pockets; in

reality, he was sifting through image files.

"Oh, here we go."

He held up a photo; in reality, he pushed the image file to Jeannie, who studied it.

"Yeah! Yeah, that's him, I'm ninety-nine percent sure! He's mostly blond now, but the rest of it's him!"

"Okay. You're where, now?"

"The Baked Bean Café, in the Golden Street Arcade, over in Imperial Park East."

"Moving up with your clientele, there, eh?"

"It pays," Jeannie declared, offended. "Better than it used to, given the guys with no bank balance *you* used to send me."

"Right. I bet it does." Gorecki leered. "I'll get somebody over there as fast as I can. Maybe we can catch the son of a bitch this time."

But by the time Gorecki could get one of his hired guns to the location – given that most of them tended to frequent the less-affluent Imperial Park South district – Ashton and his two mentors were long gone.

Much to Jeannie's chagrin, so was her impatient john.

At Rounder's home, the investigative trio spread out and explored, periodically bagging and labeling this or that item to test for the presence of virulosin. Finally Ashton stopped, irritated.

"There has got to be an easier way," he declared. "We're just guessing, here."

"What do you suggest, Nick?" Gorski wondered.

"I'm not completely sure yet, but are you two game for me trying something?" he asked.

Demetrius and Gorski looked at each other, then they both

shrugged.

"You've got a good head on your shoulders, son," Demetrius, the eldest of the three, said. "If you have a hunch about something, give it a shot."

"All right. Hang on a few minutes, here," Ashton said, and his face took on the blank expression of someone in VR.

"Dr. Botha?" Ashton asked, as the forensic physician from the Empress Adannaya III Hospital appeared in the virtual meeting room in avatar form, in response to his VR summons.

"Yes? Wait, you're the young investigator that Stefan Gorski brought with him to the rapist case, right?" Botha asked, recognizing Ashton.

"That's me. Officer Nick Ashton, Captain Investigator, IP – I mean, ICPD. I used to be IPD HQ, but I…didn't like it over there."

"Good to see you again, and I…understand. I take it, you have a question about something?"

"I do. Were you around as a forensic physician when the Sandman serial killer operated?"

"I sure was. That was a scary time." Botha's avatar stopped dead, and stared at Ashton's avatar in horror. "Oh shit. Don't tell me, he's back?"

"That, or it's a copycat," Ashton noted. "And given it's the exact same *modus operandi*, and we never really figured it out the first time…"

"Randi ka choda," the doctor cursed in a pithy tone.

"I'm not sure what that means," Ashton said in a bleakly humorous tone, "but judging by the way it sounds, I think I agree with you."

Botha let out a wry bark of laughter.

"It would be the rough equivalent of 'son of a bitch,'" he

translated. "What can I do to help?"

"From what my mentors are telling me, apparently the means of death is infection of healthy people by a specialized virulosin," Ashton explained.

"Yes, that is apparently the case," Botha confirmed. "I worked on that case, back when the Sandman first appeared – I tended one of the victims, trying desperately to find a way to stop the cascade – and was also involved in the forensics. We found a virulosin in the victims, targeted to Griggs-Andersen Syndrome, where the body's organs are failing due to – well, you don't care about that. Suffice it that, if the G.A.S.-targeted virulosin is consumed by a healthy person, it causes the reverse – it makes the organs fail in sequence, in a cascade that is, so far, impossible to stop, and fairly swift but not immediate."

Ashton pondered that.

"So...once it's been introduced into the body, the victim is gonna die?"

"Yes. The victim will die. We never found a way to stop it, though I'm sure the research is ongoing."

"You said consumed. What's the usual means of introduction to a Griggs-Andersen patient?"

"It is usually placed into a cola-like drink – preferably one with caffeine; it helps the system by pumping up the metabolism and spreading the virulosin faster – and consumed that way. Then it is absorbed through the gastrointestinal tract, and goes systemic."

"Hm."

"Yes."

"All right, lemme get to the point of this visit," Ashton decided. "Out in the field, here, us investigators are kind of grasping at straws. We don't know where the virulosin was introduced, so we don't even know where the crime scene is. I

STEPHANIE OSBORN

was kinda hoping maybe you medicos had developed a method of detecting the stuff?"

"Well, no," Botha said. "Since it's a medication, normally there's no need to detect it. It's right where it needs to be."

"Shit!" Ashton cursed with feeling.

"No, now wait, Detective," Botha said. "I–"

"It's Captain Investigator, sir, or just Officer. I haven't made detective quite yet."

"Ah, right," Botha said. "So hold on, Officer. Just because the answer to that specific question is no doesn't mean I can't help you, here."

"Oh? What have you got in mind?"

"Centuries ago, back on Earth, humans had many difficulties with viral pandemics," Botha explained. "Hundreds of thousands to many millions of deaths, with the worst of them; economies destroyed or crippled at best, as they tried to quarantine entire segments of the population. The history is...grim." Ashton nodded understanding, so Botha continued. "Even with more and more advanced medicines, detecting them was sometimes difficult. More, if the person had already had the virus and survived it, that meant the immune system was likely proof against it, but it was often hard to know who had already had it. Attempts were made to slow the spread, and were, at best, only partially effective...often at the cost of the nation-state's economy. Over time – think a couple of centuries, here – the medical community began to realize that the ability to detect a given virus or its antibody in a person or in an environment was paramount in an epidemic or pandemic. It gives us a leg up on knowing where the disease is, and how bad it is, where it's being transmitted, who needs treatment, and whose immune system is already protecting them against it."

126

"Okay. So?"

"So," Botha told him, "scientists developed a swift means of detecting the presence of a given virus based on its core nucleic acid structure. They also developed the means of detecting its antibody, but that's neither here nor there for our purposes now. So. This method is especially effective for retroviruses, where the segment of RNA contained in the core of the virion is replicated and spliced into the host's DNA, apparently in order to replicate. And this is how virulosin works. We – the medical community – use certain specific strains of retroviruses, then replace the core RNA with the segment we want replaced to cure the specific genetic disease we're trying to fix. Then we introduce the modified retrovirus into our patient, ensure the virus reaches the specific body parts needing repair, and let it do its thing."

"That's...brilliant."

"Well, it is, and I don't take any credit for it; that's not my field of expertise. *But*, since the viral detector system works best for retroviruses, I suspect it can be easily modified to look for your virulosin that's being used to murder."

"Ooo. *That* would be useful!" Ashton exclaimed. "Should I ask how that works?"

"Probably not," Botha chuckled. "Because that was not something I studied in depth, and while I could take a cut at an explanation, that doesn't mean I could get it to make sense to you."

"Heh," Ashton chuckled. "I get that. Why didn't anybody use this when the Sandman first appeared?"

"I suspect because nobody thought of it," Botha concluded. "The technology I'm referencing was still relatively new at that time, and wasn't in common use as yet. There were other methods before this technique was developed, but they were cruder and slower."

"Okay, I can understand that. So how long do you think it will take you to get hold of whoever, and get a...what do you call the shit?"

"Epidemiological Viral Detection and Early Warning Reagent," Botha said. "Shortened – a little – to E.V.D.E.W.R."

"Damn. That's a mouthful and a half."

"Yes, but you should have seen the alternative name," Botha laughed. "Anyway, I know who to call, and since it is designed to go into action early in a suspected epidemic, it's designed and set up so they can turn it out pretty fast, and one of the principal manufacturers is here on Sintar. I can have a case of what they call 'puff testers' to the ICPD headquarters in...probably about an hour or two, coded to the G.A.S. virulosin. And it will not be expensive – it is designed not to be, per an Imperial decree, so that sectors in the midst of an epidemic or pandemic can afford it – so we can send the bill through to the bean counters and they won't pass out."

"That's great! Let's do it," Ashton ordered. "We need all the help we can get, before somebody else gets hit."

"Agreed. I'll do it immediately we end this meeting."

"You're kidding," Demetrius said, once Ashton had explained. "Why didn't they use that when the Sandman showed up the first time?"

"I expect because nobody thought to," Gorski said. "And they might not even have had it yet. After all, it was the last Empress who finally got the drug companies to get off their collective asses and start pumping out the various virulosins to begin with. They were sitting on 'em because they were making more money off ongoing treatment drugs than off cures."

"That's pretty much the way I understood it, yes," Ashton confirmed. "Because I asked the same thing. The technology was brand-new at the time, and nobody was familiar with it. And older methods were too slow for an active police investigation of ongoing murders."

"Mmph," Demetrius said, stifling what, judging by his expression, would have been a particularly pithy curse. "All right. So Nick, here, comes up with the item that's going to help us locate the source of the..." he threw up his hands, "infection, for want of a better way to put it." He patted Ashton on the back. "Hell of an idea, kiddo."

"Thank you, sir."

"So should we go back to the office and wait for the...what was it, Nick? 'Puff testers'?" Gorski asked.

"You two are the experienced detectives," Ashton said, "but I don't see the point in waiting here right now. Besides, the others might have found something in the archives."

"Good point," Demetrius decreed. "Let's go."

Sitting Ducks

Jeannie's avatar was waiting for Gorecki, and this time she was in a bad mood. As soon as he appeared, she lit in on him.

"Do you have anybody working for you that has any patience or common sense?" she demanded. "That idiot you sent to me stayed maybe five minutes, then headed out, too bored to sit here and wait! Ashton just came back through, with two other older guys, one of which might have been the *other* guy you're looking for! And numbnuts didn't have sense enough to wait, to see if he might come back through! Even though I told him he ought to, just in case!"

"Roger? He didn't stay?"

"No!"

"Did he say why?"

"Something about you interrupting him while he was bangin' his girlfriend."

"Mmph." Gorecki scowled. "Son of a bitch. Okay. So we missed Ashton, and maybe Carter, too. Again. Dammit. All right. I'll take care of Roger. His girlfriend probably needs to start shopping around for a new boyfriend, though."

And Gorecki broke the link.

But Roger had thought better of the matter, and circled around until he could survey the area from a secluded spot in an alcove between buildings. He patted his pocket to make sure he was properly equipped, then settled down to wait.

He didn't have to wait long. Ten minutes later, a trio of men in casual business wear, Ashton in the middle, rode the slidewalk through the arcade toward the commuter train station. They were on the far side of the arcade street from him, but he had a decent aim.

Bingo, he thought. *Ashton* and *Carter. And the other guy is probably Imp City. Triple score. Take 'em in order, Rog.*

He smirked as he pulled his pistol from his jacket pocket. He rested it on his opposite hand, which was, in turn, pressed against the building façade, aimed at Ashton, and pulled the trigger.

The round hit Ashton right in the chest, and he went down.

Shocked, Demetrius and Gorski spun in the direction of the gun report, spotted the shooter, and drew down, yelling, "POLICE! EVERYONE! GET DOWN! WE HAVE A SHOOTER!" as the two detectives crouched and took aim. Pedestrians shrieked, and dove for cover.

The shooter ducked behind the corner of the building as both detectives let loose a short burst of weapons fire, then emerged once more to take another shot, going for Gorski.

"Get down, Stefan!" Demetrius ordered, and Gorski flattened himself on the slidewalk to present the smallest possible silhouette. Demetrius, already on one knee, steadied his weapon, aimed at the gunman – who was focusing on Gorski – and fired. Three times.

A cry came from their assailant, and he ducked back behind the building. That shelter was quickly eluding him, however, as the slidewalk carried the Imp City officers farther down the street, opening up the alcove in which the gunman hid.

By this time, Gorski had his own weapon brought back around and trained, as he lay flat on his belly. He took aim at the torso of the shooter, and fired three more shots.

The gunman fell backward, dropping his weapon and

disappearing behind a waste bin, even as Imperial City Police beat cops came running.

"Sir!" one of them said, running up to Gorski. "Are you hurt?"

"No, but my protégé may be," Gorski said, levering himself up and turning toward Ashton, who still lay on his back on the slidewalk, apparently unconscious. "Somebody stop the slidewalk and let's see to him."

"You lot! Go apprehend the shooter!" Demetrius said, pointing at a group of three beat cops.

"Yes, sir!" They saluted and headed across the street at a run.

The detectives turned to the fallen Ashton.

"Nick? Son? Are you okay?" Gorski said, kneeling beside the younger man. "Damn. I'm not seeing any blood, Gene, but there's a hole clean through…"

"I'm…I'm okay," Ashton panted, stirring and pushing into a seated position. "Body armor…stopped it. Hurt like hell, though. Knocked the wind outta me."

"Yup, thank God for body armor, but you'll still feel it," Gorski agreed. "Did he get you with more than one round?"

"Nah, just the one." Ashton poked a finger through the hole in his tweed jacket. "Damn. I liked this jacket."

"Don't sweat it. I know a good tailor can re-weave that in nothing flat," Demetrius offered, as the police officers who had gone to investigate the shooter returned. "Where is he?"

"Gone, sir. There's a puddle of blood, though, so you got him."

"We should be able to track the blood drops, then, and apprehend him," Gorski decided. "Get some blood samples, while we're at it."

"No time for that. Here come the Impies," Demetrius said, seeing several Imperial Police coming through the archway on the far side of the arcade. "We need to get Nick out of sight."

"They want him, sir?" one of the beat cops asked.

"Yes. Preferably dead. He was the shooter's target. And he's one of us."

"We have this, then," another beat cop said, as they all scowled. "Internal Imp City matter; we'll hold 'em up, you go."

"We're gone, then," Demetrius agreed.

"Can you stand, Nick?" Gorski asked.

"Help me up, and I'll be okay," Ashton averred.

The two detectives, plus one of the beat cops, levered Ashton to his feet as the others went to delay the IPD officers.

Then the slidewalk came on and they jogged along it for the near archway and the commuter train station beyond.

Roger was in a bad way. The oldest cop had hit him in the arm, and Carter had hit him in the belly. He was bleeding badly, but he pulled a kerchief out of a pocket and stuffed it into the wound, trying not to scream in pain. He figured if he could get home, he could get help...but he had to avoid bleeding out along the way.

He hobbled for the maintenance exit as fast as he could manage.

Demetrius commandeered a car on the commuter train, ensured the security monitor was killed, and he and Gorski eased Ashton into a train seat.

"All right, let's see," Gorski demanded.

"Aw, I'm doing better now," Ashton protested, even as Gorski and Demetrius stripped him of his jacket and tie. "It's just gonna bruise."

"I want to make sure you don't have any internal injuries," Demetrius insisted. "The shock wave from the impact can still cause injury – even death – even if the bullet doesn't penetrate, Nick."

"I know, I..." Ashton broke off, then sighed, and began stripping off his shirt and upper body armor. The other two men hissed.

"*Gonna* bruise?" Gorski echoed. "More like already has. Damn, Nick."

There was a big purple-blue-black blotch on Ashton's right chest, running roughly across his lower breast. Ashton wrinkled his nose in a displeased scowl.

"Shit," was all he said.

"Can you breathe okay?" Demetrius wondered. "Any sharp pains when you inhale or exhale?"

"Not particularly," Ashton decided after a moment to check. He took a deep breath. "I mean – urg. *That* hurt. Not sharp, just, you know, bruised."

"Probably even bruised some of the ribs, Gene," Gorski suggested.

"Yeah. Could be some green breaks in there, though. Maybe we need to get this looked at, son," Demetrius said.

"But the Sandman!"

"Can wait until we make sure you're going to be okay," Gorski pointed out. "He never went after another victim until the first one had died, anyway. We have some time, here. Not much, but enough. You have lungs, heart, liver, and pancreas all in the general vicinity of that hit, and any or all could have been damaged by the shock of the impact. And any one of those could be bad."

"The damn assassin must have been hot loading," Demetrius muttered. "That handgun gotta have had a hell of a kick."

"Hope it kicks him straight to hell," Gorski cursed.

Notifying Colonel Peterson of the attack in a VR message, the trio rode the commuter train to their stop, which was IUS Imperial Center. They promptly escorted Ashton to the nearest hospital, which happened to be the Imperial University's teaching hospital – which was often the one used by Imp City police, in any case. They took him straight into the emergency room entrance, showed their credentials, explained what had happened, and escorted Ashton alongside the nurses as they immediately took him back to a currently-available ER physician.

Half an hour later, and after Ashton had been scanned and x-rayed ninety-nine ways from Sunday, Dr. Anita Brand pronounced him more or less intact.

"He does have some rib bruising, and the muscular hematoma is epic," she declared. "And I'm sure there is some trauma to the lung, and maybe a bit to the liver. I don't see any heart problems; the bullet must have struck at an angle. Don't be surprised if you have some pain when you breathe for a few days, and don't be surprised if your bowel movements turn rather yellowish, or even greenish, for about a week. Oh, and expect some diarrhea."

"Bile?" Demetrius asked.

"Exactly, from the liver bruising," Dr. Brand confirmed. "It could even cause some digestive issues, because a large bile dump can seem to burn its way through your gut, so I'd recommend a low-fat, bland diet for a few days to avoid generating an even larger bile dump."

"Um, okay," Ashton murmured. "Can I put my shirt on now?"

"I'd like to pad that bruise a little, first," Brand recommended. "It would probably feel better. And I'll prescribe some topicals and a few things to speed up the healing, especially if we can get the nanites revved and working on it. I want you to watch out for a while, though, and don't dislodge any clots."

"Huh?"

"Bruises are clots forming under the skin," Brand explained to the young man. "It's the body's way of stopping the subcutaneous bleeding. But you don't want to dislodge one and have it float through your circulatory system. If it gets wedged someplace – the heart, the brain, the kidneys, the lungs, the retinas – well, it's just a very bad situation, and it can be fatal, depending on where it gets stuck."

"Oh," Ashton said, suddenly realizing. "Stroke, heart attack…"

"Pulmonary embolism, blindness, kidney failure, yeah," Brand said. "All that nasty shit."

"So we need to keep his heart rate and blood pressure down, too, right?" Gorski asked. "Does he need to go on medical leave?"

"Mm," Brand considered. "He's a detective, right?"

"Right," Demetrius said, before Ashton could correct the physician's terminology.

"Normally we come in after something has happened, not while it's happening," Gorski explained.

"Do you need him for a case?"

Demetrius, Gorski, and Ashton exchanged considering glances.

"Do you remember the Sandman murders, about ten years ago?" Demetrius wondered.

"Oh hell yeah," Brand said, expression twisting in disgust,

then she started and stared at them, horror-stricken. "Don't tell me that bastard is back?"

"Yup," Gorski sighed.

"What, did he come after you guys?"

"No, this is an old enemy," Ashton said; it was his turn to sigh. "But that was the case we were on when the old enemy came outta the woodwork."

"And Ashton, here, being an excellent detective, came up with some things for us to chase that we didn't have, before," Demetrius explained.

"Oh. So you need him. Well..." Brand pondered for long moments, eyeing Ashton thoughtfully. "Okay, do what you need to do. Just be careful. All of you. Sounded to me like that old enemy was perfectly willing to take all of you out, if he could."

"Probably," Gorski agreed. "But us two old dogs plan to stick close, and we're no slouches, with weapons or without. We'll keep him in the background and defend him ourselves if need be."

"Good. Let me pad this, get his nanites rolling, and a few scripts filled – including something for pain, to tide you over a day or two – and then you can get dressed, Detective Ashton."

Roger finally made it back to his apartment and his girlfriend, but she wasn't alone.

"Oh! Thank God! Stash! Help me. I got shot. That Carter guy nailed me. I'm hurt bad," Roger murmured, closing the door and sinking down to the floor. "Can you get me some medical help? I need to get the bullet out and get patched up..."

"Sure, Rog, I'll help," Gorecki said.

He pulled an airgun and shot Roger point-blank in the chest. He collapsed.

Roger gasped, and stared up at Gorecki in horror, until his eyes glazed and his head dropped to the floor. His body sagged as a puddle of blood formed beneath it. His pulse, just visible in the hollow of his throat, slowed, then stopped.

"OHMIGAW! YOU KILLED HIM!" the girlfriend shrieked. "You said you were his friend! His boss!"

"I was," Gorecki said, calm. "Shut up."

He turned and put two more rounds into the girlfriend, who screamed in pain and fear, then toppled to the sofa, bleeding out.

Gorecki watched until she was dead, as well.

Then he turned and left the apartment, locking it behind him.

When the IPD investigated the double shooting later that day, they pronounced it a murder-suicide, despite the lack of a weapon.

The trio left the Imperial University Hospital via the maintenance passages, hopscotching from building to building and staying well out of sight, until they were back at the Imperial City Police headquarters. Most of the team was waiting, including Peterson. Ames ran to Ashton.

"Oh dear Lord! Nick, are you okay, honey?" Cally asked, anxious. She reached for him, but then froze, and pulled back, uncertain about where he had been hit.

"I'm fine, Cal," he murmured soothingly, laying one hand lightly on his chest, where he had been hit, and the other hand on her shoulder. "I got a few good bruises here, but no busted ribs, and no internal injuries. I was wearing my body armor."

"Wish we could armor your damn head," Peterson grumbled from the corner.

"That might be possible, actually, but he'd have to wear a

wig, and he would still have a concussion if he got shot," Mott decided, thinking.

"That's better than dead, I guess," Ashton said with a wince. "Let's think about it and see what's the best we can come up with."

"That works," Mott agreed.

"Maia, have you heard from Lee?" Gorski asked then.

"No, not since I left for work this morning; why?"

"Ping him and make sure he's okay. This shooter took Nick down first, then zeroed in on me. I suspect, due to the relative ages, he thought I was Carter."

"Right," Peterson said. Her expression blanked momentarily, then she came back. "He's okay. He's been at home all day. I told him what happened, and he said he'd lay low."

"Good," Gorski averred. "Nick, you and Cally gonna be okay, there?"

Ashton gave Ames a concerned glance. She slapped on a wobbly smile, opened her mouth to speak…and nothing came out. So she nodded instead, and Ashton said, "Yeah, we'll be all right, Stefan. Listen, you and Inspector Demetrius…thanks. You two saved my ass today, and I won't forget it. That round knocked the breath right out of me, and if you two hadn't been there, I have no doubt I'd be dead now."

Cally paled, but stood firm beside Nick. She took his hand in hers, then faced the two older men.

"That goes for me, too," she said in a soft, hoarse voice. "Thank you."

Demetrius and Gorski nodded, tight-lipped. Peterson, who watched the whole exchange in silence, stepped forward.

"Let's go on through to the bullpen and see what we can coordinate on the Sandman," she suggested.

"It's a plan," Ashton agreed.

Background Work

"…So what have you guys found while we've been ducking and dodging?" Gorski asked, when the trio entered the bullpen back at ICPD headquarters, followed by the others.

"Nuthin'," Compton grumbled. "Not anything that would be useful, anyway."

"Mm. Well, let us help, maybe," Demetrius offered. "Perhaps Stefan and I can bring our experience to the matter. Are you game, Stefan?"

"Sure, Gene. It's gonna take an hour or so before the puff testers get here, so we got time to kill."

"Puff testers?" Weyand wondered.

"Yeah, Nick had an idea, and it was a good one…"

While Gorski and Demetrius explained Ashton's idea to the others, Ames signaled Nick from her desk, and he moved unobtrusively to her side.

"Hey, Nick?" she murmured. "I…I got something, here, and I'm not sure what to make of it. I only just found it when word came in you'd got shot. I wanted to run it by you, see what you thought, before I threw it out for public consumption. Especially, now, in front of the detective and inspector. But…are you up to it? I mean, damn, honey, you…I…"

"I'm fine, Cal. I swear I am."

"You're sure?"

"Doc said and everything. And she has my nanites workin' away, and I got meds and the whole bit."

"Oh! Are you loopy?"

"Nope. We made sure she gave me something that wouldn't bother me like that. She knew I'm on a case."

"Um. Okay. So I got this thing. Could you look at it?"

"Sure thing, Cal. You know I'll help, honey. Whatcha got?"

"Pop into channel 111."

"Okay."

Ashton took the adjacent chair, and they both entered VR. They were silent, sitting still with blank expressions, for long moments.

When the explanation was complete, and Gorski and Demetrius had shown the younger investigators the best way to sort and collate the information, Demetrius glanced around the room to see how things were going.

"Hm," he murmured, elbowing Gorski. "What's going on over there?" He gestured toward Ames' desk, where Ames and Ashton were both patently in immersive VR.

"Dunno, Gene," Gorski replied softly. "Maybe they're just reassuring each other in private for a few minutes."

"I don't think so," Peterson said, easing over beside the two men. "Channel 111 is active, and that's the one Cally has been working in all morning. I'd bet she's getting Nick's opinion on something, before she shows it to the rest of us."

"Well, if they come up for air soon, or if Nick does, it's probably nothing," Gorski decided. "But if they stay in there a while, I'm betting they got something."

In the VR meeting room she'd prepared, Ames showed Ashton the specific files she'd uncovered; there were quite a few. He sat down in the nearer of two armchairs and read through the files, skimming at first, then going back and rereading closer. Finally he looked up into clear blue eyes.

"Damn, Cal, I think you have something, here," Ashton said then.

"But what, exactly, is the connection?" she wondered. "I mean, there's a connection there, but...I guess I'm just not understanding it."

"Each victim of the Sandman is a close friend or relative of a member of the medical treatment approval board at, or shortly before, the time of the first murder," Ashton pointed out. "Best friend, lover, spouse, parent, or sibling. Somebody was – is – striking back at the board members through their loved ones. Because Lana Rounder is the sister of William H. Rounder, who chaired the board at the time."

"But what's the rationale? Why strike at someone close, rather than the board members themselves? And why didn't any of the board members speak up?"

"Cal, the board reports directly to Lord Falmouth, Councilor of the Department of Health," Ashton explained. "He's on the Council. The whole mess is corrupt all the way through. Have you ever had anyone that you knew need permission for a rare or expensive treatment?"

"Um, no..."

"My dad's favorite uncle did. This board is responsible for determining whether or not the treatment would work, or would be worth the time and expense. It's a kind of triage, but it's mostly driven by money and connections. If you don't have the connections, you damn well better have the money, or you won't get the treatment. Worse, if you have the connections and the money, but you're on the wrong political side, you can get turned down, too."

"Damn!"

"Yeah. My great-uncle made it...barely. Because Dad and the rest of the family managed, between 'em, to scrape together the money to pay off the board." Ashton paused. "Imagine if somebody's loved one *didn't* make it, because they didn't know the right people, or they didn't have enough money, or the board didn't approve of their politics, or whatever. That's a good motivation for a murder spree. *But* – they can't go to the police...or at least, to us, and all the Sandman murders were largely in our jurisdiction...even if they realize people close to 'em are being killed off, because that might risk exposing the corrupt way they make their decisions."

"Ooo. But what about the IPD? The bunch around here are just as corrupt as they are."

"True. And chances are, the IPD does know about it, but either they're not too worried since it isn't their circus, or they've gotten themselves wrapped around the axle with all of their own deceptions and disinformation, and they're having a hard time figuring out who's telling the truth to whom."

"Huh. So...what? We need to go back through the records of the board's approvals and disapprovals and see if we can put together a list of disapprovals, and the surviving family or something?"

"Exactly! Don't forget best buddies in that list of possible suspects, too."

"Right."

"Now, shall we go tell the others what you found?"

Ames grinned, and Ashton grinned back.

"Well, well," Demetrius decided, once Ames and Ashton had explained what she had turned up. "I think we have a thread to follow to the end now."

"Sounds like it to me," Gorski agreed. "Now, once the puff testers get here, we should be able to start narrowing down the actual crime scene for our current case."

"Those two make a good team," Weyand observed, and both Ashton and Ames flushed. The others grinned.

"Let's help Cally see what she can dig up about the board's decisions, then," Gorski opined.

The entire team set to work.

By the time the case of puff testers arrived, the team had collated a list of active members of the medical treatment approval board from a decade earlier, as well as negative decisions by that same board. They passed the data over to Callista Ames in VR channel 111, and she set to work scanning through it for possible suspects.

Eugene Demetrius opened the case of testers while that was occurring, and he pulled one out. It consisted of a small canister containing two tiny tanks, and a small bulb sprayer on the top. The chemicals in the tanks would, when combined, react with the core RNA of the G.A.S. virulosin. The resulting reaction would turn the residue a bright pink.

"This looks good," Demetrius decreed. "I think we have something here."

"Go get 'em, tigers," Smith said with a grin. "Head back to the office and the apartment and see what you can find."

"No, now wait a damn minute, here," Ashton said, annoyed. "As hard as I worked to get that stuff bagged and tagged, we got evidence right here to test. Inspector Demetrius, where's that tote with all the evidence?"

"Ah! Yes, you have a point – just a moment; I dumped it off on my desk," he said, scurrying into an adjacent room and emerging seconds later with the large tote bag of poly-bagged evidence. "Here we are. Let us spread it out on the tables and see about 'puffing' all of it. If any of it changes color, we have the source of the virulosin contamination."

They set to work.

"Damn, Nick," Smith said with a laugh, "you even bagged the leftover coffee from the cups?!"

"Well, I figured, if it had been contaminated, it would show up even better in that than in the mugs, which you notice I also grabbed," Ashton pointed out. "And there wasn't much. Just be careful and don't spill it everywhere."

"What is it with you and crime scene coffee?" Jones asked. "Didn't your first case with Detective Gorski have a couple coffee samples, too?"

"It did," Gorski remembered. "All right, so we should have two coffee samples here…"

"Yup. One with cream and one black," Weaver observed.

"Yeah, one was hers and one was her boss's, but I couldn't remember which was which, so I bagged 'em both separately," Ashton explained.

"I think he said his was the one with the cream," Gorski said.

"That fits my recollection, Stefan," Demetrius agreed.

"Well, that's what I thought, too," Ashton admitted, "but I wasn't for sure, so I figured…" He shrugged.

"And that was well done in any case," Peterson commended. "If he was also dosed, but hadn't reacted yet due to his larger frame, we'd need to know."

"Right."

As the younger investigators laid out the bagged evidence, Gorski and Demetrius moved along the tables, systematically opening a bag and puffing a considerable quantity of the viral detection reagent into the bag, before quickly sealing it, then moving to the next bag. According to the instructions that came with the puff testers, it would take this particular reagent a few minutes to react to the G.A.S RNA snippet, so they would add the reagent to all of the evidence bags, then go back around and see if any had reacted.

Two had.

"The black coffee and the cup it was in?!" Gorski exclaimed in surprise. "That was hers! So it was somebody in her office!"

"Who did she have under her?" Demetrius asked. "And don't forget that her boss had coffee with her! He may well be the Sandman!"

"True," Ashton said then, as the others clustered around. "But there's something off about that, Mr. Demetrius..."

"Gene, son, call me Gene," Demetrius said with a smile. "Everybody else does. And as well as you've done on this case so far, you've certainly earned the right."

Ashton gave him an appreciative smile, but his brain was still working on the scenario Demetrius had suggested, which seemed off. Finally it hit him.

"That's it! It can't be Witte, 'cause Witte is the vice president," he told the others. "He might get his own coffee, but he isn't gonna fetch coffee for a subordinate, too. And I don't see them leaving the review to go down to the break room themselves."

"He's right," Gorski said, one eyebrow going up. "They'd have an underling do it."

"One of the junior marketers?" Peterson suggested. "What did you say their names were...?"

"Surnames Glenn and Wall," Demetrius noted. "They're rather young to be the original murderer, though. Neither of 'em has been out of university more than about three years."

"Could be the kid of the Sandman," Weyand suggested.

"Hey, Cally?" Ashton called. "You get anything on the list of decisions by the medical treatment approval board? Any hits?"

Ames sat at the desk, staring straight ahead, and did not respond.

"She's still in full VR," Compton observed.

"Yeah. I'll go in and see what she's doing," Ashton said. "If she's got anything at all, it might help us narrow down who's our perp, out of all our suspects."

Ashton popped into channel 111 again. Ames' avatar was now seated at a desk, poring over a sheaf of "printed" papers. She glanced up when his avatar appeared.

"Hey, Cal," he said, moving to the other chair and sitting down, across the desk from her. "Damn, girl, your eyes are getting bloodshot. I didn't know avatars could do that."

They laughed.

"Hey, Nick," she murmured. "You come in to see how I'm getting on?"

"Yup. We got a hit on the victim's coffee mug, so we know the virulosin was administered in the office coffee. We just don't know who did it," Ashton said, as Gorski joined them, remaining silent. "You got anything that might help us narrow things down?"

"Maybe. I have a few possibles, here."

"Tell me."

"Well, there's Michael and Ridge Blackmoor," she said, as the avatars of Demetrius, Peterson, and Weyand appeared. Gorski's avatar shushed them quickly with a finger to the lips, and they moved silently to his side, to watch the pair hard at work. Seconds later, Smith, Weaver, and Compton had joined the impromptu peanut gallery, just as Demetrius, Peterson, and Gorski exchanged meaningful, and duly impressed, glances. Ames continued, not noticing the onlookers, so deep into the research was she.

"Michael is Ridge's father," she explained. "Michael died about twelve years ago of a rare form of cancer, when the board refused to provide the appropriate treatment. Something about him being a miner – which also means they didn't have the money to pay off the board – and they could get rid of the cancer, but it would only come back when he resumed mining. Never mind that Michael Blackmoor had retired from his profession by that time."

"Right. So, okay, how old was Ridge Blackmoor at that time?"

"Mm. About, say..." she paused, searching the files, "say thirty-eight?"

"Any kids?"

"No. Not married. Let me check..." More papers appeared on the desk, and she dug through them. "No, he never married, and there were no children."

"Twelve years is a bit too early for the Sandman, but not impossible, if he had to figure out a way to do it, I guess," Ashton mused. "That would put him at fifty now, though."

"Right."

"Coloration?"

"Um...sandy hair, kind of what used to be called strawberry blond, with green eyes. Short, kind of, of thick-set, you know, muscular."

"And Witte was a tall, slim brunet, with brown eyes," Ashton recalled, as the 'peanut gallery' watched, but remained silent. "You can change hair color, and you can wear colored lenses to change eye color, but you can't change the body type *that* drastically. So that wouldn't be Witte. Keep going."

"Mmm," Ames hummed, then fell silent for long moments. Finally she responded.

"Okay, here's a family," she said. "Sydney and Kaleb Denholm, and their son Luther. Luther died in his teens of Melsbach Syndrome. The parents were not happy."

"Why didn't the board approve the virulosin?"

"Said it was an incorrect diagnosis, and the treatment wouldn't help. It turned out to be a correct diagnosis. The boy died at age 17." She shook her head. "Judging by the description, it wasn't pretty."

Ashton smeared a hand across his face.

"Right. How old were the parents at the time?"

"Twenty-eight and thirty."

"And how long ago did that happen?"

"Uh...oh. Only seven years ago."

"Oh, that's no good. The first Sandman murder happened, uh..." Ashton paused to recall.

"About ten years ago," Peterson offered in a soft tone, meant to answer without disrupting thought trains. "The last of the murders – at least in the first wave – was about four or five years back."

"Yeah, so they're out," Ames agreed, still studying the files. "Oh. I got one more, I think. Ooo, and the time frame is right, too – ten years ago, almost on the nose. Raymond Appleton and his wife, Beryl Ellis. He was in an industrial accident. Got himself irradiated bad. Sad situation. There really wasn't anything anybody could do on this one, but she had to watch him die slowly. She swore up and down that they could have cured him if the medical treatment approval board had only ruled in his favor."

"Wow. A case where they actually did the right thing?"

"A case where, if I'm reading all this right," Ames looked up at him, and her eyes glistened a bit, "there wasn't a 'right thing' to be done, Nick. She watched her husband die a slow, lingering, horrible, painful death as his body slowly..." She broke off, eyes going wide in shocked realization. "As his body slowly shut down."

"Just like the virulosin," Smith whispered. "Damn."

Ashton pressed his lips together, face grim. "Any kids?"

"None."

"We got it," Ashton declared then. "The Sandman isn't a *he*, it's a *she*. What did you say her name was?"

"Beryl Ellis. Of course she'd be going by a fake name for all this, though..." She bit her lip, still scanning records. "Nick, there's one more former board member who hasn't lost anybody to the Sandman yet. Rasheed Singh has a son, Aarav, about to graduate from the Imperial University of Sintar..."

"Shit. How old was Ellis at the time?"

Ames scrabbled through the file, finally looking up at him. "It doesn't say."

"Any imagery of her?"

"Just one photo." Ames pulled the image out of the sheaf of papers and tossed it across the desk to him.

"Mmph," he murmured, studying it. "She looks familiar. Where have I seen...?" He glanced up. Then he spoke into the air. "Enhance image. Age ten years."

A printer appeared on the far corner of the desk, and after a few moments of humming, it spat out an image.

"Oh, good Lord," Ashton murmured in shock, and held up the altered photo so that Demetrius and Gorski could see it.

It was Lana Rounder's executive assistant, Joyce Abelard.

The team quickly exited VR, except for Demetrius, who switched channels and contacted the receptionist at the restaurant chain's headquarters.

"Ms. Hayden," he told her avatar, "is Ms. Abelard still

there? You know, Ms. Rounder's executive assistant?"

"Oh! No, sir," Hayden told the inspector, "she left about an hour ago. She was so upset! She said she just couldn't stand to look at that office any longer, knowing what was happening to 'her poor Lana.'"

"Did she say where she was going?"

"Home, I think," the little receptionist replied. "Mumbled something about having to get ready for her nephew's graduation this weekend..."

"Oh damnation," Demetrius exclaimed. "Thank you, Ms. Hayden! You've been a great help. But I need to move quickly now."

"She's gone," Demetrius announced as soon as he came out of VR. "She left work an hour ago, to 'get ready for her nephew's graduation.' She's on the way to the university. Right now, I expect."

"Contact the provost and have him get Aarav Singh out of class and into his office immediately," Peterson barked. "I'll get with Charlie and have him set up a cordon of beat cops around the university. We'll know if she enters the campus buildings."

"But how are we ever gonna round her up?" Compton wondered.

"Send out the image that Nick and Cally ginned up," Gorski said.

"I'd think that would make her more apt to flee, to try again another time," Weaver noted.

"Guys?" Ashton interjected. Everyone stopped and turned to look at him.

"If you've got an idea, Nick, let's hear it," Gorski decreed. "You've done great so far."

"Okay. She worked her way in at the restaurant

headquarters," Ashton pointed out. "According to the stuff Cally's been feeding me in VR, for each murder, Beryl Ellis took her time and got in close to her victims, either by working directly with them or by hacking their VR feed and tapping into it to follow them. Given she'd have a hard time getting onto the faculty – according to the dossier Cal compiled, she doesn't have any advanced degrees – and she's really too old to be a student in such an elite school, 'cause the student body is pretty much either Imperial scholarships or wealthy bureaucrats' kids – she's probably hacked the university's feed. And we can use that. Especially if we put out word that Ms. Rounder has already died. It'll speed up her timetable."

"Keep talking," Demetrius said. Ashton turned to Peterson.

"Chief, is Adrian Mott available?"

"I think so," Peterson said. "You want me to get him here?"

"As fast as possible, please. And Cal?"

"I'm already on it, Nick," Ames replied. "Annnd...got it."

"What do you have planned?" Gorski asked.

Two hours later, Aarav Singh left the provost's office in the University's Office Tower, and instead of heading across to the student housing building, he got in the elevator and went up to the rooftop, where a small lounge with bar gave views across the city. Only faculty, graduate students, and the occasional senior about to graduate were permitted to frequent the lounge, and Singh apparently thought he might be safe here, given it was on the Office Tower rather than the Residence Tower. He went to the bar and ordered a brew and some fries, then headed to the one empty table by himself; most of the tables already had their full complement of occupants, but he preferred a certain anonymity, under the circumstances.

He was halfway through his fries, and had ordered another

beer, when an older woman with salt-and-pepper hair and hazel eyes, presumably a faculty member, came up to him with a tray containing fish and chips and a mixed drink, as well as a bottle of water and a mug of beer.

"Hello there, young man. I'm Professor Steiner. Would you mind if I joined you? The tables are full..."

"Um," Singh began, uncertain, and the woman sat down without waiting for further confirmation.

"Thank you," she said with a smile. "Between my class schedule and my appointments, I had no chance to eat lunch today, and I'm rather hungry." She reached for her fork, then stopped and put it down. "Oh, and the bartender asked me to bring you your beer; with the crowd here today, his wait staff is terribly busy." She picked up the beer mug and set it beside his plate of fries.

"I...see," Singh murmured, and returned to eating his fries.

"It's a warm day today," Steiner declared, "especially to be sitting in the sun, like this. I do wish they would add some awnings up here. It would be much more pleasant." She picked up her bottle of water, removed the cap, and took several swallows, then gestured to his beer. "I'm surprised you aren't fairly chugging that."

"Already had one," Singh noted. "Fries are good, though."

"You should be careful not to get dehydrated." Steiner waved a hand. "Go on, drink. I won't mind, just because you're a student. I'll work on this lovely margarita, here, and sip some water so it doesn't dehydrate me."

"Perhaps you would like some of my beer?"

"Oh no, I don't care for beer, dear. You go ahead."

Singh reached into his pocket and produced a small cylinder with a nozzle and a squeeze bulb. Steiner watched in some puzzlement as he aimed it at the mug of beer and squeezed the bulb. A puff of some dusty substance emerged, hit the surface of the beer...

...And turned it bright pink.

"Singh" jumped up, ripping off a wig to reveal a shaved head.

"ICPD!" Adrian Mott cried, as the "staff and patrons" of the lounge leaped to their feet and drew weapons. "You're under arrest for murder!"

"What?!" Steiner exclaimed, rising to her own feet, shoving the chair back, and taking a step to the side. "I have no idea what you're talking about! I'm Professor Emma Steiner, and I teach VR coding!"

"There's no such person," a young man with golden-brown eyes and dark hair heavily streaked with blond said, stepping forward, weapon raised. "We've already verified. You're Beryl Ellis, the serial killer known as the Sandman, and you're responsible for eight deaths, one pending death, and one," he gestured at the stein of beer, "attempted murder."

Abruptly Beryl Ellis shoved the nearest officer aside and sprinted for the parapet, diving over it as she reached it.

"DAMN!" Ames cried, shocked. "She'd rather die than be caught?"

"She'd get to be with her husband, finally," Demetrius said softly. "According to all the information you dug up, the two of them were deeply in love. It must have been excruciating to watch him die such an agonizing death, knowing there was nothing to be done but watch."

"It sure wouldn't do me any favors," Gorski agreed. "But she's not dead."

"Do you know how many stories up we are?" Smith pointed out, astonished at the comment. "She'll be a bug splat on the pavement!"

"No, she won't," Demetrius confirmed, "because early on, two students and a professor died that very way, after a small commencement celebration up here, and much too much to drink. So this lounge has something of a security system against inebriated professors and students falling off the side."

He led them over to the parapet, and they peered over.

Beryl Ellis was tangled in a net, strung around the building's perimeter, ten feet down.

Recuperation and Other TLC

That night, Cally accompanied Nick home to his apartment for the first time. Nobody at ICPD headquarters was about to let him head home alone after the events of the day, and even so, Cally suspected they had friendly shadows accompanying. Which, she considered, didn't bother her in the least.

They only made one small detour, to pick up a shopping bag of ingredients at the grocer where Nick usually shopped; Cally planned to cook dinner for him. As they came out, Cally noticed a man across the street at the café who looked suspiciously like Adrian Mott with a black moustache. She smiled to herself, and the pair continued to Nick's apartment building, walking hand in hand.

"I haven't cleaned yet this week," Nick admitted, as he let them both into his apartment. "But I try to keep it...not too messy."

"It looks fine," Cally said, glancing around. "I like your taste in décor."

"Thanks. The furniture came with the apartment, but I did the pictures and lamps and junk."

"Okay, now you sit down while I see about fixing us some dinner, then I want to have a look at that bullet bruise."

"Aw. Lemme help, Cal."

"No, you need to get off your feet," Cally insisted. "While we were doing all that prep today, I pinged my personal physician and told her what happened and asked some stuff, and she said that you needed to just rest as soon as you could, around the case. Because the nanites can focus all your resources on healing you up, if you aren't doing anything else."

"Oh."

"Yeah. And I plan on putting ice on that bruise, and using a special cream she told me about years ago, when I was at the police academy and in the hand-to-hand training. It'll help heal the bruise."

"I don't think you're supposed to rub it..." Nick offered, hesitant. "Something about dislodging clots?"

"Oh! No, I know about that," she said. "I'll be very, very careful. And then you're going to rest, and I'm going to see what needs doing around your place, that can't wait a few days, like any tidying up you want done, and stuff like that."

"Cal..."

"Please, Nick," she told him, setting the grocery bag down and turning to face him. "Honey, let me do this. I...I need to do this for you. You...I dunno if you really know how I feel about you, but...but it scared me bad, today, when Corporal Peterson called me in to her office to tell me you'd been shot..."

Nick gazed down into the troubled blue eyes for long moments. Finally he nodded.

"Okay, Cal," he said. "I understand. And...I love you, too."

"Oh, Nick!" she cried, and flung her arms around his neck. "I love you so much!"

Dinner was late, because the kiss went on for a long time.

Cally prepared a delicious, healthful meal for "her Nick." The first course was another fresh salad, with strawberries, bleu cheese, candied pecans, and a rich balsamic vinaigrette. The second course was a creamy tomato bisque. The entrée was chicken tarragon with pan-roasted root vegetables, and a key lime tart – just one, to share – was dessert.

"You're spoiling me," Nick decided, when she offered him the last bite of the tart on her own fork.

"That's kind of the idea," Cally said with a dimpling grin. "You need it, right now." She stood. "Now, you go lie down on the couch, or in your recliner, or wherever you unwind in the evening, while I clean up my kitchen mess. Take a nap if you can. I'll look around and see what needs cleaning or straightening, and take care of that for you while you rest. I don't want you doing a whole lotta strenuous stuff tonight."

"Cal, I'll be fine."

"I know. But you'll be fine faster if you go along with me."

He sighed, and headed for the recliner.

Nick woke up an hour and a half later. He was wrapped in a cozy throw blanket – one which he had not had before – and felt relaxed and comfortable. He eased into a seated position and opened bleary eyes, to find the apartment immaculate and Cally sitting nearby on the end of the sofa, watching a VR show on his screen, but apparently listening through her VR network, because there was no sound.

"Umph," he murmured, stretching. "Ow."

Cally immediately turned to him.

"Well hey," she said with a smile. "Stiff?"

"Yeah, some," he admitted. "My chest muscles on my right side aren't gonna be happy with me for a while, I guess."

"Nope. You're gonna behave as far as the gym is concerned, aren't you?"

"Oh. Yeah, you're right. The ER doc said I needed to keep my pulse and blood pressure relatively low, and…yeah, shit."

Nick sighed, and Cally slid off the couch to kneel beside his chair.

"It's okay, Nick," she murmured. "It's only an

159

inconvenience. You could have been killed."

"I know. I'm sorry. I'm just used to being independent."

"I get it. And that's good. But we can still be a team, you and me, while you be independent."

"Can we?"

"Yeah, we can. 'Cause I'm independent too, and you know that."

He looked down at her earnest, lovely face for long moments, thinking. *She's right, I think,* he considered. *We're both independent, and we can function independently just fine, but we also make a great team...in all kinds of ways. The work, and personal stuff. And I meant it when I said I loved her. She's an investigator, and I'm an investigator. Maybe this is* right. *Maybe I finally found Her.* It suddenly hit him that he hadn't thought about Tabby in a very long time. *And that's a good thing in itself,* he decided.

"Okay, honey," he said then. "I think you're right. We'll give it a shot, anyway."

"All right!" The dimpled smile was back. "Does that make us a couple-couple?"

"I think it does."

"Good."

"Yeah."

"Okay, now let's see about peeling you out of your shirt and body armor, so I can take a look at this bruise, and maybe help it heal faster. Then it's time for your meds, and you should probably crash early tonight. I'll help you into bed, then let myself out, and go home."

Nick pondered for a minute, studying her.

"You...can stay, if you want to."

"Huh?"

"You can spend the night, if you want to. I dunno that I'm gonna be very active, but..."

Cally cocked her head to one side, looking at him, for a long moment.

"Not tonight, I think," she decided. "Or, if I do, I'll spend it out here, on the couch, so I can look after you."

"But…"

"Nick, honey, look. This is the first time I've ever even been to your apartment. And I'm honored, and it's been a wonderful night, especially when you told me you loved me! But for one, you really are banged up, here." She ran a feather-light hand across his chest. "And for another: you finally told me about Tabby, after we'd been out a few times. I'm glad you did; it made a whole lot of things about your behavior around me make sense. And I'm sorry if I made you uncomfortable at first."

"It's okay, Cal. We talked about this, way back when."

"I know. But what it means is, you've been hurt, your trust betrayed, and I'm not gonna push anything. I want you to keep trusting me, and maybe one of these days, when we're both ready, things'll happen. Okay?"

"Okay."

"Now lemme help you get this shirt an' junk off," she said, reaching for the buttons on his shirt; he had discarded coat and tie almost as soon as he'd gotten in the door.

Five minutes later, Cally was hissing in sympathy, and Nick had discovered just how stiff he really was; he seriously doubted he could have stripped to the waist without her help.

And the bruise had only expanded in extent.

"We should have iced this, this afternoon," she fussed. "No wonder you're stiff, sweetheart! And the damn shooter didn't miss your heart by much. That coulda been bad, even with the armor."

"Yeah," Nick said, studying the display of colors across his right breast. "Damn, there's colors here I didn't know living human bodies could even make."

"No shit," Cally agreed, getting up and going to the kitchen. Within moments she was back with an ice pack. "Here, let's get this iced down for a bit, then I'll see about applying that cream junk I mentioned."

"Uhn," he grunted, as she eased the special frozen pad onto his chest. "Damn, that's cold."

"That's the idea," she chuckled. "It'll contract the blood vessels and stop the hemorrhage, which is all a bruise really is, after all. Does it have enough of a cloth cover that it's not sticking to the skin?"

"Yeah, that's okay. It's just cold, dammit."

"Try to relax into it. It should start to feel good in a minute."

Nick did as she asked, and after a little, it did start to ease the pain in his pummeled rib cage.

"Better?" she asked, and he realized his face had relaxed.

"Yeah."

"Good. Just lean back, while I go fish the tub of cream out of my stuff."

Fifteen minutes later, Nick leaned back in the recliner as warm, gentle hands lightly rubbed a soothing cream into his chest.

"Huh," he grunted.

"Everything okay?"

"Yeah. That feels…really good."

"Making it feel better?"

"Yup. And my nanites are reporting that it's good, too."

"Great, then."

"Cally?"

"Mm?"

"Do you have anybody else who can walk you home from here? I mean, a guy friend, somebody from the division, or something…"

"Not really, no. My family is on the other side of the continent, you know. I guess I need to introduce you to 'em eventually. But if one of the guys from the division is available, I might get him to escort me home, I guess. Why?"

"You didn't work anything out with 'em first?"

"Nah. I figured I'd just head home."

Nick shook his head.

"No. I'm not comfortable with you doing that. Not after what happened today. If they saw you with me this evening, if they have someone watching my place, they could go after you to get to me."

"I can take care of myself, Nick. I've had the same training you have."

"I know. But…look, Cal," he said, earnest. "You've been trying to take care of me tonight, and I've let you…"

"Yeah. So?"

"Let me reciprocate. If you won't stay in the bedroom, at least let me fix you up in here, on the couch or in the recliner, here, after I go to bed. Or hell, I'll give you the bedroom and I'll stay here."

"I'm not the one who got shot today, sweetie."

"I know. But Mom raised me to know how to treat you, hon."

"Oh. Okay. I get it now," she said. Cally leaned back and studied his face while she put the lid on the tub of cream. "And you're still damn stiff…"

"Yeah," he sighed, then added without thinking, "and I'll probably be worse in the morning."

STEPHANIE OSBORN

"All right," she decided. "Nurse Cally stays, and goes in with you in the morning. I can change into one of my spare outfits in my locker, that I keep handy in case of perp interaction."

"Um, just so you know, I normally sleep in the nude, but I got some loungewear I'll dig out tonight. And if you want a t-shirt, I'll be happy to loan you one."

"That'll work. Spare blankets? Pillows?"

"I got a few, yeah."

"Deal."

Half an hour later, Nick was in a pair of lounge pants and a tee, and tucked lovingly into bed.

Meanwhile, Cally, using one of his tees as a sleep-shirt, was bedding down on the couch.

"Good night, Nick," he heard her soft call from his den.

"Good night, Cal," he responded in kind.

Then he turned out the lights in VR and they got some sleep.

The next morning was a little slow getting up to speed, but eventually Nick managed it.

Cally had the sense and thoughtfulness to help him out of bed, then into the bathroom, where she got the shower running and the temperature nicely warm, then she helped him out of the t-shirt he wore and left him to remove the lounge pants – which he simply shoved down as far as was comfortable, then kicked out of them, leaving them lying on the tile floor for the time being.

By the time he finished with a nice hot shower, he was feeling a bit more mobile. Toweling off, he headed into the bedroom, to find his girlfriend had laid out shorts and trousers for him, but no shirt, shoes, or socks. *Which makes sense,* he realized. *I'm gonna need help with those today, even loosened up.*

So he donned the shorts and slacks, and meandered barefoot through the den into the kitchen.

Cally stood in his tee, cooking breakfast. Her long legs extended below the shirt's hem, and the neckline had slid off one shoulder.

Oh dear Lord, he thought, trying not to drool. *I think I want to see that every morning for the rest of my life.*

"Scrambled eggs and bacon do for breakfast?" she asked, throwing a grin over her shoulder.

"Sounds good," he agreed. "But you look even better."

"Aw." Even her neck flushed.

She turned and dished up the food, then brought it to his dining table.

"Let's eat," she said. "Then I'll get dressed in what I wore yesterday, help you get dressed, and we'll head in to work."

"The guys may tease us, when you show up in the same clothes."

"Not when they see how you can hardly move," she retorted, and he chuckled.

Sure enough, several smirks appeared on faces when the pair appeared together, Ames clad in the same slightly rumpled clothing she'd worn the day before. But they disappeared when she helped Ashton ease stiffly into his desk chair. He grunted when he finally hit bottom, and leaned back.

"Got it?" she asked.

"Yeah," he said. "Listen, I hope you're not too stiff from sleepin' on a couch last night."

"Nah, the couch was comfortable," she said. "I'm good. And we got the bruise goop back on you before you put on your shirt today, so that'll help even more."

"Yeah. Feels better already."

"Good. Then I'm gonna run to the locker room and shower and change, so I'll be back before the morning status briefing."

"Go," he told her. "I'm sure not going anywhere."

She headed out.

Jones eased over to Ashton's desk in her wake.

"Good nurse, in addition to good cop, huh?"

"Yeah. Good girlfriend, too."

"Oh really? It's official, then? You two are seeing each other?"

"We've been seeing each other, but yeah, it's official."

"She got a ring now?"

"Not yet, no."

"Okay, man. Just so ya know, I'm happy for you two. We all are."

"Thanks." Ashton grinned, and Jones grinned back.

"And the Sandman case has been handed over to the prosecutors," Peterson told the Team, when all of the reports had been filed, later that morning. "Oh, and Lana Rounder died this morning."

The group sighed collectively, faces falling.

"I don't see that as going well for Ellis," Peterson continued, "though in some respects, I can almost see why she did what she did. I'd have had a lot less problems if she'd gone after the actual board members, though. Some of those guys...shit."

"I hear you," Ashton agreed, subdued. "I almost – almost – feel bad we caught her. Still, she was going after innocents, not the actual crooked politicos, like you said." He shrugged, then winced at the movement. "Besides, it sounds like, on this case at least, they did the only thing there was to do."

"And it is not our business to interpret the law, in any

event," Demetrius said, his tone soft. "Only to enforce it, to the best of our abilities, as honest officers of the law, when the law is just."

"And in this instance, it certainly is," Gorski averred.

"And the Sandman – or woman – is in custody, and will kill no more," Demetrius proclaimed.

It took some few weeks for Nick's chest to heal; a bone bruise was generally considered only about one step removed from a break, so it took nearly as long to heal as if it *had* broken. During that time, Cally insisted on helping him take care of himself and his apartment…which meant she walked home with him most evenings after shift. More, the Team considerately took turns escorting the pair to and from their respective apartments as needed. Sometimes she spent the night on his couch, and sometimes she headed on home – with escort – after seeing him settled for the night.

"It isn't that you can't take care of yourself," Rassmussen told her one day. "It's that…well, you're gonna be preoccupied with Nick's healing, and maybe not as alert as you might otherwise be. Plus, if they bring several of their goons, you're outnumbered."

"Yeah," Jones agreed. "And Nick…well, you're special to him, Cally. For Nick, that says a lot. This is as much for him as for you."

Cally was deeply touched, and agreed to let them escort her when needed.

By the time Nick was getting some mobility back in his upper body and the stiffness had eased, he'd made room in his closet and dresser for her to keep some of her things at his place. This negated the inconvenience of her having to get ready for work at the headquarters gym, or go home late each night to prepare her own things.

It also made their relationship even closer.

Especially after she woke up on the couch with a decidedly unpleasant neck kink.

"Enough's enough," he declared. "The bed is a damn queen. There's plenty of room for both of us, even if we decide we're not ready to go there yet. And once we are ready, then it's already a thing."

Cally considered the matter, and finally agreed. The next night, she climbed into the other side of the big bed.

They both slept like the dead, and woke rested – more than usual, since each had been subconsciously aware of the other nearby.

And Peterson and Gorski, after a private discussion, decided to keep Ashton inside the headquarters precinct until they felt he was healed enough to risk another encounter.

Unfortunately, it wasn't on a case that Ashton had his next encounter.

Ashton and Cally were headed over to her apartment together after work, with plans for Cally to make another of her gourmet French meals for Nick.

"But I think I wanna get something different for the wine," she told him. "And my usual shop doesn't carry what I want. So I want to try a new liquor store, about a block off the route home, in the next arcade over. Is that okay?"

"I guess so," Nick decided. "I don't see a reason why not, really."

"Okay, let's go."

Cally found the wine she wanted to serve with dinner, and the pair exited the liquor store, turned right…

…And nearly ran into Stanley Gorecki.

"Well, well, look who we got here," Gorecki sneered. "Looks like Ashton finally got himself another girlfriend. Hey, cutie-pie. Don't worry, you'll have a real man for a boyfriend, here, in about five minutes."

"I'm afraid you have a case of mistaken identity," Cally said, setting down her package and taking a half-step forward. Nick caught her arm, but she shook it off.

"I don't think so, sugar," Gorecki said, taking a step toward Nick as he smacked one fist into the other palm. "I know Dominick Ashton, and that's Dominick Ashton."

"I wasn't talking about him. You obviously don't recognize a bodyguard when you see one. Back up, please."

"Ha! You? You're just a little thing. I can—"

And suddenly Cally Ames showed off her top-of-her-class skills in martial arts. A chambered punch to Gorecki's solar plexus with the full momentum of her body weight was followed by a knee to the groin. The doubled-over reaction that began in Gorecki's body at the gut punch intensified with the impact to his privates. Cally took advantage of the fact, delivering an uppercut to Gorecki's jaw, snapping his head back. A quick, sweeping kick to the back of his knees, and Gorecki was on his back on the pavement, gasping.

"Shit, Cal," Nick murmured, grabbing up the bag with the wine in one hand, and her arm in the other. "Come on! While he's still seeing stars, let's get outta here!"

They ran around the corner, up a flight of fire-escape stairs to street level, and ducked into an alley, then cut across the mews between the buildings, and into a maintenance hatch.

Two minutes later, Gorecki caught his breath and sat up, cursing. He looked around, but Ashton and his "bodyguard" were nowhere to be seen. Only the odd pedestrian wandered into this or that store front.

"Dammit to hell," he snarled, getting to his feet and rubbing his jaw where Ames had hit him. "That little she-cat is next on my list after Ashton and Carter!"

He limped down the street, trying not to walk funny.

In a recessed shop doorway behind him, a shopper looked after him, stifled a snort, then headed in the opposite direction.

Cally was cooking, and Nick was setting the table, when the buzzer went off at her front door. They looked at each other, and Cally shook her head – *No, I'm not expecting anyone* – when they both got an alert in VR.

"Guys, it's Adrian," came the VR message, "and I'm alone. Just wanted to check on you two."

Nick headed for the door and let him into the apartment. He glanced both directions down the hall, but saw no one, and closed the door quickly.

"What's up?" Nick asked.

"And do you want to stay for dinner?" Cally added. "There's enough here for three."

"It's good, believe me," Nick continued. Adrian Mott laughed.

"Don't tempt me," he said. "It smells delicious. But I just came by to make sure you two made it away okay, and that Gorecki didn't have anyone waiting."

"No, we got away clean," Nick said. "Judging from the way he reacted, I think we caught him as much by surprise as he did us."

"I'd agree to that," Cally called from the kitchen. "C'mon in here, guys, so I don't have to yell."

"Good plan," Adrian agreed, and followed Nick into the

kitchen. "Oh damn, it smells even better in here!"

"So I take it you saw the altercation earlier?" Cally asked, making a quick, subtle gesture to Nick, who fished out an extra place setting from her cabinet and adjusted the placement on her little dining table, allowing for three people to dine.

"Yeah, I did," Adrian admitted. "I know you guys know that the rest of us have been taking turns watching out for you two, while Nick was recovering from getting shot, and tonight was my turn. I was just shadowing the two of you, and saw the whole thing go down. I was actually maneuvering to take him down from behind when Cally lit into him like the proverbial buzz saw."

"She did good," Nick said with a wry grin.

"She did. Gorecki didn't expect that!"

"I wasn't expecting it, either!"

"It also accomplished another thing," Cally pointed out.

"Yeah. It changed Gorecki's thinking from 'girlfriend' to 'bodyguard,'" Adrian observed. "So he's not gonna go looking for a girlfriend to hit up."

"Oh, he probably will still go looking for Cally, at some point," Nick said with a sigh. "Which is exactly what I didn't want. But yeah, she wounded his pride. He's not gonna let that go."

"True," Cally said, continuing to finish off the various dishes, and beginning to plate them. "But we've all got each other's backs, so good luck with that. And sooner or later, we gotta take him down."

"Somehow," Nick said.

"Dinner's ready!" Cally sang out cheerfully. "You two, have a seat, and let's eat!"

"But I," Adrian began.

"Sit," Nick reiterated. "We don't mind having a friend over

for dinner."

Adrian sat, and the trio chatted and laughed through a lovely four-course meal.

When they were done, Adrian escorted Nick safely to his own apartment.

First Blood to the Council

"HEADS UP, PEOPLE!" Colonel Peterson called as she came into the investigator bullpen, late in the afternoon of the next day. "We have a situation! Briefing room in two!"

Everyone scrambled for the door to the briefing room, and Peterson took the podium in just over a minute.

"All right," she said. "We've had a murder of one of the Palace staffers, in one of the apartment buildings in Imperial Park West, over near the IUS campus. You'll note that Detective Gorski isn't here, because he was here when the call came in about five or ten minutes ago, and I sent him off to handle it with a couple of squad cars, coded. That means, Nick, that you'll be involved with it pretty directly, one way or another. But to some extent, we all will…because this is top-level. I expect you all to *help*."

"Who was it, how was it done, and why?" Rassmussen, who had recently been promoted to Detective, asked.

"Vasilisa 'Vash' Medved," Peterson noted, "advisor – and personal friend – to the Empress. The Throne is gonna be involved on this one, people, so keep your wits about you. When I said top-level, I meant it."

"Aw, IPD will grab it," Weyand grumbled. "It's almost not worth taking notes on it."

"No, they won't," Peterson announced. "In fact, they tried already. Stefan called me a couple minutes ago to verify that for me; it's the only reason I waited as long as I did to call you all together. It's our understanding that the investigator and team from IPD were met by an Imperial Guard contingent…

and taken into custody by same." She paused, as gasps went around the room. "Yes, kiddies, the Empress is pissed. And apparently has reason to believe IPD may have been *involved*."

"What in hell brought this on?" Ashton asked.

"Well, given it appears to be a professional hit – a double-tap to the back of the head, while she was in the elevator and almost home, after working all day as a Palace staffer and confidential advisor to the Empress," Peterson added, meeting Ashton's shocked look with a knowing glance, "chances are, it had to do with the work Medved was doing for the Throne. I'm sure you've all followed some of the subtle little back-and-forth stuff that's cropped up in the news feeds in the last few years with increasing frequency. Let alone the big investigation on military weapons quality control and manufacturing."

Nods went around the room.

"It seems that Ms. Medved was the point on that effort. I'm not in the know, so I don't know details, at least not yet. But it would be my bet that, since Ms. Medved once worked in that industry, specifically in the quality assurance testing, more than likely she was feeding information to the Empress – or at least, the Empress' effort – that somebody didn't want her providing...and they took her out as a result. So at the very least..." Peterson broke off. "John, shut the door and everyone, initiate silent protocols."

Smith stood, closed the briefing room door, and sat back down. Immediately everyone's face went blank, as they entered full-immersion VR and met in a classified and highly secure channel – one that only those people in ICPD Investigations could access.

"All right. Now that we're all here," Peterson continued, from the podium in a virtual conference room, nearly identical to the physical one, "at the very least, since it was almost certainly a political assassination, targeted against the Empress' reform efforts, then the Council was in the know about it. More likely, the Council – or someone *on* the Council – ordered it. Directly. And since the Council's enforcers are the local IPD, you can guess who saw it was arranged."

"Damn," Ames murmured.

"From what Stefan has fed me, the IPD had an 'investigatory' team on site far too quickly, and as I mentioned a moment ago, that team has been taken into custody…with the authority of the Throne behind it. He saw it happen as he was pulling up, himself. Per his contact on the Imperial Guard, they are not in an ICPD lockdown; they are being held, incommunicado, by no less than the Imperial Guard, and their whereabouts are unknown and secure. That is classified information, kiddies, and not to leave this VR channel. Sound off and let me know you understand this."

One by one, each investigator acknowledged the security classification.

"Now to action items. Stefan has gone to meet with a representative of the Imperial Guard, to look at the crime scene, along with an Imperial Guard forensics team," Peterson went on, "and he left instructions for Nick, and in turn for as many of the rest of you as Nick decides he needs: dig into Medved's past employment records, find out who her boss was when she was working weapons quality control, and bring him or her in for questioning. It's likely that, if the former boss wasn't involved directly, he may know who was. Nick, as Stefan is our point of contact at the Palace, you're taking point on team ops. People, treat him like he was a detective already, please, because that's what we need. Given he's not far off that rank, and he's been working damn close with Stefan for a few years now, Stefan and I felt that that's how we should play it. Does anyone have any objections – including the other detectives in the room, who he may require to assist?"

The virtual meeting room was silent.

"Nick?"

"All over it, ma'am," Nick said.

"Go get 'em, tiger," Peterson said. "Dismissed."

Ames volunteered to scout out the employment records while Ashton tried to contact Gorski in VR from his office, in private.

"Oh, hi, Nick," Gorski finally responded – though it was voice-only. "You got anything for me yet?"

"Not yet, Stefan," Ashton said. "Cally is trying to pull up Medved's records now, while I contact you. She and I will go over 'em as soon as I'm done here."

"Good. I don't have a lot for you yet," Gorski said. "I'm watching the Guard's forensics team put together the crime scene right now. The husband's upset as hell, of course. It seems the victim was afraid of something like this, back when she was offered the job of advising the Empress, and he recommended she take the job."

"Aw, damn."

"Yeah, poor bastard. He's laying the blame on himself, and pretty much a wreck at this point. There was an attempt by IPD to usurp the crime scene, but the Guard headed it off."

"I feel for the poor guy, and yeah, the Colonel told us about the attempt. Listen, Stefan, you *know* who did it."

"I know who you think did it."

"Let me send you some of the stuff I've put together over the years I've been watching the guy," Ashton suggested as he requested the VR system provide a classified channel for the two of them. "Yes, I know we still have to prove it was him. And I know it's gonna be a pain in the ass to do. But just have a look. You can at least keep an eye out for anything that fits the profile I've constructed."

"All right, Nick. Lay it on me," Gorski capitulated.

The older man's avatar appeared in the small gray room that Ashton had requested in VR, and Ashton's avatar handed Gorski's avatar a folder full of papers; this represented the transfer of the electronic reports and profiles that Ashton had compiled over the years, since he first started investigating Joey Bronze in the police academy. Gorski flipped through the first few pages, scanning them, then began to read.

"Hm. You do have something here," he decided. "And yeah, this gives me some ideas about where to start looking. If I actually find something in those places, then I'll take it even more seriously. And I'll let you know immediately."

"Good. That's all I wanted you to do, Stefan. I'll let you get back to it, then, and see what Cally and I can dig up on Medved's ex-boss. Then we'll go bring him in for questioning."

"Excellent. And Nick? Thank you. I know you've been frustrated by our inability to pin anything on Bronze. But this one? You might have pointed me exactly where this investigation needs to go. Right on time to discuss it with Imperial Guard Major Dunham, too."

"Terrific, Stefan. Like the Colonel just told me, 'Go get 'em, tiger.'"

Gorski laughed.

"The old tiger and the new. I wonder which is more dangerous?"

"I dunno, but when you team 'em up, don't take 'em on in a dark alley at night."

This time, they laughed together.

"Nick?" Ames said from across Ashton's desk, when he emerged from VR. "That was pretty straightforward. I've already got the name for you."

"Oh? Let's hear it, Cally."

"Her old boss was one Bruce Peter Fairfield, Manager of the Small Weapons Test Plan Design Group in the Department of Defense. According to records, when she got unhappy about the way things were going, she told him off and quit. Um, she told him off pretty effectively, too. And in no uncertain terms." She flushed.

Ashton grinned; Callista Ames could be a bit prim and proper with him, for a fellow police officer, though she was pretty straightforward in the field, and could cuss with the best if the situation called for it. He could imagine the sort of language she was referencing, and *Screw you!* probably didn't go nearly far enough. *Maybe it's because we're putting together a private relationship that she's shy around me about stuff like that,* he considered, then got back to business.

"All right," he said then. "We need to go down to the DoD complex and see about picking him up."

"I got the address and building name, as well as his office number," Ames declared. "It's too late now to go get him, but it gives us plenty of time to plan for tomorrow."

"Good. Let's go put a team together."

"That's excellent," Peterson said, as she watched Ames and Ashton put together a team. "Because word just came down – all the way from the Empress – they want this guy brought in to the Guard."

"So it's official-official now," Ashton confirmed.

"About as official as it can get, Nick," Peterson averred. "It's late, and per feedback from Major Dunham coming through

Stefan, Her Majesty prefers we do it tomorrow, after he gets off work. That way, he sort of vanishes in between work and home, hopefully with nobody in the conspiracy the wiser about where he went, and plenty of time to vanish him. Adrian is undercover, keeping watch on him, to make sure nobody else gets to him before we do."

"That works," Ashton agreed.

"Hey, Nick," Peterson said as he came through the door the next morning. "I'm sending you over to work with the Imperial Guard and the Palace staff to see what's going down there. Per the Guard's request, they're making an attempt to locate the hit man on the street cameras we have providing security around Imperial Park."

"Right," Ashton said. "But if they're already doing that, what do you need me for?"

"Stefan wants you there, to see if you recognize Bronze in any of the imagery. You're the one that has studied him the most, so he thought that might be good. Otherwise, just answer questions if asked, and sit quiet in the back and watch. He's already arranged it through Major Dunham."

"Yes ma'am. What about taking in Fairfield?"

"You can leave sometime after lunch to go take care of that – we don't take him until quitting time, anyway. But for the time being, whenever you're not doing something else, Stefan wants you looking for Bronze in those videos."

"Okay." Ashton shook his head. "What is with all the security videos, anyway?"

"Oh, that. We had a crime wave through there about a decade ago or so," Peterson explained. "Right before the whole Sandman serial killings started, actually. It proved damn hard to solve, because there were so few witnesses, and the burglars

were pros. We did manage to round 'em up and incarcerate
'em, but we were left with the realization that the way that area
is set up, there are just too many places where nobody much is
gonna be around to see stuff go down. So ICPD made an offer
to businesses along the arcade: If you want security on your
businesses, we'll install security cameras hooked to servers for
the recordings – provided we get access for crime analysis. And
they agreed."

"Aha. That makes sense."

"it does. Now run on; they're expecting you. Park West
entrance."

Ashton arrived at the Imperial Park West entrance, checked
in with Reception, and an Imperial Guard escorted him straight
to the recording analysis team, who was just beginning their
work on the security video recordings.

He sat in the back of the room and watched quietly, being
allowed to enter VR with them when they took the analysis
three-dimensional.

They were done well before lunch.

A grim Dominick Ashton rose and went in search of Stefan
Gorski.

"So it was him?" Gorski asked.

"That, or he has a twin brother," Ashton said. "If the pattern
recognition algorithms don't dump out Josip Bronsky, I'll be
shocked. I'll also vote for firing the guy who wrote the
algorithms."

"And if we find the box, uniform, and weapon?"

"That'll probably nail it."

"Right. Never mind the *modus operandi*, because it *was* a
double-tap with a .25 caliber airgun, just like your profile laid

out. Were the analysis people sending the info over to the Marines at the spaceport?"

"What's at the spaceport?"

"Oh, that's right, you haven't been in the loop on that. The contents of the trash bins were collected by the better part of a battalion of Imperial Marines, bagged and tagged per location, and taken to their facility at the spaceport. To look for the disguise and the weapon, we'll need to go through the bags." Gorski grinned. "Wanna go help?"

"Think it'll take long? I have to be back to set up the team to take the DoD guy into custody…"

"Ooo. Lemme see. No, it's barely past 10:30 in the morning, and with all the Marines on search duty, I doubt it's going to take that long. Especially since, as you say, they've narrowed it to only a few bags. You should be back at the station by around one, maybe one-thirty."

"Then let's go. I wanna see this guy get taken down. It's been way the hell too long."

"You go ahead. I'll meet you there if I can. I have to check in with Maia first."

"Gone."

As Gorski had predicted, inside about forty-five minutes, the Marines had found all of the pertinent pieces of evidence. And one of the biggest pieces was a .25 caliber airgun.

Ashton bagged and tagged as the items were found.

He was headed back to ICPD headquarters by half past noon.

As ordered, that afternoon Ashton went to the DoD Acquisition & Testing building with a large team of investigators from the department, to help him keep an eye out and ensure that their quarry was neither missed, nor snatched from under them…or worse, killed before they could take him into custody.

They were well in advance of Fairfield's usual quitting time, and intel indicated that he was still in his office, so Ashton took the opportunity of placing his people in strategic locations to surveil the main entrance, which was also the one Fairfield always used, given all the others tended to be security airlock type portals. This would, he decided, ensure that not only was someone in position to see him, but no matter what he did, someone would also be in position to apprehend him.

More, he tagged the video security system on the building to let him know if Fairfield left through any of the other exits to the building, and ensured that he had team members positioned to cover those, as well, though they were secondary in attention, and he wanted those members largely focused on the main entrance.

Then they settled in and waited.

And waited.

And waited.

When fully an hour past Fairfield's usual quitting time had come and gone and they had seen no sign of him nor gotten notification of his departure through other doorways, Ashton checked in with their intel, only to discover that Fairfield was not working overtime, and had indeed left his office at his usual time.

"Shit," Ashton grumbled, not bothering to keep it to himself. "We missed him. Somehow, we missed him."

"I swear, Nick, we didn't," Peter Rassmussen, one of his team, declared in VR. "Every damn one of us had our eyes peeled the whole time. He didn't come out that door, I'd stake a year's pay on it."

"And I don't think he came out one of the other doors, either," Compton averred. "If he did, he disguised himself somehow, so even the pattern recognition didn't catch him."

"I gotta agree," Roger Armbrand said. "Something else went down here that we don't know about."

"I just hope the damn bastards didn't get to him before we did," Ashton grumbled.

"We didn't see anyone else on our target list go in, Nick," Ames pointed out. "I think we're good on that, unless they already had somebody embedded, like we do."

"Okay, lemme check in. Damn."

He pulled up his supervisor in the VR comm. "Colonel Peterson?"

"Maia Peterson. Nick, is that you? I was just getting ready to ping you."

"Yes ma'am. I don't have good news to report. We never saw him."

"I shouldn't expect you would. I just heard from Detective Gorski, who in turn was contacted by Imperial Guard Major Dunham. It seems that Fairfield figured out what happened from the news reports, got scared, and decided to turn state's evidence. He snuck out by a different door – likely wearing something to help hide who he was, like a hat or hoodie, though I can't say for sure, but I would in his shoes, so not even the DoD security might flag him – and went straight to the Palace and turned himself in. He's already in protective custody."

"Oh!"

"Exactly. And I assume you had eyes looking for potential assassins?"

"We did, ma'am, but only on the main door."

"Which makes sense. It's the only one visitors can enter; everything else requires one of those damn high-level clearances – one thing the damn assassins *don't* have. We had active video eyes on the others anyway, with flags on all the, uh, 'usual' faces. And I saw where you put flags on him on those same doors. The guy's scared bad, so he managed to fake *everybody* out! So pull your team and bring 'em in. Once you're here, get your shit together, then come to my office and we'll work out what needs doing next. I'll call Gorski and get a status update in the meantime."

"Yes ma'am." Ashton sent out the recall notice through VR and turned for ICPD headquarters.

On the way, Ashton filed his report through VR, checked for additional messages, then went straight to his desk. In the weeks since he had been at Imp City headquarters, some of the other detectives and inspectors had become moderately prone to dropping off handwritten notes, as well as the odd piece of 'evidence' for him to use for practice; it was known to most of them by now that he had aspirations – and significant talent – in investigation, which was one reason he was being given the task of working with Detective Gorski to round up the Empress' perps.

There was nothing for him there, and it would have waited in any event, so he headed straight for Maia Peterson's office.

Peterson had nothing in particular for him, nor were they able to determine a direction for him to go, as yet; it would all depend upon what the forensics people pulled out of what they had. So Ashton went back to his desk and pondered what he knew of the situation.

Just then, his nanites notified him of a call in VR. It was Detective Gorski.

"Hi there, Stefan. What do you need?"

"I'm over at the crime scene, Nick. I'm trying to see if I can squeeze anything else out of it that we might use to help clinch Bronze as the assassin. Unfortunately, I left my forensics kit on my desk. Is there any chance you can grab it and bring it over to me?"

"Sure, Stefan, I can do that. I'll be there in about twenty minutes. Did you leave it in the usual place?"

"Yeah, on the third shelf of the bookcase behind my desk."

"Okay. I'll go grab it and I'll be there shortly."

"Good man."

Ashton had almost reached the apartment building in which Medved had been killed, the little rolled toolkit in his pocket, when he rounded the corner and found his way blocked.

"There he is," one of Gorecki's thugs – Ashton could never remember their names; they all looked alike and were pretty much interchangeable, as far as he could tell – said with a smug expression. "I told you he'd be around this way soon enough."

"You were right, Jim," the second agreed.

"Yeah," the third remarked. "This oughta be easy. Stash said he had a girl for a bodyguard, so he can't be too tough."

Evidently Stash didn't tell 'em that the 'girl bodyguard' mopped up the sidewalk with him, Ashton thought, readying his body for what was coming, and ensuring his pistol was where it should be. *It sure would be nice if the odds were a little more even, but hey.*

A quick glance around indicated that there were no snipers or other such backup waiting for him, so he subtly flexed his muscles, prepared for whatever came.

Lackey #2 drew a knife and lunged at Ashton.

That's what comes, he thought.

He sidestepped the thrust and grabbed the goon's arm in both hands, bending it backward at the elbow until he heard several grisly snapping sounds. The man screamed as the elbow tendons failed and the oleocranon cracked.

A quick flip flung the man into one of his companions, and they both went down.

The third man snarled in annoyance, and reached for a pistol.

Ashton drew faster.

A bloom of red blossomed on the man's left chest as he gasped and grimaced in pain, then he staggered and collapsed.

Two and a half down, Ashton thought, then spun as the last of Gorecki's henchmen crawled out from under his remaining live companion, who was sitting on the sidewalk, cradling his maimed arm, and crying like a child. Ashton brought his pistol to bear.

"You want to live?" Ashton snapped, and the shocked and chagrined stooge nodded, pale. "Good. Jones, you there?"

"You saw me?" another man said as he appeared from the nearby alley.

"Yup, about two minutes after I left the building," Ashton averred. "Take these two into custody and restrain 'em, and see if that one is still alive. I've already called for transport."

"Glad to," Jones said, leering at the frightened henchman, now essentially alone and staring down two very capable… investigators of some sort, he assumed, though none of Gorecki's people thought Ashton worked for ICPD any longer.

"…Sorry I'm late, Stefan," Ashton said, as he approached the older man and handed him the toolkit. "I got accosted on the way over here."

"What?" Gorski looked him up and down. "You look okay…"

"Yup. You should see the other guys."

"Guys? Plural?"

"Yeah."

"How many?"

"Three."

"Damn."

"Timmy was performing escort duty, so I got him to help me restrain 'em. Then we had to wait for transport from Headquarters."

"Aha. Why didn't he help you?"

"No need." Ashton shrugged. "I had it."

"What did you do to 'em?"

"Shot one. Took out one's elbow. The third guy surrendered."

"Nice job."

"Eh. It made me late. Sorry."

Ashton spent the rest of the afternoon helping Gorski go over the crime scene in excruciating detail. They found nothing that the Imperial Guard's forensic team hadn't already found.

Halfway through, Peterson contacted them with word on Ashton's assailants – one died at the scene; one was in emergency surgery, and one had had his bail posted…

…By Stash Gorecki.

"I'm getting tired of that guy," Ashton declared.

Surveillance Time – Team Armbrand

"All right, Nick," Peterson said in her office the next morning, as Gorski took a seat beside Ashton, "the DNA evidence has come in, along with a request from Major Dunham. Right, Stefan?"

"Right, Maia," Stefan Gorski confirmed. "We have firm ID on one of three perps, and probable IDs on the other two, including the actual killer, based on the DNA. So now it's time to round 'em up for the Imperial Guard."

"Not for the ICPD?" Ashton wondered.

"Nope," Gorski said, with a solemn head shake. "The Empress is seriously pissed, by all accounts. The victim wasn't just a staffer but a personal friend, never mind the fact that the assassination was a direct attack against her plans and policies. This one is being handled by the Throne, not the lesser courts."

"Oh shit," Ashton said, his eyebrows shooting up. "That's serious as all hell. I sure wouldn't wanna be these guys."

"No, most likely not," Peterson agreed. "Now, I've already had reports from your team that you were really on the ball and laid things out strategically, Nick; you've got a good head on your shoulders, and show some real promise at this. So we're giving you the same team, and we need you to go get the following perps, as quickly as you can, without letting them know you're after them; we don't need one notifying the others so they flee."

"Yes, ma'am; I understand."

"I'm activating a channel in VR for you," Gorski said. "You can find the perps' files there."

"I see it," Ashton confirmed, after a moment to check. "Ohhh. Joey Bronze. They pegged him."

"Well, it isn't a hundred percent identification, but close enough to round him up and see what we get. Which you predicted. And by the way, I added the info you provided me into his official files in the department."

"Oh? Thank you, Stefan. That...is important to me."

"I know. You've followed this bastard a long time."

"Yeah. I'll be glad to finally get my hands on him."

"Won't we all?" Peterson agreed. "He was apparently the assassin."

"Why am I not surprised? Who are these other two, then? The lookouts? That couple they saw in the video?"

"Susan Kaplan, a.k.a. Suzie Q, a.k.a. Samantha Tripp, a.k.a. Sammy Tripp, a known prostitute and sometime shoplifter," Gorski noted, "and Derek Beckham, no known aliases, but he generally tends to lurk on the wrong side of the law; he's had several priors for aiding and abetting of one sort or another. Beckham is a long-time associate of Bronze, and Kaplan is an associate of Beckham. I don't know about any couple, but per what I was told about the street video, yes, those two were the lookouts."

"Aha. So they marked the target, and gave VR feedback on her movements to Bronze."

"You got it, kid," Gorski said with a grin. "You're gonna make a damn good detective one of these days. Probably sooner rather than later, if we can keep you out of trouble with the Imperial jerks."

"Hell, Stefan, he already does," Peterson said, matching Gorski's grin.

"Thank you, sir, ma'am," a serious Ashton said. "And thanks for letting me help out on your case."

"Way I see it," Gorski said, as Peterson nodded, "not only are you giving me and Dunham some serious assistance, you're getting a good bit of training and experience into the bargain, toward your next promotion. Never mind helping to train the others. Because this is a big-ass case, with serious ramifications. And for somebody with your potential, that's all to the good."

"Better here than over there, under Kershaw and the like," Peterson said, grim. "Here, he'll survive and get trained, and trained right…if, as you say, we can keep him out of their hands. Now, Nick, go round up your team, do whatever you need to do to find these guys, and call Stefan, here, when you do."

"Yes ma'am!" Ashton said, then headed back to his desk.

In the end, Ashton and his team decided they didn't have enough information to head straight out and take the assassin and his lookouts into custody immediately – at least, not without risking losing one or more of them to flight. Ashton – and the investigations department as a whole – had a certain amount of info on Joey Bronze from previous interactions, but not enough to be able to determine where he might be at any given time. And other than the nature of "work" engaged in by Susan Kaplan and Derek Beckham, precious little else on those two.

"So I think it's time to go undercover and have a look," he decided, and his team agreed. "Because we need to figure out where they are at any given time of day so we can arrest them in rapid sequence, with as little fuss as possible. We don't wanna take long, so we'll split up into teams, one for each perp. I'll take Weaver, Ames, and Compton and scope out Bronze; I got some ideas on him anyhow, after that last case he slid out of, where the guy that attacked Carter got popped. Rog, you take Weyand and Smith and check out Kaplan, and Pete, you've got Jones and Osborn to look at Beckham."

"That works," Armbrand agreed, and Rassmussen nodded.

"Then let's get in disguise and go," Ashton decreed.

The three teams worked with Adrian Mott again – they were getting good at undercover disguises, especially Ashton, but given the Throne's interest, Ashton felt it best to call in Mott, just to make sure they couldn't be recognized. Meanwhile Ames pulled the files on each perp and pushed them to the respective teams – Bronze to the "Ashton team," Kaplan for the "Armbrand team," and Beckham for the "Rassmussen team."

It was still fairly early in the morning; chances were, their surveillance targets were still at home.

So they headed out.

Armbrand's team headed into the Imperial Park South district. Susan Kaplan lived in a low-rent area quite some few blocks south of Imperial Park proper. She was a prostitute, and kept a reasonably large apartment for the purpose, since she both lived there and saw her "clients" there. But her clientele tended not to be that rich, because she wasn't from the higher strata of society, and it showed in her speech and habits. So she lived in an area where she could afford that larger apartment... which meant deep in Park South. Given that the Imperial Police Headquarters on Sintar was in the same general area, it was surprising to no one on the Team that she sometimes worked for them. At this point, it would not have surprised Ashton to find that some of the IPD personnel were among her clientele.

A quick and skillful infiltration of the building's maintenance staff enabled them to locate her specific apartment – it wasn't hard, given her "profession" – and determine that she was not awake and about as yet. Some subtle questioning of the maintenance workers – combined with a few palms crossed with several credits in coin – determined that this was normal; since she tended to be up late with the johns, she slept late to help compensate.

So Armbrand, Weyand, and Smith settled in to wait.

"Here she comes," Smith reported in voice VR, as Kaplan exited the main doors of the apartment building. "Heads up, Rog, she's headed your way."

"Okay. Yeah, there she is. Rich, she's not going in your direction; reset to down the street from me."

"On my way, Rog," Weyand's voice noted.

"Handing off to you, Rog," Smith said, as Kaplan disappeared from his view, down the street.

"Good. Reset past Rich."

"Headed out and around," Smith said, turning and heading one block down. "She headed for the arcade level?"

"Not in this part of town. That's a sure way to give up what she wants paid for," Armbrand said. "She'll stay at street level, most likely."

They trailed her from north central Imperial Park South nearly all the way to the southern boundary of Imperial Park proper; as she grew nearer Imperial Park, the neighborhood improved, and she eventually went down to the arcade level to use the slidewalks.

A couple of blocks from the Park boundary, not very far from the Imperial Mausoleum, she entered a little diner, the Waffle Stomper. Given the name, it wasn't surprising it was frequented by the Imperial Navy and Marines, which meant it was a potential source of clientele for Kaplan. She settled down at a table; Armbrand slipped inside and took a table nearby, letting the other two members of his team keep clandestine guard outside, and watching surreptitiously as she ordered two eggs, scrambled hard with Swiss cheese, with oatmeal and a cup of fresh melon on the side, along with water, grapefruit juice, and black coffee.

She took her time, spending nearly an hour and a half noshing on breakfast – or, as Armbrand noted her reference to the waitress, "brunch" – while somewhat absently watching the nearby video screens for the news of the day.

When she was finished, she paid in VR and rose, heading back out the front door. Armbrand stayed where he was, finishing his coffee, while he told Smith and Weyand in VR to follow her, and he'd catch up to them.

From there, Kaplan headed east and slightly closer to Imperial Park, then entered a grocer's to shop. She spent an hour in there, and this time, Weyand followed her in, shopping nearby, and watched her price-check her various choices; it was obvious she was pinching pennies, but she still got the makings of a large salad, as well as some farm-fresh fish.

A quick check-out, and she made what appeared to be a usual arrangement to have the groceries delivered, so she didn't have to carry them back to her apartment. Not only would that exhaust her, it would put her in danger of being mugged for the food; it made sense to spend the extra money on delivery.

Then it was off to another store...which turned out to be a very risqué lingerie store.

"Aw shit," Armbrand grumbled; all three investigators were single men, currently unattached, and none of them were comfortable going into *that* store. "Nick and Cally shoulda had this one!"

"Hell no," Weyand said. "They'd both have blushed purple! They don't even like anybody teasing 'em about the fact they're going out! It would have given the whole damn thing away."

"Well, somebody has to go in there and keep an eye on things," Smith pointed out.

"Hm. Maybe not. It's got a nice, big storefront window," Armbrand noted. "Maybe a bit of fancy footwork, here, so to speak..."

He pulled a pair of sunglasses out of his pocket and slid them on. The polarized lenses immediately adjusted for the ambient light, and Armbrand grunted in satisfaction as they cut through the window glare.

"She's getting measured by the shop manager," he told the others. "Looks like she wants some new lacy floofies."

"'Floofies'?" Weyand said, cocking an eyebrow and glancing askance at Armbrand, who flushed. Weyand grinned, then added, "Old girlfriend?"

"Um," Armbrand said, clearing his throat, "actually, no. My older sister calls 'em that. And yes, she's married."

Weyand and Smith desperately stifled guffaws.

After a purchase in the lingerie shop, Kaplan headed home. Shortly after arriving in her apartment, the windows went dark.

"Yeah, I confirm," Weyand said, hidden in an alcove down the hall from her door. "The slit under the door just went dark."

"Well, I guess it stands to reason," Smith decided. "She's gonna be up most of the night, banging johns."

"True," Armbrand agreed. "I suppose, if I was in that line of work, I'd take an afternoon nap, too."

"Then probably a shower and some dinner, before her 'guests' arrive," Weyand speculated.

"I'd say so, yeah."

"So now we're just kind of here, watching and waiting?" Smith wondered.

"Yup. Hell, if we can get a list of her johns, we might be able to bust them while we're about it."

That first night, she had four clients, beginning at 8 in the evening; the first two of them stayed two hours each, with an hour of inactivity between, and the last two clients only stayed an hour, but it was nearly continuous from 11 at night until three in the morning. And, according to Weyand, the last "client" could be heard down the hall.

At 3:30 am, half an hour after "Mr. Howler" left, the lights went out in the apartment and stayed out.

"I'm not surprised," Armbrand said, raising an eyebrow. "Damn."

Surveillance Time – Team Rassmussen

Derek Beckham lived on the unofficial boundary between Imperial Park South and Imperial Park East. It was definitely a more upscale apartment than Kaplan had, and his lifestyle showed it; it had a bit more of an upper-crust air, without being quite as expensive as true upper-crust would be.

Though he had few actual arrests to his account, and those mostly for aiding and abetting, Beckham was in fact a high-end con man, which was how he had met Joey Bronze.

The Rassmussen team surveilled him for several days, adopting tactics similar to the Armbrand team. Some discreet inquiries, accompanied by a few minor payoffs to informants, ascertained he typically rose around seven or eight in the morning and had a leisurely breakfast at home, to include a whole pot of coffee, over which he liked to linger, if delivery services comments were anything to go by. He typically emerged, fully dressed in elegant clothing – he was something of a dandy, which made sense, given his con targets – and headed deeper into Imperial Park East around mid-morning, though the informants around his apartment building didn't know where he went.

"Which means we have to find out," Rassmussen pointed out to Jones and Osborn.

Where he went, it turned out, was a fashionable café a few blocks east of the southeast corner of Imperial Park East.

"Man, that guy loves his caffeine," Jones decided, as the trio subtly watched Beckham in the café from three separate vantage points, conversing privately – and unnoticed – in VR. "Entire pot of coffee at home with breakfast, according to his deliveryman, and now he's already gone through two frou-frou coffees while reading – I didn't even know anybody still published newspapers…"

"Demetrius says it's a new fad among the nouveau riche," Rassmussen said. "It's more expensive to get your news that way, instead of in VR, so it shows off that you can *afford* to."

"I note he isn't buying the papers, just reading 'em while he drinks his coffee," Osborn said, mild disgust evident in his tone.

"Yeah. And damn! He just ordered another coffee!" Jones said. "How the hell big is that man's bladder?"

Finally Beckham finished his reading and drinking, and having paid for his coffees as he went, he rose and headed out.

Rassmussen, Osborn, and Jones followed.

Subtly.

Beckham ended up at the Waffle Stomper diner around noon. Going inside, he took a seat at the counter and ordered a huge burger topped with a fried egg and a side of fries, along with…more coffee.

"If that guy doesn't vibrate outta there, I'm gonna be shocked," Jones declared in VR as they watched through the diner windows from different locations.

"Either that, or his bladder will explode," Osborn decided. "That can't be healthy."

"It doesn't say good things about his kidneys, I expect," Rassmussen agreed.

At the end of lunch, Beckham finally ducked into the men's

room – along with Jones, to make sure nothing unusual went down – and relieved his bladder.

"Damn, guys," Jones said in VR, so his colleagues could hear but his perp could not. "It's Arntigier Falls in here! Half his belly must be bladder…"

"Anybody else in there with you?" Rassmussen asked.

"Nah. Well, couple guys in the stalls. Nobody else at the urinals. And nobody trying to make contact with him. Shit! He's *still* going!"

"Emphasis on going," Osborn said dryly.

"Okay, finally," Jones said. "He's zipped and gone to wash his hands. Heads up; he'll probably be headed out soon."

"Yup, here he comes," Osborn said. "I'm on him."

"Tag team like usual," Rassmussen ordered.

After lunch Beckham met with a well-to-do businessman named Ching, in a private club. Rassmussen called back to ICPD Headquarters to connect with the club's security manager, and soon he was able to meet with the security manager to tap into their video within the club and watch what was happening.

"What's going down, Pete?" Jones wondered.

"Near as I can tell, he's setting up a con," Rassmussen decided. "I'm reading lips and I think he's making some kind of 'business proposition' that I expect is designed to con the guy out of a fair amount of money – without being so much that the guy would be inclined to go after him legally if he's caught out."

Rassmussen kept up with the con in progress, while explaining to the security manager about Beckham's record, and was assured that the irate manager would talk to Mr. Ching in private at a later time, to warn him off of Beckham's machinations. It took some doing to talk him out of banning Beckham from the club, but finally he got the manager to understand the need to prevent flight. Meanwhile, Jones and Osborn kept a watch on the exits from the private club.

After a couple of hours of expounding on the wonders of his fake business proposition, the men appeared to strike a deal. Beckham rose, bowed, and shook hands with Ching, then departed the club with a smile, heading several blocks over, and carefully shadowed by Rassmussen's team.

There, he entered a four-star restaurant and met with yet another wealthy businessman.

Colonel Peterson had grasped what was happening upon Rassmussen's urgent call from the club, and now Adrian Mott showed on the scene with his duffel. He grabbed Osborn and Rassmussen, pulled them into a nearby mews, and proceeded to re-dress them in expensive business suits, while Jones kept an eye on the restaurant. He hit them with a whiff of the most expensive men's colognes on the market, then pointed.

"Go," he said. "Find out what's going on in there. I'll stay out here with Jones and keep watch."

"Damn," Rassmussen cursed in voice comm to the others. "Same song, verse two, only this mark is somebody named Stewart. It's even the same con."

"Well, sure," Mott pointed out. "That way, if this guy and the previous guy happen to talk, they'll be talking about the same supposed business proposal, and not only will it sound legit, it'll look like a great deal. They're getting in on the ground floor and all that, see."

"We need to make sure this Stewart knows," Osborn said.

"Nah," Rassmussen demurred. "As soon as we nail this guy and he stops showing up, his marks will either forget all about him, figure he was the crook that he is, or decide the whole deal fell through. In any case, they won't worry any more about it. Now, any previous marks that he's conned, that's a different story; we'll need to try to get any names and numbers, and see if there's anything left to be reimbursed...though I doubt it, given this guy's tastes. A huge fraction was probably literally pissed down the drain."

"True, I guess," Osborn agreed. "On multiple points."

The pair watched Beckham wine and dine Stewart with fine food and drink, while pretending to discuss business over drinks themselves, and putting their drinks on the expense account for the department.

After a couple of hours, Beckham and Stewart shook hands. Stewart paid the tab, and Beckham departed in a chipper mood.

Beckham's next stop was another restaurant, somewhat closer to home, but still a fairly expensive proposition. This time, Mott and Jones entered, dressed in classy slacks and sport coats with ties, while Osborn and Rassmussen kept watch outside.

As it turned out, Beckham was only there for dinner. He met no one, but had a very nice four-course meal with wine... and an after-dinner dessert coffee, along with...tiramisu.

"What is it with Nick's investigations and coffee?" Rassmussen wondered in disgust. "I like the stuff, but I'm starting to get sick of it."

Finally Beckham meandered back to his apartment.

The scenario repeated itself the next day, and the day after that, at different clubs and restaurants, with different rich targets.

Surveillance Time – Team Ashton

According to the information Ashton had teased out over the years, Bronze tended to be much more irregular in his habits than either of his accomplices. His day apparently depended on whether or not he had a call or an assignment from IPD Headquarters. If he did, he would be up early, either checking in with Headquarters, or scouting out his target.

For the time being, and so soon after the Medved murder, he appeared to be laying low. Which meant there was no way to tell exactly what he might be doing, except to go watch.

His dwelling was far posher than even Beckham's; these days, Bronze owned a condo in Imperial Park East. It was in the south-central part of that district, but far closer to the commuter train line than Beckham's apartment. Ashton's investigations into Bronze's finances in the course of his profiling – having hacked his various accounts – indicated he could now afford it; after proving himself on the early assassinations, he was currently paid a premium for his skills as an assassin, as well as extra for any lookouts he felt he might need, and it looked to Ashton like he skimmed from that extra, not paying those henchmen all he was given for the cost of hiring them.

Ashton ensured his team was dressed suitably for the area, which was fairly well-to-do, then they headed straight for the building in which Bronze lived.

A quick check with the management of the condominium tower ascertained that he tended to call down to the café on the arcade level for a pot of coffee and a couple of Danishes to be delivered to his condo.

"Of late," the manager said, "It's been closer to noon when he calls. He seems to be sleeping in."

"Do you know how he's employed?" Ashton wondered.

"He's a free-lance artist and analyst of some sort, according to the application he submitted when he bought the condo a couple of years back," the manager explained. "Says he works a lot for the Imperial Police, as well as some wealthy patrons. So he keeps somewhat odd hours."

Ashton stifled a snort.

After that intel, Ashton and his team quickly headed for the arcade level and the café.

"Hello, folks. How can I help you?" the host – whose name tag indicated he was the manager, one Bill Cane – asked as they came through the door.

"We'd each like a cup of coffee and one of your excellent Danishes," Ashton said with a friendly smile. "I hear Mr. Bronze highly recommends them."

"Oh yes." Cane beamed. "Mr. Bronze orders a pot of our café special dark roast and a cheese Danish every morning. Maybe not like clockwork," the manager laughed, "but he never fails. I'm glad to hear he's passing word on to his friends."

"Oh, definitely," Ames said, taking Ashton's arm in a subtle claim, thereby making them look to the manager like a couple plus their friends; behind them, Weaver and Compton grinned, not bothering to hide them. "Mr. Bronze was very complimentary. We decided to swing by on our way to meet up with some more friends for a fun little outing, and have breakfast here."

"Of course. Well, you're more than welcome; our morning rush has slackened a bit, and Mr. Bronze isn't likely to call down for Sherry to bring up breakfast for a couple more hours. What would you like?"

"Mm. How about a pot of the house blend coffee, and an order of Danishes apiece?" Ashton suggested, glancing at the others, who all nodded.

"Anything else for you?"

"Not right now, no."

"Excellent. Let me just ring that up for you," Cane said.

The manager totaled the charges, and Ashton paid for it in VR, putting it on their expense account. "You folks just pick a table and have a seat and I'll have Sherry bring out your coffee and pastries in just a moment. Do any of you want cream or sugar?"

"Both, please," Ames noted.

"I'll take cream," Compton said.

"Black for me," Ashton said.

"Me too," Weaver agreed.

"Very good. Just relax and enjoy yourselves, and it'll be right out."

"Here you go!" Sherry the waitress declared cheerfully as she stopped at their table with a tray, setting down cups, cream, and sugar before pouring each a piping hot cup from an insulated pot. She sat the pot in the middle of the table, then passed around plates with two cheese Danishes apiece. "Does that look good?"

"It sure does!" Ames declared eagerly. "Thanks!"

"I hear tell you guys heard about us from my best customer," Sherry said, and Ashton smiled.

"We sure did. Joey Bronze is well known to me and my

friends here."

"You can say that again," Weaver agreed. "If he likes it, you know it'll be good."

"Hee! Every morning he calls down and has me bring up a fresh pot, and a whole platter of pastries, usually the cheese Danishes, though he likes the strawberry too, when they're fresh in season. And I get it all together, and when I get there, he's either watching the news on the screen, or his favorite soap opera, depending on what time of the morning it is."

"Ha! Which soap?" Ashton wondered with a laugh.

"*Days of the First Empress*," she chuckled. "He loves that show!"

"I bet!" Compton laughed.

"He tips really nice, too," the waitress told them. "Sometimes, if he can tell the breakfast rush was pretty hectic, he even invites me to sit down at his breakfast table and rest. He'll get an extra cup and pour me some coffee, and we'll talk until he has to leave on business. He's amazingly attentive to me; he seems to always be able to tell what kind of day it's been." She cocked her head. "It's odd, though…usually he ends up drinking from his own cup, and I drink from the café cup. No idea why he does that."

The foursome steadfastly avoided looking at each other, but Ashton sent one word through the VR private comm channel. *"DNA."*

"What's that scoundrel been up to lately?" Ames asked then, stirring the cream and sugar into her coffee before taking a sip.

"Oh, nothing much, the last few days," Sherry admitted. "He just finished some big gig for one of his top clients, so he's resting up, and he's expecting an even bigger one to come along soon."

"That doesn't sound good," Weaver observed in VR.

"No," Ashton agreed in kind. *"Somebody else in the Palace, I'd bet."*

"I wouldn't bet against you."

"Yeah, we heard," Ashton noted. "We're sorta here under a false flag – we're planning a surprise party for him, to celebrate the gig completion."

"Ooo, that's nice! I'll be sure and not give it away," Sherry said with a grin. "...So anyway, when he's done with breakfast and I leave, he just goes down to some pub where a lot of his business contacts go to find him, and waits for another commission to come his way. It must be so wonderful to be an artist."

"I...suppose so," Ashton agreed...though his tone was rather ambiguous. *I guess some people might consider his work 'art,' but I'm damn sure not one of 'em,* he thought, carefully hiding disgust.

"Um, since you're his friends and all, I was wondering..." Sherry began rather uncertainly, "Is Joey, um, attached? Does he have a girlfriend, or a significant other, or anything?"

Ashton blinked. *Of all the things I might have expected, that sure wasn't one,* he thought in surprise. *She's interested in him. In Joey Bronze, of all people. Poor girl. She couldn't have picked a worse man to notice.*

"I...I think," he began, and cast a questioning, almost desperate glance at Cally Ames...who rose to the occasion.

"Oh, honey," Ames murmured, taking the little waitress' hand in a gentle grip and patting it, "if I were you, I wouldn't go there. He's just not the type."

"Oh," Sherry said, face falling a bit. "So...he's a, a confirmed bachelor?"

"Pretty much," Ashton averred. "He's the sort who...tends

to not want loose ends, you know?"

"Um, yeah, I think I get what you mean. Okay. Uh, thanks. Please...please don't mention that to him."

"We won't," Ames reassured her.

Sherry gathered her tray and left their table, mildly crestfallen.

Ames stared at Ashton. "Nick Ashton," she told him in VR, "if you don't give that girl a really big tip when we're done here, I will flat smack you."

"It's expense account, Cal. I can only do so much. But I'll see what I can do. Maybe I can give her an informant's fee or something. She did tell us a lot about his mornings, after all."

"Hey, Nick, do that, but then let's also see if the rest of us can't put together a few credits between us, in addition," Compton suggested. "We can add to the pot, that way."

"That's a good idea," Weaver agreed. "I can chip in five or ten, easy."

"Me too," Ames averred.

"Okay, that should make for a nice little tip, there," Ashton agreed, looking at the expense account's options for payment. "Yeah, we can do this. Lemme download the informant's fee, then you guys push me your contributions, and we'll give her a really good little tip that ought to make even Bronze's tips look picayune by comparison."

The quartet sat and noshed and sipped their coffee – which was indeed very good, and complemented the freshly-baked pastries wonderfully – and even ordered another pot, while they waited and watched Sherry.

When she and the manager put together a platter of Danishes and brewed a fresh pot of coffee, putting it all on a

206

tray and covering it with a cloche, they realized that Bronze was up, awake, and following true to form. It was nearly noon.

"Which is a little surprising, I'd think," Ames pondered to the others, sotto voce. "I'd figure he'd want to be as unpredictable in his schedule as possible, so the cops can't determine where he'd be."

"Except he's working for the cops, and the cops in question are crookeder than a shipping container full of fish hooks," Ashton pointed out. "He's generally not worried about hiding, except from us, and his IPD buddies protect him from us as best they can...which, so far, has been pretty damned good. No, he wants to be available and easily found so they can hire him for more take-downs."

"Ohhhh, good point, Nick," Weaver decided.

"Yeah," Ames agreed.

"And that comment the girl made about another, even bigger, gig coming makes me damn worried," Compton noted. "You don't suppose they might actually try to off the Empress, do you?"

"Oh shit. I sure hope not!" Ames said, horrified. "But there's other big fish working for her, you know."

"Yeah."

"Not if we can help it. On any of his potential targets. No. Damn. More. All right, let's get in position," Ashton determined. "According to Sherry, once *she* comes back down, *he* will be headed out. We need to find out where he goes."

"Right," the others agreed.

Two hours later, an unconcerned Bronze finally left his condominium and strolled down the street. With four in the team, the investigators could "leapfrog" their target for a fair distance. Sometimes Ames walked along with Ashton and sometimes they did so alone, ensuring that everything would look natural and no one would give them a second glance. The foursome followed Bronze as he sauntered through the sunshine on the street level, headed generally west, toward Imperial Park.

When he reached Imperial Park East Boulevard, Bronze turned left and headed south until he reached Phoenix Avenue, the first east-west street past Imperial Park South Boulevard.

The Fire Water Bar was halfway down the block on the left. Bronze headed into it.

Deciding not to risk Ashton being recognized, the "Ashton Team" chose to send in Compton and Weaver as drinking buddies – removing ties and jackets before they did so, in order to "dress down." Ames and Ashton stayed outside, and Ames watched the front while Ashton pulled up the schematics for the block in VR, then nosed around through the alleys and mews to verify that those schematics were correct relative to current structures.

"That's good," he told the others in VR, remaining out of sight in the shadows of a back alley. "There's only two ways in or out of that bar – the front door, and the kitchen door, which opens onto a kind of cross-alley in the back, for deliveries. I've got that one; Cal, you watch the front."

"All over it, Nick," she replied.

"What's he doing, guys?" Ashton asked.

"He sat down at a table in the corner near the end of the bar, Nick," Compton replied. "Waiter came over and he ordered off the menu, though he didn't hardly look at it. Looks like lunch. Except it looks like he's gonna drink a lot of it, if you get me."

"Mm. What did he order?"

"Uh, lemme see what I can see, Alan," Weaver said. "I got a

208

better angle. Okay, looks like some sort of meatball thing – oh! It's got a hard-boiled egg inside! He's dipping pieces in that demonic hot mustard…"

"Scotch eggs," Ashton supplied. "Mom used to make 'em. They're good."

"And maybe…blackened fish and chips?"

"Sounds like the bar's name is also a theme of the food," Ames remarked.

"Yeah, it is. But he's drinking a high-end whiskey rather than one of their signature spicy cocktails."

"Which argues that he intends to keep it up a while," Ashton speculated. "Too much spicy in alcohol can do a number on you, in more ways than one."

"Never mind the afterburn," Weaver said with a VR snort.

"Given he got a double, neat, I dunno how long," Compton observed.

"I guess we'll find out how well he holds his liquor," Ashton said.

It turned out the answer was pretty damned well…and yet not quite well enough.

After the second double shot, Bronze was obviously relaxing a lot; he was joking with the waiter and bartender, and generally seemed less attentive than he had when he entered.

"Which seems stupid," Weaver noted. "You'd think he'd be keeping a watch out, especially right now."

"It speaks to two things," Ashton decided. "One, he thinks he can't be touched. Two, he knows the staff, and they're standing guard for him. Watch your backs, guys."

"Roger," both men responded.

After the third double, however, Bronze was starting to appear mildly inebriated. The fact that he was still noshing –

nachos had arrived after the fish and chips – and had taken over three hours to consume all of it, while chatting up the bartender, explained why he was only mildly intoxicated. The fact that he had practically knocked back the second double, then promptly ordered the third, explained why he was intoxicated at all.

"This could take a while," Ames decided, when Bronze ordered fried cheese.

"Why the hell is he not the size of a hippopotamus?" Weaver wondered.

"This may be the private celebration of a successful hit," Compton decided. "I bet he works out most days, by the look of him."

"But it's been days since the assassination of Medved," Ames protested. "Going on a week."

"And apparently nobody after him," Ashton pointed out. "So he figures he's clean."

"Maybe it's time we paid the tab and got out of here, Nick," Compton said. "The waiter's come by again to see if we wanted something else."

"All right, pay the tab and head out. Is Bronze sloshed enough that he wouldn't recognize me in my disguise, do you think?"

"Does he have reason to recognize you?" Weaver wondered.

"Not really. We've never met. But I was thinking, if the IPD put out word they're looking for me, he might recognize my ID photo or something. Hell, I might be on his hit list, for all I know, and he just hasn't gotten around to me yet."

"If you sit in a booth on the far side of the room, you're probably good," Compton said. "Maybe with Cally in there with you, and you two pretend to make out?"

"That might work," Ashton decided. "Cal?"

"Works for me, Nick. Why can't we really make – never mind. We need to watch."

Weaver and Compton stifled laughs in VR.

Compton took the kitchen entrance and Weaver watched the bar's façade while Nick and Cally entered the establishment and seated themselves in a booth as far from Bronze as they could legitimately get, while looking like a couple who wanted some privacy. Nick took the seat facing the front door, and Cally sat facing the bar at the back of the pub, where Bronze sat at the nearby table.

"What can I get for you two?" another waiter asked the pair, as they perused the menu.

"I think the lady and I would like to share an order of Scotch eggs," Nick said, "and I'll have a shot of Jamesons, on the rocks."

"I'd like a Riesling spritzer, please," Cally decided.

"Right away. Are you planning on a meal here, or is this on the way to another event?"

"On the way to another event. We're early for that event – we have tickets to a show, and dinner after with friends – so we thought we'd blow off some time here," Nick said with a smile. "Never mind tide us over until after the show. It's on the way, we've heard good things about it, so we stopped in."

"Excellent, then. If you need refills, or additional snacks to nibble, do call me, and your food and drinks will be up in just a few minutes."

Compton had only been in position in the back alley for about ten minutes when an Imperial Police officer showed up, brandishing a bobby stick.

"Gonna have to ask you to leave, buddy," he told Compton,

stern and almost truculent, as if he wanted Compton to talk back, so he could get more physical. "Got a report 'bout you hangin' out back here from one o' the apartments across the way. We can't have people causing problems."

"I'm afraid you have a case of mistaken identity, officer," Compton said, extracting his badge at the same time he pushed his identification through VR. "I'm an investigator with ICPD; we had a rape in this alley about a week ago, and I'm here looking for clues as to the identity and whereabouts of the rapist."

"Aha," the IPD officer said, studying Compton's bona fides in VR. "You wouldn't happen to know a guy name of Ashton, would you? Might be in your same department..."

"No, I'm afraid not," Compton lied smoothly. "I've never known anyone with that name. There's certainly nobody in my division named Ashton. I guess he might be in some other division..." He shrugged, seeming uncaring.

"Huh. Well, maybe he's free-lancin' then. Might even be set up as a private dick or somethin'. If you see him, give us a call, okay? He's not what he's cracked up to be, and we got a warrant out on 'im."

"Sure thing," Compton lied once more.

"Okay, yell if you need help with anything. Good luck finding the rapist."

"Will do."

And the Imperial Police officer headed back out to the street.

"Nick, you busy?" Compton asked on the VR.

Ashton looked up from where he and Ames shared a whole Scotch egg – a savory dish consisting of an entire hard-boiled egg wrapped in bulk sausage, lightly breaded with crumbs, then fried until the sausage was cooked – and verified that there was nothing of interest going on in the pub. Bronze was still drinking, the bartender was prepping for the after-work happy hour, and the waiters were bussing and cleaning tables. A couple of other tables had guests, so Ames and Ashton didn't stand out, but the bar was fairly quiet.

"No, Alan, I'm just eating and keeping an eye out. But nothing's happening. Whatcha need?"

"We handed over – excuse the pun – in the nick of time. I just had an IPD officer show up with arrest on his mind – and probably a beating, judging by the way he handled his baton – and I think he was really looking for you. He asked about you by name. Wanted to know if I knew you, or if you were in our Investigations division."

"Oh. And?"

"I lied through my teeth, of course."

"Thanks for that."

"No problem. What are friends for?"

"Heh."

"But you should know – the guy said they had an arrest warrant out on you. They're trying to smear you, apparently."

"So what else is new? Arrest is the least of my worries with that bunch."

"I'll bet. They don't seem to know who you're working for, though. He asked if you were in our division, and when I said no, that I hadn't seen you in the department at all, he speculated that you might be 'free-lancing,' as he put it. Private investigation or the like, I suppose."

"Huh. Okay. Well, keep an eye out, and make sure you report that to Colonel Peterson."

"I'll do that in a couple minutes, here."

"Good. Thanks again."

"It's cool, Nick."

Bronze stayed in the Fire Water Bar, getting and staying drunk, until well after dinner. This meant that the four Imp City investigators had to play tag a bit, and even leave him unwatched for a while – at least, from inside the bar.

And after Compton's encounter, they all watched Ashton a little closer.

But finally Bronze settled his tab in VR, then had the bar host call a taxi. Fortunately, Weaver was at a table close enough to hear the conversation, and waited a full minute, then called for a plainclothes transport in VR, himself. He paid his own tab, such as it was, and left the bar before Bronze.

"Pretty sure he's headed home," he notified the others in VR. "Unmarked transport on the way."

"We could just follow him," Ames said.

"Not when he's in a taxi."

"Good call, Hugo," Ashton praised the younger man.

The unmarked transport arrived first, as Weaver intended, and by ones and twos, they climbed inside. The windows were tinted so the number of passengers – and their identities – could not be seen, but that was not unusual for the vehicles of more important citizens of this part of the city.

"What do you guys need?" the uniformed driver asked.

"See the guy getting in the taxi over there?" Ashton pointed at the decidedly inebriated Bronze practically pouring himself into the taxi with the help of the bar manager. "Follow 'em, but don't look like you're following 'em."

"All over that one," the driver said with a grin. He pulled out, into the street.

In the end, Bronze was indeed headed home. The taxi dropped him off at the posh high-rise condo building, and the unmarked car eased to the curb a little distance away. Bronze stumbled out of the cab and into the lobby entrance, and vanished.

The five Imp City officers sat and watched, as the lights on a certain floor came on, a few at a time, and moving in a wave across the floor.

Fifteen minutes later, the last light on that floor went dark.

"And Joey Bronze just crashed hard," Ashton decreed. "I wouldn't want his head in the morning."

"Now what?" the driver asked.

"It's been a long day," Ashton said. "If you could take us back to Headquarters, it'd be great; we all need to go home and crash, too. Tomorrow starts early again."

The others groaned.

The next day, Bronze was out of his condo at about the same time as the previous day. Once more, he headed southwest to the Fire Water Bar for a late lunch, heavy on the booze, lighter on food, chatting once more with the bartender and manager for well more than an hour after he finished eating.

Then he ordered a cab and headed farther east, toward downtown.

Ashton had arranged for a transport to drop them off at Bronze's building, then meet them at the bar – and his teammates ensured that he was both well-disguised, and remained out of sight of any roving IPD officer.

So they were not caught off guard when their target departed in a taxi. They easily trailed him into downtown, and watched as he entered a posh and very exclusive, members-only dinner club.

"That's a problem," Ames noted. "I don't think anybody,

anywhere in the entire Imperial City Police Department, is gonna have an in for that place."

"I don't think we have to get in," Ashton said with a wicked smirk. "After I got a feel for some things yesterday, I made sure all the perp team leads were outfitted with some special security hacking apps. We don't have to go inside; once I get into the club's security system, we can all sit back and watch."

"And stay well out of sight in a parking garage," Compton realized.

"Yup. Lemme get started, here. Hugo, see if you can find us a nice out of the way spot to sit and watch," Ashton addressed Weaver, who was behind the wheel.

"Yes, sir!" the younger man exclaimed, enthused.

216

Bronze Gets Busy

"Annnd…there we are," Ashton said, after sitting silently in VR within the parked car for long moments. "Check out channel 112."

"Got it," came the chorus of responses within seconds.

Ashton had arranged a virtual room in channel 112, in which the interior of the exclusive dinner club was laid out as a three-dimensional map of sorts. The observer, once in the room, could zoom in on this or that part of the club and see what was happening.

It turned out there was more to the dinner club than dinner. A whole lot more.

There was a "spa" area on the second floor where members could sit in saunas, obtain massages and facials, and more. There was also a very special area in the very back of the spa that partook of a bordello, as it turned out, and should the member wish, he or she could make a selection and have the same escort – male or female, as the member desired – for the entire evening, performing the massage, the facial, and more intimate functions. The escort could even dress up and join the member for dinner. And on the third floor, there was also a small gambling casino where members could enjoy themselves; some were placing very high-stakes bets against the house. And, the investigators decided after watching for a while, winning with the proper frequency to demonstrate the house was not crooked.

"Which is something, I guess," Ames decided.

"Yeah. Considering the only legal part for a dinner club is

the restaurant area," Compton noted. "The spa area is legal, but not in conjunction with an eating establishment, and the brothel and casino are right out."

"Well, the casino would be legal if it were in a different zone," Weaver said.

"True," Compton agreed.

"Surprise, surprise," Ames murmured to the others in a disgusted tone, as they finally located their target. "Where else would Bronze be?"

"In the back, getting a massage from a scantily-clad prostitute," Compton observed.

"At least she's easy on the eyes, I guess," Weaver noted.

Just then, they watched as another person, a handsome young male, entered the massage room and joined the female. He was as scantily clad, and just as easy on the eyes, depending upon one's preferences.

"This is gonna get damn embarrassing, damn fast," Ames noted in a very quiet voice.

"Um, yeah," Compton agreed as the male prostitute pulled the drape completely off Bronze's naked body.

"Hoo boy," Ashton said, eyes widening as the female prostitute grinned and reached for certain parts of Bronze's anatomy. "Yeah, we're not voyeurs, just cops. Okay, hang on a sec, guys." He went into the hacking app's controls and set up a particular sequence, then promptly decreased the image resolution until all that could be seen were general bipedal forms. Then he placed colored markers on the heads of each – red for Bronze, blue for the female prostitute, and green for the male. "We'll see about busting the establishment once we're finished with surveillance."

"That's...better," Ames decided.

"Yeah," Compton and Weaver agreed. "We can see where

they are, and get the gist of what they're likely doing, without having to see details," Compton added.

"Thank God," Ames declared.

Bronze spent several hours with his companions, apparently massaging and being massaged, as well as engaging in quite a few sessions of intercourse of various sorts. The massage room opened up to a private sauna on one side, and a bedroom on the other, and the trio made copious use of all three rooms.

Along about seven in the evening, the Imperial City investigators noted the amorous activity slacked off, and within a quarter of an hour, all three were getting dressed. Ashton gingerly increased the resolution of the three-dimensional simulacrum, and they watched as Bronze offered each "escort" an arm, and they walked down a private escalator into the dining room together, taking an exclusive table in the corner.

The club's dinner menu for the evening – most such dinner clubs varied their offerings nightly, at least in Imperial City – was a Catalonian churrascaria, a rodizio barbacoa as the Catalonians termed it, or all-you-could-eat barbecue. Grilled meats of every kind were offered, along with suitable vegetable and starch sides common to the upper-class barrios on Catalonia. Legs, loins, chops, filets, and ribs of every conceivable animal – cow, pig, sheep, goat, chicken, tilapia, lobster, and several that were rather more exotic, including rattlesnake, kangaroo, and swan – were available from rare to medium well.

"Damnation!" Ashton exclaimed as he watched. "The dinner plates are the size of platters!"

"And they're filling 'em about as full," Weaver observed.

"Plus wine," Ames noted. "Two bottles already for just the

three of 'em."

"Okay, so obviously Bronze is a hedonist," Compton decided. "But I don't get it. How does...playboy...factor into assassin?"

The others turned to Ashton, who gazed back, surprised.

"Well?" Ames demanded. "We're waiting, Nick. You're the guy who's studied this jerk."

"I've never interviewed him, or even met him," Ashton protested.

"You still know more about him than anybody else," Ames pointed out.

"Okay, okay, I'll do my best to explain, as best I understand – or think I understand," he tried. "Josip Bronsky grew up on Wollaston, and came from a broken family. His mom abandoned him and his dad for a boyfriend – they weren't married to begin with, according to records – and his dad was a con man. So Bronsky grew up in one of the poorer neighborhoods, being trained how to run cons. He got good at it."

"Okay..." Ames murmured. "Not a great start."

"No. Near as I can tell, on one of his bigger cons, he inadvertently got caught up in some of the inter-system politics that they have on Wollaston, and ended up playing one side against the other to get out of a con gone wrong. The side who helped him apparently taught him a few things about how to make a person disappear – the target of the con was killed, and the murder was never solved; the girl who helped him on that con-gone-wrong has never been found, either – and..." Ashton shrugged. "Apparently he liked it."

"What, you mean he liked the money?" Ames asked, eyes wide. The other men just listened, likewise interested, but silent, listening to the byplay between the couple.

"Oh, I'm sure he does," Ashton said. "But no. I mean he got off on it, on the hit. He apparently likes killing."

"He's a psycho?!"

"By some definitions, definitely," Ashton said. "Exactly what it does for him, I got no idea, and I don't think I want to know. But I expect it factors into the whole hedonism thing, somehow. Maybe an adrenaline rush, maybe something kinkier; I dunno.

"Anyway, after that one con gone wrong, he had to get off Wollaston fast, so he waited for the heat to die down and suspicion to get cast on someone else, then he headed here, to Sintar. He disappeared for a year or so, then showed back up, going by the alias of Joey Bronze. Very sure of himself, very confident. And with more money. I can't prove it, but it's my suspicion that he managed to get in with someone who could teach him the ins and outs of professional assassinations. And since he apparently doesn't do anything by half measures, he got pretty good at it. Because that's when what I call the 'double-tap killings' started. No gunpowder residue, two clean shots to the back of the head with what therefore was likely an airgun, and no other real evidence."

"How many have there been?"

"In the few years since I've been on Sintar? At least half a dozen that I'm aware of. All politically motivated, all people who were trying to help the then-current Empress advance her reforms."

"So he's one of the IPD's trusted assassins."

"He's one of the Council's trusted assassins," Ashton corrected her. "They just launder it through the IPD."

"Damn."

"Exactly," Ashton agreed. "And he apparently gets paid rather nicely for the work." He waved a hand at the VR imagery.

"But isn't he…? I mean, surely he's putting some aside…"

"Why? Did you read his lips earlier? They're going to the casino after dinner. He likes to gamble. In fact, he plays it big – he knows his whole life is a gamble. If a series of assassinations go wrong for him, if things don't work like he wants 'em to – hell, if even one assassination goes too far south – his bosses will have no compunctions at all about taking him out and finding someone else. Look what happened to the guy who tried to take out Lee Carter, and got himself seen by Carter instead. And, judging by the double-taps, it was Bronsky who did it." Ashton shook his head. "No, Bronsky knows it's only a matter of time. He's just playing it out for all he's worth now, while he can."

"'Eat, drink, and be merry,' huh?" Compton offered then. "'For tomorrow we may die.'"

"Pretty much, yeah," Ashton agreed. "What he's not counting on is for us to stop his roll."

Bronze was very late returning to his condo – alone – that night. The next day, however, Bronze was up relatively early; his breakfast went up at around nine that morning, and he was out of the condo by ten.

Much to the investigators' surprise, he headed for a gym.

There, he hit the cardio equipment for a solid half-hour of interval training, then added resistance training to the mix, working his legs heavily.

He worked through the standard lunch rush, then knocked off, headed for the locker room and showered, then dressed and headed for…

…The Fire Water Bar.

A quick, healthy lunch of grilled chicken over pasta with marinara – and no alcohol, just iced water – refueled his body, and the investigators watched as Bronze relaxed and rested, chatting casually with the same bartender.

After a couple of hours, during which he sucked down a quantity of water and fruit juices, Bronze rose and headed out once more.

This time, his destination was an indoor shooting range, where he spent the rest of the afternoon going through the range's arsenal, practicing with numerous types of handguns and long guns.

Dinner was at a reasonable hour, at an upscale diner near his condo.

Then he headed home.

The lights went out on his floor at eleven that evening.

Evacuate!

In the middle of the surveillance of the Medved assassin team, Jones was headed into the ICPD headquarters building one morning, running late for the morning status briefing, when he saw an odd situation – someone was placing an object near the base of the building on the side alley. Since no notice of maintenance had gone out, he eased his pistol out of his concealed holster, hooked his badge on his lapel, and slipped up behind the man...who was not dressed in a city maintenance coverall.

"What are you doing?" Jones demanded to know.

The man spun, alarmed, saw the badge, and shoved Jones away, then leaped up and ran.

Jones twisted around, bringing his weapon to bear, and fired before the man could get to the opening of the alleyway. He went down with a cry, then lay on the pavement, groaning and clutching his hip.

Jones turned and glanced at the object the perp had been placing at what was, effectively, the top of the headquarters building's foundation. When he saw the countdown clock attached, his eyes went wide, and he popped an emergency message into channel 911.

"THIS IS LIEUTENANT INVESTIGATOR JONES! EVACUATE! EVACUATE! THERE'S A BOMB ON THE SIDE OF THE BUILDING! EVERYBODY OUT! *NOW!!*"

Ashton and the other members of the surveillance team had just completed their disguises for the day, including changing hair and eye color, adding facial hair for the men, and changes of clothing suited to the locations where they anticipated observing that day. Colonel Peterson had just entered to announce the morning status meeting in five, when Jones' emergency call came in through channel 911, annunciating on the building's speaker system.

"SHIT!" Peterson cried. "OUT! OUT! EVACUATE THE BUILDING! Let's go, people!"

The Team headed for the nearest exit without question.

As police officers poured out of the headquarters building, Jones took his injured perp into custody, handcuffing him and ensuring that the bullet wound wasn't too serious, while summoning both an emergency medic unit and a bomb squad in VR. Moments later, both had arrived, and he pointed the bomb squad at the device at the base of the building. Then he gave explicit instructions to the medics – whose identification he verified – as to how to restrain the would-be bomber, and sent him off to the hospital in a medical transport.

Moments later, the leader of the bomb squad walked up to Jones.

"I can see why you'd think what you did," the woman, heavily dressed in special armor, told Jones. "But it's a fake. That's not a bomb; there's no explosive, no electronic link, no nothing. Just an empty container, a battery, and a timer."

"Shit," Jones declared, dumbfounded. "The guy fled, got himself shot, refused questioning…he could have just said it was a prank and got off a lot…oh damn. Damn, damn, damn! NICK!" he yelled, shoving past the members of the bomb squad, as he searched the crowd of cops for Ashton.

On the far side of the building, Ashton moved away from

the structure per bomb protocols, and located a barricade pillar to use as a makeshift stool. The rest of the Team was clustered a little closer to the building – still out of the mandated danger zone for protocol, but close enough to study detail and try to figure out what was going on. Ashton sighed, stretched, and eased back on his stool, glancing at the sky.

"Nick?" someone asked behind him. "Nick? Is that you?"

He turned in instinctive response.

Three people stood there. Three people he recognized from IPD, who were not in uniform. Three people he recognized from Gorecki's "goon squad."

Kendall Raines, Jane Bowie, and Marc Olestri.

Shit, he thought. *Play it, Nick. Stay calm.*

"May I help you?" he asked politely, flashing the fake badge that Peterson had had made for him some time back, to match the rarely-used alias that she'd had created for him.

"Ashton? Dominick Ashton?" Bowie queried.

"No, I'm afraid you've mistaken me for someone else," Ashton said smoothly. "I'm known as Nick, yes, but I'm Nicholas Benton, captain investigator with ICPD." He pushed them the alias credentials through VR.

"Whoa," Raines remarked. "Well, the eyes an' hair are wrong, too, though, I guess…"

"What do you mean?" Ashton asked.

"He means you look kinda like this Ashton guy," Bowie said. "We're with IPD, plainclothes like you, and we're on the lookout for him. He's wanted."

"Oh really?" Ashton asked, thinking, *You crooked scum are nothing like me.* "What's he done?"

"He's murdered several people," Olestri declared. "We have evidence on him, we've just had a hard time tracking him down."

"Is that right? Well, I'll keep an eye out for this guy. In fact, would you like to come over and tell my supervisor, Colonel Peterson?"

"Uh, no, I don't think so," Olestri said, as the trio began to back off. "Don't want to bother the Colonel; he probably already knows through channels anyway."

"She. The Colonel is a she."

"...Oh."

"Well, if I see this Ashton guy, I'll be sure to grab him for you," Ashton said cheerily. "We'll have to clear this bomb threat first, of course. But then you probably know about that, huh? Through 'channels.'"

"Um, yes, right, of course," Raines said. "Well, we need to get back on the trail. We had somebody report he was over here, but I guess they just mistook you for him and all..."

"Right," Ashton said. "Good hunting."

And they were gone.

No sooner had the trio gotten out of sight than the Team, led by Jones, Ames, and Peterson, came running up.

"Nick! Nick! Are you okay?" Ames exclaimed.

"Shush, Cal," Ashton murmured. "I just got rid of some of Gorecki's people. Claiming to still have badges, let me note."

"Damn," Peterson said then, keeping her tone low. "Tim, you were right."

"Yeah," Jones said, as the others clustered around Ashton. "Nick, man, that bomb was a fake. It was all to empty the building so the Impies could pick you off."

"They tried," Ashton said. "Apparently they've issued a warrant for me for murder – maybe more than one – and they're likely hoping a regular citizen tips 'em off where I am." He paused, then met Colonel Peterson's eyes. "Fortunately, the

'Nick Benton' alias credentials you had made for me, and entered in the system, made for some really nice use, just now."

"And that also means that we might not want you running around as you, for the time being, until we can get this shit cleared up," Peterson replied.

"Nick, has your landlord given you any problems about the apartment?" Ames wondered then. "If there's a warrant for murder out for you, I mean, well…"

The others glanced at each other.

"She makes an excellent point," Gorski noted, as Demetrius nodded. "Maia, I think maybe some of us more senior folk need to run over there and make sure his landlord – or at least, the building manager – knows what's going on, at least to some degree. They need to know that Nick, here, is being framed, and that he's on good terms with us, else he might find himself unceremoniously evicted."

"Possibly straight into the IPD's hands," Demetrius added.

"That…is a very fair point, and a good idea," Peterson agreed. "Perhaps we three can take care of that while the various teams are surveilling our perps for the big T?" she added an oblique reference to the Throne; they were still on the street.

"That works," Demetrius decided. "Stefan?"

"I'm there, but I need to be at the Palace by noon. I'm meeting with the Major about something."

"Right," Peterson said. "Nick, is your team ready to go?"

Ashton glanced around; Jones flushed.

"I can be ready in five, soon as they let us back in the building," Jones said.

"Which they're doing now, so let's go, and everybody head out in ten," Peterson decreed. "I didn't have any real news for the morning briefing anyway."

By lunchtime, the three perp teams were on surveillance, Peterson and Demetrius were back in their offices at headquarters, Gorski was at the Palace West entrance, and Ashton's apartment had been secured.

Several days, total, of surveillance indicated to the full investigative team that their perps were more or less regular in their habits, at least for the time being – except for Bronze, and even he had a certain pattern to his days.

"Which makes sense," Ashton said as they analyzed the activities, after they all reconvened at headquarters, back in their standard office appearance. "They're not gonna be doing a lot of unusual stuff, or anything to draw attention to 'em. Not so soon after a major political hit like Medved."

"It makes sense to me," Detective Gorski decided; he had kibitzed on their discussion and analysis. "It sounds like we're ready to go pick them up and take them into Imperial custody." He cocked a querying eye at Ashton, who nodded.

"Tomorrow," the younger man decreed, "we take 'em all down."

"Good," Gorski said, and headed off to see what the latest information was from the Imperial Guard.

"Hm," Ashton hummed, after Gorski left. "Now to determine exactly how we're gonna do that. Looks like we might just have a nice area overlap here, and can pick 'em off one at a time, in quick sequence?"

"That's what I'm seeing," Rassmussen said.

"Me, too," Armbrand agreed. "But it might be good if we had a couple people on the others, while we're taking down the first, and so on. That way if something happens with the others, we know right away. Especially given that Bronsky is a little unpredictable in terms of timing."

"Yeah. But if one of 'em turns into a fighter or something, we're gonna need more than three or four guys," Rassmussen observed. "And we don't have enough on the Team to do all of that. Maybe we need to call in some more folks. Some beat cops would help out nicely, here."

"Good point. All right," Ashton ordered. "Here's how we'll do this: The general team will keep the same perp assignments, but Rog, you and Pete grab stunners and tranqs and come with me. I'll see if Colonel Peterson can assign us some beat cops for extra manpower and to stake out the perimeter. Oh, and somebody be ready to take care of the VR jammer."

"I can do that," Ames said.

"Good."

"You're the boss on this one," Rassmussen said. "You're doin' a great job, Nick. Me an' Rog are damn impressed. We may outrank you for the time being, but you're gonna make detective in no time, at this rate."

"If you say so. I feel…odd…about it," Ashton admitted with a sigh. "Especially after that encounter with Gorecki's henchmen the other day. I'm a lot more comfortable here than I ever was over at IPD, but…I still feel like an add-on, somehow. At least sometimes. You know what I mean?"

"Yeah, I know what you're saying," Rassmussen averred. "You know it's not true, though, right? We all claim you. You're one of us, man."

"I know. It's only…I dunno." Ashton shook his head. "Maybe ducking and dodging Gorecki and his goons is getting to me."

"It's okay. We'll worry about all that mess later, man," Armbrand decreed. "And we got your back on it in the meanwhile. Don't worry, Nick; we'll help you figure all of it out another time. Right now, we got three jobs to do. So we need to get with it."

"Yup," Ashton agreed. "Let's go."

Busting Asses

Ashton and Smith, in departmental uniform per a request from Imperial Guard Major Dunham, waited casually outside the Waffle Stomper diner about mid-morning, confident the rest of the team was ready. Kaplan, who made the bulk of her living in the "galaxy's oldest profession," tended to keep late nights, then go to bed in the wee small hours and break the fast late in the morning as a result.

The pair could see Susan Kaplan inside, through the diner windows, tucking away a fairly substantial but healthy breakfast, just like usual. When they saw her expression go blank while she paid her tab in VR, Ashton tensed.

"Get ready," he told the others over their private VR channel. "Here she comes. We want to get her out of the way fast and without causing a ruckus if we can. We don't want word getting back to the other two. Jam VR now."

"Roger, affirm," came back the responses.

Kaplan emerged from the front door of the Waffle Stomper. Ashton allowed her to clear the door by some twenty or twenty-five meters, preventing congestion in the doorway – or unwanted backup arriving from within the diner. Then he moved forward, Smith at his side.

But as soon as Kaplan saw the two uniforms making a beeline for her, she spun and sprinted for the nearest alley, intent on getting out the other side and losing them. Ashton broke into a sprint as well, Smith close behind.

"Stun her!" he ordered. "And make sure you've jammed her VR so she can't call for help! Then block the alley on both ends!

We don't need any complications from bystanders, let alone eyewitnesses that can carry the story back to her associates!"

"Did it five minutes ago!" Ames yelled.

"Already on it!" came the responses from Rassmussen and Weyand.

A stun dart zipped from Rassmussen's concealed position, driving unerringly into Kaplan's right glute. She stumbled with a cry of pain, then fell, her right leg collapsing under her as the dart discharged, negating her nervous system response below the dart's location. Smith and Ashton, who had dropped back slightly to allow for the dart, moved instantly to her side.

"You're under arrest, ma'am," Ashton declared, as Smith bent over her with a pair of hand cuffs, intent on restraining her. "Please come with us–"

"The hell you say!" Kaplan snapped, lashing out. She caught Smith with her long, sharp fingernails, raking them viciously across his face and drawing blood. Simultaneously, she kicked at Ashton with her good leg, missing his crotch with her foot only because Ashton, farther away than Smith, saw it coming and turned, catching the blow with the side of his hip.

But when she kept on trying to kick and scratch – missing both of them, because Ashton and Smith had both quickly gotten out of range – Ashton had had enough.

"OW! Damn! Back off, back off, John!" he ordered, then added, "TRANQ HER! And get that containment set, people!"

Two college students wandered past the far end of the alley and heard screams and shouts emerging from it, as well as the sounds of flesh hitting flesh.

"What the hell?!" one of them said. "Jaime, there's a mugging going on in there!"

"Think we oughta go help, Manolo?" Jaime wondered.

"I dunno, I–"

"Everything is under control," an Imperial City Police officer said, stepping out from the shadows of the building and barring their way. "I'd advise moving along."

"But what's going on?" Manolo wondered.

"Some of our investigators are apprehending a dangerous criminal," the officer replied. "Involved in a murder. Unfortunately, the criminal is fighting back, so we've established a perimeter to ensure no civilians are injured."

"Oh," Jaime said then, uncertain. "Um, maybe we need to just leave, Manolo."

"Uh...I think that sounds good, Jaime," Manolo agreed with a shiver, as a banshee scream emerged from the alleyway.

"That is, indeed, a good plan, gentlemen," the officer said.

They went.

"BASTARDS! You damn sons of bitches!" Kaplan snarled, twisting onto her right side and slashing her nails in Ashton's direction again. "I'll tear you apart before I 'come with you'! You don't get–"

The tranquilizer dart caught her in her other glute, and she screamed in a blend of pain, surprise, and rage, continuing to fight.

"SHIT!" she shouted. "THAT HURT, DAMMIT! Let me alone, you shithead assholes!"

When she couldn't crawl because of her stunned leg, Kaplan pulled herself toward the investigators with her arms and remaining leg, trying to reach them with her clawed fingernails. But not being idiots, Smith and Ashton had immediately backed off, out of the way of the tranq dart, and remained out of her reach. The pair just kept backing away as she crawled, waiting for the tranquilizer drug to take effect.

"I ain't done nothin'!" Kaplan continued to scream, kicking, punching, and scratching. "You don't have a damn thing on me!"

"The hell you say," Ashton said. "We have you dead to rights."

"NO! I don't – d-don't...I don't...you don't have any... anyth-thing..." Abruptly her head wobbled badly, and her left leg went limp. "Oh d-damn...I don' f-feel too go-good..." She tried to pull herself toward Ashton with her arms, but they were starting to get shaky, too. She fought the sensation with all her strength, but there was no overcoming the tranquilizer used in police dart guns. At last she slumped to the pavement and lay still.

"Whoo..." Smith sighed. "Finally."

"No shit. Whole damn lotta that," Ashton agreed. "Damn, I thought that tranq would never kick in! Johnny, are you okay, pal? She nailed your face but good, man."

"Pun intended," Smith said with a rueful chuckle, as he drew the back of his hand across his face. It came away covered in blood, as more blood dripped from his nose and chin onto his uniform tunic. "Ow. Shit, that stings! I hate head wounds. They bleed like crazy." He paused, then looked up at Ashton. "She kicked you pretty good there, too. You okay?"

"Aw, I'm fine. I'll have a bruise on my ass, but I'm okay – I've had worse from a fall down a flight of stairs. She's not that big, an' she didn't have good leverage or angles anyway, on the ground like that."

"That's good. We need our leader to finish off his strategy and bring these turds in."

"Yeah. But she'd shaped her nails into points, so she could carve people up, and I'm worried about that face of yours. Hey, any of you guys rated for first aid? Johnny needs some patching up, here, before he bleeds out or something." Ashton went through his pockets, looking for anything that could be used to mop the blood that still dripped from Smith's face.

"Yep," Armbrand said through VR, as Ames released the jamming. "I see it."

"Kinda hard to miss, what with all that blood," Rassmussen commented, and everyone snorted to stifle laughter. It broke the tension nicely, and everyone relaxed a little.

"Shut up, you," Armbrand said, his grin audible. "Lemme get the kit outta the transport and I'll be right over to tend 'im, Nick."

"I'll go with, and grab the stretcher for the perp," Weyand noted. "Get the spitfire handcuffed, just in case, guys. Damn, but she was fightin' the tranq. We do not need her throwing it off and waking up!"

"Good point. Nick?" Smith said, holding out the cuffs he'd tried to use earlier. "Can you get that? I got so much blood in my eyes, I can't really see to do it."

"She didn't get an eye with those nails, did she?" Ashton worried, accepting the cuffs and restraining their perp.

"Nah. The brow bone deflected 'er, but that's the place that's bleeding into my eyes. It's just some nasty scratches. I've had worse from Colonel Peterson's cat; it's just, it's my face, so it's all bleeding like crazy. You know?"

"Yeah. Good. It doesn't sound that serious, then. Keep it clean, close it up, and it prob'ly won't even scar," Ashton decided. "Somebody bring the car around, and we'll deliver the damn she-cat to the Imperial Guard."

Moments later, Kaplan was loaded into the back of the transport, and two of the beat cops assigned to their operation were hauling her away, in the general direction of the Palace.

"Okay, that's as much as I know how to do, at this point," Armbrand said, sitting back and studying Smith's bandage-patched face. "At least I got it stopped bleeding, cleaned out, and cleaned up." He shrugged. "Rich, take John off to IUH for some medical attention, please. There's some places in that mess that really need stitches, and I'm sure he could use an antipathogen, there. No telling what was under her nails."

"Right," Ashton affirmed, as Weyand took one of the arcade carts and headed off with Smith beside him. "The rest of us, let's get reset. Beckham arrives for lunch in a couple hours."

Derek Beckham was due to arrive at the Waffle Stomper diner for lunch around noon, or about two hours after Kaplan had left it…though, unbeknownst to Beckham, only about an hour and a half after she was unceremoniously carried away, unconscious and in custody. Based on the team's undercover reconnoiter, it seemed he wasn't such a great cook; he ate out for at least ninety percent of his meals except breakfast, was seen purchasing cold cereal and milk in a grocery for that, and the Waffle Stomper was one of his favorite haunts, despite his expensive tastes. It was cheap, it was quick, it was reasonably good food, and it was long on safety for people who lived on the wrong side of the law.

"Okay, he's on the way," Ashton told the others through the team's VR channel, after getting the message through the separate reconnoiter channel. "Weaver and Compton just checked in."

"They're trailing, right?" Rassmussen asked. "With Rich and John gone, we need them for backup on this guy. If he fights the way Kaplan did, we're in trouble – he's a helluva lot bigger than she was."

"No shit, and no argument," Ashton said, "and yes, they are.

Alan is gonna be my arrest partner once he ditches the hoodie jacket he's using to hide his face and uniform tunic, and Hugo is gonna handle the VR jammer." He paused, then asked, "Any other questions?"

"Nope," came multiple replies. "We're good, Nick," Armbrand added.

"Good. Remember, we grab him just around the corner as he's headed inbound, so hopefully we'll be out of sight of anybody who might rat on us. Especially after takin' down the banshee."

Beckham was looking forward to lunch. The Waffle Stomper had been where he had first met Susan Kaplan, nearly ten years ago; she was as much of a looker now as she had been then, and he had become one of her best and most regular clients. They had soon become good friends, and that was why he had brought her in on Joey Bronze's little operation. Sometimes the pair met at the diner for what she called brunch, though it was anything but what the upscale restaurants served as such. But for some reason, his recent cons had not panned out as he had expected, and he was a little short on cash for those upscale restaurants as a consequence, so the old standby diner would do.

He didn't expect to see SuzieQ at the Waffle Stomper today, though; they had made the considered decision to avoid being seen in public together for a few weeks, to allow any activity around the assassination to die down, and avoid any accidental recognition. He had come somewhat later than his usual time for lunch as a consequence, though not by much.

So he wasn't really expecting what came next.

Beckham was right around the corner from the diner when

he was suddenly accosted by two uniformed police officers.

"Come with us, Mr. Beckham," said the tall, dark-haired cop. "Put your hands behind your back, please. You're under arrest."

"I think there's been a little misunderstanding, guys," Beckham said with an ingratiating smile, even as he attempted to raise help via VR. It was blocked, to his dismay. As the brunet cop pulled one of Beckham's forearms behind his back, the ginger cop enclosed that wrist in handcuffs, quickly capturing Beckham's other wrist in the restraint, as well. "I'm on your side."

"Look closer," the ginger-haired cop snapped.

"Huh?" Beckham responded, badly confused by this point. He had expected the Imperial Police to leave him alone, all things considered.

"I'm Imp City P.D.," the redhead pointed out.

"He's not," Becker said, shrugging a shoulder at the brunet. "He's Impie. I recognize him from the Imperial Police Headquarters, couple years back. And I'm on good terms with those guys."

"Not any more. I'm with Imp City now," the dark-haired cop replied, cold as ice. He pointed to the Imperial City Police Department patch on his shoulder. "So I'm not one of 'those guys.'"

"Oh," Beckham said lamely. His heart sank.

Much to the arrest team's relief, Beckham didn't try to fight; he came with them quietly. In short order the same two beat cops who had carted away an unconscious Kaplan were departing with Beckham in the same transport.

"Heh. The male of the species is less dangerous than the female, it appears," Armbrand joked.

"Thank God," Ashton said, sincere in his gratitude. "I wasn't keen on taking that big guy down. He stays in shape, and it shows."

"But you could've," Ames averred. "I've sparred with you, Nick. You're good."

"Yeah, I could've. But it wouldn't have been fun." Ashton shrugged. "I prefer using my brain to take 'em down...or out."

"Now what?" Rassmussen wondered.

"Lemme double-check the tail," Ashton said, his expression temporarily going blank as he contacted the remaining two members of the team, who were undercover and tailing Josip Bronsky, a.k.a. Joey Bronze. Moments later, he resumed an active demeanor. "Change of venue," he decreed. "Just like we figured, we're headed six blocks over to the Fire Water Bar, as fast as we can get there. Pack it up, people, and let's move out, five minutes ago."

Rich Weyand was back in plenty of time for the last apprehension, and Ashton sent him a call in VR to let him know of the change of venue. As he walked up to the others, Ashton turned to him.

"So how's Johnny?"

"ER doc said he'd be okay," Weyand said. "He had some nasty cuts, and the ER doc brought in a cosmetic surgeon to do the stitches; said it wouldn't scar that way. Then they pumped him fulla anti-everything, bumped up the nanites, and sent him home with some prescription painkillers; by the time the adrenaline from the fight wore off, and it bein' his face, he was kinda hurting. We notified Detective Gorski and Colonel Peterson, an' both of 'em made sure he was okay, then told him to go home and crash. I walked him to the people-mover and saw him onto it, then came on back. The people-mover station is in the arcade level of his apartment building, so all he has to do is get off the car, get on the elevator, ride to his floor, and unlock his door."

"That sounds good," Ashton said. "Sorry he's out of the tag, but he'll be okay, and that's the important part, right now. Okay, boys an' girls, let's get set up for this last one. Rich, you wanna help me take down Bronze?"

"Oh HELL yes!" Weyand responded.

With the Team in place outside, Ashton entered the bar and nosed about. When the hostess approached him, he looked up.

"May I help you, Officer?"

"Nah, I'm looking for somebody," Ashton replied.

"Someone in the pub? Are you meeting someone?"

"You might say that," Ashton replied, voice dry as dust. "I'd like to speak with the bartender, please."

"Right this way."

"Josip Bronsky? Who the hell is that?" the bartender asked, when Ashton inquired about the hit man.

"You might know him as Joey Bronze, or J.B.," Ashton noted.

"Uh, nope, never heard of him," the bartender averred. His gaze shot across the room.

"Perhaps you've seen him," Ashton said, calm and undeterred. He showed the other man a copy of Bronze's mug shot, printed from the ICPD's wanted files...then watched as the bartender's eyes flickered. *Uh-huh,* he thought. *Bingo. That should do the trick.*

"N-nope, never seen the guy," the bartender doubled down, then shrugged. "That doesn't mean he doesn't come in here, but let's face it, man – I stay damn busy, back here." He patted the bar.

"I'm sure you do," a bland Ashton said placidly. "Should you see him, however, please contact the ICPD at once. This man is extremely dangerous."

"Uh, okay. If you're lookin' for him, though, I expect he's long since left the planet."

"What's the problem here, Officer?" another man said as he walked up.

"Officer Benton with ICPD, sir," Ashton said smoothly, turning to the new man. "Just asking a few questions. And you are?"

"Brandon Travers. I'm the manager here."

"Of course. Have you seen this man in the pub?" Ashton asked, holding up the mug shot once more. "You might know him as Josip Bronsky, Joey Bronze, or simply J.B."

Travers threw a swift, almost unnoticeable glance at the bartender, then at the clock on the wall, before he looked back at the photo. Ashton noticed that Travers relaxed slightly when he saw the clock. *Good. We're timing this just right,* he thought.

"No, sir, Officer. I don't recognize the man. I doubt he's a frequenter of this establishment, if you're looking for him."

"You might be surprised." A slight, cold smile crossed Ashton's face, and the two other men hid winces. "Should you see him, please contact me at once." He handed small business cards to the two men in lieu of contacting them through VR; he didn't want these two to have anything on him that they could pass on to others, and the contact information was for Colonel Peterson, at her insistence. The two men nodded, and he headed for the exit.

As soon as he exited the pub, Ashton tagged the others in VR via voice.

"They knew him, they just wouldn't admit to it. So we

probably want to hit a sting operation in the bar later, separate from picking up Bronze; somebody ping Stefan, so he can pass that information on to Major Dunham."

"Done, Nick," Rassmussen replied. "He says he's on it, and not to worry about it. He's gonna take care of it himself. Maybe with Dunham's help, later."

"Good. Now, Bronze picked this bar because it's relatively high-end, has good food, and it only has two entrances – the front entrance and the kitchen entrance. I scoped that out thoroughly the other day. He chose it because of that very thing – he figured it would be to his advantage, as it would be easy to keep track of the comings and goings. Plus, whichever door the police enter, he exits the other way. But we're not going back in; I got his buddies at the bar thoroughly spooked. The bartender and the manager are likely to warn him off, so we'll let 'em. But we'll have people at both entrances."

"Which one do you think he'll take, Nick?" Ames asked him.

"Bronze is cocky; he's gotten away with this for a long time. I expect the bartender and the manager to want to hustle him out the kitchen entrance, so you guys back there, stay alert."

"But he's really going to…?" Jones pressed.

"Come out the front, like everything is perfectly normal," Ashton said. "He thinks he can bluff his way through all this, or that he's so good, we'll miss him, or don't have enough evidence to book him, let alone hold him. He thinks Gorecki or one of his goons will come bail him out. He doesn't understand – yet – that it isn't us he has to worry about." Ashton glanced about. "Now let's get in position, and out of sight."

"All over it, boss-man."

Joey Bronze was looking forward to lunch. It was a late lunch, but he preferred being a night owl, then sleeping in, and getting out and about later in the day, unless a hit was in the works. The Fire Water Bar had great pub food, and it was late enough that he could get a few brews with lunch and nobody would think twice.

So, confident in his cover and with his mind on the menu and what he felt like eating, he didn't notice the unusual number of people around the pub that day. He would regret that later.

Bronze entered the Fire Water Bar about three in the afternoon and headed straight for the bar.

"Hey, Dirk."

"Hey, Joey, you been a bad boy?" Dirk the bartender asked, waving Brandon Travers over.

"No more 'n usual. Why do you ask, Dirk? I got a guilty look on my face?"

"PD's been asking around after ya."

"Which PD?"

"Imp City!" Travers said, walking up. "They were in here maybe thirty, forty-five minutes ago."

"No kidding."

"Yeah, I told 'em I thought you left the planet. Ain't seen you around."

"Ah," Bronze said, unperturbed. "Long gone by now, then. Any word from the Cool Breeze Pub?"

"Not that I've heard," Travers said.

"Okay, I'll head over there instead, then. Thanks for the heads up, Dirk." He set a ten-credit coin on the bar.

"No problem, Joey," the bartender said, pocketing the coin.

"Come on, I'll take you out the kitchen entrance," Travers said, turning and waving Bronze to follow.

"Relax, Bran," Bronze said. "This ain't my first time around the block. Just lay low, don't say anything, and this will blow over like it always does. They don't have anything on me except suspicions."

And Bronze left the way he had come.

Bronze got to the corner and was about to head for the elevators to the arcade level, when he found himself between two uniformed Imperial City Police officers. He berated himself for his inattentiveness, but kept his cool. Chances were, he thought. he could slide out of this one like usual, if he played his cards right.

"Josip Bronsky?" the dark-haired one said.

"Yes, Officer?"

"Come with us, please."

"Am I under arrest, Officer?"

"Yes, Mr. Bronsky. Come with us, please."

"Of course, Officer."

Joey Bronze was the quietest of the lot, but it turned out that he wasn't the threat that day. Nor were any of the assassin team they took into custody.

Marc Olestri, one of Stash Gorecki's goons that had, with two others, tried to apprehend Ashton during the ICPD headquarters bomb threat – except Olestri was intelligent enough to be a certified shuttle pilot, unlike most of the rest – happened to be coming out of the Fire Water Bar just as Ashton and Weyand took Bronze into custody nearby.

Wait a damn minute, he thought. *Ain't that – that's Bronze. Oh hell, that's bad. But that's – SHIT! That's that bastard Stash has been hunting for, Nick Ashton! The* real *Ashton! I need to talk to the boss about this one!*

Ducking his head, Olestri got as far away as he could as fast as he could, attempting to get out of reach of the VR suppression field, then called Stash.

"Yeah, Stash, I'm sure. It was Ashton. He was in a fake ICPD uniform and everything. It ain't like they're that much different from the IPD uniforms, ya know. So he was fairly easy to recognize this time."

"Yeah, I know, Marc. I'm not surprised. We've known he was out there, he's just proven a damn bugbear to get hold of. He's a smart one, and he's got help. What was he doing?"

"Hold onto your hat. Taking Joey Bronze into custody."

"Shit."

"Yeah. Lotta that. Whole lotta that. Whatcha gonna do?"

"Two things. First, tell Stanier and Kershaw. Second, put out the word to keep an eye out for Ashton around all the ICPD precincts, 'cause if he's not working for 'em, he's gotta be working on contract with 'em. And we'll set up a hefty three-figure credit reward for locating 'im, an equally hefty four-figure credit reward for takin' 'im out. Third, we gotta figure out where they're holding Bronze and see if we can spring 'im."

"Hey, count me in. I'm gonna go back and see if I can watch where they head off to."

"Good man. Don't forget rehearsals tonight."

"I won't."

"George, we need some apps pushed to the guys," Gorecki told Imperial Police Chief George Stanier within five minutes of the contact from Olestri.

"What sort of apps, and why?" Stanier replied.

"Look, this Ashton kid – either he's trained to become a master of disguise, or he's got a master of disguise workin'

246

with – or for – him."

"Wait. So we still don't know where he's working?"

"Nah. We figure he's either put out a shingle of his own, or he's workin' with Imp City. Right now, my boys are leaning pretty heavy toward him workin' on his own, but he may be contracted with Imp City. All our efforts to find him on their records, or in their people, seem to fall through. And even though we ginned up that murder warrant on 'im, nobody seems to wanna turn him in."

"I see. Go on."

"Well, he's got some damn good disguises. If he's in disguise, you basically gotta have slept with him to recognize him."

"Watch saying that around Kershaw. That's how his niece got close to Ashton. And Kershaw dotes on her."

"Damn. I didn't know she slept with him."

"Way I understood it, yeah."

"Okay, I'll watch what I say around him. But Ashton is just…damn, George. It's next to impossible to spot him. Unless he *wants* you to spot him, I guess."

"Huh. So he's an undercover artist, has one working for him, or is training to become one."

"That's my take, yeah."

"What I don't understand is, why would he have one working for him?"

"Best I can tell, he's got his own little gang," Stash noted. "I wouldn't be surprised if he's not trying to set himself up, or already done it. Like I said, that's what my people think."

"Hm. There's an interesting take. He's set up as a private investigator, eh? With an actual team of enforcers? Maybe we can sway him into working with us, instead of against us."

"Maybe. I dunno. But he's gettin' cocky, I think. He actually showed up as himself, in uniform, to take Bronze into custody, I guess for the ICPD."

"His mistake, then. Imp City Police won't be able to hold Bronze – they never can; they're not good enough to get anything on him – and then we'll send Bronze after Ashton. I'm not so keen on the notion of bringing him to our side that I'm willing to risk it if he won't. Or if he changes his mind later. He's always got the attempted theft of the Empress' Sigil in his head, after all."

"Makes sense to me, boss."

"So what do you want?"

"We need some sorta, like, pattern recognition," Gorecki brainstormed. "Something that we can put to work on a face in VR that'll look through all the makeup and beards and wigs and hairpieces and shit and identify the real face under it."

"Hm," Chief Stanier said, intrigued. "That should be doable. Let me check; we might already have something like that in house. If not, it shouldn't take long to gin one up. Give me ten minutes to check, and I'll ping you with whatever we've got, to hand out to your people."

"Sounds good, boss."

"Meantime, make sure whoever you've got on Bronze's arrest gets over there to put a wrench in the works."

"Already goin' down."

"Good."

But by the time Marc Olestri got back to the scene of the arrest, they were all gone.

Despite their best efforts, the Imperial Police Headquarters never did figure out what happened to Joey Bronze.

Which a certain former accomplice on Wollaston would have thought singularly appropriate, had she been alive.

Interrogations

Gorski came to Ashton's desk as Ashton worked on the after-action report.

"Nick, son, have you ever seen an Imperial interrogation?"

Ashton glanced up.

"No; why?"

"We've been invited to witness the interrogations of the perps you and your team picked up so handily. That way, the ICPD can close the murder case on our books. More than likely, those interrogations will be followed by executions, and we've been invited to witness those, too. I thought you might like to see the conclusion of the investigation."

"Sure," Ashton said with a nod. "That sounds good."

"Some of it isn't likely to be pretty. Can you handle that?"

"I guess I need to get used to it, don't you think, Stefan?"

"Probably, yes. I just want you to be prepared."

"Okay. What's the schedule?"

"I think it's going to be one in-depth interrogation each day for the next three. Starting this afternoon, in about an hour, hour and a half. If you want to go, we should probably get started."

Ashton stood and reached for his jacket, hanging on the back of his desk chair.

"Let's go, then," he declared.

The pair arrived at the Imperial Park West Palace entrance. The receptionist recognized Detective Gorski, but asked for Ashton's name and his relationship to Gorski, who explained the loose partnership/protégé aspect. The receptionist nodded, then placed a call.

"Your point of contact will arrive shortly, Detective, Captain Investigator," the receptionist said. "If you would please have a seat in our waiting area, he'll be right out."

The pair sat down and waited.

It was only about ten minutes before a tall blond man in the Imperial Guard uniform and wearing the Sintar Cross, entered the reception area and came straight to them.

"Hello, Detective Gorski!" he said, shaking that worthy's hand. "I take it you're here to witness the interrogations?"

"We are," Gorski said. "Major, I have someone you should meet. This is my protégé, Captain Investigator Dominick Xavier Ashton. Nick, this is Major Robert Allen Dunham IV."

"Very pleased to meet you, Captain Ashton," Dunham said, as the two men shook hands. "I've heard a good bit about you from your mentor, here."

"And I, you, from the same source, sir," Ashton said with a smile.

"Heh. You show a great deal of promise, Ashton."

"Thank you, sir. I do try very hard. I'm pleased to make your acquaintance."

"Likewise. Let's get started; we don't want to be late. My sister wouldn't like it if we hold things up."

Dunham led the two men into an observation room. It had a one-way glass window on one wall, looking into what was patently an interrogation room. There was a table with handcuff loops on it, and two straight-backed chairs, one on each side. One was bolted to the floor and appeared somewhat larger than the other.

"The chair is equipped with sensors, Captain Ashton," Dunham said, seeing the direction of his gaze. "In essence, it is a highly sophisticated version of what used to be called a lie detector. There will be a technician and a physician in here, monitoring its readouts. We'll see what comes next."

"Gotcha," Ashton said.

"Please excuse me," Dunham said then. "I'll be back before the interrogation starts, but for now, I must see to Her Majesty."

"Your sister," Ashton murmured the addendum with an impish grin.

Dunham heard. He shot the briefest of answering grins back at the younger man, then he was gone.

A few minutes later, another Imperial Guardsman entered, along with a man dressed in a dark suit and carrying a small valise.

"Hello," the guardsman said. "I'm Lieutenant Peter Cox, and this is Dr. Morton Galway. You must be the detectives from the Imperial City Police Department." In the interrogation room, visible behind Cox, two guards brought in Susan Kaplan, clad in a prison coverall, and handcuffed her wrists and ankles to the "lie detector" chair.

"Yes," Gorski said. "I'm Stefan Gorski, and this is my protégé, Nick Ashton."

"Pleased to meet you," Cox said, and he and Galway shook hands with the investigators. "We'll be getting under way in a little bit. Oh, and just so you know, when She comes in here, you don't need to stand. Just greet her quietly. She expects we'll all be paying attention to the interrogation." He glanced at a padded chair beside the one Dr. Galway was settling into, and Gorski and Ashton stared at each other.

"Oh my," Gorski murmured in dismay. "I wasn't expecting that."

Moments later, Dunham was back.

"It's all set," he said. "We'll be getting started in just a few minutes."

Just then, two Imperial Guardsmen entered the interrogation room. One placed a padded chair against the wall beside the door, then they took alert positions in the corner, flanking the padded chair.

Abruptly, Her Majesty, Empress Ilithyia II, entered the room and sat in the padded chair.

"Ms. Kaplan. Last Monday night, a young woman in my employ was murdered when she reached her apartment building. We know without any doubt that you were one of the spotters. We got your DNA profile from the gum you discarded in a trash bin on the arcade. Someone is going to come in soon and ask you about your role, who you were working for, and who the shooter was. You will answer these questions or suffer the consequences of your refusal."

Ashton was shocked and aghast at the stream of profanity which spewed from Kaplan's mouth then, all directed at the Empress.

"Fuck you, bitch! And fuck your little redheaded bitch, too. Friend of yours, huh? Well, too fucking bad. I know my rights, and I'm not going to answer any of your goddamn questions. So you can just go fuck yourself."

"Very well."

The Empress stood and turned to the Imperial Guard officer standing by the door, who opened and held it for her. Empress Ilithyia II issued orders before she exited the room.

"Drug the answers out of her, then execute her. I'll send

down an Imperial Decree authorizing it."

A horrified Kaplan threw herself against her restraints.

"WAIT!" she screamed.

But it was too late to change her mind; the Empress was gone.

Moments later, the Empress entered the observation room and took her seat directly behind Cox and Galway, in front of Gorski and Ashton.

"Your Majesty," the room's occupants murmured, nodding to her.

"Please continue," she responded, waving off their courtesies. "Dr. Galway, I fear your services are required in the interrogation."

"Yes, ma'am," Galway said. He caught up the handle of his small valise, rose, and left the room, appearing moments later with the interrogator in the interview room.

"Lieutenant Cox, are we ready?" the Empress asked.

"Yes, ma'am."

"Good. Please notify Captain Mercer to begin the interrogation."

The first act of the interrogation was to drug Kaplan. It required two Guardsmen and her shackles to restrain her for the administration, a fact which didn't surprise Ashton in the least. He wanted to warn them to watch out for her fingernails. She screamed and cursed the entire time.

In despite of the drugs, however, the interrogation did not go well at all; Kaplan fought it the whole way. The first injection of the truth drugs did nothing – it simply wasn't strong enough to overcome her willpower.

The second dose of drug unlocked her mouth, but still did

not generate the desired information. Instead, it seemed to ramp up her ability to curse. The profanity which spewed from her mouth in those moments, like some bizarre, fouled artesian well, appalled and dismayed the young investigator. Ashton had never heard anyone make those kinds of statements before.

And there are some curse words she's using I've never even heard of, he thought, watching. *Damn. And I'm no innocent where that's concerned. I think I'm glad Cal isn't here to hear all that. She'd blush so red she'd be purple.*

When the second dose still did not elicit the necessary response, the interrogator nodded again at Dr. Galway.

"There's no coming back from this one, Captain."

"I understand, Doctor. Proceed."

Ashton knew what that meant. He was about to see someone lose her mind, though hopefully not until they had some answers from her.

He felt a slight movement at his side, and glanced down: Gorski's fingers were wrapped in a death-grip on the arms of his chair, and were turning white with the force.

Uh-oh, Ashton thought. *If that's Stefan's reaction to what's coming, it's gonna be really, really bad.*

It was.

Moments later, the key question arose. Kaplan, no longer able to stop herself, finally answered.

"Who was the shooter for last Monday night's murder?" Mercer asked.

"Joey," a disoriented Kaplan responded.

"Joey Bronze?"

"Yes."

There it was. The nail in the coffin. His accomplice had fingered Josip Bronsky, a.k.a. Joey Bronze, for the murder of

Vasilisa Medved.

Moments later, she fingered the other accomplice.

"Who introduced you to Joey Bronze?"

"Derek."

"Did Derek Beckham introduce you to Joey Bronze to be the second spotter last Monday night?"

"Yes."

As the interrogator, Captain David Mercer of the Imperial Guard, gradually drew the details of payment from Kaplan, Ashton watched as the woman grew paler, finally turning an ashen gray. Her dilated eyes rolled wildly, somehow managing to look furiously angry in despite of that – Ashton was sure her real feelings showed there – and spittle dribbled from the corners of her mouth. Her breathing became shallow and irregular.

Still she continued monosyllabic answers in a gurgling voice, prompted by Mercer's questions.

Her lips turned blue, and her body slumped farther and farther in the chair. Abruptly she convulsed briefly, and there was the sudden splatter of viscous fluids impacting something solid. Captain Mercer's nostrils flared, and his face took on an expression of mild disgust, but he kept going, and Ashton realized that Kaplan had lost control of her bodily functions. A yellow-brown sludge could now be seen dripping from her chair and running down her legs, puddling beneath her and staining her prison coverall.

Kaplan managed a couple more coherent answers, then started to babble random nonsense. Within seconds, she was making animal-like grunts, growls, and moans, and all semblance of lucid speech departed…as did the expression in her eyes, which were now dilated so much that the irises could barely be seen.

Moments later she vomited down the front of her coverall, and her body slumped completely, head lolling, eyes empty of even her anger, her mouth still moving, though nothing came out.

"That's all you're going to get, Captain. She's gone," Dr. Galway said.

"All right, Doctor. Carry out the execution."

The doctor administered one more medication to Kaplan, and ten seconds later her body sat limp and white as her vacant, staring eyes glazed over. Galway felt for a pulse, then turned to Mercer.

"She's dead."

The Empress rose and left the observation room, accompanied by her brother, Major Dunham. Neither of them spoke a word.

Mere moments later, Ashton's stomach lurched.

He leaped to his feet and ran out the door, down to the nearest men's room. He ducked inside, slammed open the door of an empty stall, and threw up into the toilet.

Less than a minute later, Gorski entered the restroom. He stood nearby and waited as Ashton purged his belly.

"Better?" he asked, when Ashton's retching had ceased.

"N-not really," Ashton murmured. "I...there are times, I guess, when having the vivid imagination required to do this job is a curse, not an aid."

"There are, indeed," Gorski agreed. "Imagined yourself inside that head, did you?"

"Yeah. A little too well, I kind of suspect. I saw this look in her eyes, once she was forced into answering the questions, and..." He shook his head. "I don't identify with her, please understand, Stefan. I just..."

"No, I get it," Gorski murmured, producing a small bottle of water from somewhere and handing it to him. "Here. Rinse your mouth and spit, then sip. No, I've been where you are, too, son. When Kaplan reacted like she did to the Empress herself, I knew it was going to be…bad. And I was worried about you, about the Empress, about…well." The older man sighed. "Some people just don't seem to understand that the laws apply to them, too. And they almost always end up like… that."

"Get used to it, huh?"

"No. I don't think you ever get used to it. You just try to realize that they were given a choice, and they made the wrong choice. Every step along their life's path, they had a choice. And chose wrong. Every. Damn. Time."

Ashton could only nod.

The next morning it was time to interrogate Beckham.

All the same people were involved, and they followed the same procedure. Gorski and Ashton showed up at the Imperial Park West Palace entrance, Major Dunham was summoned and led them to the same observation room adjacent to the same interrogation room – which had been thoroughly cleaned overnight. Ashton would have hated to have that job. *Though,* he admitted, *somebody has to do it. I wonder if Kaplan had any family.*

Lieutenant Cox and Doctor Galway were there, as well, and everyone greeted one another in a subdued but friendly fashion.

"We're gonna give this one a chance to play nice," Cox told them. "He's gonna get to watch the recording of the interrogation in immersive VR, then we're gonna give him the opportunity to cooperate."

"That will hopefully help," Gorski decided.

"Yeah," Ashton agreed. "When we busted the three perps, Beckham and Bronsky were relatively quiet, but Kaplan fought like a she-demon."

"Is that so?" Cox said, perking up. "Were you one of the arresting officers?"

"I was, yes."

"Nick, here, led the arrest team," Gorski explained. "For all three perps."

"That's promising," Dr. Galway finally interjected. He had been listening with some interest, and now chose to speak up. "I'm one of the Palace staff physicians, and occasionally I have to do something like this, but I can't say I ever like it. I swore to protect life, not take it. That said, when someone has done something as heinous as these three, I tend to view it as protecting other life against the toxicity of these lives." He shrugged. "It's still hard. But at least I can go home at night and tell myself I upheld my oath in some measure."

Moments later, Beckham was led into the interrogation room and shackled in the "lie detector" chair. Captain Mercer of the Imperial Guard entered.

"We have opened up one VR channel to you. There is a recording there you may wish to view before your interview."

Then he turned and left the room.

Beckham's face went blank in the classic non-expression of one in full immersive VR, as he watched the recording.

When he emerged from VR, he was pale and patently shocked. Beckham stared at the arms of the chair to which he was cuffed in something like dread.

That was when another Guardsman entered with a padded chair, closely followed by the Empress. She sat and gazed at Derek Beckham for long moments in silence. Seeming taken aback and frightened, he stared back with blanched face and frozen body.

"Mr. Beckham," she finally broke the silence.

"Your Majesty," Beckham said politely, bowing his head.

"Mr. Beckham, someone ordered the assassination of one of my employees last Monday as a way of derailing a project of mine. That was an act of treason. Withholding information that could lead to the capture of that person is aiding and abetting treason. Both are capital crimes. You stand accused of being an accessory to that assassination."

"But that accusation was obtained under drugs, Your Majesty," he tried, apparently hoping to cast doubt upon the accusations against him. "It won't stand up in court."

"Correct. It won't. But you do not stand accused before a lower court, Mr. Beckham. You stand accused before the Throne. I am not constrained by the rules of evidence the Throne has put in place for the lower courts. I must act in the best interests of the Empire as I see them, and your rights before the lower courts do not apply."

"...I see, Your Majesty." He paled still further.

"Yesterday, Mr. Beckham, Susan Kaplan died in that chair, at my order. We had a positive DNA identification on her from something she discarded during your assistance to Mr. Bronsky. We also have a partial DNA identification on you and Mr. Bronsky, as well as Ms. Kaplan's answers during her interrogation. And so I offer you a choice. Answer our questions, honestly and completely, and earn some leniency from me, or we will drug the answers out of you and you will die, today, in that chair, as Ms. Kaplan did."

"Leniency, Your Majesty?" Beckham's expression perked up.

He's being courteous, I'll give him that, Ashton thought. *Maybe this one will survive a little longer.*

"I have considered the matter carefully, Mr. Beckham. If we in fact determine who gave the order for the assassination, based on your answers and other sources, I will give you an Imperial Pardon for all past crimes save this one, for which I will give you a suspended sentence of death. That would mean, though, that if you are ever again convicted of a felony, anywhere in the Empire, the punishment would be the carrying out of that sentence."

"You would release me, Your Majesty?" Beckham seemed shocked.

"Under those terms, yes, Mr. Beckham."

Beckham paused only briefly to consider.

"...I will answer your questions, Your Majesty."

"Honestly and completely, Mr. Beckham." Empress Ilithyia II was stern.

"Yes, Your Majesty." He sounded – and looked – sincere.

"Be certain that you do, Mr. Beckham. Good day."

The Empress rose and left the room.

The interrogation started moments later. But this one had a cooperative subject; Derek Beckham did not want to end his life in the same fashion that his sometime lover had on the previous day. He was being given the chance for a fresh start in exchange for his cooperation, and he intended to fulfil his end of the bargain, Ashton adjudged.

Within only a few minutes, Captain Mercer had reached what Ashton considered the heart of the interrogation.

"Was Josip Bronsky the shooter for last Monday night's murder?"

"I only know him as Joey Bronze," Beckham noted with a shrug. So Mercer corrected his mode of address.

"And Joey Bronze was the shooter?"

"Yes."

"Joey Bronze hired you to be a spotter?"

"Yes."

"Did Joey Bronze also hire Susan Kaplan to be a spotter?"

"No, that was my idea. He wanted to make sure his spotters would be careful and not be identified on security recordings, so I suggested a couple would be more obscure."

"So you hired Susan Kaplan?"

"Yes. I introduced her to Joey, and he said that she was ok."

"How long have you known Joey Bronsky?"

"I'm...not sure." Beckham shrugged again. "Maybe...five years. We hang out at some of the same places."

"Have you worked as a spotter for Joey Bronsky before?"

"Yes. Twice."

"Those were murders as well?"

"Yes."

Ashton leaned forward, listening intently, as Mercer continued the questioning.

"Which murders? That is, who were the victims?"

"One was an attorney, I think. That was in Imperial Park East, about a year, year and a half back. The other was a hooker. Domino Scarlatti. I think she was blackmailing a john, and he didn't like it. That was more like two or two and a half years back."

Ashton hit the arm of his chair with his fist, producing a soft thud. Then he glanced at Gorski, who was watching him, rather than the interrogation. Gorski leaned forward and murmured in his protégé's ear.

"Looks like you nailed it, kiddo. That whole profile with associated cold cases was on the money."

"Yes, sir. I knew it was Bronze, sir."

"I know you did. And you did a good job. When this is all

over – likely with the execution of Bronze, so hold onto your belly – I'll see to it that those cases you've flagged are closed."

"Thank you, sir. I'll help where I can."

"I know you will."

They broke for lunch. The Empress disappeared, along with her brother and the rest of the Imperial Guard, though before he left, Dunham kindly told them to make use of the Palace staff cafeteria, and told them how to reach it. Dr. Galway excused himself, then entered VR to check in with his practice and tend to matters there.

Gorski and Ashton entered VR and tagged up with Colonel Peterson, filling her in on how the interrogations were progressing, then Ashton sent a private message to Cally Ames – nothing of significance, more of the "Thinking of you" variety.

Then they headed for the staff cafeteria.

An hour after lunch found them all back in the observation room – save the Empress herself. Joey Bronze was placed in the "lie detector" chair and cuffed in place, then Captain Mercer entered the room.

"We have opened up one VR channel to you. There is a recording there you may wish to view before your interview."

Then he turned and left the room.

Bronsky entered VR and watched the previous two interrogations, but when he emerged from VR, he was calm. He didn't have the same pallid, anxious expression Derek Beckham had had, and Ashton knew that meant trouble. He glanced at Gorski, sitting beside him, and saw his clenched jaw – the older detective knew it, too.

So somehow they were unsurprised when, upon the

Empress' entering the interrogation room, Bronsky usurped her place and addressed her first – and without acknowledging her status to start.

"I already know your spiel, Your Majesty. I'm not going to answer your questions." Bronze was, if anything, almost insultingly cocky.

"And die instead, Mr. Bronsky?" The Empress, by comparison, was cool and reserved.

"Why not? You're going to kill me anyway," Bronze pointed out. "There's nothing left in it for me but to deny you what you want."

The Empress shrugged.

"I'll get the answers anyway."

"No, you won't. One-word answers won't tell you what you really want to know. You know it and I know it. Make me a better deal, Your Majesty."

Ashton tried not to gape at the unmitigated gall of the man.

"I cannot allow you to run free in the Empire, Mr. Bronsky," the Empress countered.

"I don't want to die, but life in prison doesn't thrill me either, Your Majesty."

"Then we are at an impasse, Mr. Bronsky."

"Not necessarily, Your Majesty. Isn't banishment one of the traditional punishments in a system of high justice?" Bronze was negotiating for his life, gambling that the Empress didn't really want another death such as Kaplan's, and Ashton was abruptly reminded of his conversation with Cally regarding Bronsky's gambling lifestyle, and the very nature of his life.

"You mean exile, Mr. Bronsky?"

"No, Your Majesty. Banishment," Bronze clarified. "Put me on a passenger ship to some other polity. Let me be their problem. If I am ever caught in the Empire again, it is an automatic death penalty."

The Empress considered for a long moment.

"Very well, Mr. Bronsky. If you answer my questions honestly and completely, banishment it shall be."

Then she rose and left the room.

But for all his smooth negotiation, his high-stakes gamble, he misread the abilities of the parties assembled against him.

"Damn," Ashton grumbled quietly, in the back of the observing room, "has he said anything truthful yet?"

"Not much," Lieutenant Cox noted, keeping an eye on the readings from the chair. "What say you, Dr. Galway?"

"You nailed that one," Galway agreed. "He committed to an agreement with Her Majesty to save his life, but he's not fulfilling his end of the bargain. He just wants us to think he is."

Abruptly the Empress spoke.

"Lieutenant Cox, please tell Captain Mercer to pause the questioning. Dr. Galway, come with me. Bring your bag. Major Dunham, would you attend?"

"Yes, ma'am," came the chorus of response.

A grim Empress Ilithyia II rose and left the room, accompanied by Major Dunham and Dr. Galway.

The door to the interrogation room opened abruptly, and the Empress entered, accompanied by the physician.

"I've heard enough," she declared in a disgusted tone. "You've been watching the doctor's notes, Captain Mercer?"

"Yes, Ma'am."

"And you know where he's been lying, Captain Mercer?"

"Yes, Ma'am."

"Very well, Captain Mercer." She gestured to Dr. Galway.

"Drug the correct answers out of him, then execute him."

"WAIT!" Bronsky cried, shocked, even as the Empress turned to leave. She paused in the door and looked back at him, raising a sardonic eyebrow.

"Yes, Mr. Bronsky?"

"I'll tell you the truth," he said, sounding borderline desperate to Ashton's ear. "Ask me the questions again."

"No, Mr. Bronsky." She shook her head. "I'll not give you a chance to lie more artfully. We may not be able to detect it."

"But you can't do this!"

"Why not? Mr. Bronsky, are you under the illusion that I'm one of the good guys? That you can trifle with me, because I'm naïve? I assure you, I am neither. I am the Empress of Sintar. I am pledged to protect my subjects in this, my Empire. There are no rules, no morals, no code of honor to which I adhere other than that one overriding purpose. You sat down by mistake at a very high stakes table, Mr. Bronsky, and you're playing out of your league."

Bang, Ashton thought. *House wins. Game over.*

In short order, under the influence of Dr. Galway's drugs, the matter had been laid out. Stanley "Stash" Gorecki, the IPD's hired enforcer, a man with whom Ashton was entirely too familiar, had hired Bronze for numerous hits, including several that Ashton had laid out in his profile, as well as the Medved woman. Based on prior knowledge of the man, Bronze had assumed certain references that Gorecki had used meant he was doing the bidding of members of the Imperial Council and their underlings.

Damn, a fifty-thousand-credit fee ain't small potatoes, either, Ashton realized, as he listened to Bronze spilling his guts under the influence of the drugs. *No wonder he got himself a nice expensive lifestyle once he started working for 'em regularly. Then wasted it.* He shook his head in disgust.

In the end, it only took about another hour to milk Bronsky dry. When he had answered every question put to him – including a number that Gorski and Ashton sent to Mercer through VR about the other murders in Ashton's profile, and gotten confirmation on all of them – Mercer turned to Galway.

"All right, Doctor. Carry out the execution."

Galway injected one more drug, and ten seconds later, Josip Bronsky, alias Joey Bronze, alias 'JB,' slumped in the chair, dead.

"And that takes care of that," Gorski said.

Looking for Trouble

"Time for one more, Nick," Gorski said the next day. "Are you up to it?"

"Sure am, sir," Ashton replied. "You know me by now."

"You know that you were seen arresting Bronsky, right?"

"So?" Ashton shrugged. "What else is new? By who?"

"Imperial Police stooges, like usual. You've been made. Again. They're looking for you. Word on the street confirms it."

"Aw, shit. Hey, it wasn't like I was alone in the doing."

"No, but we gave you the chance to show your stuff by putting you in the lead. And it was obvious, you *were* in the lead. In retrospect, I guess we shouldn't have put you in an ICPD uniform, but it came across as more official that way, and the Imperial Guard, in the person of Major Dunham, wanted official."

"Damn."

"You still up for this? We can keep you out of sight and send some of the others."

"Nah, I wanna be in on this if I can."

"Good man. You game for us putting you in some sort of disguise to do this? Maybe even a wig and makeup? We can call in Adrian to help. It might throw 'em and they wouldn't recognize you…"

"That's…a definite option, Stefan. Yeah, we can do that."

"Good. Just…keep your head down, okay? It's a good one, and it needs to stay on your shoulders."

"Will do, sir."

Adrian Mott arrived in the Investigations office ten minutes later with a large duffel bag, and it was obviously crammed full of gear.

"What's that for?" Cally Ames wondered, wandering over as Mott put the bag down beside Ashton's desk.

"Nick got made at the Bronze bust," Mott explained. "But there's more work for him to do, so we're putting him in a deep disguise."

"What did you have in mind, Adrian?" Ashton wondered, as Gorski came up to watch, as well.

"Wig, makeup, and beard," Mott decreed. "And a change of wardrobe style."

"Aw," Ames grumbled. "I don't like beards. They scratch."

Ashton flushed, but the others laughed.

"Well, Ms. Ames," Mott declared, "you have the choice of a scratchy kiss from Nick, or a dead Nick. Which would you prefer?"

"Scratchy kiss," she said without hesitation.

"I thought so. you'll just have to get used to it for a while, at least."

"Okay. I'll deal."

And Mott set to work.

As Mott worked, he pulled this or that out of his duffel, occasionally having to rearrange things to get to what he wanted. Most of it was obvious to Ashton, but when the undercover expert pulled out a pile of stretchy black cloth in a heavy weight, he raised an eyebrow.

"What's that?" Ashton asked, curious.

"This?" Mott waved the wad of black cloth. "Oh, it's no big deal. It's a special suit for nighttime surveillance. It's matte black so it blends into shadows and doesn't gleam in the light, and it's got a lining that's essentially knife-proof. It isn't bulletproof unless you put some special shock plates in, though. But it does pretty damn good."

Ashton noted that Mott avoided meeting Gorski's eyes, and wondered.

Then Cally quickly averted her glance, and he wondered a lot more.

When Mott was done, even Cally barely recognized Nick.

He had long, curly, dark-red hair pulled back in a loose ponytail, a full beard that matched the ponytail, a ginger complexion with freckles, and blue-green eyes. He wore blown-out sneakers, ratty, ripped blue jeans with one back pocket torn off, a wrinkled, stained green tee, and a threadbare gray fleece hoodie over all.

"Wow," Armbrand said, wandering up. "You cut quite the different figure from the casual-dapper Nick I'm used to seeing, there, Ashton."

"That's the idea," Gorski said. "If you didn't know him, would you know him?"

"I...don't think so."

"Cally?" Gorski pressed.

"Um..." Ames began, uncertain. Then she looked Ashton in the eyes. "Yeah. His eyes. Even with the different color, they're still Nick's eyes. But I doubt any of the Imperial Police are gonna be gazing into his eyes."

"Point," Mott said with a grin, even as Ashton flushed again. "So I think we have something, here."

"I'd say so. Oh, and nobody call him Nick or Ashton when you're in the field with him. What's your middle name again, son?" Gorski asked, pulling out a physical badge and handing it to Ashton. "Here; use this again. Xavier, isn't it? Your middle name?"

"Yes, sir."

"Good. Everybody call him Xav." Gorski clapped his hands. "Round up the Team and go get 'em, Xav."

"Who is it this time?" Rassmussen wondered as they waited.

"Todd Whitmore," the disguised Ashton noted. "Director of Acquisitions Testing for the Defense Department. He was involved in passing on the identity of the murdered woman, Medved. Um, Vasilisa Medved."

"Ah, I remember. Right."

Just then, Whitmore stepped out of the entrance façade of his condo building in Imperial Park East. Without making a scene, Rassmussen and Ashton approached him, Rassmussen in an ICPD beat cop uniform; Ashton was in his full disguise, which made him look somewhere between a homeless person and a bum. Rather than pushing his credentials to Whitmore in VR, he flashed the badge that Gorski had given him. Not only did it allow for the VR suppressor to be used sooner, it kept his exact identity hidden.

"Todd Whitmore?" Ashton asked.

"Yes, I'm Todd Whitmore," the man responded, somewhat puzzled.

"You're under arrest, sir," Ashton said, as Rassmussen eased around to Whitmore's other side. "If you would come with me, please."

Whitmore stared at them, in shock. Obviously whatever he had expected, that answer wasn't it.

"May I ask the charge, Officer?" he asked then.

"Accessory to murder. Come this way, sir," Ashton said, then turned.

They led their prisoner to a nearby arcade cart, where they

quietly put cuffs on him before loading him into the rear and belting him into his seat. Then Rassmussen climbed into the driver's seat and Ashton got in beside him. Rassmussen released the brake on the cart, and they went through the arcade level to a police transporter. There, they loaded Whitmore into the back of the transporter; Rassmussen knocked on the side of the transport, and it shifted into gear and trundled off.

"And that takes care of *that*," Ashton decided.

"Now let's get you back outta sight...fast," Rassmussen decreed.

But before they could get back to ICPD headquarters, and in despite of Ashton's disguise, he was recognized.

A sudden *crack!* from the building façade close at hand sprayed him with masonry chips, cutting his cheek, even as a report sounded from somewhere close. He flinched, then ducked, and Rassmussen and Armbrand grabbed him by the arms and hustled him around the corner into an alley, as the others drew down and formed a flanking cover, scowling eyes scanning the buildings across the way.

By that time, Armbrand and Rassmussen had Ashton inside one of the maintenance access hatches, and out of sight.

That was only the beginning of the latest round of shell games that the ICPD had to play to keep Ashton out of the hands of a vengeful Imperial Police. After three more days of ducking and dodging and getting shot at, Gorski sat him down for a talk in his office.

"Nick, what the hell did you do to piss them off this badly?"

"I'm not entirely sure, sir," Ashton admitted then. "It only seemed to really take off when I solved this one robbery...

which is also when Lee Carter shucked me over here."

"Tell me about this robbery."

"Well, it was at a museum…"

"Oh damnation," Peterson expostulated, when Gorski called her in upon finding out about the museum robbery Ashton had foiled. "You have to be kidding me. That thing is still floating around out there? No *wonder* they want the damn thing!"

"You mean it still works?!" Ashton exclaimed in shock. "I figured, as old as it was…"

"Unless one of the Empresses since then has issued an edict to the contrary, yes, whoever holds the Sigil is considered to speak for the Empress," Gorski explained. "And I'm with Maia – no wonder they want it so badly. They could bollix up a lot of Empress Ilithyia's plans at this point."

"And they're probably still trying to go after it," Peterson pointed out. "Which is why they want Nick out of the way. He's the only one who can tell anybody that they wanted it to begin with."

"I'll see if I can't take care of that, really quick," Gorski said. "Give me a minute, here, and I'll contact Major Dunham. I'm sure he'll see to it that his sister negates *that* whole mess, in a damn hurry."

Within hours, an Imperial Decree was quietly issued, negating all prior means of representation of the Throne save a literal or virtual-reality Decree, and specifying the Sigil by name as "a delightful historic artifact, worthy of scholarly interest, but long since overcome by technology and no longer effectual or recognized by the Throne."

Which took care of that potential wrench in the works.

But it didn't stop the Imperial Police – let alone the Council –

wanting Ashton's head on a platter. In fact, if anything, it made them even more vengeful over the lost opportunity.

Tired at the end of the shift, Ashton headed home, having changed into yet another disguise, with Mott's help once more. He had kept the blue-green lenses for his eyes, and changed his wig to a sandy blond tone, along with a goatee and mustache. He was clad in the latest designer jeans and tee, with an expensive leather jacket over all...at least, that was what it looked like. Once more, Mott had raided the confiscated counterfeits inventory; even the jacket wasn't real leather...but it was an excellent imitation.

So Ashton headed out, aimed for his apartment building several blocks south of the headquarters precinct. Given that he looked like an upscale young professional, he avoided the more clandestine ways, which tended to take him through alleys, mews, and maintenance accesses, and which would look odd at best, for someone of his apparent status.

Instead, he headed down to the arcade level, took a people-mover to the arcade proper, rode the slidewalk through it, then went up the escalator to street level.

That was where they were waiting.

As half a dozen goons – none of whom Ashton recognized, this time – approached him in a semicircle, Ashton concluded that they were finding ways to run pattern recognition algorithms on his face, for no matter what Adrian did, they always seemed to find him.

"Putcher hands in the air, Ashton," one of 'em snarled. "You're the one goin' into custody this time. 'Cept you won't be gettin' out of it."

"Except in a box," one of the others snickered.

Ashton eased into a crouch; if it came to it, he would fight...

and it looked like it was coming to it pretty fast. He was badly outnumbered, but he figured he could take a couple with him. *Sorry, Cally,* he thought. *I guess it isn't gonna happen for us, honey. Stay safe.*

Suddenly fully a dozen black figures emerged from the shadows; four were behind Ashton, the rest completed a circle enclosing the Imperial Police henchmen. Dressed in head-to-toe black unitards, even their faces were covered, though the unitards showed that two were female, and at least three, possibly four, were likely mature males. They spanned the gamut of body types and heights, they were all armed, and they all stepped forward and promptly dropped into a martial arts horse stance.

"Not if we can help it," one snarled, voice an odd, electronic neuter, and Ashton realized the full-face hoods held vocal distorters.

'It's a special suit for nighttime surveillance,' Ashton suddenly remembered. *Aha. I wonder who he recruited to come along with him.*

The lead IPD stooge – who was also the closest – growled and lunged at Ashton with a knife, but Ashton stayed in shape; he was quick and agile, and he dodged easily, executing a downward block with his left hand that knocked the knife well away from his body, and in fact out of the man's hand. It clattered on the pavement.

The rest of the black-clad ninjas closed with the IPD flunkies, some moving into position for hand-to-hand combat, others drawing stun weapons.

"Run, Nick!" one of the female ninjas said to him as she sprinted by him. "We have this!"

Ashton spun and sprinted for the door of his apartment building.

Two hours later, three of the flunkies – who turned out to be gang members, responding to a call for Ashton's head on a platter – were in the custody of the Imperial City Police, oddly enough. Two were in the hospital with various levels of injury, also in custody. One managed to get away, though not without injury; he was bleeding profusely from a split over one eyebrow, and dizzy from what he suspected was a concussion. It didn't stop him from checking in with the boss.

"No, Stash," he told Gorecki in VR, panting as he hid out. "I dunno what you think he is, but that guy had his own set of goons, and they were more and better equipped than us. They beat the shit out of us. They got Gord an' Pete an' Bob, outright…"

"Dead?"

"Nah. Leastways, I don't think so. I dunno what became of 'em, I just know they got 'em. Bob was knocked loopy but not unconscious, Pete an' Gord were kinda trussed up – one o' Ashton's minions got 'em with stunners. Manny an' Scorch were down an' out. Scorch was bleedin' everywhere. I'm not sure he's gonna make it."

"And you, Jimmy?"

"Damn, Stash, one of 'em took a swing at me, so I hit 'er inna face," Jimmy said. "I–"

"Wait. 'Her'?"

"Yeah, there was guys an' gals in his posse," Jimmy explained. "An' damn if the gals didn't hit as hard as the guys! So I belted one in the face, an' she staggered back for a second and cussed at me, but before I could even laugh, she turned around and clobbered me in the head. *Hard*! Twice, even! My jaw feels like it's half hangin' off my face, plus I got a split over my left eye where she clocked me, an' it's bleedin' like a stuck pig, so bad I can't hardly see. But she rang my chimes, an' I can't half see straight nohow."

"Concussion?"

"Prob'ly. I'm dizzy as hell."

"Where are you?"

"I made it 'round the corner to Imperial Park South, an' I'm about eight blocks in, in the alley offa South Fifty-Third, near Eighth Avenue."

"Right. I'll send somebody there to come take care of you. Just sit tight."

"Thanks, Stash," Jimmy said gratefully. "You're all right."

"Sure I am, Jimmy."

The local ICPD precinct found Jimmy's body there the next morning.

He had been shot in the back of the head.

Just once.

The next morning, when Ashton arrived – as himself, but he also took the most clandestine routes known only to him and his fellows, and nobody came after him this time – several of the Team members were stiff and achy. Even Colonel Peterson was moving a little slowly.

And Cally had a black eye.

"Hm," Ashton said, in a knowing yet thoughtful fashion.

Then he ordered several dozen doughnuts for the Investigation division break room, and kitchen-sink pizzas – three – for lunch for the entire Team.

Then he called Adrian Mott and Lee Carter to come over and join them.

When they showed up, both men had facial bruising.

Ashton smiled to himself, content.

"How'd you get the shiner?" Nick asked casually, when Cally came by his place with takeout that night. "You were fine yesterday."

"Eh, no big thing," Cally said, avoiding his glance. "I got up in the night last night to go to the bathroom, thought I could do it without turning on the lights, and ran into the door."

"Ouch," Nick said. "Did you ice it?"

"Yeah. It's fine. The nanites are working on it."

"Good. After we eat, I'll get out my ice pack and you can lie down on my couch and ice it. I'll even sit on the end and hold your head in my lap if you want me to."

"That…might be nice," Cally admitted.

Nick let it drop then, and set the table for two, as Cally opened the Chinese take-out containers and sat them on the table with serving spoons.

But afterward, he did indeed sit on the couch with her head in his lap, gently stroking her hair, as she let the ice pack rest on her bruised face.

It was two more days before anything else went down, which was fortunate for the Team; they were much more spry and agile by that time. And Cally's black eye had gone through its darkest phase, and Mott had showed her how to cover it with makeup.

"The latest assignment to come from the Palace is to pick up Gorecki," Detective Gorski told them, as he, Colonel Peterson, and Nick Ashton debated how best to handle matters. "And I can't say I blame 'em. I've had enough of that loudmouthed psychopath and his henchmen myself."

"What about Wilkins? Wasn't he the next rung up from Whitmore?" Peterson asked.

"He was, but according to our sources, he's gone missing. Probably into hiding. I've already informed the Imperial Guard," Gorski said. "Based on that information, the Throne wants Gorecki."

"Mm," Peterson hummed, thoughtful.

"You know, if we get Gorecki off the damn streets and in custody, I'm probably safer," Ashton observed. "He's their head hobgoblin, after all."

"True," Gorski agreed. "But it won't be fun. I'm tellin' ya, picking up Stanley Gorecki is gonna be trouble. We've tangled with him before, more 'n once, in the dives and alleys of the South End. He is a serious, big-time pain in the ass. Never mind just being an ass."

"And a complete psycho," Ashton added. "I think the man enjoys killing."

"He does, according to Lee," Peterson averred.

"Shit. Pain in the ass, pain in the neck, pain in the…"

"So?" Peterson interrupted. "Bring plenty of back-up. This has to be done."

"You want me to lead that team, too?" Ashton asked.

"Oh HELL no!" Peterson and Gorski exclaimed in unison. "No way one of the perp's targets takes down the perp," Peterson added. "Besides, Lee would have my hide for a lampshade if I let you do that. And deservedly so!"

"No, I'll handle this one," Gorski determined. "You need to stay out of sight. Preferably in a bolt-hole someplace."

"You're taking out the guy who wants my head on a platter to present to Herod," Ashton said, "and you tell me to stay away? No way in twenty-eight levels of hell. I want to at least be able to see the guy get taken into custody." He folded his arms, firming his jaw almost truculently.

Gorski and Peterson glanced at each other.

And sighed.

In the end, Ashton had his way...sort of. He sat with Rassmussen in the latter's sharpshooting covert, there to watch from an out-of-the-way location. They were sitting in an alley across the street from where the team intended to take Gorecki into custody, and were screened from view behind a trash bin. The other police sniper on their team, Jones, waited behind a car nearby with the tranquilizer rifle.

More, Nick had talked Maia and Stefan into letting him handle the VR suppressor, so he could at least be a functional part of the team, not merely a tagalong.

They got there bright and early, just in case. Gorecki had been working into the evening for the past week or so, on what, the ICPD didn't know and hadn't been able to find out. But they'd been staking out his apartment and his office for nearly a week, and had a good feel for his hours by this time.

So no one was really surprised when it was mid-morning before Gorecki emerged from his apartment building in the South End to head into work. This was the quietest time of the day in the South End, with the revelers of the night before still in bed, and those with normal jobs already at work. Which was just the way they wanted it, Ashton considered. He triggered the VR suppressor.

Just then, Armbrand and Ames, wearing ICPD uniforms instead of their usual plainclothes look, stepped forward as Gorecki left the front door of his apartment building.

"Stanley Gorecki?" the male officer asked.

"Yeah, what about it?" Gorecki all but snarled. Then he glanced at the other officer, the female – and recognized her.

Damn, it's the she-cat bodyguard, he realized. *And she actually thinks she's gonna take me down. I can see it in her eyes. Well, bitch, you got another think comin'.*

"You're under arrest," the male officer said then. "Come with me, please."

Jones raised his rifle to the ready, loaded with a tranquilizer dart. He targeted the biggest muscles of the body: the thigh and hip.

Rassmussen also raised his sniper rifle to the ready; it was *not* loaded with a tranquilizer dart. He targeted the part of the body most likely to drop a perp the fastest, sighting carefully through the 'scope. Then he waited.

Gorecki turned and looked behind himself down the sidewalk, using the move in an attempt to hide drawing a pistol from an inside-the-waistband holster in the small of his back as he spun back to the officers.

This oughta take care of the she-cat and *her pal, here,* he thought, vindictive. *I'll catch Ashton later and put him down like a dog. Heh. Cat and dog.*

But Ashton saw the move.

"HE'S GOT A GUN!" he called. "CALLY, GET DOWN! PETE, DUCK!"

Jones promptly fired a tranquilizer dart; it hit Gorecki in the left thigh, but the big man was already moving, amazingly fast for his size, far faster than the tranquilizer could take effect.

Gorecki raised his gun, swinging it toward Ames, his intent plain, even as Ames and Armbrand dove for cover, drawing their own weapons.

Rassmussen fired. The hollow-point bullet smacked Gorecki in the temple, angling back and across the inside of the skull, expanding and spinning as it went, beginning to tumble as it penetrated the bone of the skull. The resulting carnage in both brain tissue and VR nanite networking was severe in the extreme.

Stanley Gorecki was dead before he hit the ground.

"Well, that should take care of a few things," Peterson said that afternoon, as The Team, as Ashton had thought of them long since – Stefan Gorski, himself, Peter Rassmussen, Roger Armbrand, Timothy Jones, Darrell Osborn, Rich Weyand, John Smith, Hugo Weaver, Callista Ames, and Alan Compton – sat in the investigations briefing room. "We have everybody who survived in custody, trussed and delivered to the Imperial Guard, and it's up to the Throne to take care of 'em now – those that aren't already taken care of, I suppose. If you like, I'll keep the lot of you informed of matters as I hear of 'em. Or, Stefan, if you hear from the major, you can fill us in."

"Right," Gorski agreed.

"Now, you've all been working pretty steady, including some around-the-clock stuff while you tracked down our perps, so I'm going to let you go home early for a change, and get some rest," Peterson said with a smile.

They were too tired to cheer, but they all grinned.

That night, the Palace was attacked.

Empress Ilithyia II was presumed dead.

Ashton stared at the news in his VR feed in horror.

Getting the Hell Outta Dodge

"NO!" Lee Carter decreed, as he lay beside Maia Peterson in their bed, and they discussed the horrible events of the day. "Nick was the single most promising, the most straight-laced, new recruit I've had come into IPD in *years*! Hell, watching him is what gave me the renewed backbone to stand up and walk out of that damned place! Do *not* let that boy be harmed, Maia! Get him offworld immediately! If they got the Empress, they won't hesitate to take him out, if they can get to him! Especially if the Council gets control of the Throne!"

"All right, all right, Lee, calm down," Maia told her newly minted husband; they had quietly tied the knot less than a week before. "I'll transfer him off Sintar somehow. I don't know for sure how I can do that without IPD finding out – but I'll see what I can arrange. I'm sure as hell open to suggestions, though. You got any ideas there?"

"Yeah, as a matter of fact, I do," Lee decided. "See what you think about this…"

"No," Maia decreed, sitting up and working out the details. "I'm *not* gonna wait until in the morning, Lee! Because you're right. They're gonna be on the move now, looking to take out all of the loose ends they can find, and Nick is one of those loose ends! For that matter, so are you, so you need to lay low. Again, dammit. We have a plan, here; I'm initiating it now."

"All right, honey," Lee decided. "I can't say as I can argue with that logic. Go for it, and if I can help you in any way, just yell."

282

Colonel Maia Peterson, Assistant Chief of the Investigations Division of the Imperial City Police Department, was waiting in the classic nondescript VR meeting room when another being popped in.

Kurt Walder was older, a grizzled veteran police officer in the Catalonia Sector.

And he was an old friend.

Of Peterson...*and* Carter.

"Kurt," Peterson said, "I need a favor, and it's a big one. And it's not just me asking. Lee Carter is here with me."

"Damn," Walder said, his grizzled eyebrows shooting up. "This *is* a good one. Let's hear it."

"Yeah, I think so," Walder said, when Peterson finished explaining. Carter, who had popped into the meeting to provide his input as well, stood silently, waiting and listening.

"You know I can't help out there, Kurt," Carter said then. "Not these days."

"No, I get that, Lee, and that's fine," Walder said. "I think I can handle this in a...let's call it a back-door kind of way, here. I'll get on it as soon as we're done here. Meanwhile, I think you two need to get moving and contact...Ashton? Nick Ashton, right? That was his name?"

"Yes," Peterson confirmed.

"Okay, call him and get him moving," Walder declared. "I'll take care of everything else from here. Oh, and it's a courier job, just so you two know."

"Couriering what?" Peterson wondered, puzzled.

Walder grinned.

"Information," he said.

"Ah. Done," Peterson replied, knowing.

By morning of the next day, Dominick Ashton was already on a transport to Catalonia, along with all of his personal possessions, helped to pack by the complete Team that Gorski had assembled, and which he had led in successive, and successful, perpetrator apprehensions. And of which, as Gorski pointed out, that made him unequivocally a "big brother." And they would take care of that brother, no matter what.

Truthfully, it felt like a punishment of some sort, but Ashton decided that was illogical. *After all,* he thought, *if they can reach the Empress, they're not gonna stop until they've taken me out. I was already in their sights, almost from the time I hit the streets for the first time as a cop.*

He had only just gotten to sleep, after the horror of watching the news feed about the Palace attack, and the reports that the Empress and all her family had perished in the attack, when the emergency call came in from Peterson...*and* Carter. Within ten minutes, Detective Gorski had arrived with Rassmussen, Armbrand, and several others, including Cally, and the lot had gone around his flat, grabbing his personal items and packing them into transport cases they'd brought with them, while he got dressed. Then they escorted him to the Imperial City Spaceport, refusing to stop – "Police business!" Gorski would bark, if anyone tried to detain the group – until Ashton was on the tarmac, boarding the shuttle to the Imperial Interstellar liner, the IIS *Adannaya II.*

The sun had not even risen yet.

At least they had given him some privacy when he had kissed Cally goodbye.

One man was on the commuter train to the spaceport when Gorski & Co. boarded it with Ashton. That man was one of Kershaw's informants, Mark Martin. As soon as he recognized

Dominick Ashton, he dropped into VR and sent a high priority message. Within moments, he got a response.

"Kershaw. That you, Martin?"

"Yes, sir. I've spotted Ashton, sir."

"Where is he, and what's he doing?"

"He's on the commuter train to the spaceport, being escorted by what look to be plainclothes Imp City police."

"Likely they're taking him off-planet. After a certain successful little event last night, they probably figure he's a dead man if they don't. And they're right."

"What do you want me to do? I can't possibly get through three big burly cops to get to him. Not alone."

"Follow him. You were planning on a little jaunt anyway, weren't you? You were headed for the spaceport, so you should have all the luggage you need." Kershaw paused. "I'll see you get sent on your personal trip once we've eliminated Ashton."

"Yes, sir. Sure, I can do that."

"Good. <u>Do it.</u>"

Mark Martin was half a dozen people in line behind Ashton, to board the shuttle that would take them all to the IIS *Adannaya II*.

No one recognized him.

Within hours of the departure of the IIS *Adannaya II* from Sintaran orbit, anyone to whom Martin would have reported – or who could have provided him with the personal trip he canceled to take this mission, assuming they had actually followed through with that promise – was dead. Emperor Trajan had ascended to power, and he had carried out his sister's final decrees: to dissolve the Imperial Council and execute its councilmen and staff – save Saaret, who had remained loyal – and to execute the corrupt police officials in IPD Headquarters.

But Martin had no way of finding out that critical bit of information. Not with the ship in hyperspace.

It was a direct flight; all other stops occurred after Catalonia. Therefore, it would only take about two weeks.

Nevertheless, Ashton decided to keep his head down for the time being. He stayed in his cabin the whole time, having food brought in and inspecting it carefully, while spending the rest of the time sleeping, reading, or looking up information on Catalonia in the ship's virtual libraries. He would have liked to be able to talk with Cally, but with the ship in hyperspace, that wasn't possible. So he sighed and went back to reading.

Outside the locked cabin, Mark Martin wandered by several times a day, in increasing frustration.

If anyone stopped him to ask, he was only, "…Stretching my legs."

"Yes, I know Peabody is a lieutenant colonel," Peterson told Co-consul Saaret – formerly Council Head Saaret, but he was the only member of the Council who had remained true to the Throne, so Trajan had given him the opportunity to resign before sentence was pronounced on that body; being a wise man, he had taken it – in a full-immersion VR conference, "but I know someone who is a relatively recent retiree, who has considerably more years in with the Imperial Police than Peabody has, and never besmirched his badge, either."

They were speaking in response to a communiqué that Saaret had put out in the Imperial City Police Department; Maia Peterson had seen it and immediately responded, and the current meeting was the result.

"So this is someone you trust?"

"I've known him for years, and I trust him with my life, Consul Saaret," she declared. "I trust him so much that I ended up marrying him about two weeks back."

"This sounds interesting," Saaret said with a slight grin. "Tell me this story, please."

"Well, well, then," Saaret said, at the end of the tale, which spanned several decades of service. "He does sound promising. And how many straight, honest young cops did he send to the ICPD, to get them out of harm's way?"

"I don't know for sure," Peterson said, "but I know at least half a dozen of 'em came through my Investigations division. I'd say over the years, a couple dozen, easy. Hell, we just sent one off-planet to keep him safe; did you hear about the attempted theft of the Empress' Sigil? That was one of his kids."

"I did, in fact. Really? One of his kids? That's excellent. And he himself was smart enough to play straight, and yet stay out of trouble with his superiors…"

"Yes, sir. Unfortunately, he couldn't do all that and not be at least suspected, which is one of the main reasons he never got promoted above captain. But he was still my equivalent over his people, so they recognized the skills. He had the responsibility, if not the pay grade."

"One of the reasons. Do you know of others?"

"I do," Peterson averred. "Those young cops were his kids; I didn't use that terminology lightly, or in jest. He looked out for 'em. The only reason he didn't take early retirement a lot sooner was so he *could* look out for 'em. When the attempted Sigil theft went down, it just got too dangerous with nobody there to back him up, so he got out while he could." Peterson paused, then snarled, "And the bastards still went after him."

"Aha. That's important to know. All of that."

"It is, sir. And I think he's in even better shape, because he's out from behind that desk he was stuck at, and he's maintained his certs with me."

"And you don't have a problem with it?"

"No, sir. I think it would be good for him, in a lot of ways."

"All right. Let me look into it, then."

When the IIS *Adannaya II* reached Catalonia, purely by luck of the draw Ashton debarked on an earlier shuttle than Martin, who scurried into the next shuttle, hoping to catch up to him in the spaceport.

But when he reached the gate, Ashton was already departing in the company of General Kurt Walder, head of the Imperial Police for Catalonia Sector, and a small contingent of escort police.

Well, at least I know where he'll be working, Martin decided. *I'll keep an eye on things, see where he bunks, and sooner or later, I'll take care of him. If I'm lucky, I'll hook up with some of Kershaw's people here. Which makes me think – now that I'm planetside, I need to report.*

He tried to use the QR system to link into Kershaw's VR from Catalonia, but it was odd; he couldn't raise anything on the other end. The comm tried to link, then there was... nothing.

Eh. I'll try again later, he thought with a mental shrug.

"Wait – WHAT?!" Ashton exclaimed, as Walder finished explaining matters in his personal vehicle, while his driver took them to the IPD headquarters on Catalonia.

"You heard me correctly, son," Walder said. "The Empress named her brother, Major Robert Dunham, as her successor, and in response to the patently obvious attack by the Council on the Throne using the corrupt police at IPD Headquarters, he released her Imperial Decrees condemning both organizations – but *not* the IPD Sector Branches – and dissolving the Council. Then, using the plans and preparations that Empress Ilithyia II had set in place, he completely destroyed the Council building *and* the Headquarters building, then sent in troops, and ensured that every mother's son and daughter of the lot was dead by lunchtime."

"Damnation," Ashton said, astonished.

They were silent for long moments.

"Oh," he said then. "But...so I should be able to go home now?"

"Well, I talked to Maia and Lee about that," Walder said. "They sort of want you to stay here for a few weeks, just in case. Look. Just because everybody who was at Headquarters got taken out – and frankly, and as between us, those of us who run the Imperial Police sectors were sick of those assholes, for a dozen reasons – it doesn't mean that everybody who worked at Headquarters got taken out. Because some people would be off on assignment, and some would be on other planets couriering evidence, or on vacation, or whatever. It's my understanding that they waited until the next shift showed up – often at a run – and took them out, too, at least if they weren't willing to be taken into custody and investigated. I gather there were some, like you and your former boss, who tried their damnedest to walk a tightrope between staying alive and doing the right thing, and those guys will probably manage to make it okay. Probably even be the new staffers once they start trying to rebuild it right. But Lee, especially, just wasn't sure how many of the damn snakes escaped the destruction of the snake pit. And he wants you out of the way of any pissed-off snakes."

"Aw."

"Hey, son, I've known those two a long time, and for Lee to take a shine to somebody like he did to you? That tells me a helluva lot about you. So stick close, because I gave 'em my word to keep you safe, and damned if I won't do exactly that." Walder looked at him sharply. "You're somewhere between a new detective for my sector, and a protected witness of sorts."

"Oh..."

Given the sector headquarters aspect of the precinct from which Walder operated, and the fact that some of the Imperial Police on Catalonia were transferred in from elsewhere, there was a kind of barracks annex to the building, allowing for single police officers to live within easy reach of their workplace. It was to this barracks annex that Walder assigned Ashton as living quarters; he sent several officers along with Ashton to carry his household goods – which Gorski & Co. had shipped with him – and deposit it in the studio apartment.

"It's not big, but you'll be safe here," Walder noted, as Ashton dropped his duffle on the bed. "As the sector governor has upped the ante on her political rhetoric lately, I've been upping my ante on security, as well. I have a bad feeling about that one, and I hope to hell the new Emperor knows about it. I've sent a few reports through, but given everything else..."

"Mm," Ashton hummed, thoughtful, as he recalled his few interactions with the former Imperial Guard Major Dunham, as well as what Stefan Gorski had told him of the man. "Somehow, I expect that, if he hasn't already, he will soon."

"Yes, I expect you're right, son," Walder said. "Now, if you don't mind unpacking later, I'd like to get you settled in the

290

department, and see what we can do about getting you working. I'd also like to debrief you about the shit you saw on Sintar."

"Yes, sir. I don't have a problem with that, sir."

When repeated attempts to raise Bill Kershaw failed, Martin started trying to hit up some of his other friends in the Imperial Police. When that failed as well, he began to worry that he'd been cut loose. *Which would mean,* he thought, *I'm stuck here, since I spent all my credits on changing my ticket to get here.*

Discouraged, he headed to the nearest bar. *Maybe I can at least find out what the local news channels are,* he decided, *while I get drunk. Thank God I have the credits in my pocket for* that, *at least. And I can see what's going on back home, I guess. Maybe.*

He did indeed find out what the local news channels were in VR, and he ordered a double shot of whisky to begin the process of getting drunk.

What he didn't expect was finding out exactly what was going on "back home" on Sintar.

Martin's jaw dropped as he watched video of the destruction of the Imperial Council building, and the subsequent imagery of the burning pile of rubble, taken by drones overflying the site. But it was the video of the missiles hurtling down on Imperial Police Headquarters, followed by the Imperial Marines slaughtering most of those who escaped the rubble, that shocked him the most. General William Kershaw, who fought back fiercely, was killed point-blank on camera by one unit of Marines.

They're gone, he realized in horror. *No wonder I couldn't raise anybody! They're all dead! Son of a bitch!*

And then it hit him.

I really am *stuck here! Damn that Dominick Ashton to twelve levels of hell!*

That night, Ashton unpacked his things in the little studio apartment. It was small, but was reasonably well furnished, with a bed, small sofa, armchair, desk, a separate bath, and a separate kitchenette. There was also a video screen built into the wall across from the bed, so he could lie in bed and watch VR entertainment if he wished. It wasn't his apartment in Imperial City – which wasn't fancy, anyway – but it would do, for now. And unlike the approach to that apartment, these quarters were apparently as safe as the Imperial Police sector headquarters, because they were *part* of the sector headquarters.

So he checked in with Carter and Peterson to let them know he was safe, properly set in the sector headquarters, and settling in.

"And you're sure everything's okay there?" Peterson asked.

"Seems to be fine, as far as that goes," Ashton said. "General Walder said that you two wanted me to hang out here for a while, though, just in case, to let things quiet down back there."

"Right, son," Carter confirmed. "There's a few Impies that seem to have gone underground, and we're trying to sniff those out. Once that's taken care of, we'll work out with Kurt how and when to bring you back here, if that's what you want to do by that time."

"Well, I still want to be where the action is," Ashton noted, "because that's where I can do the most good. But they had a little incident here recently – I'm still working on some of the details – but apparently there was a kook that had been listening to the sector governor a bit too much..."

"What do you mean?" Peterson wondered.

"If I'm understanding things right, the news media here is

kind of anti-Sintar," Ashton explained. "Well, anti-Throne, to be honest. And the sector governor, some woman named Renata Palomo de la Gallego – who, as between us, sounds like she's got cooties in the cranium – just eggs on the media something awful. General Walder thinks she might have certain ambitions of her own."

"Oh, that doesn't sound good," Peterson decided.

"No shit," Carter agreed.

"Anyhow, somebody got wound a little too tight on all of the political shit-talk, and decided to take out the Imperial Police," Ashton continued. "He managed to make a bomb outta fertilizer and bunker fuel from the farms on the outskirts of Catalonia Ciudad, then he started sending threats to the cops. Walder sent out his top investigative sorts to see what was going down; when they figured out who this guy was, they rounded up a team and moved to apprehend him. Problem was, he built the bomb in his home. The damn thing took out him, the older residential building he lived in, almost all of the inhabitants who were at home at the time, half the beat cops who went along on the raid, and two-thirds of the entire detective force on the planet. Most of the rest of the detectives are in the hospital."

"Damn!" Carter exclaimed, as Peterson muttered curses in the background.

"Yeah, alla that. Anyway, right now, all that's left are his junior investigative staffers, all of which are a couple ranks below me – mostly relative newbies. Some of those are coming out of the beat cop division, but even so, they're fairly green as investigators."

"So you're the top investigator, Nick?" Peterson asked.

"Sort of. For now, I guess." Ashton shrugged in VR. "General Walder has requested some more temporary transfers, but what with the shit that went down in Imperial City, well..."

"Yeah," Carter agreed. "That ain't happenin' any time soon."

"Right. So he's gonna be leaning on me kinda hard until that situation starts to resolve a little."

"It's only good for your career," Peterson pointed out. "A legitimate 'chief investigator' looks good on the résumé, regardless of the reason. Just be careful, Nick. Lee and I are starting to kinda feel like you're our kid."

Ashton grinned.

"And I appreciate that," he said. "I know Mom and Dad would, too, 'cause you're looking out for me."

"Trying to, anyway," Carter averred.

"Well, it's getting late here, and I still need to ping Cally, so lemme let y'all go for now," Ashton decided. "I'll try to keep you posted about anything of significance that happens here, and while it looks interesting, I'll be glad to get back home to Imp City."

"Things heating up with Cally?" Peterson asked.

"Hell, I dunno yet. It's good, though. And, um," he broke off, then admitted, "I miss her."

"Which is a good sign," Carter claimed. "Okay, son, take care, and we'll watch out for your Cally."

"Thanks, Lee," Ashton said, and broke the link.

Ashton promptly turned around and called Cally, allowing a heads-up notification in the call. She answered almost instantly.

"Nick? Is that you?"

"It's me, Cal. I'm here on Catalonia."

"Oh, thank God! You're all right?"

"I'm fine. How 'bout you?"

"I'm okay, I guess…"

"You're not sure?"

"I *miss* you, Nick. I–"

"You what?"

"…Never mind. I'll tell you when you come home. When are you coming back?"

"I'm not sure yet, Cal. Maia and Lee want me to stay here and lay low a while, let things get settled out there a bit."

"*Nick!*"

"I know, I know. But they do need me here, Cally. Lemme tell ya what I just told Lee and Maia…"

Ten minutes later, Cally felt a little better about the situation, and Nick had crawled into bed to finish their conversation.

"…Wow. That was bad," she said. "Really big blast, huh?"

"Yeah, it sounded like. And so they're short-handed, and if this sector governor is as much trouble as what I picked up from General Walder, when you add in the change of rule back on Sintar, things could get interesting. And not in the good way."

"Why? What did the General say?"

"It wasn't so much what he said, as the way he said it…and what he didn't say."

"Whu-oh."

"Yeah. So…" Ashton considered for a few moments, putting one bare arm behind his head and staring up at the darkened ceiling. "I watched a little bit of the local news an' shit while I unpacked earlier, and I tried to line things up with what I picked up from Walder. If I was a betting man, I'd put money on the notion that something is gonna go down around the coronation of the new Emperor."

"You think so?"

"Yeah, I do."

"Then maybe you could come home after that…"

"I might be able to, yeah."

"Okay."

"But that's gonna be a couple months. Are you good with that?"

"Yeah, I think so."

"All right then."

"Are you in bed now? You sound…horizontal, sorta."

"Yeah."

"Jammies?"

"By now you should know better than to have to ask. No."

"Ooo."

Nick laughed.

Catalonia

The next day, Ashton went out in plainclothes, sans disguise and thankful for the fact, with Sergeant Investigator Jaime Hernandez. Ashton had more investigative experience than Hernandez, but Hernandez knew the city better, so Walder decided to team them up, at least initially. Hernandez gave Ashton what he called "the ten-credit tour" of Catalonia Ciudad, or Catalonia City. He showed him the barrios in which he needed to watch his back, and took him by the governor's mansion, as well as the Imperial Government Park. It was, Ashton decided, not unlike the Imperial Park on Sintar, except considerably smaller; the entire complex, including the mansion, was only about a mile and a half long by perhaps three-quarters of a mile wide. Given the more lucrative and government-oriented businesses tended to cluster around it, it seemed oddly...dwarfed.

But that looks...like a copycat design, Ashton thought, as they walked about the park. *The governor's mansion, the mall, the departmental building...I only wonder if it was ordered by a previous empress, or by a previous governor. Some of the buildings look awfully new.*

And then Hernandez unwittingly answered his question.

"You like the design of the Imperial Park?" he wondered with a smirk. "It seems familiar, no? It was completely redone about fifteen years ago, when Señora Renata Palomo de la Gallego entered the sector governor's office. She had most of the old buildings demolished, and the Sector Governor's Mansion renovated and enlarged. All of this is new," he said, waving his hand at the governmental buildings. "It is much nicer than it was, but it was very expensive. Not everyone approved of the taxes she levied to raise the funds." He laughed. "Señora Governor Palomo likes to call the mansion 'El Palacio del Gobernador.'"

Uh-oh, Ashton thought.

Mark Martin, comprehending that he was stuck on Catalonia until he could afford to get himself off it, had spent the night in the bar, alternating between shooting cheap whiskey, sipping black coffee, and dozing in a corner booth. He had ducked into the bar's restroom to freshen up and change into clean clothes from his suitcase, then located a public locker facility and rented one in which to stuff his soft-sided case.

At this rate, he thought, *I'm gonna scrape bottom on the bank account by the end of the day. I gotta start bringing some in.*

Then he went in search of employment. If he could find a job, he could find a place to stay. It might not be much, and it might be in a bad part of town, but it would be a roof over his head and a bed to sleep in, until he could save up for the fare home to Sintar.

And take out that damned Ashton somewhere along the way, I hope, he thought vindictively. *This is all his fault.*

To his shock, however, that very afternoon, Martin spotted Ashton wandering the city with a young uniformed police officer.

"What the hell?!" he wondered, shocked. "What's he doing out here, just lollygagging?" He paused, then patted down his pockets as he stepped around the corner of a building. "Where'd I put it, where'd I put it..."

Finally he fished out a small pistol. Then he ducked into a

shaded alcove.

"Now let's see what I can do," he said with a smirk of glee.

Hernandez was answering some questions that Ashton had about the history of the city when a loud crack sounded from the masonry nearby, and a spray of stone chips pelted them. This was closely followed by a sharp report. Within seconds, the sequence repeated twice.

"¡Mierda! That was a gunshot! Someone is shooting at us!" Hernandez cried, as the two ducked instinctively, then swiftly sought shelter, leaping over a low brick wall and crouching behind it. "Where did it come from?" *(Shit!)*

"I dunno, dammit," Ashton said, once they'd placed the brick wall between themselves and the general direction from which the shot had come. "Dammit to hell! Don't tell me those jerks got people here after me!"

"You have enemies, mi amigo?"

"Yeah, and they don't seem to know when to quit," Ashton grumbled. "Their bosses are all dead, and yet they're still out to get me, it looks like." He shook his head. "Sorry to drag you into this, Jaime. I think we need to get back to the Headquarters building pronto, and get outta sight."

"I think you are right!"

"Dammit," Martin fussed. "I missed! I kept telling Gorecki I needed more marksmanship training, but no! I'm the snitch, the spy who slinks around and runs back and tells 'em. Where the hell did they go? I want Ashton bleeding out on the ground, dammit!"

Martin sneaked over to the location where Hernandez and Ashton had been standing, keeping his weapon in hand but hidden in his pocket.

But when he got there, they were nowhere to be found.

"Damnation," General Walder cursed, when Ashton and Hernandez reached Catalonia Sector Imperial Police Headquarters and reported in. "I didn't think we had any of the Sintaran IPD toadies here!"

"I might have been followed here, sir," Ashton noted. "There's nothing to stop someone from having seen me depart Sintar and catching the next flight here. For that matter, I don't know for a fact they weren't on the same ship with me. I spent the entire trip holed in my cabin, out of sight, per advice from Captain Carter and Colonel Peterson."

"Mmph," Walder grunted. "That's a possibility, I suppose. And it makes better sense than vipers already here. I've seen no sign of such at all until this. Are you sure it wasn't just a barrio war?"

"We were walking around the gubernatorial park, sir," Hernandez pointed out. "There should be no gang warfare near there; Señora Governor Palomo would not have it."

"Well...shit," Walder cursed. "That just complicated my plans by an order of magnitude or two. Lay low for a while, Ashton."

"Yes, sir," Ashton sighed. "Again."

In the meanwhile, Mark Martin managed to find a blue-collar job as a transport mechanic in a shop only a few blocks away from the Imperial Police Sector Headquarters. It only paid the base amount because it was a starting position, but he wasn't cut out for much else in the way of work available in Catalonia Ciudad, and was barely competent at that, so he had to take what he could get. At least they provided him with coveralls to work in, and that, combined with the underwear in his suitcase and the sneakers he had on, would do for everyday wear. That was all he needed for the time, anyway.

Then he managed to set up a bank account and tie it into his account on Sintar. Not that that did him any good; he'd mostly cleaned out that account in order to change his starliner tickets and come to Catalonia in Catalonia Sector instead of the pre-paid trip to Java in the Sunda Sector for his vacation. What was left had been burned on expenses while he found a job; there was only pocket change left, if that. Still, if any of Kershaw's people had survived and managed to make his reimbursement payment, he could transfer it to his Catalonia account and use it to get home to Sintar.

He considered the possibility of hiring onto a freighter long enough to reach Sintar, but that meant abandoning his vendetta against Ashton, and somehow, he felt like he was finishing off a job for Kershaw if he managed to off Ashton. Never mind his own feelings in the matter.

After that, he looked for someplace to live that he could afford, and still manage to put back sufficient funds to eventually get off Catalonia. He finally found a small room for a rental fee he thought he could manage, in an ancient house in one of the oldest barrios in Catalonia Ciudad. It wasn't much; a mildewy, rather decrepit bedroom on the third floor that didn't even have a kitchenette or bathroom of its own, just a hotplate on the corner of a tiny table.

His laundry was done in the tub in the common bathroom down the hall, then hung around his room to dry, which lent his room an atmosphere of continual slovenly disorder... especially given the fact that his coveralls very quickly developed grease stains that didn't want to come out in what he termed the "tub scrub," using the cheapest detergent he could find.

He shared that same bathroom with the four teen males of the household – he assumed they were all from the owner's family, though he wasn't sure – whose bedrooms were on that floor. They carried bright red bandannas all the time, and he suspected them of being gang members. They certainly eyed him like predators. He tended to watch his back in the house, and always locked door and window before going to bed.

He reached the room via a rusty old outside fire-escape stair, and climbed through the sole window to enter. The room accessed the upper hallway of the rambling old house, but since he wasn't family, he wasn't allowed on the other two floors. He idly wondered sometimes if the family was involved in illegalities, but didn't much care.

He wasn't able to find a lot that he could afford to eat – especially given how much he was trying to save to get back to Sintar. The nature of the various original polities that made up human space was based on the original nation-states of Earth, and many kept a good bit of the culture from which they originated. The Catalonia Sector had once been the star nation of Catalonia before a huge interstellar war had broken out; many of those same star nations essentially collapsed in the wake of that conflict, and the Sintaran Empire had absorbed them. But Catalonia had been settled largely by those dubbed Hispanics on Earth, and much of the culture remained, even to a prevalence for Spanish in the local language and cuisine.

Unfortunately, while the basic cuisine tended to be inexpensive to acquire and prepare, most of it disagreed with Martin's belly rather violently. And the longer he ate it, the worse it seemed to get.

It didn't help that it was just one more chunk out of his paycheck to buy food, and one he did his best to minimize. He could stuff himself once he got back home. As a consequence, much of what he did consume was poor quality at best, and half-spoiled, at worst. He had never heard of ergotamine poisoning.

He walked several miles each day, to and from the mechanics shop from the barrio where he lived. He couldn't afford to take mass transit – which, in Catalonia Ciudad, unlike most of the other planets in the Empire, required payment… which went into the Sector Governor's coffers.

And so week after week, Mark Martin grew thinner and thinner, and his health poorer and poorer. As this happened, his mental state, in turn, deteriorated severely.

Thus determination became obsession.

Ashton, meanwhile, worked with Walder to develop a functional investigatory division within the sector department. Walder tried to use Ashton in an administrative role as much as possible, since it tended to keep him off the streets and thus less of a target.

But occasionally Ashton got sent on cases here and there, usually with a forensic team of some sort, the members of which were always charged to watch out for their investigative lead.

When nothing else happened for a couple of weeks, both Walder and Ashton drew deep breaths of relief.

But the forensic teams were still instructed – by Walder personally – to keep an eye out for any attacks on Ashton, and prevent them if at all possible.

As the time for Emperor Trajan's coronation neared, the media push against him in the Catalonia Sector ramped up in intensity. Finally the sector governor consented to an interview. When she was pressed by the reporter regarding the new ruler, she opened up at last.

"This just will not do," Catalonia Sector Governor Renata Palomo de la Gallego said. "An Emperor, not an Empress? No, no, no. And he's her brother! We all know that the Throne of Sintar is not hereditary! It has never been passed within a family – ever! This makes the succession troublesome at best, if not outrightly illegal. Do we even know if this brother was our beloved Empress Ilithyia II's actual choice for ruler, or might that terrible destruction that killed not only the Imperial Council, but the thousands of people in the building, have been a ploy to kill the rightful successor, and cement this 'Trajan's' illegitimate rise to the Throne of Sintar? After all, there is no actual, real, tangible evidence that his counter-attack was ever anything more than a fit of pique. We've seen no proof at all that the Imperial Council or the Imperial Police were even involved in the assassination. It is entirely possible, perhaps even likely, that her own brother was responsible, and chose this means for clearing his way to the Throne!"

"Son of a bitch!" Ashton expostulated, sitting forward and jabbing an accusing finger at the screen. "That's a flat-out lie! I met Major Dunham and the Empress in my last case on Sintar! They were all but twins in everything but age! Even as an Imperial Guardsman, it was obvious he loved his sister! There's no way in twenty-three levels of hell he'd ever have done anything to hurt her! And the Council and the Imperial Police Headquarters were as crooked as an entire shipment of springs! It's why I'm *here*!!"

"¡Hijo de puta!" Jaime Hernandez exclaimed. *(Son of a bitch!)*

"You know that," General Walder noted. "And I have no doubt that she knows that. But the average inhabitant of this sector? They have no clue. The majority only know what they are told about such things. And Ms. Palomo is ensuring that she is doing the telling – directly, or indirectly."

"Damnation."

"Exactly."

The interview with the sector governor continued.

"...So I am forced to consider what kind of ruler this 'Trajan' will be," Palomo declared. "A man that would kill his own sister has little if anything in the way of a heart. I do not expect benevolence. I fully anticipate despotism."

"Are you considering what to do about it? Is there anything you *can* do about it?" the reporter queried.

"That is under discussion with my advisors," Palomo admitted. "We believe there are steps we can take, yes. And we are prepared to take them. I will not have my people," here she swept her hands about, as if to gather the entire sector into her embrace, "fall victim to a tyrant."

And the interview ended.

"This isn't going to go well at all, is it?" Ashton asked then.

"No, son, I don't think it is," Walder agreed. "This may not have been the best place to send you to keep you safe. If matters go south under her regime – and make no mistake, she wants a regime, she just doesn't have it quite yet – then we may end up under siege here, or even under attack. I've heard rumors she's working on suborning the military commanders assigned to the sector. Both Navy and Marine, but I think the Navy commander is already in her pocket."

"Damn her to hell."

"I'd like to, yes."

"Is there anything I can do, sir? Something to help?"

"I don't know yet, Nick. I'm watching and waiting, and

STEPHANIE OSBORN

doing my job while staying in the background as much as possible. When you get down to it, we may be the police force, but we're grossly outnumbered by the population as a whole, and if that population turns nasty toward anything to do with the imperium, and if the naval forces back them instead of us, we're in a great deal of trouble."

A few days later, Ashton was on his way back from a quick investigation for Walder; the assumed perp had been caught at the scene of a robbery, but Walder wanted Ashton to give it a once-over to verify that the arrested person was indeed the suspect. It hadn't taken him long – not all such criminals were exactly masterminds, after all – and Ashton was headed back to Imperial Police Sector Headquarters.

When he rounded a corner into an alley shortcut and came face to face with a wild-eyed man holding a pistol on him.

"Whoa!" Ashton said, taking a step back. "Sir, please don't brandish a weapon like that. You could accidentally hurt somebody."

"Oh, I'm gonna hurt somebody," the man practically snarled. "You're a dead man, Ashton."

"Ah. So you're the one," Ashton said, heart sinking. *Damn. I thought this was finally over,* he thought. *Instead, I let my guard down, and I'm caught.*

"Yeah, I'm the one that shot at you right after you got here," the man said, shaking lightly. "Because it's your fault I'm here at all!" He flexed his free hand absently, and Ashton noticed the man's fingers were swollen and peeling, and the nails were dark. A quick check of the gun hand revealed the same condition there.

"I...don't understand," Ashton said, now studying the other man carefully. He noted the coveralls, and the name patch on

306

the left breast. *Martin,* he thought. *Shit, is this the informant Kershaw kept, Mark Martin? What the hell is he doing here? And damn, is he skinny. Doesn't look like he's been eating that well lately. I wonder what's up with that. But those eyes, and the spasms...has he gone 'round the bend? He definitely isn't well.*

"Dammit, Ashton, do I gotta spell it out for you?!" the man demanded, incensed and frustrated. He waved the pistol around wildly, and his head jerked to the side repeatedly in a tic-like spasm. "I'm here because of you! I saw you, reported it to Kershaw, and Kershaw sent me after *you,* you bastard, instead of on my vacation! I spent all my cash to change my tickets to follow you, with the promise that Kershaw would get me back on track and the money reimbursed! Then all your cock-sucking, shit-nosed pals killed him! Killed all of them! Every last damned one of 'em – except me! So he NEVER REIMBURSED ME, DAMMIT! Here I am in this Godforsaken hellhole of a shit planet, with only a suitcase fulla resort clothes, no cash, no place to stay, no way of even gettin' to my damn home! Because of YOU! YOU KILLED 'EM! You stranded me here, you sonovabitch!"

"Um, okay, wow," Ashton said, faking dumbfoundment, all the while realizing, *Yeah, this is Martin. And he was never the brightest bulb in the box. Sounds like he's teetering on the brink now. Maybe he's already gone over the edge, by the sound.* "So you're gonna...what?"

"I gotta kill you," Martin declared, waving the pistol at him. "It's your fault, see. And I'm the only one left. Bill Kershaw wanted you dead, so I gotta do this. There's nobody else left to do it. Then I can concentrate on goin' home."

"But why?"

"Huh? Ashton, what the hell are you talkin' about now? I gotta do this. Just shuddup an' lemme finish matters, so I can go home."

"Hold on," Ashton said, holding up his hands, deciding to run with his gut and Martin's ramblings. "I see what the problem is, here. I think I can help you out."

"How the hell can you help me outta this shitty situation?"

"Simple. You don't wanna do this. I can tell. You give me the gun, it's over. We walk away from here, and I tell nobody. I don't arrest you, I don't report you, I don't put out a warrant for your arrest. You're free and clear."

"Huh?"

"Well, you feel obligated, right?"

"Hell, yeah…"

"And you're angry about it. Because they set you up in a no-win situation."

"DAMN STRAIGHT THEY DID!" Martin yelled. "That damn bastard Kershaw! Two-timin' sumbitch! I bet he never had any intention of gettin' me offa this damn asshole of a planet!"

"Probably not," Ashton agreed, calm. "Stranding you here was mild, really. Hell, I saw him and his pet bulldog, Stash, kill off lots of their loyal guys, once they got 'in the way.' I used to work for 'em, you know. That's why I don't, now. And why they wanted me dead. I just got in the way. So I got out of the way, and they *still* came after me."

"Really? You…you know?"

"Sure do. Firsthand," Ashton said, holding out his hand, palm up. "That's why I'm offering to let you off their hook. Gimme the gun, we both walk away from here, nobody tells anybody anything, you're free."

"You mean that, man?"

"I sure do. Gimme the gun, I tell nobody. We both walk away free." He waggled his fingers. "All you gotta do is give me the gun."

Martin paused with the gun lowered, searching Ashton's face. Finally he nodded and laid the pistol in Ashton's open palm.

"Okay," he said. "Here you go. It's all over, right? It's gonna be okay now?"

"Sure thing," Ashton agreed, slipping the handgun into the pocket of his jacket. "I won't tell anybody, won't send anybody after you. You're free."

Ashton turned and headed out of the alley.

"HEY!" Martin yelled after him. "What about getting me home to Sintar?"

"Oh," Ashton said, slowing as he neared the mouth of the alley, with sector headquarters in sight. "I never said anything about that. That's up to you. And Kershaw, I guess."

And he disappeared around the corner.

"DAMN YOU, ASHTON!" Martin yelled after him.

Coronations and Assassinations

Finally, after a considerable amount of tension, especially in Catalonia Ciudad – though, thankfully, no serious incidents – the day of the coronation arrived.

Ashton sat with a couple of other police officers, watching the coronation from their offices, on a screen showing the VR feed. They saw the coronation of Trajan, followed by the secession speech of the "new Empress of Catalonia," then the declaration by Emperor Trajan.

"People of Catalonia.

"You have been the victims of a deception. You have been lied to by your sector governor and by her paid minions in the Catalonian press. I am not an illegal occupant of the throne of Sintar, I did not execute the Council without cause, and I am not a tyrant.

"When my sister, the Empress Ilithyia, named me her heir, it was perfectly legal, although not traditional..."

"Yeah," Ashton told Hernandez then. "This is the Major Dunham I knew."

"He is a strong man," Hernandez decided. "He survived the death of his family, his wife, the destruction of his world, when the Council and the police headquarters attacked. And now he carries on his sister's wishes. Alone."

"Yes," Ashton agreed. "That's the man I met."

"And this is the man that idiota wants to supplant," Hernandez said in disgust. "Feh."

"...And yet," the video continued depicting Trajan's statement to the Sector. "People of Catalonia, if this is the path you wish, and not just the ravings of a madwoman, then I must take your desires into account. But you must also know that, if Catalonia leaves the Sintaran Empire, it leaves behind the benefits of being a part of the Empire. The medicines, the technology, the rule of law, the peace of Sintar.

"To that extent, it is your decision. I will not fight against a secession that has the popular support of the people of Catalonia. I will not lay waste to a portion of the Empire I hope to rule. I will not kill the very people I hope to serve.

"The moment of your decision is upon you. As a taste of what you would be missing, though, the Empire will no longer support the VR system and QE radio network that is only a small part of the Empire's benefits.

"I await your decision."

Ashton laughed silently to himself; Major Dunham – now Emperor Trajan – had definitely played a trump hand on that one.

And then the VR feed onscreen went dead.

Ashton blinked in shock. *Wow, he really meant it,* he thought, surprised. *Like, immediately.* A quick check revealed that the IPD internal comm was still operational, but nothing was coming in or going out of the headquarters building, not even to the Governor's Mansion. *And,* he sighed, *since that's only for official business, I can't even call Cally to find out what's going on there. In terms of the people I love and care about, I'm completely incommunicado.*

Coming out of VR, he looked around, and saw the others looking puzzled and glancing about as well.

"What do we do now?" Ashton asked then.

"Wait," Jaime Hernandez said with a shrug.

The end of shift came and went, but General Walder kept everyone at their precinct buildings, and called in all the off-duty shifts. This included Ashton, whom Walder kept especially close.

"Because I gave my word to Maia and Lee," he told Ashton, "that I'd look after you, mentor you, and keep any of the corrupt bastards from Sintar off your back. We already know they sent somebody after you; we don't know how many others. And right now, there's a hell of a lot of 'others' on the streets."

"And they're not happy," Ashton agreed.

"No, they're not," Walder affirmed. "Besides, I've already had...word...from Sintar. Just sit tight and let's see how this plays out."

Some five and a half or six hours after the coronation, along about sundown, a call came in from the sector governor's mansion from one of the staff there. Renata Palomo de la Gallego, sector governor and would-be empress, was dead, apparently shot by one of the enraged crowd. Walder called Ashton over.

"Nick, I want you to head up an investigation team," he said. "At Captain, you're currently my top-ranking active investigator, and from what I've seen *and* been told, have eyes like the proverbial hawk. I'll pull together the team for you, but you're in charge. Be careful, but go find out what really happened, because somehow I don't think it happened like we were told."

"Yes, sir," Ashton said.

The shuttle hangar facility was across the side street from the sector headquarters building, and Ashton led his hand-picked forensic investigation team out the side door and toward the shuttle, which was already warming up for takeoff.

Since Coronation Day tended to be a holiday in most of the Empire, and all means of communication, news, and even financial transactions had been shut down by the VR removal, the streets were now very crowded with a lot of confused, frustrated, and angry people, and Ashton and his team had to carefully but politely elbow their way across the sidewalk, into the pedestrian-filled street, and through the gate into the hangar facility. This resulted in a certain amount of yelling, foul language, and catcalling by said pedestrians, who were by and large well on their way to thorough inebriation, but since the police officers were courteous, nobody complained too much. In fact, some even tried to help part the crowd for the group to pass, apparently thinking that the nicer they were to the Imperial representatives, the sooner they might get their VR and QE comms back.

Until one man, very drunk, shoved his way toward the fenced landing-pad gate.

"DOMINICK ASHTON!" a painfully thin Mark Martin yelled, jerking and slurring his words badly, his hands nearly black; he had been fired from his mechanic job when he'd lost all dexterity. "YOU DAMN COCK-SUCKING IMPERIAL SCUM! What the HELL do you mean, doing this to me?! I'll KILL YOU, do you hear?"

By that point, however, the investigative team had already boarded the shuttle, which was spinning up with a loud whine; there was no chance that Ashton had actually heard any of it, let alone seen or recognized Martin.

But as he ranted, the crowd around Martin grew quiet.

Deadly quiet.

Finally, as Martin's inebriated rant died off, a big, muscular man addressed him.

"Hey, hombre, ¿qué haces? Don't go pissin' off the Imperial Police, man! The bitch in the mansion done enough for us on that account already! Just shut up!" (*Hey, man, what are you doing?*)

But Martin wasn't in a mood to be told what to do.

"*You* shut up, chico!" he yelled. "I ain't s'posed to even be in this hick dump, an' that guy's responsible for me bein' here!" (*boy*)

"What? Did he drag you here, hombre?" the big man asked, squaring his shoulders. "I didn't see nobody draggin' you here. Why you here, man?"

"I was sent after him! He's a cock-sucking suck-up, and he got all my bosses killed!"

"Killed how?" someone else asked.

"Executed!" Martin wailed. Members of the crowd glanced at each other.

"Este tipo es un ladrón," someone murmured. (*This guy is a crook.*)

"Sí," came several responses.

"Y está loco in la cabeza, un poco, tambien," someone else added. (*And he's crazy in the head, a little, too.*)

"And he wants to kill the Imperial Police detective," the first man said.

"Is not good," another responded. "Esa cabrona en el palacio has done enough already. We don't need more shit goin' down right outside Imperial Police headquarters." (*That bitch in the palace*)

"You need to shut up and go home," the big man told Martin.

"I WON'T!" Martin yelled. "I'mma follow that shu-shuttle an' find Ashton an' I'mma kill 'im!"

He shoved the man, pulling a knife…but he fumbled it in his gangrenous hands, and it clattered to the sidewalk.

Seeing the knife, the man backhanded him. He was nearly twice as big as Martin, in his emaciated condition.

Martin's feet left the pavement as he flew through the air and smacked against the main gate post, hitting the back of his head against galvanized steel. There was a mushy thud, and Martin bounced off, face-planting the pavement.

He didn't get up.

The street rapidly cleared of pedestrians.

An hour later, one of the Imperial Police officers glanced out the window and noticed the body lying in the street.

The team headed from Imperial Police headquarters in the Catalonia capital on an official Imperial Police shuttle. They set down on the shuttle pad on the grounds of the sector governor's mansion, where they were met by a staff member with an electric cart. He drove them around the back to a door, and led them to the sitting room in the residence portion of the mansion in the early twilight.

The body of the sector governor lay in the middle of the floor, shot three times in the chest. A pool of blood had formed under the body and spread, staining the tile flooring and the corner of a nearby area rug.

"Hello. Anyone here?" Ashton called, seeing no one else. A scrabbling sound came from behind a sofa against the wall, and Bernardo Palomo de la Gallego, husband of the deceased – Ashton recognized him from various media imagery – crawled out from the cubbyhole behind it.

"Thank God, you're here!" he exclaimed. "It was terrible. We were talking, and then someone came in from the balcony and shot her. I ran for my life, and he missed me."

Ashton raised an eyebrow.

"All right, Mr. Palomo de la Gallego," he said. "Just have a seat. We'll need to get a statement from you."

"Of course, of course," Palomo agreed, placating. "Poor Renata."

But Ashton noted that he moved to the far side of the large room before sitting down.

Ashton met with Sergeant Fernando Garza and made sure that the forensics team was organized and under way with the investigation, then he went over to Palomo and sat in an armchair; Palomo had chosen another sofa. Ashton pulled out a small device and placed it on the end table between himself and Palomo, activating it in VR.

"What's that?" Palomo asked, gesturing at the object with his left hand.

"Oh, it's an audiovisual recording device," Ashton explained. "It'll enable me to record my interview with you so I have it on file. It's intended to protect you and me from inaccurate memories and accidental transcription errors."

"Ah. I see."

"So, Mr. Palomo de la Gallego–"

"Just Mr. Palomo."

"Ah. That *is* easier. Mr. Palomo, please tell me exactly what happened."

"But I already told you. Someone came in from the balcony and started shooting."

"In detail, please. What were you and your wife doing?"

"We were talking. I told you already."

"About what?" Ashton asked, thinking, *This is gonna be like pulling teeth. And just as much fun.*

"Um, about the crowd outside," Palomo said.

"What about the crowd?"

"Oh. We were wondering when General Walder was going to send some troops to disperse the rioting crowds."

"Riots? Is that what you call a riot?" Ashton wondered, amused.

"Well…yes. Wouldn't you? They were not happy," Palomo pointed out. "They were yelling and screaming insults at us. We could hear them from inside."

I'll bet you could, Ashton thought, and let the distinction slide, for the time. "And then what happened?"

"And then a man shot from the balcony," Palomo said, his eyes starting to wander to and fro. "We had the doors open for the breeze, you see, and he apparently climbed up and over the railing, and starting shooting. Renata went down almost immediately, but I ducked and dodged, and then ran for my life! I don't know how I managed to avoid getting shot, too! He finally ran out of the room, back onto the balcony, and I hid behind that sofa–" he pointed at the sofa behind which he'd been when Ashton's team arrived, "until you got here."

"Who called us about the attack?"

"I don't know. I guess it was one of the staffers who heard the gunshots."

Palomo's eyes were still dodgy, darting here and there, and Ashton bit his tongue to stifle the sarcastic comment that wanted to come out.

"I see," he did say, deactivating the small recording device and stowing it in his jacket pocket. Then he waved over one of the regular beat cops that Walder had sent along for just such purpose. "Officer Mendez, please take Mr. Palomo into an adjacent room and watch over him while I see about finding the staffer who called us." A quick, subtle hand signal added the command of, 'Stand guard, and don't let him out of your sight.'

"Yes, sir," Mendez said, as she escorted Palomo out of the room.

Ashton wandered up to the forensics team. "What have you got so far?" he asked.

"No bullet casings, and no weapon," Luis Garza, the lead forensic scientist, told him. "Powder here and there, by the look. We'll have to wait until the autopsy report comes in to determine caliber, but I don't think it was a very large-caliber weapon. Something a bit more than a plinker, but not much."

"We've got bullet holes in the wall, there," Ashton pointed, "so we ought to get some caliber estimates off that."

"Oh damn, how'd we miss that?" Garza said in disgust.

"Probably because of the dead body in the middle of the floor, and the guy hiding behind the sofa. The fact it got dark on us hasn't helped." Ashton glanced out the balcony door, then rolled his eyes. "Talk about melodrama."

"Yeah, no shit. Patricia, hit the overhead lights, then get over there and see what you can find on those!"

"Yes, sir!" the junior investigator said, heading to the wall with the pockmarked surface.

"Is there anything else you see, sir, that my team hasn't?"

"No, I don't think so. More a case of wanting to know some specific things, Sergeant," Ashton decided.

"Name 'em."

"Since we don't have casings – likely an old-style revolver was the murder weapon – I want to know where the gunpowder is, exactly, to the best of your ability. I want to know where it stops, where it starts, and what the angles are on every one of these bullets. I want the security video checked, I

318

want the security staff checked, and I want everyone inside the house or on the grounds checked for residue. Anybody who would have been in a position to fire the weapon at Ms. Palomo."

"Yes, sir."

"Finally, I want a search of the grounds in case an intruder is still here, or in case he – or she – ditched the weapon somewhere," Ashton added. "No, wait a minute."

The puzzled forensics team leader stood and watched as Ashton headed for the balcony, stepping out into the dark. He turned back and called to Garza, "Sergeant, could you have the staff turn on the outside lights for the rear yard?"

When the exterior lights came on, Ashton stood and stared out into the landscaped yard. Garza joined him.

"What are you trying to do?" he asked Ashton.

"Find the murder weapon," Ashton said.

"But it's dark!"

"I know. That's why I wanted the exterior lights on."

"But surely the murderer carried it away with him," Garza pointed out.

"I don't think so, I – there!" Ashton pulled a small but powerful flashlight from his jacket pocket and shone it into the shrubbery, some twenty or twenty-five feet from the edge of the balcony. A long, intermittent scrape mark in the sod led to something glinting under the shrubs, and he climbed over the railing, eased himself as low as he could, then let go, falling to the ground and landing on his feet. He pulled out a small imager and took *in situ* imagery, then walked over to the shrub where the glint had appeared, donning gloves as he went. He bent, reached under the manicured bushes…

…And drew back a small revolver.

A quick sniff of the weapon revealed the scent of fresh gunpowder; Ashton carefully placed it in an evidence bag. Chances were, it had been emptied of bullets in the attack, but he wasn't taking chances in the near-dark.

"It's been fired recently, by the smell," he told Garza as that worthy leaned over the rail to accept the bag Ashton passed up. "It's an old-style revolver, so the casings are still in it. And now that I'm down here, I can tell you for certain, there's no easy way to get up there from here, unaided." He looked around. "And no sign of anything to aid a climber in getting up there, either."

"Now what, sir?"

"Go back and get the room taken care of as I instructed, and I'll go around to the door," Ashton said. "Have someone waiting to let me in, please. And if you can set someone up to get the staffers lined up for questioning, it would be good."

"Yes, sir."

"...What? No, sir," one staffer told Ashton as he questioned the workers in turn, in a small room down the hall from the sitting room. "That's not what happened at all. I heard the gunshots, two bursts of three, from inside the sitting room. I ran in – I'd just been in there not long before, so I wasn't far away – and Ms. Palomo was just lying there, staring at the ceiling, with blood all over her and the floor, and the horrid stink of gunpowder in the room. And Mr. Palomo came running in from the balcony and said, 'Did you see him?' I said, 'See who?' and he pointed at the French doors and said, 'The shooter. He was on the balcony.' Well, I didn't see anyone – at least, besides him and Ms. Palomo – and I told him so. Then he told me to call the police and report that the governor was dead and to send help. And I rushed out, because I was going to have to send someone, what with the VR down and all."

"Wait," Ashton said. "So Ms. Palomo's body had the eyes open when you saw it?"

"Yes, sir."

And they're not open now, Ashton realized, recalling the scene as he had first seen it upon entering the room. *So someone closed them. And Bernardo Palomo was neither cowering, nor fleeing, according to this staffer. Who, unlike Bernardo Palomo, shows every indication of telling the truth. I think perhaps Mr. Palomo's story needs looking into a little deeper. Surprise, surprise.*

Just then, a message came in for him through the Imperial Police VR channel. He dropped into a voice channel.

"Ashton here."

"Ashton, this is General Walder. I have Imperial instructions. I quote, '…You are to hold Mr. Palomo on an Imperial Warrant as the investigation proceeds. In addition to the murder investigation, you will investigate the financial records of both Mr. and Ms. Palomo. The Throne is particularly interested in payments to individuals in the press.' For what it's worth, I do have our forensic accounting people already on the latter."

"Oh; that's good. And yes, I already have Mr. Palomo, uh, under guard. He thinks it's for his protection, but what he doesn't know doesn't hurt."

"You suspect him?"

"Aside from the fact that he and his wife participated in treason? Yes. His story doesn't align with the crime scene or the story told by the staff members at the governor's mansion. I'm still looking into it. I fully expect to place him under arrest for the murder of his wife before all this is over, though."

"Keep going, Ashton. This sounds good. Fill me in with the details as soon as you can."

"Yes, sir."

"Walder out."

"Ashton out."

By the time Ashton had finished interviewing the on-shift staff and returned to the crime scene, Garza and his people had it laid out.

"Well, that's interesting," he said, noting the bright dye markers that had reacted with the gunpowder on the floor, and the lasers aligning the various gunshot angles. "A nice little right-angle layout. With nothing coming even close to the balcony doors."

"No, sir," Garza said. "Why did you think – oh."

"Right," Ashton said with a grim smile. "Looks to me like Ms. Palomo was shot from a distance of about ten feet."

"That's what it looks like, yes, Detective."

This time, Ashton let the mode of address pass; Walder always emphasized his status as the ranking investigator anyway. He was more interested in the implications of the layout in front of him – more so, given that neither Garza nor any of his team had actually heard any of the interviews with Palomo or the staff.

"And there are four lines of powder residue that were ejected from the gun – one big one for the victim…that argues for all three shots fired from the same place…and smaller ones for each of the bullets in the wall, forming a right angle to the victim's line. Oh, were you able to pry any of the bullets out of the wall?"

"Yes, sir," Patricia spoke up then. "I got all three, after I did *in situ* imagery and measured the diameters of the holes. At initial analysis, the caliber appears to match the weapon you found in the yard."

"Excellent. And none of those firing lines point toward the balcony."

"No, sir," Garza verified. "Now, the shooter could have run into the room to about this point here," he indicated the intersection of the gunpowder lines, "and unloaded, then run out. But I'm still trying to figure out how he got onto the balcony to begin with. Like you said, it's one thing to get down there, but another entirely to get up. Never mind the stupidity of running so far into the room, where he might have been caught if, say, someone was around the corner from the balcony. Still, the crowd outside is agitated, half are drunk, and somebody has to be on the low end of the intelligence curve, after all."

"What did the security imagery show?" Ashton asked.

"No one around the house within the fenced perimeter who shouldn't be there, sir."

"Only external video?"

"Afraid so, sir."

"Mm. Thought so. How about checking the personnel for residue?"

"No residue on any of the staff, sir."

"Has anyone checked Mr. Palomo yet?"

"Not yet, sir. We...weren't sure if you wanted him checked too, or not, given he might have residue from where he was shot at."

Garza is good at laying out the crime scene, Ashton thought, stifling a sigh, *but he has* no *imagination or insight into it.*

"Yes, I want his hands, cuffs, sleeves, and shirt front checked, please. And do be very thorough."

Fifteen minutes later, the appropriate team members came back.

"Sir! Mr. Palomo's hands are clean, but his left shirt cuff and part of the sleeve show definite signs of powder residue."

"And he's left-handed," Ashton said, remembering the instinctive gesture Palomo had made at the recorder when he had interviewed the man. "All right. Keep him in custody while I pull up General Walder and report in. The Throne is interested in this one, so we may need specific instructions."

"Yes, sir."

"General Walder? This is Nick Ashton."

"Ah. Do you have something for me, Ashton?"

"I do, sir. It was Mr. Palomo, without doubt."

"Lay it out for me."

"All right, sir. Angles showed the shooter was at a distance of only about ten feet from the sector governor when she was shot. This is inconsistent with Mr. Palomo's story of a shooter at the balcony doors. He would have had to walk well into the room – say, fifteen to twenty feet – to be within that distance of the location where we found the body, and that would give either of the Palomos a chance to call security. Further, there is no ready access to the balcony from the ground, or any other direction except the room in which the crime was committed. The weapon was, however, found about twenty or twenty-five feet away from the end of the balcony, underneath a landscape shrub, on the side of the shrub next to the house."

"Where it could have easily been thrown from the balcony," Walder speculated.

"Exactly. Yes, sir. With a scrape mark in the dirt pointing at the balcony. And the initial field analysis indicates that the bullets fired were of the same caliber as the weapon. Further, there were no casings found at the scene, and the weapon found was an old-fashioned revolver, smelling strongly of gunpowder. We then looked for powder residue on the floor from the various shots. There were four lines of powder drop along the floor – one for each bullet hole in the walls, plus a much heavier one back from the body. This would be consistent with multiple shots from the same location. None of it extended toward the balcony doors, but the wall shots were at approximately ninety degrees from the body – roughly, given that they were somewhat spread out – making the story of a shooter from the balcony much less likely."

"All good so far."

"Would you like for me to set up the crime scene in VR, so you can see it in three dimensions, sir?"

"No need. I can see it in my mind's eye, as you describe it. Keep going, Ashton."

"Yes, sir. In addition, while there was no powder residue detected on Mr. Palomo's hands, he had plenty of time to wash his hands – according to the staffer who reported the murder to us, he had time to close her eyes–"

"Wait, what?"

"Oh. According to the staffer who ran in right after the shooting, then ran to contact us, Ms. Palomo's eyes were open and staring at the ceiling, and Mr. Palomo ran in from the balcony, claiming a shooter had just come in from there, shot her, and ran out. More, he apparently was not agitated and fearful, according to the staff member, but rather incensed. Yet when we arrived, Ms. Palomo's eyes were closed, and Mr. Palomo was hiding behind the sofa, claiming to have been shot at and to have fled and hid in fear of his life."

"Oh, now there's an inconsistent story."

"Isn't it, though, sir?"

"Keep going, Ashton, this one sounds good."

"All right. So he had plenty of time to wash his hands; there is a washroom – what is sometimes, and singularly apropos for our purposes, called a 'powder room' – just off the sitting room, in fact. So that would readily explain the lack of residue on his hands. But our rapid arrival did not allow him time to change clothing, and so there were powder traces on his shirt, particularly on the left cuff. And per my observations, Mr. Palomo is left-handed.

"Finally, none of the staff saw anyone else, and the really very extensive and efficient security camera setup around – but not within – the sector governor's mansion shows no evidence whatsoever of any intruder approaching the mansion. From *any* direction. All individuals in the security recordings were on-duty security people, and their hands and clothing all tested negative for powder residue. As did the household staff."

"Oh, very interesting. It sounds fairly open and shut to me, Ashton."

"Me too, sir. Have you had any feedback on the financial transactions?"

"As a matter of fact, I have. They aren't anywhere near finished yet, but that looks rather damning, too. Lots and lots of little payments to friends in the media. Oh, and we also have the payments to the team hired to create and uplink Palomo's 'coronation' video. And possibly the contract for same."

"Ooo."

"Yes. I think I have plenty to report to the Throne, here."

"I believe so, sir. If you have the chance to talk to the Emperor yourself, please tell him that 'Detective Gorski's protégé says hello to the Major.'"

"I doubt that, son."

"Well, it was a thought."

"Arrest Mr. Palomo and bring him in, please. I'll see about passing the information upstairs and determining what needs done."

"Will do, sir."

Palomo did not like the idea of being arrested, but Ashton had a big enough team that his personal protests and attempts to get out of it were of no avail. All the police officers scorned the bribes he offered, and the staffers at the Governor's Mansion had long since had enough of the couple, ignoring his attempts to order them to his aid. Palomo was thoroughly searched for hidden weapons, handcuffed, loaded into an electric cart, and trundled off to the shuttle. The team loaded up and headed back to Catalonia IPD headquarters.

Upon arriving at headquarters, Palomo was promptly led off to confinement – which, given the Imperial death warrant, wouldn't last long – but General Walder was waiting for Ashton.

"Go get your things, Detective. It's time to send you back."

STEPHANIE OSBORN

Unexpected Welcomes

It took a bit longer for Ashton to arrive back on Sintar than it had for him to get from Sintar to Catalonia, by about a week. When he arrived at the Imperial City spaceport, there was a welcome-home group waiting for him in the main concourse. This included Detectives Gorski, Rassmussen, and Armbrand, and investigators Jones, Weyand, Compton, and Ames.

It also included Maia Peterson and Lee Carter.

As soon as the group spotted him, Cally Ames let out a delighted squeal and ran straight for him. Ashton suddenly found he had an armful of very shapely girl, and he dropped the bags he had been carrying without another thought as soon as she planted a big wet one on him. When she finally let him come up for air, he looked her in the eyes and simultaneously they murmured, "We have to talk."

"Later," a grinning Peterson said, as the others walked up then. "We have some business that needs taking care of, and we need to get you out of here to do it. Let's go."

Once they got Ashton back to the Imperial City Police headquarters, only a few blocks outside Imperial Park, Peterson pointed at his old desk.

"There. We kept it for you. Park your stuff there, and let's get a few things worked out."

Ashton dropped his luggage beside the desk, then turned to Peterson in puzzlement.

"Okay, Chief. What's up?"

"According to what we've been told by General Walder, the

328

mandate for the police to swear allegiance to the Throne came down after he sent you back," Peterson said. "So you probably haven't done so. Am I right?"

"Uh, this is the first I've heard of it," Ashton said, startled, "but you know me. I don't have a problem with that at all." He shrugged. "I kind of had my own private oath going anyway, I guess you could say."

"Stand straight and salute, then, son," Lee Carter told him, and Ashton obeyed. "Maia, go for it."

"What's your full name again, Nick?" she asked.

"Dominick Xavier Ashton, ma'am."

"Good. Repeat after me," Peterson said. "'I, Dominick Xavier Ashton, do solemnly swear that I will, to the best of my ability, preserve, protect and defend the Throne of the people of Sintar.'"

"I, Dominick Xavier Ashton, do solemnly swear that I will, to the best of my ability, preserve, protect and defend the Throne of the people of Sintar."

"Welcome to the police force of Emperor Trajan, Detective," Peterson declared.

"Wait – what…?" Ashton almost stammered.

"Yes, you heard her right," Gorski grinned. "We heard about the work you did on the governor's assassination. It was good work."

"It was mostly interpreting the forensic team's work," Ashton protested.

"Yes, and said forensic team, per Kurt Walder, has about the same imagination as a sea slug," Carter noted with a chuckle. "He said he was spread thin, especially with some of the shit the sector governor had set up to pull, and you stepped up and functioned as a full detective with no issues whatsoever. Solving a governor's assassination is a big deal, Nick."

"Well...I've had some good teachers over the years," Ashton noted, modest. "Most of whom are in this room."

"Besides, the promotion – which the ICPD chief approved, by the way – was necessary to discuss what Lee wants to talk about with you," Peterson added. "Come on, let's us three go into my office."

"...Whoa, whoa, wait a minute!" Ashton said, surprised. "I thought you were *retired*!"

"I was," Carter said. "I'm not now. I came out of retirement for this. The Emperor needed someone to rebuild the force locally, someone trustworthy. The few survivors of the dissolution of the IPD Headquarters on Sintar are iffy, at best – including the personnel held in the Throne's custody through the short little civil war that we didn't even know we had until it broke out and ended within a single day."

"So...you're asking me to come back to the IPD," Ashton confirmed.

"I am. Under me as Chief. And I need detectives. Right now I have exactly three, and one of those is the detective who's been in custody of the Throne during the big brouhaha that killed an Empress and the Imperial Council, one more is 'old-school' who was on vacation during the mess, and a third is someone I coaxed in from Odessa Sector headquarters, and he's a provisional detective – he hasn't quite made the promotion yet. Frankly, right now the only one I trust for sure is the guy from Odessa Sector. I need someone I can pull in that I trust. And that's you, Nick."

"But I don't want to work under a chief of investigations who's as bad as it used to be, Lee. Uh, Chief."

"You won't. Right now I have no inspectors. I've already told the guy who was vacationing that I'd be accepting his early retirement come this Monday, and while it took a bit of strong-arming, he finally agreed. Peabody was head of investigations under the previous regime, but not only did I oust him from taking over the Sintaran headquarters, he's been busted down to sergeant. And I don't mean just sergeant; I mean sergeant investigator. That came down from Consul Saaret, and Peabody wasn't at all happy about it, but he admits there's some trust to be earned back, there."

"Wait," Ashton said. "Did you poach any of the guys here at ICPD?"

"Other than you? No. They have a tight-knit group, and they're needed here, in any case. I'm hoping, given what we're trying to put together, the new IPD Headquarters and the ICPD will work together, instead of at cross purposes, from now on. And that's one reason why I want you as my top detective."

"Oh shit," Ashton whispered. "Lee, I'm not ready for that."

"That's not what we've seen," Peterson declared. "Nor what Kurt Walder saw, either."

"I'm not asking you to head up the Investigations division, son," Carter said. "I'm asking you to be my top, most trusted, detective. Right now, you'll be reporting directly to me until we find someone who can step into that leadership role in Investigations. We're rebuilding, basically from the ground up."

"What, um," Ashton broke off.

"What-what?" Carter asked, confused.

"He's wondering about Cally Ames," Peterson told her husband.

"Oh, that. It won't be a problem," Carter said. "She and I have talked, and she's decided to stay here, so she can still work with you on cross-department things, but there isn't any risk of someone getting accused of nepotism. Especially if the two of you get married."

"Oh!" Ashton exclaimed, flushing despite himself. "We, uh, we haven't even…"

"Then what are you waiting for, silly?" Peterson asked with a huge grin. She elbowed him lightly. "That woman is not only a great catch, she's nuts about you."

"I, er…" Ashton broke off, and a grinning Carter nudged his wife in turn.

"Hush, Maia," he said. "The boy – the man has his own timetable on that. Let him do it his way."

"I'm just sayin'," Peterson said with a shrug.

"Yes, well, that's none of our business at this moment," Carter noted. "We're still talking police business, here, not advising Nick on his personal life. And to that end, Nick, do you need to think about my offer?"

Ashton, at a loss for words, shot a questioning glance at Peterson.

"Nope, it ain't a problem, kiddo," she said, interpreting that look. "You came to us to stay safe, and we kept you safe, knowing you might go back when the time came – assuming it ever did. I'd say the time is here, and we're proud one of ours is going to help rebuild the division and the department, and do it right."

Ashton nodded.

"You said you talked to Cally," Ashton said then. "Did she have a problem…?"

"She's so proud of you she could about bust," Carter said with a smile. "She seemed to think you should do it."

"Then…pending my talking to her myself…I think you have a tentative yes, Chief Carter," Ashton declared.

"That's what I hoped I'd hear," Carter said, relaxing.

They were back at the Laughing Cat, in the little corner booth, screened off from the rest of the backmost back room.

"So did you accept Chief Carter's offer?" Cally asked, after the waiter departed with their order.

"I said I wanted to talk to you about it, but yes, I tentatively accepted," Nick told her.

"Why did you even need to talk to me?"

"Well, we're kind of a couple now," he pointed out. "And I figured, if I'm gonna do something that big, I needed to at least verify with you personally that you're okay with it."

"I'm okay with it. In fact, I'm so proud of you I can hardly stand it."

"Aw."

They were silent for a few moments, sipping their drinks.

"Listen, Cally..." Nick began.

"Yes, Nick?"

"You know...I really missed you while I was on Catalonia."

"I missed you, too."

"And if I go back to IPD, and you stay here, we won't see each other every day anymore."

"True. But no, Nick, I'm not transferring with you. My place is here, at least for now."

"I know. That wasn't what I was gonna ask."

"What, then?"

"I was going to ask you to marry me. I think that would be a really good thing all around. Besides, I..."

His voice cracked, and he broke off. Cally smiled.

"Finish it," she said softly.

"...I love you, Cally."

"I love you, too, Nick Ashton. And yes, I'll marry you."

She got up and moved around the table to his side, where she leaned into him and kissed him.

He slipped his arms around her and kissed back.

They never even noticed when George, with a huge smile on his face, brought their food to the table.

Please review this book on Amazon.

Author Notes

I want to thank the usual suspects, plus some, here. There's beta readers Evelyn Zinn and Dr. James K. Woosley; they always help me catch any wupsies in the course of the writing. Rich has his own readers as well; I don't know you all like he does, but believe me, I appreciate you all.

Additional thanks go to: Robert R. Murphy MD, Dave Martin, Susan Powers, Pat Viebey, Karen Calvert, Jon Glenn, Jolie Lachance, Bob Buelow, Joe McKeel, Richard D. Cartwright, Dan Hollifield, Scott Kuntzelman, and the other denizens of Lady Osborn's Pub on Facebook, for helping me come up with henchman and other bad-guy names!

A *very* special thanks goes to Richard Weyand, who trusts me with his characters and his universe. I've tried hard to do well by him on that. I love both of his series, so this is fun for me, too.

Stephanie Osborn
April 2020
Huntsville, AL

www.ingramcontent.com/pod-product-compliance
Lightning Source LLC
Chambersburg PA
CBHW061324170626
46817CB00001B/304